NONA ~~THE NINTH~~

The Locked Tomb Series

NONA
THE
NINTH

TAMSYN MUIR

A TOM DOHERTY ASSOCIATES BOOK

NEW YORK

NONA THE NINTH

Copyright © 2022 by Tamsyn Muir

A Tordotcom Book
Published by Tom Doherty Associates
120 Broadway
New York, NY 10271

www.tor.com

Tor® is a registered trademark of Macmillan Publishing Group, LLC.

Library of Congress Cataloging-in-Publication Data

Names: Muir, Tamsyn, author.
Title: Nona the ninth / Tamsyn Muir.
Description: First edition. | New York : Tordotcom, a Tom Doherty
    Associates, 2022. | Series: The Locked Tomb Series ; 3
Identifiers: LCCN 2022011660 (print) | LCCN 2022011661
    (ebook) | ISBN 9781250854117 (hardcover) |
    ISBN 9781250865830 (signed) | ISBN 9781250854124 (ebook)
Classification: LCC PR9639.4.M84 N66 2022 (print) |
    LCC PR9639.4.M84 (ebook) | DDC 823/.92—dc23
LC record available at https://lccn.loc.gov/2022011660
LC ebook record available at https://lccn.loc.gov/2022011661

Our books may be purchased in bulk for promotional, educational, or business use. Please contact your local bookseller or the Macmillan Corporate and Premium Sales Department at 1-800-221-7945, extension 5442, or by email at MacmillanSpecialMarkets@macmillan.com.

First Edition: 2022

Printed in the United States of America

0 9 8 7 6 5 4 3 2 1

for pT

◆

DRAMATIS PERSONAE

GUEST LIST

(as transcribed by C. Hect.)

Dogs to invite to birthday party

- Brown one by the fish shop, average sized, four legs
- Stop It, name assumed, lies under counter at dairy, red colour, big sized, four legs
- White-and-black one seen once in the park, average sized, tail curled twice, three legs
- Noodle, king of dogs in secret, white-adjacent, small sized, six legs
- Spotted beach dog, often on beach, large sized, huge ginger eyebrows, three legs

Members of gang to invite to birthday party

- Hot Sauce
- Honesty
- Born in the Morning
- Beautiful Ruby
- Kevin

Teachers

- The Angel?

Blood of Eden

- Crown Him with Many Crowns (No.—C.)
- The Captain, maybe (Not possible.—C.)
- Cell Commander We Suffer and We Suffer, although actually she might be Wing Commander, I don't know which it is (It's both, and no.—C.)

- And you three (Good to know.—C.)

One for the Emperor, first of us all;

One for his Lyctors, who answered the call;

One for his Saints, who were chosen of old;

One for his Hands, and the swords that they hold.

Two is for discipline, heedless of trial;

Three for the gleam of a jewel or a smile;

Four for fidelity, facing ahead;

Five for tradition and debts to the dead;

Six for the truth over solace in lies;

Seven for beauty that blossoms and dies;

Eight for salvation no matter the cost;

Nine for the Tomb, and for all that was lost.

You told me, *Sleep, I'll wake you in the morning.*
I asked, *What is morning?* and you said,
When everyone who fucked with me is dead.

When everyone we loved has gone or fled,
That's morning. Empty's just another word for clean.
Let's put this first-draft dream of mine to bed.

In the appointed hour
I'll pull up your sheets. I'll kill the light,
Lie down beside you; die; and sleep the night.

This time will be the time we get it right:
Forgiveness not so hard, nor anger long;
Our graves will be less deep, our lies less true.

You held aloft the sword.
I still love y

NONA ~~THE NINTH~~

JOHN 20:8

IN THE DREAM, he told her the words about where he took his degrees, his postdoc, his research fellowship. They were his noise and not really for consumption. More like meditation; like even his mouth knew the pointlessness of it, and just wanted to recite. Dilworth. Otago. Auckland. Overseas to Corpus. (She likes the word *corpus;* it sounds nice and fat.) Then another year abroad, where he got the grant and met the men who would make things happen. Special pleading with the New Zealand government and Asia-Pacific Environmental, at his suggestion, then back to the facility outside Greytown. They mocked it up to look like a freezing works. We all thought that was funny, he said.

He said: We just wanted to save you. You were so sick.

He said, It was me and A— and M— at the start. It wasn't that they didn't have the money for a bigger team; we were simply the only ones capable of what they were asking. M— for medical, A— because he was the glycerol-6 genius. He could've gone anywhere but he stuck with me . . . and thank God for that, because he handled all the shareholders. I was there for everything, but those meetings were like dying. I'll never love meetings. C— was brought on by the oversight execs for contracts, you know, checks and balances, but look where *that* ended up, she was on our side before the first year was over . . .

He said: You have to understand that right up until that last year we believed they were going to see it through. We *knew* the plan could work. The Mark-R cryo cans had room for eleven billion people, easy. We'd got the procedure down to five hours per person with

13

a trained team of four. Assuming an existing medical degree, that training could take as little as weeks, manpower wasn't an issue if we started *now*. Sure, the maternity stuff wasn't totally ironed out, but we were nearly there, and the packing was perfect. Of course they bitched about the timeline, and they bitched about the money, but they were always going to bitch about the money. Our rule was, nobody knowingly left behind.

He said: Even when they were constructing the other ships we got told straight-up that it was nothing, they were being sent off to the Kuiper installation to be on point for the full-population evac. IAF were involved, Pan-Euro Astronautics gave it their blessing, it was all so benign. We even lent them G— at the time because they wanted to talk about coating. M— said that she didn't like it, she smelled a rat, and you know what I said? You know what I told her? I said, *Don't let it get to you* and I said, *Don't get paranoid!* I fucking looked her in the eye and said, *This is the way we're getting out, and you know that the moment half a dozen trillionaires realise it, they're going where the oxygen is.* That's what I always told her. *They're going where the oxygen is. Wealthy men head for the exit.*

He said: When they called me up and said the cryo project was over she looked at me and she just said, *There they go, John.*

In the dream they were sitting on the beach. He had made a fire from damp driftwood. The smoke made a black mark where it touched the tarpaulin, at the top, where it was stretched over their heads. The ash was still falling. It made them sick, but only ever for a little while. Anything that hurt them only ever hurt them for a little while.

In the dream, she was sat next to a bundle of meat he'd cut, thighs mostly, for when they felt hungry, which happened rarely and always simultaneously. When it did happen they would be side by side, eating until their stomachs were sore. They would drink from the sea like dogs.

He said after a pause: You know the worst part? She cried. She and A— both cried. In each other's arms, like babies. They were so fucking scared. And I was right there, and I couldn't do piss. Everything I was and everything I had done, and I couldn't do a damned thing.

He was quiet for a long time. The sea ate at the sand. The waves glowed a little even though there was no sunshine, only thick yellow cloud.

She prompted: So what did you do?

He said: A damned thing, didn't I.

She said: When is the part where you hurt me?

He said: Soon. It's coming up.

She said: I still love you.

And in the dream he rubbed his temple with his thumb and said: "You always say that, Harrowhark."

DAY ONE

Regarding Nona—Hot Sauce Is
Watchful—the City Has a Bad Day—
Nona Gets a Bedtime Story—Five Days
Until the Tomb Opens.

1

LATE IN THE YEAR of nobody she really thought about that much in particular, the person who looked after her pushed the button on the recorder and said, "Start."

She squeezed her eyes shut and began in a practised hurry:

"The painted face is on top of me. I'm in the safe water—I'm lying down, I think. Something's pushing at me. The water goes over my head and it's in my mouth. It goes up my nose."

"Does it hurt?"

"No."

"How do you feel?"

"I like it. I like the water, I like her hands."

"*Her* hands?"

"They're the things around me—maybe they're my hands."

The pencil scratched loudly on the paper. "How about the face?"

"It's the picture face." The sketch they'd made for her, the one locked in the secret drawer where they put all the really interesting things, like cigarettes and the fake identification cards and all the money they said wasn't legal tender and couldn't be used. The pencil obligingly scribbled its way across the page. It was hard not to open her eyes and look at the person opposite, so she amused herself by imagining what she would see: tanned sure hands on the notebook, head bent over it, the fringe pinned up waiting for haircut day. Imagining was better than looking anyway, because the battery lamp wasn't switched on.

She said, "What are you writing?" because the pencil was still going. Most of the time the writing was interesting, but some of the time it was just boring descriptions of how her face was changing when she talked, like *0.24—Smiled.*

"Incidentals. Keep going, you woke up late."

"Can you change the alarm song? I can sleep through 'Good Morning, Good Morning' now."

"Sure. I'll drop a wet sponge on your face instead. Keep thinking."

She kept thinking.

"The arms go really tight around me. They're her arms, definitely."

"Is she familiar?"

"Maybe. I don't know."

"How do you know they're 'her'?"

"I don't know."

"What happens after that?"

"Don't know."

A long pause. "Anything else?"

"No. It's gone already. Sorry, Camilla."

"Not a problem."

Camilla Hect depressed the button with a bright and final plastic *clack.* This was the cue, so she exploded into action. The rule was that she had to lie still and concentrate as hard as she could from the time that the button went down to the time when the button went up. When it went *up,* pyjamas came *off;* under the pale, wavering light of the tiny torch taped to Cam's clipboard, she undressed and dressed herself at the same time, which required a lot of contortions. She wrestled out of her nightshirt with her arms and stretched on her trousers using her ankles, in the move that Camilla called *worm with problems.*

Being the worm with problems did not worry her. Just being able to dress herself was charming. In the bad old days she used to have to be helped even with the nightshirt, because she couldn't be trusted not to get stuck with it halfway over her head and get all hot and upset from claustrophobia. It was incredibly important that she not get upset like that again. She had only ever had two tantrums in her life, but it would be humiliating to have a third. Her fingers fumbled a little with the vest, but she was fine pulling on the UV sand shirt, even with arranging the cuffs, which could be complicated and if you got it wrong you had to stand in the bath to take it off again in showers of yellow dirt. The canvas jacket with the toggle closers didn't slow her down at all. When she finished Cam said, "Good. Quick," and she was so exhausted from the praise she collapsed back on the mattress.

"I'm doing my stretches now," she announced hastily, before she could be told to do anything else. She swung her legs upward until her feet were pointed flat at the ceiling, and as she'd been taught, rotated her toes from that angle to circle around the water stains she could see on the plaster. The winter wet was over, but the huge patch of black damp in the corner hadn't dried up yet. She had told everyone that she should really talk to the landlord, but it had been communicated to her that if she could even *find* the landlord she would get a gold medal.

Camilla had not said anything in approval or censure, so she said more emphatically, "My *legs* are really *tight* today," in the immortal hope that Cam would take her ankles in her hands and walk them forward. Cam would do this until her knees were touching her chest and her hamstrings were stretched so taut she was convinced they were about to go *ping* and snap. It was the best thing in the world. If she was *really* lucky Camilla would rub her calves, which were always sore from walking, or even sometimes her back, though that was usually after practise. But Camilla was busy writing and did not take the bait no matter how much she wiggled her toes. She even repeated herself, and added, "Wow, *very* tight, goodness gracious," in a slightly louder voice.

Cam said, not looking, "Walk it off."

"I think I might have a cramp. I think I can't move."

"Guess you can't go to school, then."

She knew when she was beaten. "I'm up, I'm up."

To prove how *up* she was, she arched her back and rocked up to stand, having only pushed herself up a little bit with her arms: she'd been practising, and when she straightened up with only the slightest wobble she was delighted. But all Camilla said was, "Don't hyperextend," crushingly, and worse, "Go see if Pyrrha needs help with breakfast."

"Okay. She's probably done though, we took forever. Maybe the food went cold," she added, misty with desire.

Camilla briefly looked up from the notebook with a critical eye at her bedhead, which had not been improved with stretches or jumping, and she added: "Get her to do your hair. I'm going to talk."

"Oh, good! I'll time."

"I've got a clockwork."

"Cam, that sounds strange, nobody here calls it a *clockwork,* they say *watch.*"

"Good to know. Stop trying to miss breakfast."

She hedged cunningly. "At least please can you write down, *I love you, Palamedes,* please, from me? At least write, *I love you, Palamedes, from Nona.*"

This Camilla Hect did unblushingly, though Nona had to take it on trust. When she squatted down on her haunches, following the strokes the pencil made, she could not make out a single word. She could not even make out a letter, not of any alphabet she'd ever been shown, which interested everyone except herself. But you could always trust Cam. When the pencil stopped and the message was obviously discharged Nona leant into her and said, "Thanks. I love you too, Camilla," and: "Do you know who I am yet?"

"Someone who's late for breakfast," said Camilla.

But as Nona straightened, she turned and smiled her rare brief smile, the one like the sun catching the glitter of a car on the motorway. Cam smiled so seldom now that Nona immediately felt it was going to be a good day.

It wasn't any lighter in the kitchen. There was thin blue light coming through the joins in the curtains, and an orange glow from the worn-out hot plate mostly blocked by the other person she lived with. There was a baby wailing in morning-related outrage a few apartments away, so Nona walked on the balls of her feet to not add to the noise. The people underneath hated it if you walked loudly, and Pyrrha said they had militia links and not to piss them off because they were also hungover ninety percent of the time. This was unfair, because the person *above* them never took their shoes off inside, which surely meant they were allowed to complain about that. But Pyrrha said they shouldn't piss *them* off because they were a cop. Pyrrha called it the shit sandwich. Pyrrha always seemed to know everything about everybody.

"All done? Good timing," said Pyrrha, without turning around.

Pyrrha was holding a can of spray-on oil whose nozzle she directed neatly into the pan, where she wiped the pale froth around with a spatula. She was wearing pyjama pants and a string vest and no shirt, so the orange glow of the hot plate ring lit up all the scars on her wiry arms. She was feeling around for the breakfast things in the cupboard with her other hand, so Nona came and took the mesh basket and started counting out plates for her. "Is that pikelet mix?" she said.

"Get bowls. It's eggs," said Pyrrha.

Up close Nona could smell the spray-on oil and watch Pyrrha agitate a fork in a beaker of violently orange liquid, radioactively orange even in the dark, before tipping it into the pan to sizzle. Yellow lacework immediately formed where it splashed against the hot edge. Nona replaced the plates with two chipped bowls, and Pyrrha said, "Doesn't that school of yours teach counting?"

"Oh, but Pyrrha, it's so hot. Can't I have something cold?"

"Sure. Leave them to get cold."

"Yuck, that's not what I meant."

"The eggs aren't optional, kiddie. How's the dreams?"

"Same as normal," said Nona, reluctantly taking another bowl. "I wish I could dream something different for once. Do *you* dream, Pyrrha?"

"Sure. Just last night I dreamed I had to give a briefing, but I wasn't wearing pants and my backside was hanging out," said Pyrrha, hacking the shocking orange curds into clumps with the edge of the spatula. During a pause in Nona's gurgles of mirth, she added solemnly, "It was no fun, my child. I knew I'd be okay so long as I was hiding behind the podium, but I didn't know what I'd do once I had to sit down again. Die, I guess."

"Are you being serious or joking with me?" Nona demanded, once this fresh pleasure had subsided.

"Deadly serious. But go put another mark under *ass joke* anyway."

Nona was happy enough to get up from the table and cross to the big sheet of brown paper tacked up on the wall; to take the pencil and wait for Pyrrha to say, "One higher, one left, stop right there," so she could make a blobby tally mark.

She counted up the tally marks and said, "That's the seventh one this month. But that's not fair when you keep making them. Palamedes will say you're skewing the data."

"I never could help giving the girls what they wanted," said Pyrrha. She turned off the hob and upended some of the pan into Nona's bowl, then set the pan back on the hob with a cloth over it to keep it warm. She wiped her hands and said, "Eat. I'll do your hair."

"Thank you," said Nona, grateful for the understanding. "Cam said to ask. Can I get braids?"

"Whatever the lady wishes."

"Can I get one big braid and two little braids coming off it at the sides?"

"Sure, if we've got time."

"They don't come loose and the plain plaits do." Nona added in the spirit of truth: "And I can't help chewing the ends with plaits. I want to steer clear of Temptation."

"Don't we all? I need to stop torturing myself by staring at the cigarette drawer."

"Don't start the secondhand smoke argument again," said Nona in alarm, but then, figuring she'd been harsh: "Anyway, they're bad for you and I love you, Pyrrha."

"Prove it," said Pyrrha, which meant she had to eat the eggs.

Nona ate while Pyrrha brushed out her hair in short, brisk strokes, letting its fine black sheets fall over Nona's shoulders. It went almost to the bottom of her back now, and it was soft and thin as water: every fourth haircut day they cut it, but not *every* haircut day because it was a pain, and because people noticed your hair growing less when it was already long, Camilla said. Camilla and Pyrrha both got to have short hair, which she envied. Cam's was dark brown and bobbed off sharply at the chin and it felt nice against your cheek, and whenever Pyrrha didn't shave her head quick enough she got a little flat cap of dark terracotta, the colour of wet red earth at the building site. Most of Pyrrha was the colours of the building site: deep dried-out browns, dusty hunks of clay, rusted metal. She was raw and ropy and square-shouldered, and Camilla was long and shadowy and lean. Nona thought they were both exquisite.

Camilla came in when Pyrrha was fixing up the first braid and when Nona had gotten as far as *chewing* the eggs, which was an agonising step on the journey to *eating* the eggs. Camilla said unhappily, "Eggs? Have we not invented a new protein?" which meant it wasn't Camilla at all.

The easiest way of telling who was who was in the eyes. Palamedes had soft cool eyes of brownish grey, like bare ground in the cold mornings when Nona had been little, and Camilla had the clearest of clear grey eyes like storybook ice, not like normal cloudy ice at all. But Nona could tell them apart from across the room, which she was proud of, because their body was otherwise exactly the same. The difference was how they stood: Camilla couldn't stand still, ever, not without shifting her weight back and forth on each knee or popping her knuckles, and Palamedes stood like he was playing a game of Hot Chocolate and the tagger was looking right at him. Hot Chocolate was in fashion with her friends at the moment and Nona wanted to get really good at it.

"Meat's black-market only right now," Pyrrha said, starting in on a second braid. Palamedes was spooning gritty black spoonfuls of instant coffee into mugs. He said absently, "Coffee, Nona?" even though she always said, "No, but thank you"—Palamedes liked giving you options—and he even waited until she said, "No, but thank you" before he poured the boiling water twice. No milk, because they'd run out of packets. He put one mug where Pyrrha could reach it— she was currently leaning over to the counter for a hairpin—and kept one for himself. They sat and steamed in the muggy air, and Nona sniffed at the nice bitter coffee smell. Pyrrha continued, "Anyway, you're paying for the meat roulette. The stuff the butcher's keeping back is only ten percent upholstery, the rest is livers and gristle."

Nona wanted to know. "What part's the upholstery?"

"A very nutritious part," said Palamedes.

"The part that hung out in my dream," said Pyrrha.

That set Nona off again, so she had to get up from her eggs to make another mark on her tally sheet. Palamedes stared, distracted, and said: "Dear God, two in a day? Why are we even remotely in doubt? Forget the meat, I was being facetious. We wouldn't have upholstery money even if I wrote hardcore pornography for a living."

Pyrrha said, "Wish you'd try. These nicotine patches are killing me."

"If that's meant to make me feel guilty, I feel nothing, thank you," said Palamedes. "Cam's body is a temple. She's the one who's banned me from a life peddling poor-quality erotica. Says she doesn't want our last gift to the universe to be tales of people mashing birthday cakes beneath their bottoms. Speaking of, Pyrrha—do you have a minute? You came in too late last night to talk."

"We're over time, is why," said Pyrrha. "The damn drills stop every half hour so we can take cover."

Nona felt the pin securing the last little braid to her head, and then the braid being patted flat with one weathered hand. Pyrrha said, "Empty that bowl, Nona," and took her mug of coffee as Palamedes spooned himself some eggs. She and Palamedes went back into the bedroom with their breakfasts and closed the door behind them.

In their absence Nona considered the eggs. They were a uniform yellow colour, with dusty black flecks of pepper. You were allowed to put as much thin, fiery red sauce on them as you liked, but it wasn't the taste Nona minded. She then considered the window beyond the curtains, which was open a crack, at the very least enough for a spoon; Pyrrha had, after all, said to empty the bowl. But Palamedes said that she could handle abstract concepts and therefore literal interpretation was not a defence. She considered the eggs again. As a virtuous compromise she put three spoonfuls in her mouth and

walked soundlessly over to the shut door. It was unnecessarily harsh
to expect her not to listen *and* to eat.

"—verdue for a chat about the due date," Pyrrha was saying.

"If they want her early, want can be their master. They gave us a
year."

Then they both moved away from the door, which made things
more difficult.

"—nything from your si—" Palamedes was speaking at the bottom
of Camilla's voice.

"—aying some guys to comb over Site B . . . push maybe tomorrow
we—"

"—promise in Site C: we know they own the build—"

"—afe sites first. The closer we get to the barracks . . . to being
rumbled that we're searchi—"

There was more talking, but they had both dropped their voices
past Nona's comprehension so it sounded like *mnah mnah mnah*.
She held the eggs in her mouth silently and pressed her ear to the
door as hard as she dared, and was rewarded with Palamedes saying:

"—could've made inroads on the barracks at any point. They're
holding off. Why?"

"You know why," murmured Pyrrha's voice in response. "The moment they go in there and clean out the last poor bastards busy div-
vying up the rats and the sedatives, that's going to put a big black
mark on the negotiations. The Cohort dies like anyone else under
siege . . . eventually."

"Then this is our last chance to make a difference. Give us *orders*,
Commander."

Pyrrha was audibly chewing. "Stopped being that when I died,
Palamedes. It was a courtesy title, anyway, and there's an embarrassment of commanders here if you want 'em."

"Pyrrha," he said, "why are they running now? Why would Blood
of Eden run when they have the best hand they were ever dealt? Why
would they run when common sense, good tactics, and foreknowl-
edge must tell them all that this is the best moment to make a stand?
The time you've spent—the insights you've had that nobody else has

been privy to—and you're truly telling me you don't even have an *inkling*?"

"You're not a prude. Feel free to say it," said Pyrrha, and though her voice was its normal deep, comfy, slightly hoarse self, there was a little undercurrent in it that Nona couldn't quite parse. Nona would have understood it more if only she'd been able to see Pyrrha. "I spent all that time sleeping with the enemy with very little to show for it, right? Blood of Eden is a house with many rooms, and I was only ever visiting one of 'em. Sure, I've got *inklings* aplenty."

"Then you've *got* to brief us—"

He was cut off by a metal-on-plastic noise, like eggs being spooned from the bottom of the bowl. "No. Not if there's any risk of you two undergoing interrogation."

"Neither of us appreciate being treated like children."

"Children? I'm treating you like the Sixth House Warden and his cavalier, neither of whom have been trained to survive a Blood of Eden hot seat," said Pyrrha. "Don't think because Camilla's carrying you that you'd have an easy ride. You have no idea what BoE torture is like, and we don't have the five years I'd need to teach you."

"Pyrrha, stop saying you don't have time to teach us things and *start teaching*. We're quick studies."

There was a definite slurp of coffee being drunk. Pyrrha always did drink loudly. She said she still wasn't used to her teeth. "I could teach you some bits and pieces, sure. I'd need my necromancer to teach Camilla."

"Why?"

"Because you need teaching to be an asset, and Cam wants teaching to be a killer." There was a brief silence, until Pyrrha said slowly, "Or you could take me up on my first offer, which would solve a lot of your problems—"

Palamedes spoke at the bottom of Cam's voice, which made it harder to catch. "It was a beautiful offer, Pyrrha, and almost completely useless. There's no retiring our forces in a search-and-recovery op. In any case Eden would turn on us completely, even our own cell. We need to fight clever."

"If you wanted to fight clever you'd focus on search-and-recovery and not on the barracks. It's not helping Cam. She's mad as hell—even madder than you—and it's getting you nowhere."

"Thank you for your insight regarding my cavalier," said Palamedes politely. "It's appreciated."

A snort of laughter. "He ices over . . . I'm too old to know not to be offensive, Palamedes, so forgive me quickly for telling you your business and let's move on. I'll say it outright. Forget the barracks and stop trying to be the people's hero. We've lost that fight."

"Lost? There could still be two hundred people holed up in th—"

"—optimistic—"

"If there were *two* I'd do it. It's a rotten way to die, House or not. What's more, once it's over—the deluge."

"Hey, we might get some breathing space. It might drain the boil."

"You can't truly believe that."

"No, I don't. It'll be first blood," said Pyrrha, and made another slurp. "I know how it is. You should have heard the demo crew yesterday. These people are beside themselves waiting for kickoff, waiting for the Houses. One guy tells me this'll all be over once the barracks get cleaned out, another guy tells me he'd welcome the Cohort regiment with open arms if they just brought supplies and broke up the gangs. Half my guys would strangle the other half on a pretext. This is what happens when you force refugees from twenty different planets to live cheek by jowl and you keep thinking people unify under a common threat . . . She always made that mistake. I told her twenty years ago. Works beautiful in the short-term, but you've got to give them a future to really keep 'em glued. Palamedes, we made this mistake ourselves. You can have the barracks *or* your people—or neither. You can't say 'I choose both' like a wet towel and expect the universe to fall into line."

"Pyrrha, this is sounding perilously like giving up."

"Is it? You *know* I'm ready to give up. This is a shitshow. You know I'm ready to get Nona safely off-world the moment you accept the way things are."

"There's *no way* off-world—"

"It's called a ship—"

"If you're hiding a ship in your dungarees, please share it with the rest of the class." His voice now raised a little. "Bypassing the question of *how*, where would we go, Pyrrha? What would we do?"

"Anywhere," she said. "Anything. I've been out of commission for ten thousand years . . . I'm ready for pretty much anything else."

There was a brief silence, then a slurp. When Palamedes picked up again, his voice was earnest. "It's a false dichotomy, you know. We're all of us in one layered hostage situation. Three million people squatting on a thanergy planetoid millions of kilometres away from us. Nine million people in this city alone . . ."

"Who aren't *yours* by any stretch of the imagination."

"*Nine million*, Pyrrha, that's equivalent to the whole of the Seventh and the Eighth put together. Three million people, plus nine million people, plus sixteen. We refuse to leave any of them behind."

"You're big-minded. Know who isn't? Blood of Eden, and me," said Pyrrha. "If you asked me to pick between the three of us and those twelve million plus sixteen, I'd pick us without turning a hair. You're not listening to me. BoE are *making* that choice, Palamedes . . . We Suffer's lost. The Wakers and Ctesiphon Wing can't protect us. Merv Wing's got the glue, which is *a way out*. The Hopers call the shots now . . . and I've met leaders like Unjust Hope before. They're the guys who come to the fore when people want leaders who don't count the costs. We're heading for a purge, Sextus. This is the Blood of Eden who don't give a fuck."

"I wouldn't have called them too generous with fucks before."

"You've got no idea. Listen to me. You've never met this Blood of Eden, not really. *This* Blood of Eden has spent their entire existence gambling everything on staying alive for one more day . . . and I don't know if I even want to find out why anymore. 'Cause you know what? Gideon's dead, and I don't give a fuck either. Not if I can save our skins."

"I don't believe you."

"You should. I know a little moon that's only half-flipped. It's got great soil, breathable air. Gideon used to think about running away there. I know how to farm . . . I can teach you and Cam and Nona. I can teach you how to wait. That's my speciality. And the moment I get my hands on a ship, that's where I'm taking us."

There was another rustling: but then the timer bleated in a soft, muffled way, as though it was coming from inside a pocket. Palamedes made a sound under his breath that Nona knew was a rude word. He said quickly: "My time's up."

"That's the best part, right? Getting out of rough conversations." And, almost immediately, more quietly: "Forgive me the joke, Warden. I forget you're not used to it."

"Never will be. You understand. Look, you'll be late for work and Nona will be late for school."

Pyrrha's voice dropped so that the only thing Nona caught was: "—ing her go to—?"

"I want her to remain as calm as possible. Can you push for Site B?"

"I'll do it by end of day, even if I have to finish it off myself. Don't worry."

Nona looked at the last lumps of yellow in her bowl and silently scraped half of it up to put in her mouth, figuring that if she swallowed all at once she wouldn't choke or taste. She could not have made the slightest sound, but Camilla—she could tell it was Camilla again—called from within: "How long were you listening, Nona?"

"You were pretty loud, so nearly the whole time," said Nona, through eggs.

"Then that damn breakfast had better be eaten," said Pyrrha.

Camilla stood by the kitchen counter and tore through her half-eaten breakfast mechanically as Nona unwrapped a sterile tablet in the bucket of greywater for the dishes. Pyrrha balanced a mirror on the table and shaved her face. Nona loved the clean, bright smell of shaving soap, and to see Pyrrha swiftly and expertly scrape the dark russet-brown stubble off her cheeks and from around her mouth, and the little wet red marks that appeared. When she reached over to touch one freshly smooth cheek, the marks were already wrinkling up and disappearing. Cam was stationed by the pegs at the door saying, "Hats," prompting Nona to dutifully take down and hand round the hats, and, "Masks," for the same. The hats were hideous, large-brimmed, with cloth panels that came down behind and strings to tie beneath the chin: Nona often thought about burning hers, and it wasn't as though they needed either hats *or* masks. That was the whole problem, wasn't it? Nona wouldn't cough even if the wind blew the smoke straight into her face, and Pyrrha wouldn't burn any colour other than her deep cool brown. Camilla was busy untucking the back veil on her hat, so Nona let her attention drift to the side of the window, where light was thickly glowing through the little rips in the tape, and the sky was visible through the worst tears.

The sky over the city used to be a thick yellow butterscotch colour. Now it was only like that at the very edges of the horizon, as the blueness had spread like a stain on carpet, touching even the light. Nona took a moment to surreptitiously twitch the curtains, peeking between the broken antisniper striping to catch a glimpse of the world outside. The blue light got stronger, and Camilla said sharply, "Nona," and she hurriedly let the curtains fall.

Pyrrha, now masked, paused before the door with her wiry knuckles: "Roll call. What's this week's *all scatter* word?"

"Lowdown," said Camilla.

"And the *all clear*?"

"Deadweight," said Nona.

"Perfect. What are your stations if that thing in the sky even *looks* like it's about to stop periscoping?"

"The underground tunnels by the fish market," said Camilla.

"The big underpass bridge dugout," said Nona.

"Ten points to you both. And what do you do once you're there?"

"Hide until you come," said Nona, and then added, truthfully: "And rescue any nearby animals so long as they don't exceed the size of the box, and are woolly rather than hairy."

"Half points. No animals, hairy *or* woolly, I don't care. Cam?"

Camilla had finished with her hat, and now she was easing the big dark glasses onto her face—the ones she kept specially, despite the fact that they were a little unbalanced on her nose and her ears. They made both Palamedes and Camilla look chilly and clinical, but as

Palamedes said, they solved the problem of the ghost limb. Without them he was everlastingly pushing something up his nose that wasn't there. And Nona thought Camilla privately rather liked them.

She settled them on, considered the question, and said: "Fight."

"No points. Camilla, if you engage with a Herald, you're not coming home."

"That's your theory," said Camilla.

"There's data behind it. Hect—"

"If Camilla gets to fight, *I* should get to keep adjacent dogs," said Nona decidedly. "Even if they're hairy."

Pyrrha turned her eyes up to the ceiling in mute appeal. Her exhalation rasped loudly against the vent in her mask. "I used to run the whole Bureau," she said, and she didn't sound like she was addressing either of them. "Now I'm up against wannabe heroes and hairy dogs. This is the punishment she would've wanted for me. God, she must be pissing herself laughing . . . Let's go, kids. Like hell am I walking in this heat."

PYRRHA WORKED FOR NONA, Camilla looked after Nona, and Palamedes taught Nona, all on the understanding that she was not simply a person, but probably one of two people. Nona did not know either of her real possible names. Palamedes said not to lead her unnecessarily. One of the reasons they had called her *Nona* was that the first thing she had said, when they saved her and brought her here, was *No, no. Nono* became *Nona*, and *Nona* meant *Nine*, and nine was an important number.

What she definitely knew was that her body belonged to one of two people, and she was interested in her body. When she looked in the mirror she had skin the colour of the egg carton, and eyes the colour of the egg mixture, and hair the colour of the burnt-out bottom of the pan. More to the point, Nona thought she was gorgeous. She had a thin, complicated face, and a mouth too easily unhappy and too easily discontented; but she had nice white teeth in a smile that looked sad no matter how happy she was, and arched black brows like she always wanted to ask someone a question. Nona talked to herself in the mirror even now. When she had been earlier born, and less self-conscious, sometimes she would rest her face against the mirror's face, and try to reach her reflection. Camilla had caught her kissing it once, and had written about six pages of notes on that, which was humiliating. It was hard enough not to be allowed a single solitary secret, without a book being written about whatever you did.

If Camilla had six pages of notes on her kissing herself she had about twenty regarding eyes. Nona's egg-yellow eyes belonged to the other person—the other girl; that was how all of their bodies worked, not only hers. All four pairs of their eyes belonged to other people. Pyrrha's deep brown eyes really came from her dead best friend, and Camilla's clear grey eyes should have really been Palamedes's, and vice versa with his wintertime irises. Nona's eyes were a deep, warm gold, the colour of the sky at midday—or at least the colour the sky had used to be at midday.

"You see," Palamedes had said to her, "the eyes are a dead give-away. When you give yourself to someone else, their soul shows in yours by the eye colour; that's why you'll never see me looking out of Camilla's face with my own eyes again."

"So someone's inside me, then? I mean—I'm that somebody?" She always stumbled over this.

"Maybe yes, Nona, maybe no. Eyes can also show that a soul is in someone else's body temporarily. Your amber eyes could mean that you're like Camilla and me, or it could mean something else. But you seem to have had . . . a big shock."

"Maybe I've just lost my memory," said Nona dubiously.

"It happens," agreed Palamedes—not convinced.

She didn't care whose eyes were whose; but she was a little vain, and cared about being nice-looking. Nona knew early that other people thought she was pretty too. Once a long time ago when she was waiting in line to pick up some detergent and Camilla was getting something else they'd forgotten, the person in the line behind her had said, "Hey, pretty thing, where have you been all my life," and laughed a lot when Nona said truthfully that she didn't know. Then they had stood quite close to her and touched her on the hip, where her shirt was tucked in. The shop was very crowded and there were a lot of people waiting to get things, and the aisles were packed high with stuff, and there were people the shop paid to make sure nobody stole things, and they added to the crowd. Nobody was paying them any attention.

When Camilla came back the person was still trying to talk to her, and Nona had to translate what they said to Camilla, and Camilla looked the person deep in their eyes and casually touched the hilt of the knife she kept down the waistband of her trousers, and then the person moved to the back of the queue.

"If someone touches you again, and it's not me, and it's not Palamedes, and it's not Pyrrha," Camilla had told her later, "move away. Get one of us. You don't know what they want."

"They wanted to see me naked," said Nona. "It was a sex thing."

Camilla had made a sound, and then pretended it was a cough, and drank a whole glass of water. After the glass of water, she said, "How did you know?"

"That's just the way people look when they want to see you naked and it's a sex thing," said Nona. "I don't really mind."

After a moment, Camilla had told her it wasn't a great idea for Nona to let people she didn't know see her naked, and not to encourage sex things. She said sex things were right out. She said there were enough problems in the world. Camilla said it was bad enough that she had used to help Nona in the bath. Camilla had also written down a lot more notes.

That was after Nona could talk, but before she started making herself a useful member of society. It was difficult living with Pyrrha and Palamedes and Camilla in those early days and feeling as though she couldn't contribute much. They worked so hard for her. Pyrrha was an excellent planner and good with her hands, and if you gave her five seconds to talk she could make any*one* believe any*thing*, so they ate quite a lot off the money she won at cards. She ran them all with what Cam said was military efficiency. Pyrrha was the one who made them learn code words for *all clear* and *danger*, which changed every week. Nona got to be the one who picked them on weekends because that helped her to remember. Pyrrha also gave them special emergency code words for *someone following* ("red ribbon") and *someone listening* ("fritters"). They even had a code word for *important resource, come help me get it* ("fishhook"), but Palamedes said Pyrrha needed to stop treating cigarettes and liquor as important resources, so they hadn't used that one in ages.

Pyrrha could cook, and she was tough, and if you went up to the roof of the apartment building and put a marble on top of a certain column, she could close her eyes and raise a rifle and shoot the marble from the other side of the rooftop. She wouldn't do this lately even if Nona asked, because bullets were expensive right now (but a lot cheaper than meat). So Pyrrha could earn money *and* fight with a gun. She was also very wonderful with a sword, but she never lifted a sword unless all the curtains were drawn and the door was locked. They hid the swords behind a false board in the cupboard.

Camilla could fight with pretty much anything, and especially knives—she wouldn't do the marble trick with her knife because she would just say, "What did it do to me?" and then smile her tiny beautiful smile. Palamedes said that was typical. It seemed like there was nothing Camilla couldn't do after a few tries—the laundry, or starting up a truck, or opening a door when she didn't have the keys, or telling the drunk man at the bottom of their hall that none of them liked it when he hit his partner, in a mystical way that caused the man to move out of the apartment forever.

Palamedes could think. He said it was his party trick.

But Nona couldn't shoot *or* fight *or* think. All she had was a good nature—that wasn't true all the time, but Nona didn't want it bruited about that she had a *bad* temper when she had only ever thrown two tantrums in her life and couldn't remember either of them. Even if she'd been proud of those, you couldn't brag about two tantrums. Every day she held a sword until she seriously didn't care about swords anymore, but she still couldn't fight with one, no matter how big or thin it was. Camilla had wanted to teach her properly, but Pyrrha said not to, that they wouldn't be able to tell if anything suddenly came back.

Nona couldn't do the forbidden bone tricks either, even though Palamedes did nearly the exact same thing with big grey lumps of bone as Camilla did with the sword. She had to hold them, and listen when he told her to do nonsensical things—"Pretend you can stretch it; stretch it now," or "Pretend you can touch the insides; split it open." He never made Nona feel bad for not being able to do any of these things, only acted like it was interesting that she couldn't.

In the beginning she hadn't been able to do much for herself at all, but over time she had remembered how to button her shirts, and tie up her laces, and soap herself in the bath, and pour water into a glass so that her hand didn't tremble and the water didn't slop out. It shamed her, remembering how little she could do at the start. She had been so frustrated, in those slow early days. But now she could do nearly everything. She knew important facts like what was expected and what was unexpected at different parts of the day, and that people's ears weren't so interesting that she had to put her fingers inside them. In those early days Palamedes and Camilla and Pyrrha had often looked at her in a sort of stupefied shock; now they were still stupefied but they were not so shocked, and often she made them laugh.

And now they touched her, sometimes not even by explicit request. Pyrrha would roughly hug her in one big suddenness, or sweep Nona up in her hard, wiry arms before setting her down on the sofa; Palamedes would pull the blankets up over her if she was getting into bed and tuck them in softly at the corners. If she slipped her hand into Camilla's, when they were walking down the street, Camilla would hold it. Nona didn't understand how the others could walk around and go through their lives only touching each other as much as was necessary. When Nona asked, Camilla said that this was because they needed to get the washing-up done.

Nona could do all the basic things now, but there was still distressingly little that she was good at. Nona was good at:

1. touching,
2. wiping dishes,
3. running her hand over the flat cork carpet in a way that got all the hair out of it,
4. sleeping in lots of different ways and positions, and
5. speaking any language that was spoken to her, in person, so she could see the person's face and eyes and lips.

It turned out that Palamedes and Camilla could only speak one language, and Pyrrha could speak all of that one and some of another two and a little bit of about five more. The one language all three were fluent in was a kind people used for business transactions, so it wasn't strange that they used it—but it was falling out of favour, because it was a language used by awful people. Even then, the dialect spoken in the city didn't always make sense to them, or the pronunciation was strange. Nona understood everybody, and could speak back to them so that they understood her, and nobody ever said she had an accent. This confounded Palamedes. When she first said that she could speak back by watching them talk and making her lips look like theirs, it confounded him so much more that it gave Camilla a headache.

There were lots of different languages and dialects around because of all the refugees from other planets, and because of all the resettlements—Nona knew about resettlements because it was all anyone talked about in a queue—and if you spoke someone else's language they were nicer to you, and assumed you had come from the same place they had come from and lived through what they'd lived through, which was helpful. Many people were suspicious of other people because they wanted a good resettlement and were afraid that other people would somehow get them a bad resettlement. Many people had lived through at least one bad resettlement already. Everyone was crammed on one of three planets now, and they all agreed that this planet was easily the worst, though this always made Nona feel a little bit offended on the planet's part.

And so Nona lived with Camilla, Palamedes, and Pyrrha, on the thirtieth floor of a building where nearly everyone was unhappy, in a city where nearly everyone was unhappy, on a world where everyone said that you could outrun the zombies, but not forever.

You were not allowed to say the words *zombies, necromancers,* or *necromancy* outside her house, or really inside it either. Nona said they talked about everything else, so why not those words, but Palamedes said superstition for the latter and indignation for the former, which Nona did not understand. This had been the case for Nona's entire life, which would be six months next week, and Pyrrha had said as a treat she would take everyone for a birthday trip to the beach (if nobody was setting up a mortar on it).

Nona was so grateful to have had a whole six months of this. It was greedy to expect much longer.

HARDLY ANYONE WAS SUSPICIOUS OF NONA, even in the early days. They assumed she was the way she was because she had been through something terrible. They had all known at least *one* person who had not been through something terrible. When she asked Camilla how she came across to other people, Camilla said unworldly. Pyrrha said she acted like she had given away one of her two brain cells already. Pyrrha said to keep going, that people loved it if you were good-looking and dumb.

Nona didn't want to be just good-looking and dumb; she wanted to be useful. She was dimly aware that she was not what anyone had wanted. This was why she had gone out and got herself a job, even though it wasn't a paying one.

About four months in, when Nona had learnt enough to be allowed outside and to talk to strangers and to do up her own shirts, she was permitted to visit not merely the garage beneath the Building but the surrounding three buildings too. There was a school behind her building that used the first two floors of an old beat-up office block for classrooms, and Nona liked to hang around near the fence and watch the children play during break time. This caught the attention of a nice lady teacher who asked Nona why she wasn't in school herself. She said truthfully enough that she did lessons at home, and the nice lady had made a face and asked Nona where she lived. When she heard that Nona lived in the Building, she didn't quail, but wrote down the floor and apartment number on a piece of paper.

When the nice lady teacher turned up one evening and told Pyrrha and Camilla how wonderful the school was and how it had almost twenty other children and reading and writing at all the levels and an hour of the sciences *every* day *and* games, and talked about how it was even more important for children in the refuges to have a routine so why didn't they want that for Nona, Cam had to tell the nice lady that Nona was nearly nineteen.

The nice lady was totally foxed.

"But she's such a dot."

Pyrrha explained without missing a beat that what with everything Nona had gone through she had been ill and still didn't eat very much, which was why she was so knobbly and undergrown. The nice lady said that yes, many of the children had problems like that, but it was still hard to imagine Nona was anywhere over fourteen, wasn't it? The nice lady added that she obviously didn't get her build from her father, and she smiled at Pyrrha. Before anyone could stop her, Nona laughed and laughed and said, Pyrrha wasn't her *father*. The nice lady got suspicious—Nona could see it in her hands—and suggested that Nona should come anyway, could even be a Teacher's Aide, someone who helped the other children with their lessons. They told her Nona couldn't read *or* write and the nice lady said, Oh.

But at this point Nona felt the lure of not only an hour of the sciences every day *and* games but also the glory suggested by the capitals of a Teacher's Aide, and she said: I want to go, please and thank you.

The nice lady asked why didn't they try it out the next morning and see how it went. Nona was delighted. The lady said she was the main teacher, but they also had a wonderful science teacher and it would be lovely to have someone else on the team. Their last Teacher's Aide had tragically died. Pyrrha said, Were the kids that bad then. The teacher's mouth thinned and she said, No, the water plant explosion, and so Nona said, Yes she would go! before Camilla or especially Pyrrha could say anything else. Then Pyrrha, much to Camilla's disgust, flirted outrageously with the nice lady teacher until the nice lady teacher left.

After Pyrrha saw the nice lady teacher out, Camilla, who had been pacing around the kitchen, looked up and said coolly—

"What was that?"

"Getting us out of hot water, my naive beauty," said Pyrrha, collapsing into a chair with an appalling creak. "She paid you and junior the compliment of thinking you were working girls, and that I was your pimp. God knows I'd have had better luck pimping out Augustine and Alfred."

Nona wanted to know: "What's *pimp*?"

Instead of getting to know what *pimp* was, she got in trouble for giving anyone their door number and house number. Nona cried, lavishly and immediately, but Camilla and Pyrrha wouldn't budge. They also agreed that no way, no how was she going to school, not then and not ever. Camilla said it was too dangerous, and Pyrrha said it was a shame but they were going to play it safe. Nona went to lie down on the bed and be angry.

Then much later on, when Nona was having her bath and Pyrrha was watching out for her, because back then there was still the danger that she'd have a funny turn and drown in six inches of water, Pyrrha said casually to Nona: "You're allowed to go to school for half days, on trial, and only as long as you practise answering questions with us first."

Nona was ecstatic.

"Why? How? Truly?"

"Palamedes talked to me—then he convinced Hect."

"Oh, I *love* Palamedes," said Nona, and thus fortified dunked her head under the water, which she didn't like normally because she was mortally afraid of getting soap in her eyes. When she emerged, spluttering, she had presence of mind to ask: "Why did you flirt with the teacher, even though you didn't like her?"

Pyrrha's hands stilled from folding laundry, sitting next to the tub.

"How'd you know I didn't like her?" she asked.

Nona still didn't have the words to explain. "Just where you put your body—you only looked at her sometimes, that's all."

"Wish I'd had you in the Bureau," said Pyrrha, but she didn't answer the question.

That was why Nona was allowed to go to school, on the understanding that she would say she was living with her sister and a friend of her father's and that everyone else was dead. This was an answer so ordinary and boring that she soon wished she had been given a more interesting one, for cultural cachet.

Although Nona was officially a Teacher's Aide, she quickly learnt that she was really only interested in three parts of school. The first was games; the second was the Hour of Science; the third was the coloured markers that you could write on the squeaky whiteboards with and then rub off with a cloth so that you could mark again, which she was allowed to do to her heart's content. In fact, she only loved the Hour of Science because that was when she was allowed to look after Noodle, the science teacher's dog, who was a dirty white creature with six legs and a gentle disposition. She looked after Noodle while everyone else had to wrap ice cubes in socks and the normal nice lady teacher, Joli, marked books or drank big cups of hot tea; then during games she watched to make sure nobody hit balls through any of the windows in the abandoned building next door. If they did, the ball was lost, because there were still mines and burnables all over. Neither of these duties was particularly hard, and she considered her lot a happy one. It was all unpaid, of course, but when she was at the dairy or talking to the people who weeded plants in the park, it was such fun to say, "I work at the school" when they asked her what she did. Everyone always said she was doing good work and they couldn't ever even think of doing it themselves but well done her.

It was just as hard to make Nona learn any facts as it was to make her learn the sword or the bones—harder, probably; as she explained all the time, as sweetly as she could, her brain simply wasn't interested in them. It was as though someone had probably told her everything before and she had already forgotten it. Every lesson she sat in on, at a rickety desk with an old plastic chair at the back of a class full of kids, she could feel exiting her ears as soon as it entered them with the ring of old familiarity—it *felt* and *sounded* as though she had heard it all before. The teachers were amazed when they found out about her being able to speak all the languages, but Pyrrha had schooled her to say that she had had "lots of resettlements," which seemed to suffice. The nice lady teacher abandoned trying to teach Nona, and instead treated her like a good, simple colleague who could be relied upon to clean whiteboards and look after extraneous dogs and explain to the littlest children, in a variety of languages, where the bathroom was— which was really all teachers wanted.

At school, after the first week, Nona was cornered by five children who informed her that she was now their friend.

"Okay," said Nona.

"Hot Sauce wants you," she got told.

Hot Sauce was the oldest child, at fourteen, but would have been the authority no matter her age. She was queenly for her years and spoke very seldom. She had burns on most of her body and had got to hold a gun in a war. If you were new to the school her group always eventually found you and said, "You have to come and see Hot Sauce," and took you to Hot Sauce, and Hot Sauce would lift up her shirt and hoick up her shorts and show you the burns. This was intended to instil a sense of reverence in the fresh meat, not disgust, but the group was just as proud if the new child broke down crying or didn't want to look.

Hot Sauce herself was blank and unmoving in her moods and did not seem to have many strong passions, except that she was violently disdainful of every subject but the Hour of Science.

Nona wanted to know why Hot Sauce wanted her.

"You're old and can get us drugs," said Honesty, who was twelve and served as Hot Sauce's lieutenant. "You live in the Building."

None of them was crestfallen when Nona told them that she was not allowed to get anyone drugs; they took it with stoic acceptance. "What's special about the Building?" she asked.

"It's banned," said Honesty.

One of the other children, Beautiful Ruby, said: "My mother says that if you get caught downtown or you shoot at the wrong window you get taken to your building."

"But you play in the garage all the time," said Nona. "I've seen you. You were one of the ones who hit a car with one of the big hard balls and the alarm went off for three hours."

"Ah," said Beautiful Ruby wisely, "but that isn't *in* the Building.

That's the garage. You can see out through the struts, so it doesn't count as being *in* the Building."

"You need to show us the secret room where they keep the bodies after you're taken to the Building and shot, or you can't be our friend anymore," said another child, Born in the Morning, who was the group's negotiator.

"I can't," said Nona, in agonies. "I only know the cupboard in my place where the hot water cylinder is."

The children got together and agreed that this was complete shit, not good enough, and not up to expectations. But when they petitioned Hot Sauce, Hot Sauce simply said: "She talks to the Angel. She gets to look after Noodle."

The Angel was what they called the nondescript, washed-out, dusty-haired personage who came to teach the Hour of Science. Why they called her the Angel was unclear, but Hot Sauce idolised her: she was widely liked by all the children, because she was calm and even-handed and the same day in and day out, but for Hot Sauce and therefore the others it was more like an obsession. Nona got to look after the science teacher's dog and knew its name and could report on how its fur felt (nice) and how its breath was (awful). She received such pearls from the science teacher's lips as: "Was Noodle a good boy for you today? Thank you, Nona," which made her an elevated personage.

Facts about the Angel were in short supply. Where the science teacher lived was a mystery, and Nona's hours were such that there was no way she could follow the science teacher home to see where home was or what she did there. Camilla came and picked Nona up every day after lunch, when school shut down in the afternoon heat, and the Hour of Science happened before lunchtime.

So all in all, Nona's worth to the children was universally agreed to be minimal. She ranked very low among them, definitely below Honesty and Beautiful Ruby and only fractionally higher than Born in the Morning. The only person Born in the Morning outranked was the seven-year-old, who was just Kevin.

Those were really all their names—even Kevin—but nobody ever told Nona why Hot Sauce was called Hot Sauce. Hot Sauce had no parents, so she couldn't ask them. The other kids had thirteen people at home between them, but the numbers were skewed by Born in the Morning, who was saddled with five fathers: Eldest Father, Second-Eldest Father, Brother Father, Younger Brother Father, and New Father. More importantly to Nona, Beautiful Ruby had a new baby at home, and sometimes Ruby's mother brought the baby to the school foyer and she could look at the baby's fingernails, which were small.

Nona explained all this to Camilla and to Pyrrha and sometimes to Palamedes over dinners, usually in the hope that she could talk so much nobody would notice she wasn't using her mouth to eat. They all agreed that whatever made Nona happy at school made Nona happy at school, but the bottom line remained that she shouldn't buy anybody drugs.

"I don't," explained Nona. "Honesty found someone else to buy him drugs, so I don't have to."

"Is his name really and truly *Honesty*?" Palamedes wanted to know.

Nona struggled.

"That's how I hear it. Anyway, he shouldn't be called *Honesty* at all, he tells huge lies and he's trying to teach me too."

Nona longed to lie, but didn't know how to stop her body from showing the truth; at first, she had triumphantly caught every one of Honesty's lies, until he took her behind the bike sheds and said he would give her a cigarette a week if she stopped. He was lying, but she could see how much it meant to him, so she stopped. And when she *did* get a cigarette, she slipped it to Pyrrha.

Most of the best things she learnt from Pyrrha, and Palamedes and Camilla, whom she loved and trusted with all her numbered days; but in those early times when she wasn't used to living, the schoolchildren had taught her everything else. New words, mostly, which were always enlightening, but also how to spend time doing nothing.

They made doing nothing an art: squatting on stoops or loitering in parks beneath splintering trees, running like crazy if they heard shots, running like crazy even if they didn't—so hard to keep up!—hunkering beneath the roofs near the sanitation ponds, going where nobody cared if they went, fighting over scraps of shade near the huge cemetery hills where they had dug all the bodies out of the cracked sand and concrete and put them in a huge pile, which still smelled terrible. One of their favourite ways to hide was to clamber up a dusty mound of rocks and rebar right at the very edge of their part of the city—they had to do this carefully because they could easily slice themselves open on a piece of rusty metal, and that meant Nona had to be doubly more careful than anyone—and sit around on the second floor of a building that had been blown wide open to the sky. There was plenty of stained old office furniture to squat on, and they could watch the enormous stretch of road that ran all around the city. There was a huge expanse of it: Honesty said you could fit twenty vans on it at a time and there used to be a train track in the middle, with turn-offs and turn-offs for the turn-offs that led to a nest of tunnels beneath the city itself. In the tunnels you could drive and drive and drive for hours and never see sunlight, said Honesty, but hardly anyone used them now. There were special fleets of gunners in cars that patrolled down there and shook people up for money, or scavenged the cars that had never made their way out. Every so often an absolutely enormous earthquake rumbled beneath them, and when Nona first asked what it was, Hot Sauce said, "The Convoy"; and because it was Hot Sauce and not Honesty, she knew it had to be true.

How wonderful it sounded—*The Convoy*—so big and mysterious and subterranean. Nona had no real idea of what a convoy was or what it looked like for a very long time, but she joined in with the others when they felt the rumble in the old office-space hideout and competed to be the first to say, "The Convoy," and have the others question, or jeer, or confirm.

"Can't feel it."

"That's a fart."

"No way, no way, that's right. That's the Convoy, I can feel it, my shoes are off."

The whole broken building would rumble and shake, and at the end they would chorus, "Convoy gone."

Nona was frankly disappointed when she asked Pyrrha what

a convoy was, when Pyrrha was half-absorbed in melting slag for dummy pellets in her little bullet-shaped crucible, and Pyrrha explained that it was a bunch of vehicles driving in a line, probably very big ones. But she never quite got over that little shake, that tight vibration of the stomach when the Convoy was near, how it excited her somehow. It was like she could feel something wonderful in it.

They often stayed in the abandoned office building until the glowering dusk, because nobody wanted that space or threw chunks of brick at them to make them leave. Nona loved to watch the moon tremble in front of the big broken hanging blueness in the sky, careless of it, while Honesty prised bullet casings out of holes in the walls and Kevin played with his dolls. Beautiful Ruby and Born in the Morning whiled away the time with a deck of playing cards that had too many numbers for Nona to join in. Sometimes Hot Sauce would play too, but mainly Hot Sauce silently and majestically held court as the city honked and smouldered and yelled.

Nona liked to sit near Hot Sauce; it was good to be quiet. One time they were sitting there and the Convoy rumbled beneath them, with the others hooting and hollering and Kevin putting his hands over his ears patiently waiting for the Convoy to go away, and when the last rumbles had died, Honesty looked over and said—

"You'll join, Hot Sauce, won't you? Hot Sauce will join."

"Join what?" said Nona, the ignorant one.

Which made the others do their usual chorus of—

"Nona doesn't know."

"Nona doesn't know *anything*."

"Tell Nona."

And Honesty, who had been very nice since the cigarette arrangement, said: "When we leave school, we're going to kill zombies, we're gonna kill necromancers."

"You shouldn't say the *word*," said Nona, forgetting in a panic that that was a Nona rule, not a school rule.

All Honesty did was drum his heels on the floor next to the wheelie chair that the stuffing was coming out of and exclaim: "Who cares? I'm not scared. This isn't class, I can say what I want."

Born in the Morning said with an air of old rehearsal, "I threw a rock at a necromancer and it died," and Kevin crowed, "No, you didn't! No, you didn't!" and Beautiful Ruby said, "That's such a bullshit story you tell," and Honesty, easily and hypocritically, said, "You are *such* a liar, my man."

Born in the Morning protested, "I *did* throw a rock and it *did* die," and Nona said, "What, the rock?" at which the others paused in order to jeer at her. Then Beautiful Ruby explained that the rock had been thrown at one of the cages and the necromancer had been almost all the way on fire, and the question of whether or not the rock had even hit the necromancer or the bars was still a live one, but the rock could have helped. A rock hits you in the head you're going to die, aren't you.

While the others litigated whether or not the rock still counted if the necromancer was almost all the way on fire, Hot Sauce, sitting with her legs dangling over the side of the broken floor, had gone very still. Nona always noticed when Hot Sauce was still, because her stillness was peculiar: it wasn't the stillness others got when they were thinking about things in class, markers paused as their brains furiously combed over some answer. It was the stillness of someone *rejecting* thinking. Midargument, Ruby's voice rose over the others— "There aren't any necromancers here anymore, they're all dead."

Born said, "Not all of them. My dad says they're all in the barracks."

"Which dad? You have like seventy."

"Don't say I have like seventy, you know how many dads I got."

"If I had the amount of dads you got, I'd sell some of them," said Ruby.

"You *think* you would, but you *wouldn't*," said Born wisely.

Honesty said, "Some of the zombies go spying outside the barracks, they ain't all mad. That's why you got to make sure you see all your friends eating and bleeding, or, you know—*bam*, you're dead, or bones, or worse."

"*I* eat," protested Nona.

"Nobody's saying *you're* a zombie, you dumbass," said Honesty.

"I'm saying hidden zombies, you know, spies. You're pretty stupid for your age, you know that?"

"I watched Nona eat a pebble," Kevin volunteered, bending one of his doll's legs into position. Then: "And a marker top."

"Don't squeal, Kevin," said Nona, offended and on her dignity; she had just learnt *squeal* and therefore used it constantly. "And Honesty, don't call me a dumbass. At home they said if you called me a dumbass again I should tell you that they know what you look like and they'll beat you up."

"Okay. I don't want to piss off your folks, you live with a pimp," said Honesty.

By that point Nona knew what *pimp* was, and was so annoyed she knew she was on the road to a tantrum. But before intragroup violence could erupt or get contracted out, Hot Sauce raised her voice and said—

"The necromancers will come back. They may already be here."

Everyone subsided into reverent silence at Hot Sauce's proclamation, even Nona, who took the opportunity to do five breaths in and out like Camilla had shown her.

Eventually Beautiful Ruby broke the silence and said, "What about Varun, Hot Sauce? What about Varun the Eater?"

"It's here for them," said Hot Sauce.

They looked up through the big crack at the blued sky respectfully. Then Honesty said— "You'll join up, right, Hot Sauce? You going to go over?"

But Hot Sauce didn't answer, and then Kevin wanted to go to the bathroom, so they had to call out "Not me," to see who had to escort Kevin to the bathroom. He was a big boy and easily old enough to go to the bathroom by himself, but Kevin had such a huge facility for freaking out and locking himself in places that you had to wait until he'd finished peeing to make sure you didn't need to bust a door lock open with half a brick. By the time that had been agreed on (they concluded Ruby had said *not me* last) the question had been dropped, and there was Hot Sauce, very still and looking at the sky.

Nona whispered, "Join what, Hot Sauce?"

Hot Sauce didn't answer her. When she *did* say anything, she asked a question instead, which was irritatingly like Pyrrha. "You like it here?"

"I love it here," said Nona sincerely. "I wouldn't want to be anywhere else."

"You're sweet," said Hot Sauce.

That settled it, Nona knew. If Hot Sauce thought Nona was *sweet,* she was going to be part of the group no matter what. From that day nobody bothered to question Nona's presence no matter what she said or how old she was or how little facility she had for buying anyone drugs. She was one of them, which gave her enormous pleasure. She was born to the untold wealth of belonging to Camilla and Pyrrha and Palamedes, and now added the beauty of being friends with Hot Sauce and Hot Sauce's friends, which gave her high status in the world, even considering Kevin. She loved Camilla and Pyrrha and Palamedes, but the thing about being with Hot Sauce and the others was that you could be completely and entirely alone.

Eventually, when it got dark enough, all their families would come looking for them—Cam always came *horribly* early—except for Hot Sauce, who had nobody to come looking for her, and Honesty, whom nobody ever remembered about. But even with this flaw in paradise, Nona could do nothing but hug her knees to her chest and feel fantastically, wonderfully lucky, luckier than anyone else who had ever had the pleasure of being born.

4

THE MORNING ROUTINE was that they would walk together until Pyrrha had to split off, and then Cam would drop Nona off at school and go off to do her own thing, clean the house or do crimes that Nona wasn't allowed to partake in. Nona liked the walk, but the early morning was as cold as the afternoon was hot, so to keep warm she had to stamp her feet and put her hands in her pockets. They walked alongside all the other workers—the ones who didn't get picked up in the morning in the worker vans, or didn't have a job that merited a worker van, or didn't have a job but lived in hope—and they all trudged slowly through the street in clusters, parting only when a truck ground through, the driver leaning on the horn if someone didn't move out of the way quick enough.

Nona's breath was misting on the inside of her mask and escaping out its cracks in ghostly grey puffs by the time they made it to the park, comfortable but not talking. It was always the same route—straight down the street all the way to the gates of the thing that had used to be the big park—and then Pyrrha would say something like, "Let's cut through, it's so smoky," or she'd say, "Let's not. Park's full of mercs," and then they'd go around. This morning she said, "Let's go through the park. Move with the crowd," so Nona took Camilla's hand and moved with the crowd.

The plants filtered out some of the clinging smoke, and Nona loved to look at the trees and the bristly, curving shapes of the shrubs and bushes. Much of the vegetation had been turfed up, some in an attempt to make a community garden, some of it into shanty houses skulking against the big concrete fence. Another place had been cleared and ineptly concreted over, and they put the cages there. The cages were bone-cold and they'd been almost fully cleaned, but Nona didn't like looking, so she spent her time gazing at the mist of trailing vines on the tree trunks instead.

Once they were out of the park and out of the crowd, Pyrrha kissed the top of Nona's head and said, "Be good," like she always said. She did not kiss the top of Camilla's head but told her, "Good hunting, you two."

"Good hunting," echoed Camilla.

Pyrrha melted into the crowd in her big steel-toed boots and her over-the-shoulder bag with her helmet and extra batteries for her helmet light and her gloves and her lunch. It was easier now than when Nona had been very new and Palamedes said she had no object permanence, but Nona still always felt a pang watching Pyrrha walk away, commingled with the pride of having Pyrrha, the familiarity of seeing someone and knowing they belonged to you. Camilla drew her back to the pavement with a guiding hand on the small of her back, and said the magic words: "You'll be late for school."

Then it was one right turn, one cut through an alley, and one pause as Nona pointed out to Cam a building that had been fine only the other day and now had a huge hole in it ("They used a very big gun," was Cam's explanation) before they got buzzed into the school building by the nice lady teacher and went up two flights of squeaky linoleum stairs. Camilla always turned down the offer of a warm drink in the tiny staffroom, and turned it down quicker the more compassionately she was asked, and then she melted away into the street like a grey shadow. Nona often watched her from the window.

"Kevin's here already, so he can help you take down the chairs and clean the whiteboards," said the teacher.

This was absolute stupidity on the teacher's part, as Nona knew Kevin would not help take down the chairs nor clean the whiteboards, nor do anything but sit on the cushions where the stuffing was leaking out in drifts of off-white beads. Then the teacher said, unexpectedly: "Hot Sauce is here too."

Not even the teacher knew Hot Sauce's real name. Nona said, "That's early."

"Yes. I asked her why, but she wouldn't say. Check on her, won't you?" As though *Nona* could check on *Hot Sauce*. "I'm worried about her, living alone. I've tried to tell her about the sheltered accommodation, but she's too independent . . ."

Nona was still laughing over the idea as she went into the classroom and started taking the chairs down off the desks. Kevin was, as she'd predicted, lying flat on one of the cushions doing something social and complex with two stuffed rodents; but there was Hot Sauce, feline and still next to one of the schoolhouse windows, her burns rippling neatly beneath the electric light when Nona turned it on.

"Turn it off," said Hot Sauce, so of course Nona turned it off. "Come here."

Nona took the plastic, chlorine-smelling box of whiteboards and the rag and the spray bottle with her, and she squatted down next to Hot Sauce, wetting the rag with the stuff in the spray bottle. Hot Sauce said, "Don't let them see you from the window."

"Who's watching?"

"Don't know. Green building. Fourth floor."

Nona was smart enough to catch herself getting up to look, which she privately congratulated herself upon. She placed the cleanly scrubbed white square on the threadbare carpet, which also smelled like chlorine, and started on the second. She remembered about Blood of Eden and all the talking, and it gave her a sudden worry. She said, "Do you think they're watching *me*?"

At least Hot Sauce took her seriously. She went *hmm*, which was how you could tell. "Why would they be watching you?"

"I don't know."

"They were here before you. So. Doubt it."

Nona said, "Who are they?"

Hot Sauce didn't say anything for the longest time. Then she said, "I'm investigating."

Once Hot Sauce said that she would do something, all you could do was wait for Hot Sauce to do it. She would not invite you to help, or ask your opinion. Hot Sauce's failure to ask anyone's opinion on anything she did was probably the reason she was the unquestioned authority in the school, over and above the teachers. Nona had told Palamedes about it and Palamedes had said, Lead researcher material, certainly. So now there was nothing for Nona to do but clean off all the whiteboards and lug the box of them over by Kevin, and when invited examine the silent discourse between the stuffed rodents, which was conveyed by mashing them together. Nona searched for the right words and said, "They're having a baby, aren't they?" and Kevin seemed pleased.

By the time the whiteboards were cleaned and all the chairs were taken down and Nona had emptied the bins, most of the other children had streamed into the classroom. They all sat at their tables, with Nona at a special table at the back for her and any of the smallest children who were feeling wet or vulnerable and wanted to sit in her comforting presence. This morning Nona was left alone, which she liked; Hot Sauce had put the wind up her. She listened with only one ear to the teacher taking the morning roll call, and she took the whiteboard she was allowed to use and drew squiggles on it with only half her brain. The other half of her brain was plagued with questions.

Who is watching the classroom from the green building?

How will Hot Sauce investigate?

Then her mind wandered.

What will Pyrrha check out for Camilla today?

Why is the seat such a nutritious part?

Who am I?

So her drawing wasn't much good, and was further harmed midway through the lesson, when the teacher was taking Honesty and Hot Sauce and Born in the Morning for integers while the nursery class copied things down off the board. One of the tinies who didn't like going to the bathroom alone tugged on Nona's sleeve, so she ended up standing in front of the cubicle lost in thought, and then she got distracted looking at herself in the mirror. It was such a relief to be pretty, and to have the braids that Pyrrha had given her look so dark and juicy and glossy. Cam said her hair was drying up and she had white spots on her nails, but Nona couldn't see it. When the tiny emerged from the toilet Nona helped it wash its hands and return promptly to the numbers on the board, and by then the Angel had arrived.

The Angel looked less like an angel than ever that morning. Nona always liked the science teacher's face, which was sort of snub-nosed and thin and crinkly around the eyes, but that morning she was frankly untidy. She was a gallant little person of fortyish who gave the impression that she had learnt a lot early in life and discovered late that it was no real good to her or anyone else. This lent her teaching a weightless, secretive feeling, like it was really all for fun at the end of the day. She liked to wear button-up shirts, often with suspenders to hold up the trousers, and a dust jacket to keep her clothes neat walking through the city; but that morning her shirt looked like yesterday's shirt and her face looked like yesterday's face—careworn, with her freckles fading into the background of her skin. All of the Angel was tinted in soft greys and browns, but she had delicious reddish freckles scattered on her cheeks and nose which added life and vivacity to her face; not so much today. As Nona led the tiny by hand into the classroom, Hot Sauce had paused on integers to say, "Good morning, sir," which caused a reverberation around the classroom of equally respectful *Good morning sir—Good morning*s; but the Angel's answering "Good morning, everyone" was distinctly pallid.

Hot Sauce noticed that. Nona watched as Hot Sauce never fully returned to integers, but quivered at the front desk with the others, her eyes constantly flicking back to the Angel. Nona thought the Angel was moving like someone who hadn't slept well. Sometimes Pyrrha went out late at night and came back smelling like alcohol, and Camilla would say nothing at all, but if Palamedes was there he would say, "Really, Pyrrha?" and Pyrrha would just say, "Really, Sextus," and then the next morning she would be walking in that same rumpled, weary fashion—though Nona thought she exaggerated it for effect. Nothing Pyrrha drank could really hurt her. She had even drunk the contents of the bleach bottle once. When Palamedes had asked why, Pyrrha said she had realised she wasn't used to being tortured while immortal and wanted to get a head start, and Pala-medes said *bullshit* because he thought Nona had not been listening. Nona wondered if the Angel had been drinking too, albeit not bleach, which had given Pyrrha some sensational hiccups. She shared this thought with Hot Sauce and the others at break time after numbers and reading, when they huddled in the corner with their sliced fruit.

"What, hungover you mean?" said Honesty. "Give us your fruit, Nona."

"I already promised it to Ruby," said Nona, whose portion was al-ways promised before class started, sometimes days in advance.

"Fuck you, Ruby," said Honesty. "You *know* I want it when it's stone fruit."

"You shouldn't always get whatever you want," said Beautiful Ruby.

"I never get whatever I want," said Honesty, inconsolable.

"If you swear again I'll make you go and put your name up on the board," said Nona.

Hot Sauce said—

"The Angel doesn't drink."

Born in the Morning wanted to know how Hot Sauce knew. Hot Sauce simply said, "Because I know," which ended that line of ques-tioning.

Beautiful Ruby, perhaps buoyed by being that day's fruit recip-ient, held out cupped hands for the foodstuff in question and said: "Hey, you don't look so well lately, Nona. You look kind of sick."

Everyone turned to look at Nona, who writhed beneath this judge-ment, and they agreed that she had not looked well for, like, weeks. "I *do*," she said indignantly. "Look at my braids—I look wonderful," which thankfully replaced their worry with a group effort to squash her vanity. They often took it in turns to squash Nona's vanity, which never worked. Beautiful Ruby, the best-looking out of them all and therefore the authority on looks, had once said, "You got the face of a rat and the body of a dead person," but Nona knew she was beau-tiful and was complacent about it. Even if they *all* assured her that she was nothing to write home about, she could say, "Who cares? I can't write," and then they had to switch tack and squash her for being proud that she was so goddamned stupid. Nona quite liked this really; it made her feel like she belonged. They were all proud of her stupidity, in the same way that they were proud of Honesty's rampant crimes and of Hot Sauce being the most important person in the universe.

Ruby ate all of his stone fruit and nearly all of Nona's too, then he magnanimously said, "I'm full. Honesty, you take the last bit. I get fruit at home."

Honesty was not overburdened with shame. "Lucky boy, lucky boy," he said, and he tossed the fruit up in the air—the rest of them shouted—and caught it in his mouth, which he always did. Honesty had the widest mouth Nona had ever seen. He chewed and did not bother to finish chewing before he said, "I don't mind telling you I need the blood sugar. I've got a job after lunch."

Born in the Morning scoffed, "*Real* job or *Honesty* job?" but Born in the Morning was always a bit of a stickler.

"Real job, sunshine, real job. *Underground*," he added, and tapped his nose mysteriously.

Hot Sauce said—

"Dangerous."

"I know; those tunnels is hell," said Honesty baldly. "But I'll be in a car the whole time and no shooty-shooty, it's just stripping stuff off the pipes again."

Beautiful Ruby was impressed. "You should've said, I would have given you half if I'd known."

"I'm not a boy who boasts," said Honesty.

"God, you're a liar," said Born in the Morning.

When the class teacher clapped her hands together and announced the Hour of Science, which meant Nona was about to get the Hour of Noodle, Hot Sauce dawdled behind. She looked Nona dead in the eye, the ripples of her burns making pretty ridges up and down one cheek, and she said— "You're right."

"That I'm beautiful?" said Nona.

"No. About the Angel. The Angel's worried."

"Okay," said Nona.

"Stay on the grounds today," said Hot Sauce. "When you take Noodle."

It was getting hot. When she took Noodle down the side stairs of the building and went out through a side door to the rubble out back, the heat hit her like a slap—not as uncomfortable as it would be later, but enough that it wasn't hard to do as Hot Sauce said and keep to the shade with Noodle. He gamely ran a few times around the fenced part, all six of his legs moving in wonderful concert, but then he tired out and came and sat next to her and panted. Nona shared water with him from a bottle and looked around—looked up at the next building and listened to the sounds on the road, all the carolling honks and people calling out to one another—but there was nothing abnormal at all. This was almost worse, because she had been waiting for it. The most interesting sight was someone lounging in an alleyway opposite the school building, sitting in a busted-up chair next to an overflowing bin, and Nona watched intently, trying to decide if they were dead or not. She decided *not* dead, because they were wearing quite a good jacket and faceguard and nobody was coming around surreptitiously trying to take either.

She was somewhat disconsolate and cross by the time the main teacher called out to her from the second-storey window, but she cheered up at the handover: Noodle licked her hand, and the Angel said, "Nona, you are a little lifesaver," and there was the pleasant, after-class dopey feeling of half the children preparing for lunch and sleep. The blinds were being drawn, and a couple of parents were there to pick up children who had food and naps elsewhere, but Hot Sauce and her friends were all dragging their mats together, claiming the coolest and darkest corner of the room.

When Hot Sauce saw her she said, quietly, "Anything strange?" and Nona reported everything, including the possible body, and Hot Sauce seemed satisfied even though there was so little to tell. She said, "Okay. Nothing. Good work, Nona," and Nona was happy again, and forgot all about the body, or anyone watching anything.

CAMILLA WAS WAITING FOR HER in the vestibule where the coats and masks and the bathrooms were. When she asked how school had gone, Nona was able to say "Good!" with perfect truthfulness, and then they sidled away before the main teacher could try to slip them a pamphlet and look Camilla over for bruises, and they walked home in complete amity on the shadiest side of the street. As they went out of the school building Nona looked quickly in the alleyway for the person she'd seen in the coat and mask, but they were gone, which meant either they really had been alive or someone else had gotten to them already.

The heat made the backs of Nona's knees blister with sweat, but Cam, unlike Palamedes, was always merciless about keeping her going. In a way she was glad that it was Cam today and not Palamedes, because even in his short appearances Palamedes liked to ask probing questions about exactly what the teacher was teaching, and to say things like "My God, *that's* how they teach mathematics?" and cluck Cam's tongue in a way that was impossible to answer. Camilla was just quiet and nice and held Nona's hand, and once they got into the Building gave Nona a long drink of ice water from the cooling cupboard.

Nona enjoyed the water, but wilted a little at the sight of Camilla removing a carton of more sliced fruit from the cupboard. She and Pyrrha and Palamedes had gotten it into their heads a month or so ago that Nona could be tempted with fruit, which was true then but not particularly true now. Nona had decided that she was fine with

61

having eaten fruit, but not with *eating* fruit; but she was too cheerful to disappoint Camilla, so they both ate slices of sweating orange melon until it was time to tack up the thick black sheeting on the windows, and then Cam barred the door and gave Nona the bones.

Nona sat cross-legged on the floor and chose to arrange them into a sort of snaking spiral, smallest pieces in the centre and biggest pieces on the outside, as Camilla sat nearby and sketched what she was doing on a brown sheet of butcher's paper.

"Where did you go?" Nona asked, once she had taken the time to admire her handiwork. "When I was at school, I mean."

The pencil stilled briefly. "Seeing people."

"About Site C?"

"Keep going. There are some bones left."

Nona added a big greyish knobble of bone to the spiral, but with no great interest. It was only a bone. Nice to nibble at, boring otherwise. "Done," she said, then guessed, "People like Crown?"

The pencil had been put down. The eyes had shadowed into earthen greys. "Crown," said Palamedes pleasantly, "isn't our friend right now. Okay, take that smallest piece there and try rolling it in your fingers. Feel all the little indentations in that scooped-out portion."

"*I* love Crown," Nona protested, giving the smallest bone a desultory grope.

"Why do you love Crown?"

Nona thought about it.

"She has lovely hair. And when she hugs you she smells like cinnamon, and her breasts feel nice, and she's so big and pretty."

Palamedes looked at her, and then he took the notepad out of Camilla's capacious pockets. Nona despaired: there was always a tick somewhere if she mentioned *breasts*. "That's not exactly *love* as I would classify it," he said. "That's simply a list of things most red-blooded human beings like about Crown. How do you know what cinnamon smells like, Nona?"

"Oh, I don't know. I just do. Is your timer on?"

"Yes, it's on. Thank you for asking. Why don't you pick out the piece of bone you like best, and tell me about it?"

She looked at them all: there were long treelike pieces with branches coming off them, and little wedged pieces and a long smooth piece with a jaggedy end. Nona picked the jaggedy piece and ran her thumb over the prickly splintered end, liking the bright itch. "Am I not allowed to love Crown?" she said.

"I could never stop you from loving anything. I don't have the right. Nobody has the right to tell you who to love or who not to love, and equally nobody's obliged to love *you*. If you were forced into loving them, it wouldn't be love . . ."

Nona liked that.

"That's why I love Hot Sauce and Honesty and my friends so much. They don't *have* to like me, and it was a huge surprise when they liked me, but they do."

"Being unexpectedly loved is so wonderful or terrible, isn't it?"

"Wonderful, I think," she said. Then she said, "Well, *I* still love Crown, anyway."

"She's used to people loving her *anyway*," said Palamedes, with the air of someone not wholly paying a compliment.

"Do we still like the Captain?" (Even Nona couldn't quite *love* the Captain.)

"I pity the Captain to the very depths of my heart, and never did like her much," said Palamedes. "I pity Crown not at all, and like her terribly; that's the problem. Why don't you try to make that end smooth?"

Nona pressed her thumb down hard on the jagged end of the bone piece. The pad of her thumb began to feel warm. The tiny splinters of bone broke her skin, and a pinprick of red blood bubbled up. Nona stuck her thumb in her mouth. Palamedes carefully drew it away— "Good thinking, that's antiseptic, but I can do better," he said—and, with fine lines appearing at the side of Camilla's mouth, the minutest fragment of bone popped out from the blood. Then the wound was gone, and the warm feeling with it.

Nona said curiously, "Does that hurt Camilla?"

"No, thank God. I'd never do it if it did."

"Why is it that the blue light in the sky hurts—other people," said Nona, "but not you and Cam?"

She had asked this upward of a dozen times, especially lately, but Palamedes always answered unhesitatingly no matter how many times he had been asked before. "She's got the wrong kind of body. She and I can cheat . . . for now . . . draw on *me*, not *her*, for the unusual kinds of things that I do, with the downside being that our time is very limited. If I was in her body for too long, I'd hurt her and the blue light would start to hurt me. But in summary, nothing will hurt Camilla so long as I stick to the time limit. Make sense?"

"I think so," said Nona, and deciding: "Yes. That's a relief . . . I wouldn't want anything to hurt Camilla. I love Camilla."

"And why do you love Camilla?"

Nona struggled with this a little. It was like asking why you breathed air.

"I love the way she moves," she said pitifully.

He said, "Me too."

"Do you miss seeing her?"

"Dreadfully. But the recordings are nice."

"Is the blue light going to start hurting Pyrrha, Palamedes?"

Another question she had begun asking again. Camilla said it was anxiety. Palamedes said gently, "No. She's immune to the blue light and it's not going to start hurting her. She's got the right type of body to be hurt by it, but the wrong soul. She was made to be immune to the blue light."

"So do I have the wrong kind of body, or the wrong kind of soul?"

This was the only question Palamedes ever hesitated on.

"We don't know. We were worried that the blue light was hurting you when you first came to us, but you're fine. This could mean that you're like Pyrrha, and that you're immune because your soul is protecting your body. But . . . there are a lot of factors, Nona."

"Is that why—Blood of Eden don't want me?"

"Oh, they want you," said Palamedes. "They want you very badly. Look—are you scared by the conversation Pyrrha and I had this morning?"

"Not really. I mean, I know things are getting worse," she said, wanting to sound worldly. "I know I'm not fixed and we only have a few more months to fix me, and who knows what's going to happen in the meanwhile. But I'm not scared of We Suffer. I like We Suffer."

Palamedes quirked Cam's eyebrows in the way that meant he was amused.

"Just because the commander gave you a sweet the once?"

"It wasn't just that," said Nona.

It was *sort of* that. We Suffer had given her a sweet early on when she had not been having a good day, and she had said, *Keep at the mission, Nona.* The sweet had been *too* sweet—she had to apologetically spit it out after about five sucks because it got too much—but she had liked *Keep at the mission, Nona.* It had made her feel full of purpose.

"In another time and in different circumstances I would also have liked We Suffer," said Palamedes. "Hell, I might have liked all of Ctesiphon Wing. Right now though . . . Tidy up the bones, let's stop for today."

They stopped then started tidying up the bones together, putting them in the false bottom of the big box that was otherwise filled with canned beans.

"Sometimes," she found herself saying, quite meditatively for her, "I don't like it when you do—the necromancy word—" ("You just said it," said Palamedes) "—but it feels nice at the same time. It's mixed up. It's like when you do that, it makes me sad—not sad that you did it, but sad that you *can* do it. Did I say something wrong?" Nona added in a rush, seeing Palamedes's face.

"No," he said, gently, after a moment. "I don't understand yet, that's all. Not even a little. I have so much to learn in the ways of not understanding."

Then he got the expression he only got when he was thinking about doing something. This was the expression that isolated him the most from Camilla's face: Camilla had the same look on her face when she was doing something and when she was thinking about it, which was what made Camilla so hugely unexpected. Before he could do whatever it was though, the timer bleated in his pocket. "Time's up," he said. "Give this to Cam for me, will you?"

And he spread Nona's fingers like he always did, and he quietly kissed the second right-hand knuckle.

Nona always paid so much more attention to the lessons of the hand and the mouth than she did to the lessons of the bone and the sword: they were significantly more interesting. With the bone and the sword she faintly got the impression that she was being read a boring bit out of the newspaper, or one of the two-for-one books Pyrrha sometimes bought from the back of somebody's truck. Whenever she was read to from one of these she was asleep in minutes. But she was good at this, whatever *this* was; she didn't even know; nobody would give her the words, and she didn't have them herself. The first time Palamedes had asked her to do it, quite a long time ago, and the first time she had raised Camilla's hand to her mouth and done it—pretty much exactly as Palamedes had, making the same shape as his mouth had done like she did when speaking languages, and touching the same way as his hands had touched—Camilla had looked at her, and then she had gone away to sit in the bath by herself in the dark for almost an hour, even though there hadn't been any water in the bath.

Now when Nona waited for Camilla's eyes to clear, and she lifted up Camilla's hand to press her mouth to it, all Camilla said was, "Thanks." And she almost didn't flinch.

PYRRHA WAS WORKING LATE THAT EVENING. They were demolishing a big building that everyone was worried was about to come down and squash all of the surrounding streets flat and go right through the road to the tunnels. The work kept on being stop-start stop-start because people couldn't decide who was responsible for paying the workers: the militia or the old civic government. Down at the local dairy one of the old men had grumbled that at least with the Houses around you knew who was paying who and the other old man had said, Is that all you care about, you shameful old bastard, and then they realised Nona was there and to cover up their mutual embarrassment they had asked Nona what *she* thought. She said she didn't mind what happened so long as Pyrrha got paid, because she wanted a birthday present. Then they chucked her beneath the chin and laughed a lot and Nona didn't know why, because she had been perfectly sincere. They each gave her a coffee coupon, and she was so excited that she nearly dropped the coupons twice on the way home.

Now that the last of the heat had died, Camilla was uncapping fresh water to put into the tank so that they could have a bath. Nona had her scrub-down in front of the sink, hopping cold despite the heat, eager to get into the warm water; the door was cracked a little so that she could hear Camilla moving around, sloshing the water around with a stick to make sure there was nothing blocking up the pipe. She said: "Will you read to me?" They were still getting through old news sheets where people wrote in questions about problems they were having and the editor suggested things they could do. They were written half in a language Cam could read and half in one she couldn't. Nona loved these sheets. Nobody in real life would ever have the problems those people in the paper had, and the suggestions were even worse.

"Piece of melon gets you five minutes" was the reply.

"I can eat two," Nona decided. "That's ten." And: "When's Pyrrha coming back?"

"Bedtime, probably. We won't wait up." Then she shocked Nona deeply by saying, "Nona, would you ever want to leave here?"

"What?"

"Live on a farm with the Warden and me. With Pyrrha. Out of the city. Away."

"No," said Nona, startled and not at all pleased. "I love it here."

"Would you love a new home too, if we were all there?"

"Maybe," said Nona, now startled *and* suspicious.

"Is there anything you're not telling me?"

It was the first time ever that Camilla had asked that question. It was such an abundantly awful question to ask. The silence drew out between them in a way that made the tips of Nona's ears feel hot. It felt as though it lasted a very long time.

Then— "Yes," said Nona, faintly.

There was another long pause. "Do you promise to tell me or Palamedes if you get scared about something, or don't know what to do?"

That was more like Camilla. "Sure," Nona said.

"Thanks. We appreciate it." The door opened a fraction, and a plastic saucer with two slices of melon appeared. Nona began rinsing her soapy arms. A voice cleared outside the door, and the sheet rustled. *"Dear Aunty. When my boyfriend and I get into an argument, he goes to the bathroom and then makes me apologise to . . ."*

Nona sat in the bath and ate one and a half slices of melon, which was one and a half slices too many, and got about seven minutes of the letters from people with problems. She laughed a lot. She couldn't read Camilla anything in return, but Camilla liked having baths by herself, so Nona amused herself in the front room taking strips of paper and folding them into little crinkles and streamers the way Honesty and Kevin had shown her. Kevin was very good at folding paper into shapes: he had small and nimble fingers. Despite having waited and waited, it was still hot when they both settled down for bed, but there was a breeze and the windows were open, and they were both comfortable with wet hair and lying with no covers on.

Nona tried to doze as the water dried on her body, listened to a muffled siren falling and rising somewhere beyond the blackout curtains, but she and Camilla were both fidgeting too much—Camilla with some discipline, stretching her legs out, pointing her toes at the ceiling, Nona trying to get comfortable on her back. She waited for Cam to tell her off for being restless, but eventually Camilla asked, "Should I read another letter?"

This was such a nice offer that Nona was pleased and sleepy immediately.

"Cam," she said, snuggling up into her back, "can't you tell me a story instead, like you used to? I'll rest my eyes while you talk."

"You haven't wanted stories in a while. Said you were too sophisticated."

"That was because Beautiful Ruby made fun of me when I said what I did to get to sleep," said Nona.

That had been early on. It hadn't even been that Beautiful Ruby hurt her feelings; it was that the others had shushed him immediately and Honesty had said in a much louder voice than was necessary, "Shut up, lad, Nona can do kiddie things if she wants to," which was a *much* better way of letting her know she was being an appalling baby. And Hot Sauce had looked at her in a way she really hadn't liked.

"Hmm," was all Camilla said. Then: "What kind of story?"

Nona thought about it.

"Tell me the story about how you met me again. Neither you nor Palamedes have told me that one in ages."

"Okay."

Camilla's curt, sweet, low voice took on the tones of recital: "We met you when the Warden saved you, after you were hurt."

Nona supplied, "And it was the first time he showed he could do things like that because he didn't have a body, and you were amazed," and Camilla said, "Who's telling this, me or you?"

Nona subsided. Camilla said, "It was the first time. He and I . . . were trying to talk. He was stuck, not having a body that talked. At the time we knew you were in trouble. You'd disappeared. We'd been trying to get you. We found you and Pyrrha. You were hurt. Pyrrha helped us escape from an attack. We lost people. Ships. Something very important. But we got you away, and we wanted to keep you. Other people said no. But you didn't know what was happening. You weren't a threat to anyone. Neither was Pyrrha. But not many people believed me, or the Warden. Many people said you were too dangerous."

Nona said, "And everyone paid attention to We Suffer, who said, 'I trust them. They will not betray us.'"

"Yes . . . back then We Suffer trusted us. We Suffer even let Pyrrha live. Pyrrha talked fast. Then I found a way for the Warden to come back. That was a relief. He wanted to evoke the break clause . . . which means, he wanted his family away from the Houses. You weren't awake yet. You only woke up for very short periods and you couldn't speak properly. We looked after you. The Warden convinced the Oversight Body, convinced the Sixth House to come with us. We showed them the secret of the installation. We helped them find a stele that would anchor such a big thanergy transition . . . which means, we helped them move. Then the Warden picked sixteen people to talk with Blood of Eden. To discuss the future. You were waking up. You met me for the first time."

Nona said, "What did you think of me?" knowing the answer.

"I thought I didn't know you at all. You were new."

Nona always loved this answer unreasonably; the idea that *that* was when Camilla met her, that was her birth. She said, "I don't re-member much about back then."

"Not surprised. We didn't let you meet many people."

"And we lived here and I got better and Pyrrha went out to work and you taught me how to speak. And then things went wrong."

That had been a hideous time.

Camilla said, "Yes. Then things went wrong. The light appeared. We found out Blood of Eden had lied to us . . . or at least, didn't have the power to look after us anymore. That's it."

Nona stretched her toes out until her ankles burned.

"That was still the kiddie version," she said, faintly accusatory. "I'm more sophisticated, Cam. I can understand more."

"Okay. Keep in mind I never had to practise an adult version."

"Can I ask questions?"

"Go ahead."

"I don't understand why We Suffer hates Pyrrha."

"Pyrrha's best friend killed We Suffer's boss."

That made sense.

"Why did you want to take your families away from the other place?"

"We didn't feel we could be there anymore . . . not until we really understood what we were doing, morally. The Warden is our leader, and our families listened to what he had to say. We voted on it . . . made promises we couldn't keep."

Camilla's voice was bitter. Nona was sorry.

"If I remember who I am, can't I help to find them?" she said.

"That's up to you," said Camilla.

"Will your families like me? Will they say, 'Well done, Pyrrha, well done, Camilla, well done, Palamedes'?"

Camilla smiled audibly.

"No," she said.

After that Nona slept, or thought she was sleeping: she lay in the heat feeling it itch across her body, rolling over to find the cool part of the pillow where Camilla had tucked the frozen blocks in the pillowslip like she did every night. She heard Camilla breathing and felt nearly completely at peace, happy despite everything. Sometimes it was hard not to be happy; sometimes it was so difficult when everyone else had that hard, hurt look at the corners of their eyes that meant they didn't quite know how to carry on: the men at the dairy, Pyrrha, Palamedes, the nice lady teacher at school, Kevin.

When she was 90 percent asleep, she heard the door very quietly unlatch and close. Then she counted, and at the end of five counts there was Pyrrha at the door saying, "Ah, my darling hearts, my sleeping babes, Daddy's own treasures," and Camilla saying without opening her eyes, "Go to bed. I just got her to sleep."

Nona fell asleep and was happy.

JOHN 5:20

I N THE DREAM, she said, "But that's it? They shut you down—it was over?"

They were standing at the top of a hill now. She couldn't remember moving. At the bottom of the hill there was a great swept-out plain, as though somebody had cupped their hand over the landscape and scraped everything to one side. Like filth off a table. It was clean to their left, and to their right, where the invisible hand had stopped, was a huge confusion of rubble and metal and foliage—trees and structures; stones and metal.

He sat down on a patch of brown grass and laughed a little, and said, "Beloved, it wouldn't be over—it wouldn't begin—for a *year.*"

He said: It was the thin end of the wedge. He said that official paperwork claimed they'd decided to pull back and think things through again, but he'd always known they'd reinvested in something else, he just didn't know what. He said when the leak happened everyone suddenly knew everything, their project was all over the news, everyone had a fucking opinion. Then it suddenly dawned on the general public that this was the next move—we really were in the endgame, you weren't going to last the distance—and everyone started to panic. The economy tanked. It hadn't been in great shape to begin with.

A— was panicking because our kill-fee money was suddenly worth nothing and what if the banks crashed and that nothing went too? C— was panicking because with the project over she was getting recalled to England and didn't want to go, she'd got N— and didn't want to leave her, refused to admit they were dating even though we all knew. M— was panicking because we had a health

73

board and someone from Energy coming to talk about shutdown and what the hell were we going to do with all the dead bodies we'd collected to test on?

He said, It was the last one that was getting to me. I knew all those bodies by name. Funny to say, but they were my mates, you know? I'd worked on them for such a long time, and they'd given us so much, and now they were going to get dumped in some concrete skip because after what we'd done to them they couldn't be cremated or buried safely. I hated that.

I didn't have to worry about the public or the media—we had a pet cop, P—. She'd made detective by that point; was going on to big things in the MoD. Knew G— from way back, and G— and I were both hometown boys, so P— kept the heat down for us. We got a lot of attention at first because they wanted someone to blame, wanted to rubberneck, wanted to write up think pieces about it. Wanted to know who we were. M— and A— could've walked into new jobs in a heartbeat but I was irradiated, I'd never work in the industry again. I sure as hell wouldn't be allowed to work on anything else to do with you. I told M— and A— to go and that I'd shut up shop, but they wouldn't leave me. None of them left me.

He said: It was such pandemonium. I mean, the worst was yet to come, but it was like the crisis had been announced all over again. Like you'd sprung this on us out of nowhere, like you'd never said you were sick. We went through the same old shitty questions of what to do. What about the Mars installation, what about the fusion batteries? We've still only got room for five million tops up there, guys, and we haven't worked out how to feed them either. What about the Kuiper platform, what about Uranus, what about the shell we're building there? And it's like, we knew that was going to be slow twenty years ago, before we knew we were fucked. The only way out was to dump the population on an exoplanet. The cryo cans would have let us get everyone to Tau Ceti in my lifetime. Then we could work backward from there. It was about giving you breathing room, you know? I knew I wouldn't live to see you get well, but I wanted to stop you hurting.

He said: I wasn't panicking with the rest of them. I know I should've been. But I wasn't. I kept working on the plan even without backing. Kept refining the canister mixture. It was like I knew more every day about how it should work, what the little niggles were. I was having six breakthroughs a day. They'd all expected me to go nuts. A— kept saying, Are you sleeping, are you okay, are you taking any Class As, you know you can tell me. But I wasn't taking anything. I was sleeping like a baby. I was looking at those guys on the slab and something in me was like, I know you, I know this.

He said, Told M— that. Huge mistake. She was like, *Oh my God, you're drinking, aren't you. You're on amphetamines. You are on coke. You are on amphetamines* and *coke.* I was all, *Yeah . . . Coke Zero.* She didn't laugh. *I* laughed.

He said, I guess I've always thought any pun was automatically funny.

After a while he said, Problem was the electricity guys were all, look, we sympathise but we cannot keep diverting three percent of the country's electricity to your vats. He was a nice guy. The health board man was a dickhead though. Kept saying we had to dispose of the bodies on site, had to do it now, could we liquefy, could we put the fluid in a concrete chamber and bury it. You would've fucking loved that. I was like piss off, those are our friends, we need to treat them with respect. I mean . . . I guess it was me saying stuff like that, which was worrying A—. G— kept saying I was fine, but he was the voice in the wilderness. G— always thought anything I did or said was fine. Not necessarily right, but fine.

And then out of nowhere they said, No more prep. We're shutting you guys down tonight, lights off. And we knew that out of the cans the bodies would degrade immediately. We only had the demo cans; the mass-produced ones were made in a Five Eyes factory in Shenzhen. No question of getting any of the corpses that far. I had to let them go. I went around to everyone, talking to my favourites—I know it was weird having favourites, but let's bloody face it, I'd gone weird—not even saying goodbye, just saying it'll be fine, hang on for me, kia kaha, kia māia. C— made appeal after appeal after appeal.

No dice. They shut down our power to the vats one night, one minute after six. We were all there, waiting, when they turned them off.

He fell silent, and she prompted— "What happened, Lord?"

He smiled out over the hillside, over the flat plains and the twisted rubbish, a strange fleeting thing with teeth.

"Most of the bodies got the melt, like we thought they would," he said. "Damaged beyond repair. Their brains liquefied almost immediately. But, Harrow . . . all the ones I touched, all the ones I loved . . . they stayed incorrupti

DAY TWO

MUSH FOR BREAKFAST—HONESTY'S JOB
GOES TERRIBLY WRONG—THE CITY HAS A
WORSE DAY—CAMILLA-AND-PALAMEDES—
"KEEP HER HOME TONIGHT"—FOUR DAYS
UNTIL THE TOMB OPENS.

7

Nona's dream cut off abruptly. Something wet and heavy and awful had been dropped on her from above, right on her face, splattering drops everywhere. She squealed so loudly that someone above them stamped on the floor, at which point she had to stop squealing. Camilla was inflexible: she had pressed the button, and she had said, "Start."

Nona closed her eyes so hard that she could see bright lights at the fronts, little lightning patterns.

"It's the sitting part. My feet are in the nice water, the safe water. The water's in my boots. My socks are full of it. I'm talking to her but I can't see her face. I tried to, Cam, but it's what always happens, I don't manage to look at it, it just doesn't work."

"That's fine. Keep going."

"We have a talk."

"What do you talk about?"

"I don't know. I can't really understand. I hear the words. Sometimes I open my mouth and words come out and I know I'm talking."

"Sensations? What are you touching?"

"I'm touching her hands. She's touching my hands. But in the dream it's always *my* hands, remember, Cam, I'm touching my own hands but they're not mine."

The pencil scribbled furiously.

"Okay. I know how it is. Keep going."

"There's eyes all around us, red eyes. In the darkness. I remember this time, they're red."

"Do you have any thoughts?"

"Yes," said Nona. "I'm hungry. In the dream. Really hungry."

The pencil stilled.

"You're hungry?"

"I'm *so* hungry," said Nona.

The pencil didn't move. Nona realised Camilla must have been waiting for her, must have been disappointed, so she added in tones of slight injury: "I probably would have remembered more, except then a wet cloth falls on my face and I go 'Ahhh' so loudly that the militia person above us stomps, so Pyrrha's probably going to get another rude letter about us, so really I think the wet cloth on my face isn't a good idea and can you change the alarm?"

"Well, you didn't wake up," said Camilla. "Anything else? Anything else at all?"

"Nothing."

The record button got pushed down with its big bright *clack*. Nona, still rubbing her face where the sponge had hit it, panicked herself out of her clothes. Her arms and legs seemed even more unwilling to move in the same direction than normal, which meant she probably didn't even look like a worm with problems but more like a spider who was about to go terminal. She didn't like the T-shirt waiting for her, even though she had been the one to lay it out. It depicted a cheeseburger with little legs. The tinies liked it, but today she found it juvenile and unprofessional, not the kind of thing for a Teacher's Aide at all. Camilla shone the little light at the end of the clipboard on her so that she could do up the button on her trousers and then the cinch, and Nona spent some time mopping her wet fringe.

"Sorry I gave you a fright," said Camilla. "With the sponge. I didn't mean to."

All Nona's resentment melted away.

"No, I'm sorry I didn't get up," she said, contrite. "If you drop a sponge on me tomorrow I promise I won't scream about it."

"I won't do the sponge again. Failed experiment."

The pencil worked away at the paper. Nona patted her hair down to make sure that the braids were still tight, that nothing was coming out, and when she stood up and peered at herself in the mirror comforted herself on that part: her hair still looked great, at least. There were dark circles under her eyes, and she rubbed them with her thumbs.

"Nona, when you're looking at your hands . . ."

That startled her. Camilla rarely asked anything after Nona had recited her dream.

"Yes?"

"Who do they feel like they belong to? Do you like them?"

Nona chortled. "Not one bit." Nona hated having hands.

But Camilla didn't ask for any reason why; she just squinted a little as though she was trying to figure out what she could make for dinner out of a limited number of ingredients, and said, "Sure. Thank you."

"Was that a clue? Are we any closer? Do you know who I am yet?"

"No."

"That's okay. I love you. Tell Palamedes I love him too, don't forget," said Nona, and, very pleased with herself, went off to brush her teeth and eat her breakfast without even being told; that session had been nice and short.

She was so early that Pyrrha hadn't even started cooking breakfast yet; or maybe Pyrrha wasn't going to cook at all because she hadn't got out the little beaker to fill up the heat ring, and she *was* getting out a big covered dish from the refrigerator.

Pyrrha emerged from the fridge and said, "Cold mush all right? I covered it with fruit juice last night. Threw a handful of dried sultanas in there too, so go hunting."

"Better than eggs," decided Nona. "How was work?"

"Excellent. Two of my guys got in a fight because someone said the fighting at Prithibi had been tougher than the fighting at Antioch. Had to peel them off each other. Ear-biting stuff. Here—take some water, it's going to be a scorcher today."

Nona took the water from Pyrrha's brown, work-chapped hand and even sipped it. It was blisteringly cold.

"Silly thing to fight about."

"Absolutely, but there'll be more of that before the end," said Pyrrha. "They would have just yelled at each other three months ago.

Now they'd happily kill each other over who spilt whose beer. There's more dead bodies in the streets now then there were at the first barracks massacre. You see them lying around, dead, not of exposure either . . . just dead. Creeps me out. How is it at school?"

"None of *my* friends want to kill each other," said Nona. Then she amended: "I mean, they say it all the time, but they don't really. None of the little kids have bit each other in weeks, and when they argue too much Hot Sauce says, *Quiet,* and they're quiet."

"Hot Sauce is a girl with a future, so long as she gets a new name."

"Honesty says there's a really special and wonderful reason behind her name and I should ask her sometime," said Nona, trying to select the smallest possible bowl to have mush spooned into. Tiniest one for her, middlest one for Pyrrha, biggest one for Camilla and Palamedes. Then she remembered last night.

"Pyrrha—why does We Suffer hate you?"

"Because I remind her that her God was just a human being who could get tired and fuck up," said Pyrrha instantly. That was the wonderful thing about Pyrrha: she didn't waste time saying things like "What made you think of that?" or "Why?" She went ahead and answered. In a way though, it was also a bad thing about Pyrrha, because she lied and told the truth at exactly equal top speeds. "I like to think she doesn't hate me so much anymore . . . now that she's seen my famous charm, that is. Now she probably says to herself, 'Of course, how could anyone have resisted it?' Because I'm charming, Nona, that's what I am."

"If you're that charming," said Nona, "how come you're single?"

Pyrrha struck an attitude, with a spoon over her forehead, that looked much too melodramatic for her wolfish, ribby body.

"I've got a broken heart and I'll never love again."

But even though Pyrrha was being ridiculous, Nona thought that she was saying it more truthfully than she wanted to—that if Nona looked at the way the red-brown eyes crinkled at the ends, Pyrrha really *was* brokenhearted somehow; which made complete sense, if she thought about it. Pyrrha had used to be like Camilla and Palamedes and now her equivalent of Palamedes was gone—really dead—killed by a terrible monster that nobody would describe to her. It seemed impossible to think of Camilla and Palamedes being apart. Of course they *were* apart, separated forever by a matter of minutes; but Nona knew they talked to each other in pages of letters and letters and letters. Nona had seen the stacks. Camilla didn't lock them up because Nona couldn't read and when she said to Pyrrha, *Are you going to read my correspondence?* Pyrrha said, *Not unless I need to induce vomiting.*

Nona was pushing mush around with the spoon when Camilla came in, rolling down the rolled-up cuffs of her shirt, and said: "Oh, God, we're on baby food," which of course meant it wasn't Camilla at all.

"Delicious num-nums for baby," said Pyrrha. "Anyway, it's this or beans and dried fish flakes."

"I thought you were bringing home groceries last night."

"I'm on half pay until they find someone to foot the drill bill," said Pyrrha.

"Yes, but what happened to that half?"

Pyrrha spooned the softened mush into the big-size bowl and handed it to Palamedes. "You're going to make someone a really irritating wife one day, Sextus," she said pleasantly.

"Dve, if I thought you were drinking all of our money away I would sleep a peaceful and easy sleep." Palamedes brandished the spoon in her direction. "Who, and whyfor, did you bribe?"

"Some guys. Site C," said Pyrrha succinctly.

"For God's sake, Pyrrha, if it's that hard to access I'll swap you Site B, Cam and I have ways and means of accessing—"

"I would pay any amount of money to stop you taking that risk you take," said Pyrrha, digging a spoon into her mush and placing it squarely in her mouth. "Mmm, mmm. It's so swallowable."

"Pyrrha," said Palamedes, "we only do it when we have to, and we'd do *anything* for a clue."

Pyrrha dropped her voice very low.

"Who gives a shit about clues? It's a thalergetic fuckfest you're subjecting that cerebral cortex to, is what it is. Every time you overlap, son, you're subjecting her thalamus to appalling stress—"

"I greenlight it every time, I thoroughly scan her for—"

"You should be draining and replacing her fucking brain fluid," said Pyrrha. "When Gideon and I designed that trial, I used to crack his skull and sieve it myself, just as a control variable. It's aggregative. I doubt you're testing her white blood cell count either. The only other people I put through that damn trial were Mercy and Cris, because only Cris didn't mind being trepanned on the regular. Fucking around with *souls* is the problem, Sextus . . . you can't ever get the full data on souls."

Palamedes ate a spoonful of mush very deliberately and thoughtfully.

"So you think I trust myself too much," he said.

Pyrrha said, "I think that you can't be your own checks and balances, and you shouldn't try."

"Sometimes you remind me of my mother," he said.

"A woman I'd kill to meet," said Pyrrha.

"Let's hope you get the chance," said Palamedes. "Then again . . ."

Nona teased a soft, swollen sultana to the top and mulched it between her teeth, trying to eat it very delicately. The mush wasn't bad, only too sweet and a little gritty, but she always had to decide which bits of it she could eat without either bringing it back up or anyone else working out what she was doing. She said, "Are you two fighting now because everyone else in the city is fighting?"

Both Pyrrha and Palamedes looked a little hunted and guilty.

"Don't get too cute to live, kiddie," said Pyrrha, but after all she had said *kiddie*, and given one of her plaits a twitch. "We're stressed, that's all. Eat your mush . . . God, this stuff's awful."

Funnily enough, Nona didn't mind it too much; it was so different from normal food that it was easy to swallow as much as she possibly could without thinking about it, which got her cheap praise from Pyrrha and Palamedes both. Palamedes ate his with a mechanical fury—"Can't starve Cam," he said—and then once he had just about finished with the bowl his timer beeped and he said, "Thank God! I did it," and then there was Camilla. Camilla looked at Nona and said, "Update?"

"Palamedes hates mush," said Nona.

"We had mush?" Camilla looked down at her plate, and then looked up at Pyrrha, who had reserved all of her sultanas for last and was spooning them into her mouth. She said, "What happened to the food money?"

"I'm not fighting over this twice," said Pyrrha.

After that there was still lots of time before school, so they did one of Nona's favourite things. Nona got to stand on Pyrrha's feet as Pyrrha and Camilla both lay down and did their morning crunches, their sit-ups, and their stretches, with Pyrrha helping Camilla to stretch both her legs to the point where Nona was afraid she would go *snap*—and then they ruthlessly stretched out Nona too, making her touch her toes, making her stretch out on one leg, stretching *her* out too until she *did* hear a lot of little things go *snap* and felt brief, bright sizzles of pain. "Got to keep your muscle up," said Pyrrha, "this is brute-forcing it." At the end she got her back and her calves rubbed, which was the best part. She felt breathless and sparkling by the time they started downstairs, more tired than she dared admit, but by the time they hit the street and wandered past the big steaming vents with the rest of the crowds Nona felt better.

They went down the street all the way and didn't take any turns until Pyrrha said at the park gates, "Too busy. Let's go around," and so Nona took Pyrrha's hand and they went around. They turned left at the dogleg around the park, past all of the braver stall owners and merchants setting up their wares, smoking cigarettes, setting down long untidy cables attached to exhaust fans to blow smoke away from their shoppers. Nona hung back a little on Pyrrha's arm to see all of the rows of thin synthetic shirts and plastic-coated boots until Pyrrha said, "What d'you want from the cheap-jacks, No-No?"

"Oh, nothing—except it *is* my six-monther soon," she reminded Pyrrha.

Camilla said, "You can get a present once it's been a year."

Nona was alarmed; if she didn't get a present *now* there was a good chance she would not get to have one later.

But Pyrrha said, "God, you think she's ever gotten presents? I visited her hometown back before Anastasia got settled, and it was grim as fuck *then*. Just spooky caves all the way down . . ."

This interested Nona, except Cam said sharply, "Don't lead," and Pyrrha said, "No leading, ma'am, I understand. What do you want for a gift, Nona?"

Nona seethed in a welter of greed.

"I want a pack of coloured rubber bands to tie my hair up with so that you can put one colour on one braid and another colour on another, like Beautiful Ruby has."

Pyrrha said, "I said a *present*, Nona, something that costs something."

Nona was puzzled. "That's why I picked it, it's cheap so you can probably get it even if you have to pay the demo crew half your money. You don't earn much in the first place."

"Domestic life," said Pyrrha to Camilla, over Nona's head, "is immensely depressing and has a lowering effect on the ego."

"Sometimes," said Camilla unexpectedly.

Once they went down two streets and back to where the park cut-through usually led them, Pyrrha kissed the top of Nona's head and said, "Be good," and to Camilla said, "I'll be home for dinner, honey, so don't go out with your girls and get your nails did."

"Try to bring home something useful this time," said Camilla.

Nona felt a pang to see her go, sauntering off with her lunchbox and her helmet and her spare jacket, whistling a tune like she was any other worker. Then Nona was turning right with Camilla, hustling through an alley, past the building that now had the hole in it because of the very big gun. There was only one change, in that Camilla picked a different road to go down because she spotted a pair of legs sticking out underneath a parked car and decided to go a different way, and then Camilla and Nona got buzzed into the school building by the nice lady teacher and stood in the vestibule shaking their boots. Nona was just in time; the move around the park meant she wasn't early at all. Cam stopped before Nona went to mount the stairs.

"I'll come to pick you up at the usual time," said Cam.

Nona said, "Aren't you coming up?"

"Not this morning." Then Camilla was gone.

Which was a little puzzling; but as Nona stood in the cloakroom and unbuttoned her sand jacket and unrolled the sleeves, her attention was caught by the voices of her friends already in the classroom, and that of the nice lady teacher. When she peeked in, the nice lady teacher was leaning over Honesty and applying a cloth to one side of his face, with Kevin and Born in the Morning gathered around. A cluster of tinies who had come early were watching the proceedings in fascination

"Hi, Nona!" Honesty bawled, in some agitation, when he saw her. "Miss, let Nona do it—Miss, this is hurting my dignity."

The nice lady teacher was plainly stressed. She looked at Nona with relief and said, "Nona, could you come and hold this? I don't trust Honesty to keep it still."

"It's too fucking cold is why," said Honesty.

"Language, thank you," said the teacher coolly.

"Sorry, miss," said Honesty, "only it *is* so f—f—it's cold as hell is what it is."

The teacher removed the cloth as Nona approached, fascinated. Kevin said, "Honesty's face smashed in," and Born in the Morning hastily said, "It's nothing, it's just a black eye."

But *what* a black eye! Honesty's whole eyeball was alarmingly bloodred and the bit around the eye was already turning startling colours, red and purple and blue. Nona was glad enough to take the cold, tingly-smelling cloth and put it back over the whole mess. Honesty whined, "For God's sake," but the teacher said— "Hold it there until the bell goes. Born in the Morning, wipe the whiteboard, please. The rest of you, give Honesty some space immediately. Books out—things ready—then down on the mat waiting for the bell."

Awestruck, Nona kept peeking at the eye, then remembering she was a Teacher's Aide and reapplying the cloth hastily. Honesty asked, "What *is* that stuff?"

"I don't know—medicine probably," said Nona. "Honesty, *what happened*?"

"You should see the other guy," said Honesty, very loudly. Then he said, in lowered tones, "Shut up, Nona. Haven't you seen a black eye before?"

"Not really," said Nona honestly. Whenever Pyrrha got hit hard in the face it was better in seconds, and neither Camilla nor Palamedes ever got hit hard in the face, and of course *she'd* never gotten any kind of black eye she could see. She said, "It looks awful—your eye's all bloody and your cheek's huge."

Honesty puffed up at this.

"I guess it's hideous."

There was no sign of Hot Sauce, not until the Angel came in with her tie on squiff and her shirt buttons all done up into the wrong holes, still wearing the same trousers that she had been wearing yesterday. She wasn't late today, but she looked more tired and lined than she had the day before. Somehow she even looked shorter, more hunched and defeated, but she rallied magnificently when she saw Honesty. She paused in front of him and Nona and said, "Go on, let me have a look at it."

Nona peeled away the cloth to reveal the damage. "Nasty!" said the Angel appreciatively.

"Think I'll get a scar?" said Honesty.

"No, it just looks disgusting," said the Angel, looking him over. She reached over to probe gently at one of the swollen bits as Honesty flinched. "It's going to hurt like fury, though."

The main teacher came over with a relieved expression, having seen off a parent.

"Oh, thank goodness you're here. I wouldn't have the first clue what to do. Does he need to go to the clinic?"

"No, nothing's detached or broken, as far as I can tell," said the Angel, draping the cold cloth back on his face. "Once he's had ten minutes with that we'll get him an icepack wrapped in a towel. What in living memory hit you, Honesty? This wasn't a fist."

But Honesty glared at her truculently out of his other eye.

"How do *you* know? You weren't there. It might've been a fist. Might've been two."

"Honesty, she's a doctor," said the nice lady teacher.

"Well," said the Angel, straightening her lapels in a funny way, "I am *adjacent* to being a doctor, and I'm getting a good crash course in, er, triage. Anyway, Honesty, if you don't want to talk about it that's your lookout. I don't like violent stories myself."

"I'm not squealing to anyone. I'm not Kevin," said Honesty.

"Sure. Nobody here minds. Be good for Nona, she's doing you a favour."

The nice lady teacher looked as though she *did* mind, but she followed along in the Angel's wake, chatting inconsequentially about traffic, which left Nona to hold the damp cloth to Honesty's eye and shield him from goggle-eyed tinies until the bell was rung to start the school day. The Angel got him an ice pack wrapped in a staffroom dish towel and he seemed quite glad to hold it to his face, really.

Hot Sauce had trailed in behind the Angel at a suitable and careless distance. She passed by her own seat and ousted a tiny who sat near the window, and when questioned about it the tiny peeped up that they had *wanted* to swap with Hot Sauce anyway, so all the main teacher could say was that they would swap back please after the break. Nona rather doubted whether this would happen, and in any case it was a silly idea to pit your will against Hot Sauce's. Hot Sauce was always going to win and the whole class knew it.

This was illustrated at break. All of the gang were inclined to fawn over Honesty with his wound—Nona's fruit had been promised to Born in the Morning but Born in the Morning didn't even raise an issue when half that portion got slid along to Honesty—and most of the class had clustered around too, out of their seats when they weren't meant to be, asking him if his eye was going to fall out. Hot Sauce told them, "Scatter," and they scattered.

Then she said—

"Who did this to you?"

"You don't have to go apeshit, Hot Sauce," Honesty said sulkily. "I don't want to talk about it. I *can't* talk about it. I promised."

Hot Sauce sat down on the cushion in front of him. She waited, resting her elbows on her knees and her hands in her lap, and she stared with her eyes open, not blinking, not watering. She did the thing she only did every so often, and only when they all begged her to—made her eyes go very wide and the corners very white. Because the stiff greyish-roseish ripples of her burns didn't move when the other bits of her did, this made her suddenly lopsided and terrible with waiting. Born in the Morning and Beautiful Ruby and Nona all stopped eating and got very quiet. The only one who kept eating in perfect serenity was Kevin.

Honesty swallowed and said, "Come off it, boss."

Hot Sauce said, "You keeping secrets from me, Honesty?"

Honesty shrivelled. "Nah."

"Okay," said Hot Sauce.

Even shrivelled, Honesty still wavered, which Nona found impressive.

"Boss—maybe not in front of, you know, the kids—"

"We don't have secrets from each other," said Hot Sauce.

Honesty swallowed again. He bent his head toward the rest of them and stared at the floor. At this cue they all put their heads together, even Nona, despite the fact that Camilla had said not to do that if at all possible because of nits.

Honesty dropped his voice so low that they almost couldn't hear it. Then he said what had hit him. Nona, who was good at hearing whispers, didn't have to strain to make it out, but Hot Sauce said, "Say that again," probably because she didn't believe it.

This made Honesty go red, and he hissed— "A *streetlight*. I'm not fucking kidding you here."

Born in the Morning's voice was shrill with astonishment. "My man, how'd you let a *streetlight* hit you?"

"Keep it quiet," Honesty said, and Kevin said, "It fell on you."

"No, I ran into it with my face, so hard I fell on my ass and blacked out and when I woke up some wino who felt sorry for me had dragged me into their alley, so that's how low I fell, I got babied by a tramp," said Honesty. Then he said more reflectively, "Probably saved my life though. They were good tramps. Didn't understand what the fuck they were saying. They kept checking my eyes and my mouth and miming going 'Ahhh' and fucking biting at the air. Wonder if they were on something new, I gotta know for market economics."

Honesty was talking very fast. When he had taken a couple of breaths and put a piece of fruit in his mouth for comfort—it was tiny sprays of green berries, the slightly soggy kind you had to suck off the stems—he said, "Anyway, I was out of my fucking mind scared."

Hot Sauce said, "The job?"

"Yeah." Honesty fidgeted with the empty spray and picked between one of his teeth with it, which seemed to give him courage. "It was a fucked-up job. I'm not doing odd jobs with those guys anymore. Well . . . can't anymore even if I wanted to, come to think of it."

Now Hot Sauce was very quiet and gentle when she said—

"Tell what happened."

Honesty took another spray to fortify himself. It was one of Beautiful Ruby's sprays, but Beautiful Ruby didn't even complain.

"I thought the job was to go down into the tunnels and get the stuff off the pipes, but it was van guys," said Honesty, very fast. "I said no sir, not if we're knocking off a gun vehicle, but they said no, they were gonna grapple for air-con units off the tops of megatrucks— you know, circuit boards and coolant and shit. They said the trucks don't even notice until the next pit stop if you do it right, the driver just thinks a gasket's blown or something. I dunno, one of the old chicks explained it, but I didn't get it. And I wasn't gonna be grappling, I was gonna be put in one of the overheads holding out the net so the grapplers could get back up. I don't get sick around heights."

He suckled one of the sprays completely free of berries and chewed them. This close up there was a little bit of saliva so everyone went, "Ugh," and leant back, but then they leant back in.

Honesty said, even more quickly now, "It was a neat job, right? They drop on the van from the top of the tunnel, they unscrew the unit, then down the end of the street we're there with the net and we scoop up the guy *and* the unit. The timing's sweet as hell."

He looked at Hot Sauce, implacable and opposite, and he swallowed again and said, "Worked fine first two times. Then they were like, let's do a third, let's do a third, and their guy in charge was like, well we don't have a timetable but okay, we'll get into position and if something comes along we'll do one last run. So the guy gets in position and so do we . . ."

He stopped.

"Keep going," said Born in the Morning urgently. The rest of them *shush*ed him, Hot Sauce included, and even Kevin. Honesty didn't join in. His eyes only met Hot Sauce's eyes now.

"Then we heard the noise," whispered Honesty. "I thought it was an earthquake, I—I just about pissed myself. Just about. I saw them go beneath me—the heat nearly fuckin' roasted me and the other guy, but we'd skinned up and I always slop extra thermal, like you tell me, I'm the good boy, I burn like fish in a rowboat, don't I. We had on masks so we didn't choke, even me, they're professionals, but—but the guy had fuckin' *dropped* for them. I don't know what the fuck he was thinking, why did he drop? Why did he drop for *that*? Fucking nuts man, fucking nutter, just braindead, just out of his ears."

This was all pretty incoherent and Nona didn't quite follow it, and Honesty's voice had risen in a kind of strangled way and broken a little too and nobody had even made fun of that either. Then Hot Sauce reached out and put her hand quietly and firmly on Honesty's shoulder, and that calmed him down, but he was sweating, he was warm. He smelled like overheated animal.

"So we pick him up when he beeps us. We get the net out," Honesty said, more slowly, more methodically. "We get him up and he hasn't even got shit. He's like, go. Go. Lead guy's like, get out, get back to the car. So we climb up the pipes and we get out to the vehicle and we stash everything else and I get in. I'm in the car with the guy, and his boss is there over the radio, and this guy—this guy's fuckin' crying. He's a grown man. He's all like, I fucked up, I fucked up, and the boss is like, who did we hit, and he's like, I dunno, and then he tells us this fucked-up story—says he dropped onto the back and it was real sophisticated, he climbed down into the vent pipes to get the unit, pay dirt he said, real good stuff, but then he . . . he pulled up a vent, and he saw down into the cargo trawler, and he said he saw . . ."

Honesty broke off. A shiver ran down Nona's spine. Nobody asked him to continue.

"People with no eyes," said Honesty.

Born in the Morning said unsteadily, "He was bullshitting you."

Honesty ignored him. He said, "Said the eyes was all white. But he said he was moving quietly, real quietly, and these guys—they're all just sitting around—they all look up . . . they all look at him . . . with these white-out eyes . . . they all look up *at the same time.* They look at him. He kept saying that," he said suddenly, breaking off. He said, "Kept saying, they saw me, they saw me, oh my God."

His voice took on a more normal cast and he said, "Then he said that someone in the van behind started taking potshots at him so he called for pickup. The boss was all, calm down, calm down. But then . . . then the driver said we were being followed . . . and the guy goes crazy sobbing and apologising, saying he fucked up, he got us in trouble, and then one of the old chicks is like, get the kid out, and . . . and they stop the car and there's another two big trucks pulling up behind us, militia trucks with guys, and . . ."

For a moment Honesty couldn't talk. They all sat there together and breathed as one, Nona matching her breath to Hot Sauce matching her breath to Honesty and Beautiful Ruby and Born in the Morning and even Kevin, all in one tight and sweating circle.

Then in a completely normal and even brassy voice, Honesty said, "Then I ran like fuck and I bonked my head on a pole so bad I probably got brain damage, so you have to all be very nice to me."

The whole group absorbed this. Nona reached down for one of the empty sprays and chewed at the ends, wanting *something* to chew on, if not to eat, liking the way the tough fibrous stem felt between her teeth.

Then Born in the Morning said, "You just said like forty-two swears."

"Oh my God, man, shut up," said Honesty.

"It's not fair if I swear and get in trouble with Nona and Honesty doesn't," said Born in the Morning.

"Shut up, Born in the Morning," said Kevin.

And because Kevin never told anyone to shut up, Born in the

Morning shut up. But that was okay—that broke the atmosphere. Hot Sauce kept her hand on Honesty's shoulder and said, "You think they're following you?" and Honesty said, "Nah. Nah," and then: "I'm your boy, right, Hot Sauce? I'm your best boy?"

"Yes," said Hot Sauce gently, "you're my boy. I'll take care of you."

Then there was the main teacher standing over them, and they looked up guiltily from their huddle, but she was only smiling at them in the way teachers did when they thought they knew what was going on and didn't really.

"Group meeting, is it?" she said, kindly. "Honesty, here's one of the shelter pamphlets, okay?"

Honesty was so affrighted that he just said, "Yes, miss, thank you, miss," and took it.

"Don't worry about a thing," she said. "Clean up, everyone, it's nearly class time. Nona, could you ring the bell? Then you'd better leash up Noodle. I want to mark some books."

Nona jumped up immediately. "Yes, of course."

But she didn't go *right* away. She went back down into a crouch as the rest of them picked up fragments of stem and crushed berry from the floor—not so many crushed berries, they weren't stupid—and she volunteered, "I'll take care of you too, Honesty."

"Who wants you to take care of me?" said Honesty cheerfully, getting to his feet. "You're dumb as a box of hair, Nona."

Nona was indignant, but Hot Sauce said, "How many vehicles?"

"I dunno," said Honesty. "I wasn't counting the whole way and the guy picked the middle one, middle-ish. Over ten. Could've been twenty. Megatrucks, all of 'em. I tell you what," he said, and he brushed his trousers off, and he said heavily: "*I* know what it was. I hang out with you lot. I know the deal. Nobody ever asks poor old Honesty . . . Honesty could've told him not to try and knock off the goddamned Convoy."

8

HOT SAUCE APPROACHED NONA before the Hour of Science and said, "You're still on lookout."

What with all the fuss about Honesty it had completely escaped Nona's mind that someone was watching, or that Hot Sauce was investigating. But that was Hot Sauce for you; Hot Sauce never forgot.

Nona said, keeping a weather eye on the Angel, chatting to some of the smaller kids as she got out a bucket of ice cubes and socks (they were finishing off a unit on temperature): "She still *looks* tired."

"Yes."

"I should make her a coffee," Nona said decisively. "I'm a Teacher's Aide, I need to look after the teachers too." And: "Did *you* know she was a doctor?"

"Yes," said Hot Sauce, without explaining. And: "When you're out there today, I want you to pretend to do something."

"Okay. What?"

"I want you to pretend you've got a radio," said Hot Sauce, "and you're making a call."

As Nona had never used a radio nor made a call in her life, she said dubiously, "It's not going to be very good. There's nothing out there shaped like a radio so it'll have to be a pretend radio, and I'm not like Honesty, I can't do mime or anything."

Hot Sauce tapped her foot impatiently, her gaze still outside the window for some reason.

"Pretend it's small. Hand sized."

"What do I say?"

"Make something up. But hide your mouth."

When the Angel approached with Noodle's leash in one hand and what looked to be six weird little cups in the other, she said, "Don't stay out in the sunshine any more than you have to. He'll want to walk, so can you put his pattens on? My old man doesn't need burns on his feet. Noodle's used to the shoes, but tell him to stop if you see him chew his feet and he'll stop. I'd keep him inside, except we'll be using the hair dryer today and he always cringes at the sound. Thanks, Nona, you are my hero. Hot Sauce, can you set up the stations?"

Nona left the Hour of Science behind her and went down the stairs. She checked to make sure the light above the door was still red, which was one of her jobs, as the nice lady teacher always warned her that people would try to come in if the door was unlocked, and they probably wouldn't be dangerous but if they had *another* teaching building get taken over by squatters she simply had no idea where they'd go after that. Then Nona tried to put the shoes on Noodle. It was by far the most difficult thing she had ever attempted. It would have been easier to do the weird bone things that Camilla and Palamedes loved her to attempt. Noodle *didn't* want to have his pattens put on. He kept staring at Nona over his shoulder every time she wrestled a tiny, dirty white foot into a patten—it was like a little sock over a plastic grate—and there were *six* of them, she even had to do the legs he often stuck up or folded in at the middle. At one point, Noodle cunningly wriggled his way out of one shoe using another foot and Nona could have shrieked. She said, "Noodle, how *dare* you?" and he didn't look guilty at all.

When the pattens were on, he clattered out into the courtyard. He sounded like one and a half horses. He bucketed disconsolately around, smelling things, doing his business, and then drinking from the bowl of chilled water that Nona poured for him. Then he politely clattered away to lie under the big stone seat in the shade, panting.

Nona ambled around the dusty courtyard for a bit herself until she simply felt too hot to live. The heat and the sweat were making her feel faint. She squatted in the shadows close to Noodle's seat and listened to him breathe, and then she tried to pretend she was taking a very tiny radio out of her pocket. She cupped her hand to one ear, and she walked out into the sunshine, because she loved Hot Sauce and wanted to do it right. The heat made the backs of her knees panic.

"Hello, hello," she said into her hand. "I am having a conversation with Crown." Nona remembered that she was meant to be covering her mouth, and did so. She said aloud, "How are you, Crown? Things are fine over here. I wish you were around more. You haven't come to see me outside of meetings for months and months. I know you said you visited me before, but I was too young and I can't remember it so it doesn't really count. Would you like to come to my birthday party on the beach? If I don't get really mad it'll probably still be able to happen. You don't have to bring me a present, but please wear your hair down. Anyway, I love you, so, bye."

This was as much conversation as she could think up. She pocketed the fake radio and took her hand away from her mouth, then she settled down on the bench in the shade to think. The smoke had cleared and so the air outside wasn't making her cough, and there were little insects haunting the nearby dead-brown bushes, murmuring busily. There was no bird song, but every so often there was the nice comfortable noise of a car backfiring. Nona put one foot down on the ground to anchor herself, and worked the other foot out of her shoe, and only felt slightly guilty that she was allowed to do such a thing and Noodle wasn't. It was so hot, and her eyelids felt very heavy, and the stone beneath her was very cool.

JOHN 15:23

HE SAID: ON THE FIRST DAY A— BELIEVED. On the second day so did M— and G—. By the third day everyone believed, because of my eyes.

He coughed wetly and, once he had recovered, said: A girl in my high school once told me I had pretty eyes. I was puffed up over that until I was like thirty. You wouldn't believe how stupid guys get over compliments on our looks, I was vain as. But my eyes weren't anything special—light brown, not even hazel, yellow on a sunny day. The morning after the lights went out they lightened to dark amber, then they went the colour of new lager, and on the third day they were gold.

P— said I looked like a Māori TV Pink Panther. C— said I looked like Edward Cullen from that old *Twilight* movie, if Edward Cullen had the body of a history teacher. A— said I looked cool. He was the only one.

He said, And all around us, those corpses refused to rot.

In the dream, they were hiking up a big hill of brown, sun-blasted grass, crunching like paper beneath their feet. Below them the waters were rising, but they ascended without hurry, unpanicked by that bubbling, churning, brown morass: those stupefying eddies frilled around the edges with trash of all kinds—broken trees and big sheets of steel; bobbing, groaning constructions of tires and frames that he had pointed out as cars. He had spent some time pointing at things that were being claimed by the water, though she felt less that she was being taught their names and more that he was naming them for himself. Someone's Honda. Someone's Mazda. Someone's four-wheel drive. Someone's shed. A Macca's sign. The rain would turn on and off. The clouds were strange, and in the far distance, a twister danced on the neon surface of the sea.

They found a bench to sit on, though they didn't need to catch their breath. It was warm despite the rain, and the air around them was moist and prickly. It made the skin on her ribs sweat. And he said, "There it all goes again. I can't stand it," and for a long time he cried, unashamed.

Once that squall had passed, he said: In the beginning we moved those corpses all over the place . . . M— was so frantic to prove something in the science had gone wrong, or right. I think she thought if we'd achieved some scientific breakthrough, I'd get a job again and everything would go back to normal and we'd keep doing cappuccino Tuesdays. We picked two of them—two people, different sexes, different deaths, one got their neck snapped in a car accident and the other was smoke inhalation. Same age though, for control; they were born twenty days apart. Then we played dolls with those two kids for a week.

He said, They wanted to see if we could make them rot. We left them in the boiler room. Left them in the morgue. Left them outside overnight, exposed, all over dew in the morning. Nothing changed. Their internal temperature stayed regular the whole time. It wouldn't change even with A— and C— holding hair dryers over their damn bodies or us wrapping them in solar blankets and putting them in the sun. Poor C—. You should've seen her heave every time we unwrapped the blanket. She was a good sport about it, but it wasn't in her remit. Contract law doesn't set you up for rolling a couple bodies into a pond.

He said, But she didn't need to worry about it. They didn't change. Not one thing about them changed. They were perfect. All those corpses were perfect.

He said: I'd been sleeping in the facility already. I refused to go home. A— and M— moved in with me, and G— set up outside; he was sleeping in his ute. C— was staying with N—, long days. She left us early in the morning and came back the next day with sausage rolls for breakfast. I didn't realise it at the time but she'd already gone AWOL from the stakeholders. She was doing freelance for us: so translated, she was unemployed. But she was the reason we could even stay in the building. She'd massaged all the contracts and told the cops we needed to be in there to make sure disposal and records were handled properly, which gave us a grace period of a whole month. How we got through that I'll never know. I don't know if we would've got away with it if we hadn't had our pet cop. And if the whole world hadn't been freaking out every time you did something unexpected and people thought you were going to kick the bucket early. Nobody was looking at us back then, and we got lucky. It worked.

He said, more to himself: Fuck, it was a weird time. I wasn't eating much. I only wanted to be with my bodies, like if I took my eyes off them the magic'd stop. I started knowing what room they'd been stashed in even if no one told me. C— said it was psychological clues in their body language, but I wasn't convinced. I could feel them—I could feel everyone in the building—it was like having the lights turned off. You hear all the sounds outside. You hear all the cicadas in the grass, you hear the dogs in the next town over barking. You hear the moreporks in the trees and the possums skittering over shed roofs. It wasn't that I hadn't been able to hear them before, but I couldn't separate the noises. Like hearing a chord without knowing what notes go into it.

He said, A— was trying so hard to bring me back down to earth, trying to get me to pay attention to the outside world. He'd swapped with M—. She'd stopped freaking out, she didn't ask me where my pills or the drink was anymore. She just took notes, helped with all the trials I wanted to do, squabbled with A—. At least that made me feel normal. That was their usual double act. It was only when they felt the same thing that I knew it was serious.

He said, I just wanted to be in the lab. It felt like I could sit by those two bodies, those two kids, and make time go away. I could sit next to them for six minutes, I could sit next to them for six hours. Just listening. They were my moreporks and possums. I was hearing their bodies in all that silence, all the bacteria that weren't growing . . . what wasn't building up in the gut, what wasn't pooling at the joints. They were my silent night. I should have been doing paperwork and closing reports, but I hadn't opened the computer in days. I couldn't stop thinking about their palms, their hands. I touched their hands so often. I'd touched their hands before, but not like this. Even when I wasn't touching them I could feel their skin on my skin, that temperature that wouldn't change. I kept thinking I was touching them when I wasn't. M— said I should probably get tossed in a rubber room, but she wasn't scared I was nuts. She was scared I wasn't.

He said, You know, I can't even remember how it came together now. There was no catalyst, no revelation. I was too far gone for *revelations.* It was like I'd been dozy and now I was waking up. So, my two kids, the guinea pigs, they were U— and T— on their certificates, you know, their old names. I thought about using those but it didn't seem appropriate. They weren't around to say yes or no. I was starting to really care about that. What they would've thought, what they would've wanted. My two kids with their frozen brains and their perfect internal temperatures. There wasn't a place on the poor bastards I hadn't breached with a thermometer, and now I was knocking before I came into their room. Yeah, I was nuts. But I was waking up.

He said, I can't remember how or why I brought M— and A— into the room. I was like, *Hey you two, I want you to meet someone.* I wasn't trying to be a dick. I think I hadn't slept for two days.

So I brought them into the room with the bodies and I was all, *Let me introduce you to . . .* Ulysses. *Let me introduce you to . . .* Titania.

He thought about it and added, I better say that it was Titania from *Midsummer,* Shakespeare, but Ulysses was for a dog my nana had when I was a child. I worshipped that dog. He was the bravest dog I'd ever met. Half Chihuahua, half pug. Nan called him Ulysses S. Grunt. Died from eating too much pizza. The dog, I mean. Nan died of pneumonia when I was a teenager.

She said: "But what about the bodies?"

He said, Well. When I said, *Ulysses,* I moved each of his fingers and his thumb into a fist, curled them into the palm. And when I said, *This is Titania,* same thing, I placed each of her fingers and her thumb into a fist.

And I was laughing and laughing like I'd kicked out a chair before someone sat down. Like, good joke. But M— threw up.

"Because, Harrow, I'd done it from the other side of the room."

9

NONA JOLTED AWAKE with a start when she felt a tender slobbering on her ankle. It was Noodle's terrible licky tongue investigating the bit where the bone of her foot made a bump, which he obviously thought was a friendly gesture. She could have only been asleep for a little while—the sun hadn't moved and the big hot blue shadows of the courtyard were shimmering in the same position they always had—but she startled herself upright anyway, freaking out that she had snored away most of the Hour of Science without taking care of Noodle or even looking for whoever was watching the building. She checked Noodle to make sure his pattens were on, retrieved the bowl and the bottle, and took the dog inside.

She was very relieved to hear the Angel's voice coming through the door and floating down the stairs, explaining why the ice cube in the sock had melted more slowly than the ice cube not in the sock. She sat down on the stairs and began assisting Noodle out of his pattens. Nona had assumed Noodle would be grateful, but he still turned around and showed her the whites of his eyes despite the fact that she was now taking him *out* of the pattens rather than putting them *on*, and he wriggled. The cloakroom door opened and out came Hot Sauce.

"What did you *say*?" she demanded.

Nona was bewildered. "What did I say when?"

"Out in the courtyard."

"Oh—nothing," said Nona, barely able to remember. "I wasn't good at pretending to talk at all. I just pretended I was talking to someone else and I only talked for like ten seconds because I felt silly."

Hot Sauce did not look convinced. "Better come inside early. We've used the hair dryer."

"What happened? When I talked on the radio?"

Hot Sauce hesitated, then said: "The watcher took off."

"Well, that's good, isn't it? Right?"

"I need to investigate."

"But it's useful to know, isn't it?"

But when Hot Sauce shrugged, Nona could tell she thought Nona didn't understand, knew that Hot Sauce was keeping things back: something she didn't mind as *much* when Hot Sauce did it but still minded a *little*. It was shitty being able to tell when people were holding back from her. Hot Sauce just said, "Come inside."

It wasn't a great end to the school day, and it seemed to jinx everything from there on. Nona, sitting at the back with Noodle, found she couldn't follow what was happening in the Hour of Science, which culminated in a lot of ice cubes removed from strange places to triumphant shrieks from the crowd. And *then* there was the familiar *pop-pop-pop* from the street, really close, so they had to close all the blinds and the nice lady teacher had to go downstairs to make sure everything was locked up and they did everything sitting down away from shot lines from the window. They'd all done gunfire drill a million times and hardly any of the tinies got scared, even when the dreary siren started up outside. It was more boring and hot than it was terrifying. Even the Angel only seemed annoyed.

"That's too close for comfort," she commented. "Probably a one-off."

But it wasn't a one-off, it kept happening. They cut off any plenary time and mopped up ice water and the main teacher read to them from a book after a vote. The tinies outvoted everyone to select a book that wasn't even good, a soppy tale about some children who went to the beach and weren't eaten by anything. Another sign of the afternoon being cursed, Nona thought dolefully. At least school was nearly over for her.

People's parents snuck in despite the fact that there was still shooting going on a couple streets away. Some of them said that it had been like that for hours and their child wouldn't come back for afternoon school, even though both the Angel and the nice lady teacher tried to get them all to stay until it was better. They were still arguing when Camilla came to pick up Nona, and even though the lady teacher's eyes brightened to see Cam—Nona could see her pamphlet hand twitching—Cam bundled her out of there before she even got a proper goodbye. The last thing she saw was Hot Sauce sitting by the blinded-up window, thoughtful and still as a statue in the park, only her head was still on of course.

Camilla led Nona by a *very* circuitous way home. They stopped at the street their building was on, and Cam ducked into a bakery and came out with a warm and probably radioactive paper bag of pastries that had been under the bakery light the whole time. When Nona asked how she got the money, Cam said, "Never mind."

Nona was annoyed.

"You can just *say* you stole some, Cam, I don't mind."

"I sold something," said Camilla.

Light dawned on Nona back home, after she had choked down some of the meat roll. She tried not to complain about it, but did the thing where she drank water until she said, "I'm full," and Cam said, "Then we'll wait. You haven't had any protein today," and she had to eat it anyway. She peeled off the casing and ate the stuff inside and hated the experience, but at least then it was over. While Cam was cleaning up she checked the secret drawer and found that the cigarettes were all gone.

When Camilla came back in to tack up the blackout curtains, Nona said, "You sold her stash. Pyrrha's going to freak out."

"Pyrrha will deal," said Camilla. "Start stretching."

Which meant it was time for swords. When Nona said passionately, "I hate swords, you don't even teach me how to use them," this just got written down on the clipboard as though even her complaints were only useful for research. Nona felt very bitter about life.

But her bitterness slowly ebbed away, as it always did, and turned into something a little more like misery. Pyrrha was late coming home that evening. It had used to be that after the bones and the swords Nona would spend sultry evenings out at the harbour, to swim if the beach was empty and if there was nobody there to see, or to dig clams and cockles out with a stick if there were people. Walking made her tired, but she could swim in the salt water for hours and never get enough of it. It was comfortable and private. Unfortunately, these days if she said, "Cam, can't we go swimming?" Cam would say, "Remember what happened the last time," and won every argument that way. That was because what happened the last time was that Camilla had got sick, and less important, Nona had got shot.

* * *

What had happened was that after the bones one day Palamedes said she looked peaky and made her eat crackers and spread until Nona worked herself halfway to a tantrum. In the end Palamedes had to promise her a swim for a whole twenty minutes before she would do anything, eat anything, or agree to anything. It was bad behaviour, but Nona *had* been a whole month younger. Promises made, Palamedes got to go away, saying, "Tell Cam I said it was a water cure," to which Camilla remarked that Palamedes was an enabler. It didn't matter to Nona. She had already got her towel and the old shirt she used to swim in—much easier to go naked, but the others had all objected to this, and Cam had said it would make her a sniper target—and her jandals, and then after masks were tied and hats put on they walked to the beach in the low dusk.

That evening they had walked around the long way, which meant it took fully half an hour to get there, but often they walked different routes to throw off anyone who might have gotten interested and tried to follow them. On this walk they ended up spending a little time by the city graveyard. All the concrete tops had been sledged open and the buried coffins had been dug up, piled high, and burned. The smoke still clung to the sides of the buildings and made Nona gag. Pyrrha had told her this was business as usual; Pyrrha said the first thing that happened was all bones got burned, whether they were moving around or not.

By the time they had gotten to the beach Nona was depressed, but it only took her feet being in the salt water to make her happy again. Camilla never came in with her. This was because there were heaps and heaps of jellyfish in the harbour, with their beautiful bodies transparent at the crown and deep indigo at the very tips, and they weren't at all afraid to come up near to you and brush you. On Nona, this made the place they touched tingle a little, but nothing else. That was why Nona had always swum at dusk, because Cam said the jellyfish sting killed most people within minutes. The water seethed with them because the harbour was closed, and nobody was fixing the barrier nets.

Instead Cam sheltered near the concrete pillars of a jetty out of sight lines with a beat-up paperback book. It had been earlier in the spring, and night had fallen fast. There was no electric light, so she had a little torch. The first time Nona had asked to swim they had let her without cavil: she had barely known how to explain herself, then, but her hunger was so terrible that she had made them all understand. For security, Camilla had taken handfuls of rocks and sailed each one up into the centre of the lamps that shone down from the pier, with a terrific smash of plastic and the brief snappish yowl of a busted wire; and nobody had come around to fix them since. They wouldn't have had time—the blue light had appeared in the sky soon after.

It had been high tide that night. Nona had gone wading out into the shallows immediately, picking her way over the big pockmarked rocks and the slippery seaweed clumps floating haplessly in the surf, until she was up to her thighs, the shirt billowing around her. Then she plunged into the salt water. She let herself go under and felt the huge, rocking cradle of the waves rolling her forward to the beach, nearly weeping with relief—like going to the bathroom when you were really desperate, or drinking when you were really thirsty, or hearing the door open when you were really lonely. The black water sank right down to the roots of her hair, right through the braids, and made her ears go *pop* as water blocked up the canals. Bubbles rippled across her face as her laugh came out as oxygen. She kicked up to the surface and her hair and her shirt floated all around her in the water, and she bobbed there, in the dark, avoiding the inviting yellow squares of light that the other jetty lamps made on the roiling surface.

Then she had clung to one of the wooden legs of the pier—bubbled all over with barnacles and crusted with salt and plastered with dried-out fans of seaweed—and watched as blue jellyfish moved about her, squirting through the water or drifting there, looking dead, until suddenly they would undulate forward in delicate blue squiggles of movement. She *did* get stung, but the sting only gave her pins and needles in one foot, which was soon over. She pushed off from the pillar again and into a wave, and let the tide carry her forward, slowly, to the rocky shore.

Salt water had always relieved her: salt water made her feel as though, if there was someone in there with her, she would suddenly know the words to tell them everything. The sea was so kind after a hot concrete-smelling day, and she knew the water had runoff in it but it seemed so clean anyway. The sea was a big, grinding, unchangeable machine. The only terrible part was an awful longing to let her head go below the surface, to lose all buoyancy and lie at the bottom like a flat fish. Nona didn't want to die, but she wanted to sit in the water and drowse, which she was forced to admit was the same thing eventually.

That fatal evening she lay with her arms and legs spread out and her middle only a little submerged, shirt plastered flat to her belly and chest. She stared up at the glowing blue circle in the night sky: it crowded out the stars and looked much like an incandescent jellyfish itself, crowning in a black ocean.

Nona had been very happy when she turned around and kicked back toward the jetty and the shore, slipping among the waves and the foam and the floating plastic rings people used to keep bottles together. It felt so easy to be good when you were happy. Nona had been ready to eat as many meals as Camilla wanted her to, so long as the number was less than three. She had made it to the end of the pier and Camilla was clear in her view, and a big shock went right down her spine when she saw her: not because it was Camilla, but because she was not alone.

There was a little cluster of figures in tatty coats spread out on the beach on the side they'd come in on. Nona counted six of them. They looked black-headed, but when Nona squinted she saw that they were wearing goggles and caps or wraps around their heads. One of them was holding one of those little motorized bikes that you often saw going *plut-plut* down the streets of the city. It was turned off now except for the lamp, which was on full brightness. The suds and the waves filled her ears and she could not make out what anyone was saying—if they were saying anything. It was impossible to see their mouths. Easy enough to see Camilla, silhouetted in the lamp of the *plut-plut* bike, strung across one of the supports beneath the pier like a sinuous night animal. The beam was hot and white and bright, and Camilla hovered within it like a moth.

Nona assumed it was the police. Only the police got to have those bikes but still couldn't afford good jackets. Each one had a shoulder holster, which meant each one had a short gun, and they stood in a kind of triangular gaggle with one right at the point before Camilla. Nobody's guns were drawn, but the holsters were out in the open, each a kind of glittering mechanical bulge at the top of the chest.

Camilla had put her hands out in a beseeching *no guns here* kind of a way. The light made the wrist-strap watch on her arm glitter. She swung her legs down off her pillar to land in a little puff of sand, with one hand still raised; she rummaged around in her pocket—threw something down on the ground—backed off. One of the figures ducked forward and picked it up. Nona kept the water right up to her eyes and began to approach—made it to the next pole in the jetty, and the pole after that—but Camilla tucked her hair behind one ear, as though she was nervous, and flashed her palm out to the jetty. One thumb tucked in; four fingers spread. That was the sign to *stay put*.

Nona hesitated, then stayed put. There was a lot of discussion in the triangle about whatever had been picked up. It could have been a perfectly ordinary conversation, albeit a conversation between six people with guns in a triangle and one person with her hands up. Camilla was so bad at staying still: even as they talked she stretched in that cold white circle of light, one foot pressing down into the sand and then the other, slowly and deliberately and liquidly. Nona swam to the nearest pillar, found her footing on a big metal screw, and waited, buffeted by the waves and the brushing lappets of three comfortably stinging jellyfish.

She still couldn't make out what they were saying. One of the police (?) had thrown the object back down into the sand in front of Camilla. Nona could see it better now; it was Cam's wallet. Had they asked for papers, or something? Camilla didn't retrieve it. Then all at once, one of the cops at the back drew their gun—Nona threw herself forward into the water—and shot. The muzzle flashed.

Camilla hadn't fallen down. She hadn't been hit. The bullet had gone wide past her shoulder and she hadn't moved, hadn't ducked, hadn't done anything except keep her hands up. Nona kicked silently to the pillar in front, where she could hear snatches of conversation—

"—said *scare* her—"

"—did what y—"

"—speak House," Camilla was saying.

The figure at the front made their mouth look different and said, exaggeratedly loudly and clearly, "Try again. Unjust Hope says—" but the waves took the rest.

Camilla said something Nona didn't catch at all. The cop turned around and said, mouth different again, "—ut a bullet in her this time."

The one with the gun responded, sounding garbled, but the first figure said clearly, "Get the knee. I'm sick of this—" and something else.

Nona had broken. Her only use was translating, and there she was, listening to the most important conversation that had ever been had, and she was not translating. She had surged out of the water and shrieked, "*Run!* They're going to *shoot you,*" and instead of shooting Camilla, the cop with the gun aimed right into the dark water, and shot Nona.

It felt like someone had punched her in the shoulder—hard. Nona did as Pyrrha had taught her, and went completely limp. For a moment her shoulder felt hot and awkward, and there was a hot burst of blood over her arm, feeling weird against the cool salt water. A yellow light shot through the waves like a dropped egg, and she writhed in its silhouette briefly before deciding to sink right to the bottom. The light arced back and forth, swinging around, never finding her.

She counted to twenty, glad she had taken a big breath, waiting there at the bottom and clutching the black rocks. It was very murky. Every so often a questing jellyfish would bob into view, and she had to bat it away from her face. She thought she heard a brief report, coming thickly from far away, as though maybe someone had pushed the part of the bike that went *honk*. Then there were weird white lights—quick, darting, moving lights, like very small fireworks—but Nona kept what Pyrrha called firing discipline. Only at the end of the *long* twenty seconds did she kick away, launching herself forward along the rocky bottom until she hit one of the jetty pillars.

By that time the pain and the weird feeling were over. The bullet had gone clean through the topmost part of her arm, which was good, and there wasn't even a hole to show where it had been. She felt a little sick, but that was all. Nona had never been shot before. She inched up the pillar until her head broke water.

The beach had gone very quiet. The *plut-plut* bike's headlight still shone out in her direction, blinding her a little. As Nona's eyes adjusted she saw Camilla, squatting on the sand. Everyone else was fanned out, lying down around her, as though they had all decided to take a schooltime nap.

Nona waded through the water, heart racing, struggling through the surf—thrashing upward through the shallows, pulling herself to stand. Her feet felt numb, but looking back that was probably the jellyfish. Each and every single person who wasn't Camilla was down on the ground. Their unholstered guns were still clutched in their hands or scattered loosely near them. The sand underneath each one was oily black. It hadn't been that hot, but wisps of steam curled up from the dark, wet sand.

Camilla was crouched down, wiping her knives on one of their jackets. When she looked up, Nona was electrified. One of her eyes was a pale, pearlescent grey; the other one of her eyes was a deep, cool stone colour. Nona understood in a sudden shiver what she was looking at.

"Stay calm," said Camilla-and-Palamedes. "Five breaths, if you need it."

Camilla-and-Palamedes's voice was strange to her, cool and efficient, distantly kind. But Nona wasn't angry. The air smelled strongly of smoke and burnt meat. It made her deeply unhappy and very hungry, even though she had forced down all those crackers.

"I thought if I played dead," Nona began, and stopped, because a big lump had come into her throat. She felt stupid; she felt she was being ungrateful; when Camilla-and-Palamedes smiled that strange new person's smile, she suddenly felt very shy.

But Camilla's clockwork interrupted with a series of urgent beeps: the *BEEP-BEEP-BEEP-BEEP* of a timer alarm, faster and more panicked than the usual time's-up sound. Camilla-Palamedes got up all of a sudden, as though they wanted to get *getting up* over and done with as quickly as possible, and swayed backward and forward a little. The blood on the beach was steaming. Their hands were steaming. Nona struggled forward to catch her—them—the new person; but then Camilla straightened and blinked furiously, and it *was* Camilla. Her eyes were pale grey again and she shuddered like herself.

She said, a little hoarsely, but in quite normal Camilla tones: "Not your fault." Then she equally normally set to putting her knives away—sticking them in the bands down her thighs, inside her trousers—and normally seeing that made Nona want to laugh, but that night she felt as though she might vomit instead, which would have added insult to injury.

Camilla said, "Shoulder?" She didn't sound angry at all, but strangely quiet and tight.

"It's fine—I'm fine. Cam, what did you *do*?"

"No questions. They didn't have silencers. We need to go. Get the bike."

Nona wasn't able to help herself. She burst out with, "What did they *want*?"

"Intel. They were Merv Wing. Turn the lights off."

The spotlight was still shining out over the ocean like a very small moon. Nona righted the *plut-plut* bike and turned off the headlight, which left the beach blue and cold. She kept looking at the fallen cops—at their necks and at their chests—but Camilla gently drew her chin up and away, urging her forward, putting the towel around her wet shoulders. It felt nice and dry and scratchy. Nona mechanically wheeled the bike over the sand. Cam threw down her jandals and she squeezed her feet into them, the sand gritty on the bottoms of her heels.

Camilla didn't say anything. She had zipped up her dark jacket even though the night was still warm, and Nona thought she understood; she was cold too, colder than she ought to have been even when wet. Camilla kept her arms folded tight over her chest as though she was thinking. Nona was too sodden with regret and self-hatred and sea water to think anything but that Cam must have been very angry with her for calling out, and so she was blind to the truth of the situation until they wheeled the bike off the ramp and weaved it through the poles that were meant to prevent you bringing bikes onto the beach and Camilla suddenly staggered to a halt. She leant hard against the wall and shuddered. Nona nearly dropped the bike.

"*Cam?*"

"Towel," said Camilla, very calmly. And: "Don't scream."

Nona was about to be indignant, but then Cam unzipped her jacket, and she nearly screamed. Cam's thin cotton top was sodden with blood. The tops of her pants and her whole jacket were already black and wet from spray, so it hadn't really showed the blood coming through. The worst part was that the blood was coming from *everywhere*, with no wounds, or bullet holes, or stab marks. It was coming out of her skin.

Cam rubbed the towel down both of her arms, briskly. The towel came away bright red. "Blood sweat," she said, unsteadily.

"Get Palamedes," was all Nona could think to say. "Get Palamedes— he can fix it."

"No," said Camilla. Nona noticed that her lips had gone the same colour as the skin around them, a sort of ashen rosy brown, instead of either skin or lips being normal. Cam's voice was still very even and calm, but it was quiet, and came out strangely punctuated as she took in breaths. "He can't. Not this. Make it worse."

"But—"

"Get us home," said Camilla. "You can do it. On the bike."

The *bike*! Yet it was not to be borne that Nona would say, "But my car sickness"; if Camilla said anyone could do anything, they could do it. It was not the kind of thing she said often, or at all. It was more buoyed by the sucker-punch of Camilla's belief than through her own confidence—she suddenly needed to go to the bathroom, which Palamedes always said was her displacement activity—that Nona got on the bike. Her courage had nearly failed her when Camilla got behind her and wrapped her arms around Nona's middle, very tightly. Nona had realised then that Cam was worried about falling off.

Even thinking about it now, how Nona drove Cam through those black streets she did not know—ignoring all the traffic signals, slowing down laboriously to turn into the little side alleys, the lone truck breaking curfew that chugged along the street next to her like a massive animal of hot wind and noise—but she did, and it took both forever and no time at all. Camilla was very warm and solid behind her with her arms unflinchingly tight. She never released the grip, which was nice until Nona realised that half the warmth was the blood seeping through the towel. She was about to guide the bike into the garage beneath the Building before Cam said, "Dump it. Here," in a voice barely more than a whisper.

Here was behind a big rubbish cache next to the Building. Cam stood herself against the wall and Nona wheeled it into the gap behind the cache and the wall, then covered the gap up with boxes. She was pleased with the neatness of it until she came back to Camilla and saw the deathly pallor of her face: the stillness that was not Palamedes, but Camilla conserving all of her blood for silence. In the black nighttime of that alley the towel around Camilla's middle was black with blood, and the sea water and blood had dried on Nona's clothes. She put Camilla's arm around her shoulders and they crept into the garage, each breath from Cam's mouth high and tight. It was so strange to hear Camilla breathing at all.

Somehow they made it up the stairs—of course the elevator didn't work—and Nona was almost too slippery and panicky to knock. When Pyrrha opened the door all Nona was able to say was, pitifully, "No, no, no," like the baby she had been: but what a relief it was at the time, to give things over to Pyrrha. Pyrrha had carried Camilla to bed in her big brown arms like Cam weighed nothing, was less than Nona. Pyrrha said, "What happened?" and Nona told her, and Pyrrha wasn't even angry, but when Nona told her about Cam's eyes she looked at Nona and said a completely new swear word. It was such an unusual swear word that later on Nona was able to swop it to Honesty for five whole cigarettes, he was that impressed.

Pyrrha sat down with Cam's head in her lap and pinched her awake, and then made her drink little sips of water. Cam's eyes were almost closed, like an animal's when they weren't quite asleep.

The water brought her around a little. Pyrrha kept saying, low and steady, "Don't black out, kid. You're in thanergy shock. Stay awake, come on." After about five minutes of that treatment, Cam's eyes opened all the way, and she drank the rest of the water mostly on her own. She let Nona give her a painkiller, but just a cap, not a needle.

In the end Pyrrha said in a calm, dead voice— "You can't do that ever again, Hect, *never.* Synthesis is a one-way ticket—I walked the Eightfold, I should damn well know. I'd give Palamedes the hiding of his fucking life if he wasn't renting an ass with you."

Camilla, cradled in Pyrrha's arms, with all the towels bright red, looked up at Pyrrha like Nona wasn't even in the room. Her eyes were chill and grey and gleaming. She whispered—

"Don't tell him I was weak."

"He's going to know, Hect. You're killing each other."

"It's our choice."

"He's going to *ask.*"

"Do what you're good at," said Camilla. "Lie."

"Hect, you're not listening. It's killing him too—"

"It was good," said Camilla, and her eyes closed. "It was good. We were happy."

Pyrrha stayed put until Camilla fell asleep. The expression on her face was one Nona had never seen her wear before. Nona stayed too, except to go occasionally to the bathroom out of prolonged stress. Finally Pyrrha told Nona to go make up her bed next to Pyrrha's on the fold-out part of the couch, and when Nona asked if Camilla was going to be all right, Pyrrha said—

"No."

But when she saw the expression on Nona's face she put on a smile—produced one, like she would produce sweets or coins or little magazines—and said, "Don't worry about it, junior. I don't mean we're going to find her dead in the morning."

Then she had gone to the kitchen and poured herself a little glass of clear grain alcohol. She crossed to the taped-up window, bottle and glass in hand. To Nona's awe, she twitched the blackout curtains aside—stood bathed in the hyper-blue light from the sky as Nona held her breath—and she said to the window, "Here's to Camilla Hect, yet another of devotion's casualties," and knocked back the glass.

Then she said to the light, quite gently, "No, I don't blame *you*, man . . . He was always looking for things to throw himself on."

Then Pyrrha settled down on the bed she had extended for Nona and knocked back two more little glasses of alcohol. She let Nona taste a little bit of the second glass when Nona asked, but Nona thought it was awful: it tasted like petrol and felt like sunburn. When she lay down, she kept wiping her lips to take the taste away.

"If Cam's fine," she said, "why did you just say goodbye to her?"

"How'd you know it was goodbye?" When Nona opened her mouth, Pyrrha said: "Don't answer that. Go to sleep." And after that, there had been no more swimming.

1̄0̄

GOING TO THE *BEACH* THOUGH, if there was still lots of light and plenty of people, was another matter. Nona tried her luck.

"No beach," said Cam, drying dishes at the sink. "I didn't like the city today. Two people got shot in the centre while I was there. Someone else got dragged out of the river."

"Drowned?"

"Strangled. Neck snapped—all the way around."

"Gross," said Nona. And, struck by an idea: "Cam—can't I go back to school for the evening?"

"School? Why?"

Nona tried to think up a really intelligent and persuasive reason. "Hot Sauce is worried about something," she said. "She said someone was watching the classroom and she wouldn't tell me about it. I want to make sure they're all okay."

It wasn't that Camilla didn't take this seriously: she could see right away that Cam had taken it a little *too* seriously. Her dark brows drew together a fraction, and she placed another plate in the rack, and one of her legs folded up beneath her so that she was standing on one leg and resting the other foot at the top of that thigh. "Not in the dark," she said. "Not after the gunfire today."

"But it's not dark yet. And the sky's always sort of light now."

"It'll be dark enough by the time school's over."

Nona grew desperate.

"But I'm a Teacher's Aide. I've got a responsibility."

"I know," said Camilla, lowering the foot, then raising the other. "It's also your responsibility to keep yourself safe. Responsibilities clash."

Nona felt hot and cross.

"It's hard to feel responsible for the other two people I might be," she said, knowing she sounded crabby and not knowing how not to. "I don't know them. But I feel *very* responsible for Hot Sauce and Honesty and Ruby and Born and even Kevin, and I've only got so much time, you know. Maybe the other two people I am would feel incredibly responsible for Hot Sauce and the others too, Cam."

"Oh, one of them, definitely," said Camilla. "And maybe the other. I don't mean you've got a responsibility to *them*. You have a responsibility to me and the Warden and to Pyrrha."

In desperation, Nona flung herself down on the soft mat on the floor she and Cam had been using for stretches.

"Cam, responsibility just means you can't ever do anything you think is really important."

"Yes," said Cam simply. And: "Let's stop waiting for Pyrrha and go pick up dinner."

They walked to the fish shop so that Nona could look longingly at the ocean, and listened to the fishmonger explain the latest about the port riots so that Nona could later translate for Cam. Nice girls with no guns needed to stay inside, urged the fishmonger. The space elevator had gotten breached about an hour ago because too many loyalist soldiers had been rerouted to the barracks siege, and the old workers had busted through with a key card trying to hijack a shuttle off-world. Most of them had been shot, and there were no shuttles there anyway. There were no shuttles anymore.

When Nona relayed this to Camilla, she said: "Hope Pyrrha takes the back roads."

"Will Pyrrha be okay, Cam?"

"Pyrrha's a survivor," said Camilla.

But she let Nona slip her hand into hers and they walked shoulder to shoulder all the way home, with the plastic foam container of spicy rice and oily fish hot and steamy in the crook of Nona's arm. It had been very cheap; people weren't eating the harbour fish, because they said that the blue light got into them. They said the blue light got into the air too, and they wore masks for that, though Palamedes said that was nonsense. Cam ate most of the fish and rice as Nona picked at the edges, and then there was all the fruit they hadn't eaten for afters. Nona's plate was left still mostly full, despite one genuine effort to eat and two not-so-genuine ones where she faked it.

"You can eat three more mouthfuls, or two and drink some water," said Camilla inflexibly.

"But I've eaten so much today."

"You ate gruel and a sausage roll."

"But I'm full, I'm really full."

"Have you been eating sand again?"

"I haven't eaten sand in months," Nona protested, then more truthfully: "Weeks," and more truthfully than that: "One week."

Nona eventually took the deal where she drank a glass of water and ate two more mouthfuls; as it turned out though, she never had to eat the second, because the special knock sounded—five short, two long, which they changed often—and Cam unlocked and unbarred the door for Pyrrha.

Pyrrha looked terrible. Her deep skin was powdered with concrete dust and shiny with smoke, splotched with rusty patches on the front that it took Nona a moment to realise were blood. She reeked of petrol and sweat. Cam recognised the red stuff immediately and started trying to check Pyrrha over, tugging at her overalls, her arms—Pyrrha said swiftly, "It's not mine," and dropped into one of the chairs at the kitchen table.

Nona got up and went to pour her a glass of ice water from the covered jug. Pyrrha said, "Thanks, Nums," and drained the whole thing. Nona, fascinated, watched the brown column of her throat move as she swallowed. There was already a fine dark rust of stubble beneath her chin, amid the dust and the dirt, and when Pyrrha caught her looking, she felt there with her hand and said, laughing, "I know, I know . . . Gideon always had a five o'clock shadow at three o'clock. Sextus, can't you fix it? If you kick the sebaceous glands back a notch you can interrupt the hair cycle. Quick injection of thanergy below the root'll freeze the growth."

Pyrrha's eyes were hot and shiny and her pupils blown wide. Nona hadn't even seen Cam and Palamedes switch. Palamedes was busy rolling up one of Pyrrha's sleeves, examining a slimy patch of scabbing-over blood, and he said briskly: "No thanks. I had the joy of working on a . . . on a body like yours, the once, and I don't want to repeat the process for anything smaller than a brain haemorrhage. What hit this forearm?"

"Vehicle shrapnel. They were taking pot shots at the police, and the police took pot shots back, with a munitions launcher." Pyrrha held the glass out beseechingly to Nona; Nona went and refilled it. "Don't worry. I squatted in a public bathroom and forked everything out myself. It's mostly closed up already."

"Did you . . . ?"

"Saved who I could, left the rest to be buried," said Pyrrha. "Or burned. Lots of 'em were burning. Couldn't do anything for them . . . People notice when you don't burn, is the thing. There was an audience. Others have been killed for less."

Palamedes said nothing; he pushed at a pair of glasses that didn't exist, made a noise of annoyance, and swept his hand lightly over the arm. Nona, fascinated, watched the blood peel away and frizzle to nothing, leaving a long zigzag of clean open meat on Pyrrha's arm that was wrinkling shut as they watched.

Nona said, "Was it the port riot? Were you there?"

"You heard about that, kiddie? No," said Pyrrha. "It's just after-shocks. I was on that side of the city, is all."

Palamedes said, "Is it finally kicking off?"

"Not yet." Pyrrha curled her arm inward, examining the disappearing wound, and took the cool glass from Nona's hands. Her fingers had left dirty fingerprints on the glass. "I know that sounds ridiculous, but not yet. Even though they're chucking bombs at the cops and yelling shit about *No deals, no lords, no zombies,* and *Cops love zombie money.* When it kicks off, nobody will be yelling anything.

This is anger, not fear. False labour pains . . . Do they still do gravid carry where you come from?"

"On the Sixth, only for research," said Palamedes.

"I helped at a birth once. There's a lot of noise and run-up before the real thing happens." Pyrrha necked the second glass of water all the way down and wiped her mouth with the back of her hand before she could think better of it. When she saw the result, she grimaced. Nona fetched a damp cloth without being asked so that Pyrrha could start to clean up. "This has been a *shit* day . . . I'm having a cigarette. I'll smoke it out the window."

Nona froze, but Palamedes said calmly, "No good; Cam sold them. Said they were our most liquid asset."

She expected Pyrrha to get very sarcastic. Pyrrha didn't yell, ever, but Nona experienced so much yelling among her friends that she deeply preferred it. Pyrrha just sighed, deeply.

"How much did she get?"

"Maybe a third of what they were worth."

"What an entirely haunted time to be alive," said Pyrrha. "Nona, my sweet, can you draw me a bath? My filth's got filth."

Nona sprinted to the bath and put the plug in the plughole and dutifully started grating the soap bar into fine, dusty flakes to put in the hot water, not even minding leaning over the sweaty hot-water tap; but she pricked up her ears when she heard, in the other room, Palamedes saying softly, "I'm going to let Camilla look you over. Tell her what you told me," and Pyrrha saying, "Wait a moment, Warden. Wait. I want you to hear this first . . . not Hect. I need you to stop Hect, okay? I need you to hold her back."

Nona shut off the hot-water tap. It wasn't as though she was deliberately trying to eavesdrop; she was still carefully holding the paring knife and trying to make the longest unbroken rind of soap that she could, watching flakes disappear and dissolve into white scum on the surface of the water. Her hair was itchy with sweat. She heard Palamedes say, "Oh, God, Pyrrha, just tell me."

Pyrrha said, "In the chaos, they found some . . . people . . . to take to the park tonight."

There was a very long silence, or else Nona couldn't hear. Pyrrha said, "I saw them for two, three seconds. In the back of a truck. Three adults. It was dark. Said they'd taken them off the cops. One person I asked said they'd been in the barracks, another one said they'd found them wild."

Nona couldn't wait anymore; she ran the cold water tap before she died of being too hot, and let the water run over her wrists and her palms, like Camilla had taught her. Wrists were the best place for cooling down. That meant she only caught fragments, until Pyrrha and Palamedes helpfully made their voices louder—

"You versus *two hundred motherfuckers* with machine guns! *Camilla* versus two hundred motherfuckers with machine guns, Sextus! I know you and she are doing some ungodly tricks with soul manipulation, but what do you think you are, a damned Ly— L-word? You're not even a fraction of one, you're only a step in the theory. The poor fools they have probably aren't even—"

"How many people do you leave to burn tonight, Dve?"

"You say that because you think it hurts, and because you're frightened," said Pyrrha coolly. "The answer, my boy, is *multitudes* . . . so long as it doesn't include you and me and Nona. We're all three of us in enough trouble as it is. Don't make me repeat myself."

"Pyrrha, they tape their arms to their sides and they put them in those cages and they douse them in petrol, in gasoline . . ."

"Yes, and then they set them alight, and it's terrible, and usually somebody shoots them long before the fire takes them. There's always some softie in the crowd, Sextus, even for zombies. And it won't be 'zombies.' Listen to me. What I've been trying to tell you this whole night is that me and the boys combed Site C and I found nothing: no bodies, no blood, none of your people. No sign they were even kept there by Edenites. This is the public taking it out on a couple of poor bastards they pick up who are insane, or drug-addled, or who said the wrong thing and gave someone a wonderful opportunity to get them out the way. You *know* that's been the vast majority of the cage deaths since the initial flush. Even if it is one of yours then

Number Seven'll have them so out of their tree that they'll hardly notice when—"

"This isn't about House loyalty," said Palamedes quietly. "It's about three people being burnt to death."

There was a big silence. Nona made a number of tiny noises, cleaning the paring knife, cleaning her hands, making sure Pyrrha's towel was dry.

Pyrrha said, "Keep Camilla home tonight. I'll call it quits for the cigs."

Palamedes said, "Do you know she has a half sister? Did she tell you? It's not my secret to tell. They're quite fond of each other. Camilla's ten years younger. Kiki's a member of Oversight Body, junior fellow. She was one of the group that came to negotiate with Ctesiphon Wing."

"I didn't know that, no," said Pyrrha.

"Alongside fifteen other of the finest minds of my House," said Palamedes. "Led here by my conviction and Camilla's hand. My colleagues, my friends. My family . . . The people they put in cages will be someone's family, someone's friends."

"*Keep—Camilla—home—tonight,*" said Pyrrha. "That is all I am saying. Keep her home. No heroics. I'm not moved by sentiment. Whatever it takes. Don't feel. Just do."

"Tonight I hate almost all the human race," said Palamedes wearily.

"That's a feeling," said Pyrrha brutally. "Kill it."

Palamedes did not seem to notice when Nona crept back into the kitchen, drying her hands on her front; he had ducked into the bedroom. It was just Pyrrha, peeling her bloodied shirt off and putting it in the sink to soak; Pyrrha with her naked chest so moth-eaten with scars that even Camilla and Palamedes couldn't guess the cause of. Nona always felt soft and tender when she saw Pyrrha with her shirt off, and liked to rest her head on her back, between her prominent shoulder blades. But tonight she just said humbly: "Can I go into the corridor for five minutes?"

Pyrrha raised one eyebrow. "Does Cam let you do that?"

"No—but I just want to sit outside number three-oh-two. They play the radio, and we don't have one."

"Sounds harmless. What's Camilla's objection?"

"She says they're maniacs."

"Go. Take five. I won't tell her if you don't get shot," said Pyrrha.

Nona unlatched the door and tiptoed outside, even though she had been granted permission. The desire to listen to the radio at number 302 was only a *mild* blind. She knew that if she hung around the question of the remaining mouthful would come back into play, and she wanted a moment to walk by herself and think by herself. The corridor lights were dimmed and the cool linoleum under her bare feet felt sticky with each step, and condensation left perfect Nona-shaped footprints on the squares as she went.

The windows were all blinded and boarded, so she could not crack one and get a breath of fresh air, but she lolled outside number 302. The radio was on, and was playing something mournful she could not really translate; Nona always found listening to the radio much harder to understand, with no mouth and no eyes. She sat there in the moist dim corridor night, thinking escapeful thoughts. She wondered if she *quite* had the bottle to go down the stairwell and down to the garage and check to see if anyone she knew was down there; but that felt like more of a betrayal than she wanted to truck with.

Outside number 302 she found a window that had only been taped up most of the way and peeled it off just a little bit more with her fingertips. The sun had set. The nighttime light was blue from the sphere that hung over the city, and she let the light touch her eyes and her lips and felt better for it.

This was a secret that Nona kept from Pyrrha and Camilla and Palamedes, almost the only one she kept from them, but one too beautiful to tell. She knew the luminous sphere hanging above the city, high in space, had kicked off all the riots, and was making everyone scream, and had caused the siege in the port, and made people throw themselves in front of buses, and made everyone say the end of the world was coming soon. It was making everybody's lives horrible, and it had given Palamedes and Camilla the same grave, pensive expression, and Pyrrha slapped on an extra nicotine patch every time the fog burned away and it hung like a great blue ball in the sky.

But Nona loved the blue sphere as much as she loved everything else. She, and nobody else, could hear it sing.

"Good night, Varun," she said.

When she tiptoed back down the corridor—the whole building seemed still tonight, as though it were tucked into a dark corner hoping nobody would notice it—she opened the door as quietly as she could. There was nobody in the front room. Nona heard the slopping sounds of Pyrrha in the bath. She walked on the balls of her feet to the bedroom, and she found Camilla in front of the recorder with the single lamp on—Camilla with her arms clasped around her knees, her chin sunk down to the tops of her thighs, staring greyly out into space.

Nona lay down on the mattress. She felt very tired and sad all of a sudden, seeing Camilla tired and Camilla sad. On some impulse she opened her arms, and Camilla unexpectedly lay down next to her and crawled inside them—not quite letting Nona hold her, but letting Nona put an arm around her, putting an arm around Nona in return. It was hot, but Nona didn't mind.

"Cam," Nona whispered.

"What's up?"

"I could go to the park for you," whispered Nona, desperately trying to sort through the words, say the correct thing, communicate the right desire. "I could help . . . really. You know what happens when I get hurt. That's got to be worth something."

Camilla said, "Is that your plan? Getting hurt?"

"Well, it might freak them out," said Nona. "And I'm not scared of dying. Really truly, Cam, I'm not . . ."

"Why not?" said Camilla.

Nona thought about it. "Because I like letting go of the pull-up bars and falling off," she said. "I don't like the part just before you let go and I don't like the part where you hit the floor, but I like the letting go."

"I don't let go," said Camilla. "It's my one thing."

Nona was amazed at that—the idea that Camilla, who could do so much and do it so fluently, could sum herself up as having *one thing.* Amazed too, a little, that anyone might not love the weightlessness when your fingers slipped off the metal and you hung, unsuspended, in midair. Camilla's hand wound itself around the end of her braid and held it, as though to find some kind of leash or safety rope, as though Nona really might fall.

She was half-asleep by the time Pyrrha finished with her bath (and rinsed the bath down twice); this meant it was Nona's turn to take a bath, so she undressed herself half-asleep and would have been all the way asleep in the water once she got in if Camilla hadn't been there saying, every so often, "Not yet." Which kept her awake, because it would have been terrifically stupid to drown at this point.

She was three-quarters unconscious pulling on the shirt she slept in, and stumbled out of the bathroom but didn't quite get it all the way so that Pyrrha had to say, "Tits, Nona, don't give Camilla a heart attack," which jolted her awake enough to lie down on the mattress and rebutton her shirt from the bottom. She reached nearly all the way up before she fell deeply and completely asleep.

JOHN 5:18

I N THE DREAM, night had fallen, or what she assumed was night. They were lying atop the hill they had climbed and he was pointing out all the constellations that they would be able to see if it weren't for the thick green cloud and the softly falling flakes of ash. They were lying head-to-head, their eyes aimed at the right part of the sky to see, or in this case *not* see, the Southern Cross. The stars were sweet and familiar, but she did not know their names, though they seemed to be at the tip of her tongue. She asked him why it was called the Southern Cross. He said that was just one name for it, but the stars were in a cruciform pattern and it was only visible from the southern hemisphere. He said when he was little he'd been taught it was the anchor of a ship. He still preferred that, he said. Liked the idea that the Milky Way was pinned down and couldn't go anywhere. Said when he was a kid he hated change, any change at all.

She had quite liked change—mostly. But he did not want to dwell on that. So she asked him about the fingers trick, and he was happier to talk about why it had upset everyone so much.

He said, Keep this in mind: it was the first time anyone had ever done it. You couldn't explain it away. There were no strings or magnets. No illusion of the witch or whatever. I could repeat it for anyone who wanted to walk in and deal with M— dry-retching in the corner. And I did. Everyone had to come watch, the whole gang. And by then . . .

He said, By then it was easy. By then I had Titania and Ulysses sitting up. By the end of the day they were walking around with me, sitting down when I sat or standing when I stood. It gave the others the absolute shits. Again, I didn't mean to be a creep. I just wanted them close so I could look after them—it seemed so important. And A— was right, I wasn't operating on a lot of food or sleep.

He said, Everyone had a big fight over what it meant. C— and G— took it fine. Funny in hindsight that *they* were the ones who were the least weirded out. C— had been raised little-England Anglican and G— 's grandparents who raised him had been religious as hell, White Sunday and suit and tie for church, that kind of thing. It was M— who couldn't take it. M— had been hard atheist since she was twelve. But she got over it; she was a walking contradiction anyway. Her best friend in the whole world was a nun. Also, at some point A— gave her a benzo and a shot of whiskey, so that helped.

He said, But you know what? They *wanted* to believe. All of them. We all wanted a miracle. Everyone wants to believe that God's randomly made them one of the X-Men. We all thought of you right away, what it could mean for you. P— was worried that this was some kind of zombie apocalypse, but Titania and Ulysses weren't zombies. They were . . . extensions. Constructions without a soul. They hadn't woken up, they hadn't resurrected in that sense of the word. Their bodies moved when I wanted them to move. And then I stopped having to hold the strings—I could say, *Go here*, or, *Go there*, and they'd go like I'd programmed them to. You had to make sure you told them to stop, or they'd keep walking into things. It wasn't like they could talk or bite you, you know? I wished they could've. But they were just me.

For a moment they were both silent, brushing ash off their faces, their hair. It was falling thick and fast like snow. They took shelter beneath a burnt-out tree and watched the ash hump up against the rocks and branches. Some of it got in their mouths.

After a moment, he said: I *knew* it was fine. I knew I'd touched something, come away with something, that could be used for good. Could be used to fix everything, used for *you*. I only had to figure out how. There was so much to figure out. But I'd got a dream team on tap, eh? People who could think. C—'s N—, she was on board. C— was still pretending they weren't dating—she was an artist, so that was cool. If you have two scientists and an engineer and a detective and a lawyer and an artist you're pretty much sweet as. Sounds like the start of a joke, right? Two scientists, an engineer, a detective, a lawyer, and an artist walk into a bar to help me become God.

He said: They put me through my paces. I was exhausted all the time. We all came up with trials to figure out what I could do, what I couldn't do. There was too much to go on. We figured out early that what really helped was if I was near the dead bodies, if I was in the facility. Back then we thought maybe there was something about the ground, something about our particular patch in the Wairarapas, but if we loaded up the ute with a bunch of bodies and looked out for the cops we could do the same thing anywhere else. The corpses were what mattered. They were my batteries.

He said, So of course, what do M— and A— do, they go raid a fucking graveyard. I was pissed off with them about that. So was P— but, like, mainly because it was illegal and she had to cover it up. But *that* proved it wasn't that we had a load of specific magical corpses on our hands. I could take a body that had been dead for twenty years and do the same thing. Can't believe we didn't get caught.

He said, At that point we knew that was the biggest risk: getting caught. Getting hushed up. Getting flown to some government facility in America. Or weaponised—given to another group of stakeholders or bought by another magnate son of a bitch. I guess we'd seen too many movies. We assumed that we'd all go missing. Get disappeared. Get used for evil.

He said, So we figured that what we had to do was make as big a noise as humanly possible, turn to the public. Find out if anyone else was like me, if there was someone out there who could do the same thing. And there *was* a way we could do just that. It was a different time back then. I didn't want to do it. It felt too—kill switch, too awful to contemplate. Too grisly. Too shitty. But it was the only trick we had up our sleeves.

He sighed and said, "We had the internet. We decided to stream."

She said, "What is this *internet*?"

And he said, "See, I *did* make a utopia."

DAY THREE

11

THE NEXT MORNING CAMILLA pushed the button and said, "Start."

Nona did not close her eyes this time, but stared hard at the black mould marks on the ceiling, as though for inspiration, and began: "I'm holding something down in the water. It's the same water, the good water. But whatever I'm holding doesn't want to stay down, it keeps coming back. To the surface, I mean."

"What are you holding?"

"The girl with the painted face."

"Tell me about the girl."

"She's under the water. She's not drowning, she's lying there. Her eyes are closed, I think. The water's cloudy. But then there's the arms still around me . . . I think. I'm mixing parts up."

"Show me where."

Nona wriggled around in an attempt to embrace herself: she rolled over frontways on the mattress and attempted to get one arm slung over her neck, the other over her waist. Camilla said to these efforts, "Demonstrate on me."

Delighted at the opportunity, Nona immediately sat up—ignoring the brief wave of dizziness—and wound her arms around Camilla. She paused halfway and said, "It's a bit—are you sure?" and Camilla said, "You've shown me before. Show me again."

Nona concentrated on how it felt in the dream, as strange and multibodied as it was: she was good at the hand and the mouth, she was good at this, but she hesitated. She said, "I can't do it by myself," and took Camilla's arms. She put Camilla's hand on her hip, put Camilla's other hand on her other hip, splayed her fingers, said, "More. No—there," as Camilla kept up, then reached out to Camilla—like she was drowning; like she wanted to drown. It was nice to be this close to Camilla. Camilla's hands on her were a little clinical, a little unsure.

"Okay," said Camilla, once they were locked in this clinch. "Anything else?"

"No. Was that useful?"

"Everything's useful."

Camilla detached one hand from Nona's hip to reach out and depress the button of the recorder, but kept the other in place. Nona liked seeing Camilla up close: liked seeing the lines of her collarbone through the unbuttoned part of her shirt, the naked parts of her arms, her ears. Camilla was so sweetly handsome and good. Nona always wanted to be close to her. Pyrrha said it was puppy love, but Nona knew that puppy love was different, it just made you want to open the puppy's lips and play with the puppy's teeth.

"It's pretty nice like this," Nona said now, and a little doubtfully. "It's funny—I never feel like that in the dream."

"Hmm," said Camilla, and: "But you've said you like it."

"It's not *sexy*, though."

Camilla's eyebrows went up a little way. "Since when do you use the word *sexy*?"

"The other day Honesty said he thought nice shoes were sexy, and Beautiful Ruby said what just the shoes, and Honesty said no there had to be feet in them, and Born in the Morning got mad and said that Honesty was just being cheap, everyone had feet."

Camilla tilted her head, unwound herself from Nona—Nona was a little disappointed, Cam's hair smelled so much like nice dust—and took the clipboard back. "Okay. What do you think is sexy?"

Nona cheered up immediately at being asked.

"The huge old poster up on the side of the building at the end of the street—the one the dairy's in. The old poster for shampoo."

Camilla looked at her for a few seconds too many. "The painting of the two flowers," she said.

"I think they're very sexy flowers," said Nona. "All right, your turn! Tell me what *you* think is sexy."

"Eating breakfast," said Camilla.

Nona lifted up her voice in despair. "You don't. It's not fair. We're having a heart-to-heart, I'm sharing deep personal thoughts, and you just want me to eat."

"Yes. I'm going to talk to the Warden."

"Well, ask him what he thinks is sexy."

"No. I already know."

That made sense. "Tell me! I'll eat the whole thing if you tell me," said Nona, enchanted, starting to pull on her trousers but deeply distracted. "Oh, Cam, please, please. I've been so good lately. And when I haven't been good it hasn't been because I haven't tried. Yesterday was awful. I need to know—I know it'll help my memory. It's like a *deep need* inside of me, it must be my real self *wanting* to know, right? So this is work, right? What does Palamedes find sexy?"

Camilla took up the clipboard and the pen and wrote, serene and tranquil, underlining something once—twice.

"Strong work ethic," she said eventually. "High test scores."

Nona buttoned up her shirt and wriggled on one sock, then the other, contemplating this. "Okay," she said. "Wow."

"Go get breakfast—tell Pyrrha I'll be along in a moment. How's your hair?"

"My braids are still okay," Nona decided, and then: "Do you know who I am yet? Did that help?"

"Not yet," said Camilla, and bent her head back to the paper. It was a dismissal.

Nona waited, hoping for another smile like the one she'd got the other day. Camilla did not glance back at her, and no smile came. This filled Nona with sharp pangs of disappointment. It wasn't as though the smile had kept things perfect up till now—obviously a lot of terrible stuff had happened in the interim—but that smile had been a kind of guerdon, a safeguard against anything terrible touching *them*. Camilla had stayed home. Pyrrha had come home. Nobody had come to hurt Noodle or the Angel. Nobody had come to get her.

Thinking about Noodle and the Angel made her forget about Camilla's face and how good the day would or wouldn't be. She fled to the front room where Pyrrha, fully dressed, was whisking powdered milk into a jug of water. Her posture—the way her arms were set; her shoulders, a little stooped—brought Nona up short.

"You didn't go to bed last night," she said accusingly.

Pyrrha looked over her shoulder; she smiled that easy smile that always seemed so strange on her strong-jawed, weather-beaten face, set the jug down, and crossed to close the door to the bedroom very, very casually. "Sure I did, slept like a baby," she said, but her smile didn't crinkle her eyes. They were very alert and brown and watchful. "What were you and Camilla talking about? Sounded fruity."

Nona in that moment remembered that she had not told either Palamedes or Camilla she loved them. She glanced at the plastic jug of pale brown-flecked powder and wanted to become happy again, but there was a shadow over her joy now. Pyrrha saw her looking and said, "Hey, you said you wanted pikelet mix. I *can* be trusted to bring home groceries sometimes, you know."

"Where have you been?" said Nona. "You've been crouching. Your right arm's stiff."

Pyrrha, who had picked up the spatula, set it down again. Nona wondered how anyone would ever believe she'd slept. There was wakefulness in her eyes, in the short dead russet of her hair, in the bunching-up of her shoulders—so stringy in her clothes, really, not a spare scrap of fat or softness to her, but she seemed bigger than her body gave her rights to. Her body was a rubber band, but she moved like an animal—like the big dust-coloured cats that lived on the outskirts, the ones with venomous whiskers and ruffs. She moved to the bottom of her voice, and she towered in front of Nona, and said: "I'm putting you in my circle of trust. Can you do that for me? Is it going to be hard for you?"

"Yes," said Nona, automatically dropping her voice to match Pyrrha's. "No."

"I went to the park."

Nona thought about this for a while. Camilla hadn't smiled at her, and now she was being asked to keep a secret. These flags were serious ill omens, even if there *was* pikelet mix. Even two weeks ago she would have become really and genuinely excited for pikelets: she liked scraping the canolene on them and watching it melt into bright yellow puddles, and they were easy to get down, they were so soft. She whispered slowly, "You know you shouldn't have done that."

"Since when have you been my keeper?" Pyrrha just seemed amused. "I don't think you've ever criticised me before. This is rotten. I was about to marry you."

"I wouldn't marry you even if you asked," said Nona apologetically. "I love you, Pyrrha, and I think you're wonderful and very beautiful—" ("Are you kidding?" said Pyrrha. "I look like two elbows.") "—but I don't want to be married to you. You'd never act like you were married to *me*."

This briefly corpsed the person who went to work for her. Pyrrha leant against the sink and seemed pleased that the question of the park had passed, then shook the jug with the powder and the reconstituted milk in it until they were all mixed together. Then she poured it expertly into perfect circles in the hot pan, each puffing up quickly in the heat, big bubbles swelling like magic in the pale brown batter.

"It's the job," Pyrrha said. "You can't take the woman out of the job."

Nona kept her voice at its very lowest register. "Pyrrha, why did you go?"

Pyrrha did not answer. Nona persisted, "Did you save anyone? Because you can tell Camilla and Palamedes if you did *that*, you know they'd like it."

"No," said Pyrrha. "Not how they'd understand it."

"Then, Pyrrha—"

"And I wasn't the only one," said Pyrrha, flipping one of the pikelets over. Nona stared at its perforated yellow top, which was a little bit darker brown everywhere a bubble had touched the pan. "Don't ask questions, Nona. But do something for me . . . Be very careful about those kids at that school, the ones you hang out with."

This blew all the smoke in Nona's brain in the other direction.

"My *school*? What's wrong with my friends?"

"Shh-shh," warned Pyrrha, then said: "Not all your friends . . . That kid with the burns, that's the one I mean. The one with the stupid name."

It took Nona a moment to realise who was being referred to. None of her friends had stupid names; she had to remember what burns were.

"Pyrrha, I'm not sure I like you being mean about Hot Sauce," she said, feeling redder and more bewildered and unhappier all the time. "She has a wonderful name with an important and exciting reason behind it."

"Mean? Not my intention," said Pyrrha. "Nona, all I mean is, your friend Hot Sauce was there last night at the burn cages and she was keeping some pretty ferocious company."

The world revolved. For one moment Nona couldn't think, and couldn't feel, and couldn't stop her body. Pyrrha said, more gently, "Sit and take five," so she sat and took five breaths, in and out, and felt better for it. She concentrated on taking deep bruisy lungfuls through the nose and whistling them out her pursed lips, and by the time Pyrrha had counted out, "Five," she was at peace again.

This was due less to the breathing than it was to the force of her belief in Hot Sauce. If Hot Sauce had been at the burn cages she had a good reason for it. Nona was one of Hot Sauce's friends, a member of her gang. She wouldn't even say a thing until Hot Sauce wanted to tell her about it. That was all. She relaxed.

"Are you mad at me?" said Pyrrha. "You know it's okay to be mad at me, right?"

"No," said Nona. "But I'm not going to stop being friends with Hot Sauce."

"I'm not saying *don't be friends*, I'm saying *be careful*."

Nona decided it was time to change the subject. She hated feeling cross with Pyrrha. And there was *getting mad,* and then there was *having a tantrum.*

"What do you think is sexy?" said Nona, in her normal voice.

Pyrrha seemed pleased to think about something different, and waited until the bubbles were getting really big before she took the spatula and slid it under a rising patty, flipping it over. Nona had come up by her elbow to watch.

"Do you want what I *really* think is sexy, or what I'd tell someone if they asked and I wanted to impress them?"

Nona was pleased that Pyrrha understood.

"The first one."

"Landmine people," said Pyrrha, and when she saw Nona's brows cross in confusion, she said: "Some people were put into the universe to rig it to explode, then walk away . . . I always fell for that."

Nona thought she got it, but she was unsure on a few points.

"But you can't really tell that about someone when you first *look* at them."

"Oh, you can," said Pyrrha. "You haven't looked for it." She flipped over another pikelet, looked grave and intelligent for a moment, and then said: "I mean, also redheads. *Love* a redhead."

Apart from Pyrrha, whose hair was a very deep dark russet, Honesty was the only redhead that Nona knew, and Honesty had big, pallid blue eyes that he could make float in different directions, when one wasn't smushed. He also had skin like a horrible ghost's. You could see all the veins in his eyelids. Nona said, "Okay. *I* don't think redheads are very sexy."

"What? Hang on," said Camilla, opening the door—no, Palamedes, opening the door, busy buttoning himself into Camilla's jacket—"That's a very interesting thing you just said, Nona. Let me write that down. Is that pikelets, Pyrrha? You're a legend."

Nona wondered how Palamedes couldn't see the hitch in Pyrrha's shoulder, nor all the crinkles in her posture or her clothes that screamed *PARK . . . PARK . . . PARK,* but took her moment.

"Palamedes, what do you think is sexy?"

"Those little outfits nurses wear," said Palamedes promptly.

So Camilla had been lying, after all.

Breakfast that morning was a dismal affair, pikelets or no pikelets. Pyrrha and Palamedes didn't seem to have much to say to each other, though Palamedes was cordial—he ate Camilla's pikelets, saying, "She said she wasn't hungry," which filled Nona with a new hot envy wishing she had someone to eat food for her. But Palamedes could never stay long, and so there he was resting his hand on Nona's shoulder, saying, "Take care of everyone for me, Nona," which was Palamedes all over. Never *be good*, or even *be safe*, but leaving you in charge, like he really thought you'd be up to it. Nona always loved him for that.

But then once he had gone Camilla was grey-eyed and quiet and wrathful, and breakfast became almost entirely silent and Camilla paid far too much attention to what Nona was eating, which was uncomfortable.

Nona had negotiated her way through one and a half pikelets and a piece of yesterday's melon and a glass of water when the door burst open despite the fact that it had been locked and a gun made that *ker-KLUNK* noise that Pyrrha had explained meant it was ready to spin small pieces of metal through you at high speeds, and a voice, through a tinny layer of plastic, said: "Heads down, hands up. The first sign of zombie shit and I blow your brainstems."

12

THE HOUSEHOLD HAD BEEN very well drilled, even better drilled than her classroom with the gunfire. Nona hit her melamine plate with her forehead and shot her hands in the air, and there was the answering clatter of Camilla doing the same opposite her—of Pyrrha, who had gotten up to refill her glass, hitting the deck, facedown on the floor. Booted footsteps filled the room— Nona knew without looking that it was six sets of feet: they never came with fewer than six—but as she felt her chin jerked up, and felt the rough, dark plastic weave of the hood working over her head, she couldn't help but give a muffled protest: "But I've got to go to *school!*"

But Blood of Eden never cared if you had to go to school, or clean the whiteboards, or examine the psychodramas Kevin was playing out with two erasers that Born in the Morning had drawn faces on.

In the Building people did not come to look when they heard booted feet down the corridor, or a door flung violently open. As had happened many times before, Nona and Camilla's wrists were taped to their sides with cut lengths of silver tape even as Pyrrha, lying facedown, kept saying calmly: "Cool it, Ctesiphon, you know we'll do what you say. There are too many of you, we don't want to get hurt," but got handcuffed anyway—Pyrrha always got tape *and* handcuffs. All three of them were patted down for weapons in their clothes. Almost all of the knives Camilla had strapped to her got taken away, but not the very hidden knife, or at least the one hidden knife Nona knew about. There were probably more. And no one ever found anything on Pyrrha, which didn't necessarily mean that Pyrrha

141

didn't have anything, although when Nona had asked her the once she had said, *What would I have?* and winked. Then they got two people on either side of them to march them down the hallway. All of the doors were shut tight that morning. One door opened a crack, but nobody emerged.

All three of them were taken downstairs via the big concrete stairwell with the fizzing broken lamps, and then came the part that Nona really hated, when they would emerge in the cool garage space below street level and be bundled into the back of a big white four-wheeled car.

The seats at the back of the car had been taken out, and Nona and Camilla had to lie down and Pyrrha got locked in the boot. This was ostensibly so that if anyone shot through the windows they wouldn't get hit, but as Camilla said the car doors weren't exactly armoured and there was every chance they'd catch a bullet and then things would get interesting. Their hoods got pulled off, and even in the darkness of the garage everything seemed very bright. While they were lying down one of the people in the masks waved a little machine that went *parp!* over them, and another took a temperature measurement from their mouths and under one armpit. Camilla said they did this to make sure that they were alive, and not something else. Nona resentfully reacquainted herself with the carpet flooring on the car. It was made of very scrubby, itchy fibres, and it reeked of the fuel they put in the car engine and the mud on people's boots.

The windows of the car were tinted and hard to see out of. In the early days they had kept hoods on Camilla and Nona the whole way, but this had always contributed to Nona getting violently carsick, so they didn't anymore. Nobody talked. Nona found that if she twisted her head and buried her face in her shoulder she could smell her shirt instead of the car gas, which at least smelled like sweat and the laundry powder Camilla used, and that made the time go away a lot more quickly.

They *did* hood them again when the car finally stopped. Nona counted her footsteps and Camilla's and two other Edenites' as they were walked down a crunchy gravel road. A door was cranked open and they were inside somewhere dark, and then they were sat down and their hoods were taken off, though the tape was left on, and they were sitting in a little waiting room. Pyrrha wasn't there. They never left Camilla and Nona alone with Pyrrha.

It was always a different little waiting room. Nona found them quite glamorous: Camilla and Palamedes, who were both still obsessively trying to work out the route, said in all likelihood it was some old government building. The insides were all brushed steel panelling and clean white floors, and glossy red-and-green plants in pots with thick juicy leaves that Nona always longed to chew on. The leather on the sofa covers was worn and old and shiny, and the metal tubing of the elegant chairs was a little bit scratched, but she always felt untidy and out of place in those office rooms. It was like a picture from an old magazine.

They did not talk because Camilla had made the little sign with her thumb that said, *Keep silent, we're with strangers.* They did not even look at each other until the door opened and someone said, "Test reports are back. They're clean," and in came Crown, and Nona's motion sickness and vague need for the bathroom went away.

Crown, in her heavy boots and stained zip-up jacket and tough canvas trousers with bulging pockets, was the most beautiful woman in the city and maybe on the planet. She filled up the doorway like a light-up sign. She had skin like amber and wonderful hair exactly the colour of golden sugar, and if she had ever been in a queue to get something from a shop *everyone* would have asked her where she had been all their lives. You could have sold tickets to see her. When she smiled at Nona, like she did now, her purple eyes crinkled up at the corners. She was always happy to see Nona. Nona was regularly the only one happy to see her.

Crown turned to Nona. "Come on, cutie. Let me get that for you," she said, and took a knife from her pocket and cut through the tape holding Nona's arms to her sides. Once Nona had been freed, she hugged Crown. Crown was fantastically tall and big and gave wonderful hugs, the type where she put her arms around you and really squeezed. The only uncomfortable part was that with their height difference, Nona was always poked by the gun holstered at Crown's right hip and the sword scabbarded at her left.

"I'll tell them to use the plastic ties for you next time," said Crown, once Nona had withdrawn and was working the tape painfully away from her wrists, where it took all the hairs off and reddened the skin. "Your turn, Camilla— Oh!"

For Camilla's bonds were already gone, even though both her arms had been taped squarely to her thighs. She must have used the very secret knife. Crown's mouth tightened. Camilla was peeling the last remnant away, not making eye contact. All she said was, "Where'd you put Pyrrha?"

"The others only deal with the Saint after he's scanned. You know that," said Crown.

"She's not a Lyctor."

"Not everyone's got that clearance. And it's not like you know the whole picture either."

"She isn't hiding anything."

"You don't believe that," said Crown.

Camilla fell silent. Then she said, "You're still wearing the sword."

This seemed to put Crown back on more comfortable ground. "Of course. Makes me think of home."

"You're not even wearing it for anyone."

Crown said, smiling, "I didn't take you for a traditionalist. I don't *have* to wear it for anyone. Anyway . . . it's an aesthetic."

"It doesn't belong to you."

"I'll give it back if its owner asks, but otherwise, finders keepers," said Crown lightly. "You sound like the Captain, you know."

"They haven't put her down yet?"

If this was meant to hurt Crown's feelings too, it didn't appear to hit very hard. She said cheerfully, "If *I* haven't put a pillow over her face, they won't anytime soon."

"Won't be a pillow," said Camilla. "It'll be head and hands off and the burn cage at the park."

A silvery laugh. "Ooh, she'd love that. Head and hands, like a Cohort martyr. Can you imagine? Can't you just hear her say, 'I regret that I have only one life to give'?"

"You sound like your sister."

"Do I?" Now Crown sounded gratified. "Thanks. I could use some of her gravitas, honestly. I always think I sound too flighty for command . . . I feel like a schoolgirl every time I give a briefing. Everyone else around here feels so old, even if they're three years my junior."

Camilla said, "Are you trying to disgust me, or yourself?"

Another laugh. "Because *you* know me so well, sweetling—"

"I don't know you, Coronabeth," said Camilla. "I don't know you at all anymore."

They fell silent. After a while Crown said, quietly and somehow more truthfully, "It's good to see you, even if you don't feel the same," but Camilla didn't say anything to that either, only rubbed her wrists where the tape had been. Nona's skin was already back to its nice normal colour, and the fine dark hairs on her forearms had regrown themselves. Camilla's skin still looked red and sore.

Crown said, "They're probably finished now. Don't worry so much. The Cell Commander wants to see you in private this morning. This isn't official . . . just a chat."

"I'm missing school right now," said Nona, reminded of her grief. "I'm a Teacher's Aide, Crown, and there's lots of stuff going on."

"You've got to skip sometimes, or they won't know how much they need you," advised Crown, smiling—but Nona could tell she didn't sympathise that much. There was a worry pucker right in the centre of her forehead, and it wasn't a worry pucker for Nona. "I could write you a note."

Camilla said, "I am no longer interested in whatever the Cell Commander has to say."

"I know," said Crown—and there was that worry pucker again. "I know. But *try*, Camilla . . . I know you refuse to see it anymore, but We Suffer's on your side. We're not the hardliners. We want the same things you do."

"You really don't," said Cam.

Camilla reached down into her shirt pocket to take out a hard-shell case. She retrieved the pair of worn dark glasses with big smoked lenses, and slid them up the bridge of her nose. Nona didn't like the way they looked on her face: they made her look like one of the people who would sit in the back of an armoured truck with shiny rifles covered in blazes of orange tape, chewing bubble gum, waiting to get hired by people who wanted to go shoot something up but didn't have enough friends to scare the militia. Hiring them cost a little bit more than bread. They whistled at you if you had gone swimming and were wearing damp shorts and still drying your hair, and Camilla didn't stop them the way she stopped other people. When Nona asked why Palamedes said he had made Camilla promise to never stop them, never get their attention, never make a fuss. He said Nona needed to do the same. He said for one thing they only had so many towels at home.

Crown murmured, all her annoyance gone, "Be careful, Sixth, We Suffer's not stupid," but Camilla just said—

"Let's get this over with. I had things to do today."

"You have no idea" was all Crown said, mysteriously.

Nona had been to "debriefings," which were always extraordinarily strange and uncomfortable, and they always escorted you to the bathroom nearly into the cubicle, which was hell. But they had never been seen in private before. Crown led them down unfamiliar corridors until they reached the usual long, dusty corridor they always walked down, and the room they were always led to—the tall narrow room dominated by one long table, covered in wood veneer and cracked in several places, though very clean. There were still pens and loose scraps of paper on the table, as there always were, which gave you the feeling that you were walking into a meeting right as the last one had ended. The ceiling was multi-holed ventilation panelling of a type Nona longed to throw pencils at, to see if they would stick in the holes. The only decoration was a series of portraits, clustered at the far end of the table.

The portraits were of people from the shoulders up. There were little shelves inset at the bottom of each frame where people had left flowers, dried or plastic, and long burnt-out joss sticks in little glasses, or coins that didn't look like any kind of legal tender Nona ever handed over in return for a bottle of milk. What distinguished most of the portraits was that they were paintings, and very old, all except for one: a photograph of a woman with ferociously red hair and an expression that said she was about to hit the photographer. She blossomed out of a thicket of dusty plastic flowers more numerous than those her painted associates got.

Pyrrha was sitting in the special chair they always got out for Pyrrha. It was a hard chair made of bent metal tubing and scratchy matte plastic pads, and they always strapped a thing to her neck that made soft *klik ... klik* sounds whenever she moved her head back and forth. This was because if Pyrrha made too many sudden movements it would blow out her spinal column automatically. It made a soft *klik* as Pyrrha turned back her head to look at them: she had been staring at the portrait of the lady who looked as though she were about to hit the photographer.

There was another *klik,* more of a *click,* as the door locked behind them. This startled Nona; she hadn't seen anyone walking with them and Crown down the corridor. Crown didn't seem to care, but Camilla tensed up.

There were people already in the room when they got there, dressed the way Blood of Eden always dressed. Nona was forever amazed by their get-up. Everyone she ever met at the meetings covered their heads like they were in a dust storm, and wore masks that varied wildly—gas masks and surgery masks and festival masks with teeth drawn on, and welder's goggles that covered the eyes, and dark glasses that let you see in the nighttime—everyone had visored eyes and swathed themselves in layers of fabric so that it was hard to tell what lay beneath. When they talked, their voices sounded flat and muffled, or breathy and tinny if they were wearing gas apparatuses. Some people with bigger masks had voices that did not sound like any voice that had ever come out of anyone. Palamedes had said they were using tech to hide what they sounded like.

Usually there were a dozen people like this at the meetings; today there were only two.

It was easy to tell which person was the more important. They were sat right in front of the portrait, haloed by that thicket of plastic flowers. A kind of bodyguard stood a little to their left, a long gun slung over their back and a big machete strapped to each thigh. Nona used to think that was cool, but Camilla said it was completely stupid and not cool at all. Palamedes then said Cam was a big hypocrite. The two-thigh-machetes person had their face obscured with an air cleanser toggle mask and welder's goggles, which made them look quite frightening to Nona, like a monster picture. Two-Thigh-Machetes was hooded and wore a long jacket and gloves, so not one bit of their true self was visible.

The sitting person was less frightening in a white mask, the kind they had a box of at home, and quite ordinary black goggles and a deep black hood. You couldn't see any forehead or ears, or any skin at all. This was the commander. In heavily accented House she said, "Please sit."

The soft panel lights at the sides of the room had been dimmed, which made the overdressed visages sitting with them at the table all the more indistinct and weird. It also made Crown's beautiful face more beautiful, lending her eyes a softness and her laughing mouth a tenderness that bright light sometimes took away. Camilla and Nona sat down at the very end of the table and Crown sat on Nona's left. Camilla took one of the click pens from the table in front of her and rolled it between her fingers very slowly, making it flip from knuckle to knuckle, her hips angled forward on the chair.

Crown pressed one hand to her chest in a formal salute and said, "Crown Him with Many Crowns Thy Full Gallant Legions He Found It in Him to Forgive, representing Ctesiphon-3, acknowledges We Suffer and We Suffer of Ctesiphon-1. Troia cell reporting in, Cell Commander."

"Let's not be so formal. I have had three emergency meetings today and I am pretending this is, how you say, a coffee break," said We Suffer and We Suffer. "This is . . . a personal discussion. So please consider all information here limited to Troia cell, not to be mentioned in outside chitchat."

"Have you checked the room for bugs?" asked Pyrrha pleasantly.

"Please try to do a little less of the telling me my own business, Ms. Dve," said We Suffer.

"Just wanted to make sure," said Pyrrha. "Because this *is* off the log, isn't it? We're in one of the old buildings on the southeast, in a district Blood of Eden doesn't hold. You're outside your zone."

Two-Thigh-Machetes drew the big gun from their back and it made the ready noise. They said— "The Lyctor knows too much."

Only their air-toggle mask had some kind of vocaliser on it, so they sounded like a pissed-off robot suffering an occasional blast of static, sort of THE LYCTOR ZZT KNOWS TOO MUCH.

"At ease," said We Suffer, not even looking at Two-Thigh-Machetes. Two-Thigh-Machetes did *not* move to being at ease. We Suffer kept her eyes on Pyrrha. She asked, "Did the drivers take the southern motorway, with the bumps?"

"It's a giveaway," said Pyrrha.

"Goddamn it," said We Suffer. She waved her hand again; Two-Thigh-Machetes slowly lowered the gun. She said, "Yes. We are not on our A-game today. Let us move on from playing games with how clever and how old you are. I am not impressed, and they annoy my colleague."

Camilla popped the nib on the pen and said, "Who armed the dockworkers who busted through Port Authority yesterday?"

Two-Thigh-Machetes said, "Here we go." This became HERE WE ZZZT GO.

We Suffer steepled her fingers together and said, "We have a great deal to discuss and that is not really relevant," and Camilla said— "Let me make it more relevant. Did you know about the Port Authority assault beforehand, or didn't you?"

Before We Suffer could answer this question, their bodyguard said intensely: "Did you have an *objection*?" (ZZT?)

Camilla said, "Twenty-two people were shot," and the bodyguard said, "No. Nineteen people were shot, and three zombie loyalists got put down. Get your maths right. Do you care about the nineteen? Or the *three*?"

Because of the mask it came out very flat, like DO YOU CARE ZZT ABOUT THE NINETEEN ZZT?, which didn't work at all. Nona longed to point this out, but Crown got in first— "If you question Troia cell's loyalty you're questioning *my* loyalty, agent. Are you? Because Blood of Eden states I've got right of recourse, and I can take that recourse right here, right now. How about it? Bet you've never been challenged before. How does it feel?"

Even through a plastic mask and some goggles and a hood We Suffer was starting to look distinctly pained, and when the bodyguard intoned, "JUST GREAT. LET'S GO ZZZT," We Suffer said: "That is much more than enough. You are trained soldiers, not dockside rabble two beers down. There is no right of recourse here. I would rate you both, except that we have no time for that whatsoever."

The bodyguard and Crown fell silent. Crown's eyes were hot and angry, and her lips were pressed together: as per usual she looked great. When Nona was very angry her cheeks went red and her voice got squeaky; she felt deeply envious.

We Suffer said, "Please listen calmly to what I have to tell you, Hect. The negotiator is in orbit."

Camilla stood up.

Pyrrha said gently, "We were expecting this. Get the intel," and Camilla sat down. From the side Nona could see her eyes were angry in a different and less magnificent way than Crown's. They were blank, as though everything Camilla in them had been erased: perfectly grey and glassy and still.

Pyrrha said, "You could have saved yourself half an hour and us a round trip by telling us this back at our digs, Commander."

"What I do is watched very carefully, Ms. Dve," said We Suffer. "So I am being very casual . . . very by the book . . . so that I can get a chance to talk with my Troia cell, in the normal way, quietly. The negotiator arriving throws us all into disarray. Many factions did not expect them to dare to come, not with the blue madness."

"How's consensus?" asked Pyrrha.

"Currently there is an emergency meeting I am not attending

about whether to blow the negotiator out of the sky. The numbers are now not so in favour of that that I am especially worried," said We Suffer. "They are the anarchists who propose this in any case, not the hardcore. They would blow most of the planet up as a middle finger, but they do not have the support. Officially I am willing to be led. Unofficially I am wildly delighted by this. As time goes by . . . as we dither and panic here and lose more and more on Antioch . . . the antinegotiation sect loses momentum. And this is a huge boon in many ways as far as we are concerned. The picture, please."

This was said to Two-Thigh-Machetes, who crossed to the left side of the table and vented their feelings on a cord dangling from the ceiling, making a length of white sheeting come tumbling down the wall. Then they returned to the other side of the room behind We Suffer and started to fiddle with the projector box embedded in the table, mumbling darkly all the while, which sounded through the air circulator a lot like they were fizzing.

Nona grew vaguely excited, because she did like seeing projector box displays. With Blood of Eden all you normally got to see were maps, or numbers, or pictures of dead bodies dumped on one another, but you took what you could get.

"Thank you. Let us get this thing loading," said We Suffer.

Crown said slowly, "You didn't show *me* a picture, Commander."

"No," said We Suffer. "I am showing you now."

The guard flicked the switch. In response, the projector hummed to life and the white screen exploded into greys, but the image projected came into focus so slowly that it was barely a picture at all. It looked as though it was being painted on the screen row by row, from the top to the bottom, every row constantly redrafted with higher resolution and sharpness. Nona made out something lumpy on a darker background, but that was it.

"The limits of technology. Excuse it. We are using shortwave," said We Suffer, with a touch of impatience. "I knew I should have loaded it before . . . I have been in cars all of last evening, all the night, all this morning. I will get a thrombosis. Let me give you a little preamble.

You are about to see a stellar craft sighted"—We Suffer looked down at a folder in front of her—"six hours and twenty-five minutes ago. It is in orbit as we speak."

The grey-on-grey blob resolved into a shuttle. Nona had seen shuttles planetside before the sky changed: big boxy cargo launchers with hooks on top so that they could attach to the space elevator and launch from the geostation. They looked like cake tins with company pictures etched on the sides. This looked sleeker and it wasn't etched at all. There were bones inlaid in the sides like fossils in a dried-out riverbed: whole skeletons curled up as though they had fallen in the shuttle mould, beautifully and intricately set. And it had windows of dark glass. No cargo launcher had *windows*.

The moment the image came into view Camilla's fingers had stilled on the pen. She clicked it so that the nib appeared, and then idly doodled on the paper, except that Camilla was never idle and was physically incapable of doing anything that sounded like *doodle*.

We Suffer said, "You understand that this image caused serious consternation."

"Should've eased your minds," said Pyrrha. "That's not a reinforcement craft."

"I agree. It is not a troop carrier. It is maybe ten metres across," said We Suffer.

The bodyguard said hotly, "I can cram a battalion into ten metres. Give me time and I'll cram two." (ZZT TWO.)

We Suffer said, "Mmm. Perhaps stacking them lengthways?"

"The soldiers will do as I say," said the bodyguard.

"Then how relaxing it is for the soldiers that we have removed you from active duty," said We Suffer. "Crown? Let your people comment."

Crown and Camilla exchanged a significant look. Camilla's stilled fingers had returned to playing with the pen. Nona snuck a look at what she had been drawing; it looked like nothing more than three squiggles and a tiny heart.

"How long has the Second House installation been abandoned now? Station Red-as-Blood?" asked Cam.

We Suffer said, "Ah. I see where you are going with this, the line of questioning you are bringing. The answer is three months since the troops of the Empire abandoned it. I received word yesterday of an investigation last week. It was reported empty. You are wondering about point of origin?"

"Yes. That ship's not big enough for a stele. Don't know if it's big enough for subluminary travel, even. How did it get here?"

Crown leant back in her chair, staring at the projector screen, head balanced in the crook of one golden arm. Nona noticed that her biceps showed even through her shirt, and that there were rubber bandages wrapped around one palm. She said, "Oh, that's big enough for subluminary travel, Millie. See the double struts, and the massive exhaust? That's a *Ziz*-class."

It was hard for Camilla to hold anyone's gaze behind the dark glasses, but she inclined her head a little way toward Pyrrha, who was staring at the picture. Pyrrha shrugged and said, "Crown's the expert. This is all after my time."

Crown continued, "The *Ziz* isn't Cohort standard. And it's not as big on the inside as you think. Look at the windows—see how there're none on the back end? It's mostly engine. Not plated either. It'll get to sublume without many problems . . . but it definitely doesn't have room for a stele. Camilla is right. It can't travel by obelisk anchor."

Camilla had started writing on her bit of paper before Crown finished talking, somehow managing to write and stare intently at the same time. The bodyguard did not even try to hide their interest in Cam's paper, craning their head to stare in open suspicion, but did not seem to find anything to be hostile about.

We Suffer said, "Ah! Are you secretly an expert on the stellar craft of your people, Crown? That is a very useful piece to have in our box of tricks," but Crown just laughed.

"Oh, only secondhand, Commander. I had a massive crush on a boy who was really into shuttles," she said, and added wistfully, "He had a great body. A dancer. *Loved* shuttles . . . didn't look at me twice, so I fell head over heels. Story of my life."

The bodyguard said, "What happened? You eat him?"

Crown said, "A boy like that? Not all at once."

"You're foul," said the bodyguard.

"Yes. Good. The intel, I mean, not anybody's romantic history, which I abhor," said We Suffer. "Let me change my numbers. Lower our estimate to seven to eight metres—yes?—of troop room. That is even better."

But the bodyguard said urgently, (ZZT!) "Seven metres. Six metres. It doesn't matter, Commander. It would take five trained zombies to blow a hole in us. The city's only just starting to get over the fear of having their bones come out. If that confidence gets hit again, we're pushed *months* back on the barracks, and they'll regroup. Let me talk to the antinegotiation faction, you know I've got pull."

"Have you forgotten Varun the Eater all of a sudden?" asked We Suffer mildly. "Have you forgotten hive exposure and blue madness, for the sake of your argument?"

"Who says they haven't come up with a cure for that? Who says they haven't figured out magic, or a pill or whatever, that stops them throwing up and screaming? Have you forgotten *Assume the worst, ignore the best*?"

For some reason, Pyrrha smiled a little, like she was thinking of something. The bodyguard's head had inclined briefly to the portrait hanging behind We Suffer.

We Suffer said: "Have *you* forgotten: *do not catastrophise*? I heard that often from her own lips. I have no time for worst-case scenarios. We must play with the cards we have been dealt."

Pyrrha said suddenly, "Crown. How's the fuel consumption on a *Ziz*-class ship?"

"Thirsty," said Crown, brightening up at being asked. "Its cell would be totally drained after a day in subluminary. It only takes the powerful stuff too—thalergy-enriched, not just hydrogen blend. Hydrogen blend stuffs up the engine."

"Back to point of origin. Either this shuttle's derelict, or—it dropped through the River," said Camilla.

The bodyguard said, "What *River*?" but We Suffer interrupted: "That is above your security clearance. Ignore."

"Then I should *have* that bloody security cl—"

Pyrrha said, "Then who exactly is the negotiator?"

"That is what we would all dearly love to know," said We Suffer. "This has delighted many factions, Unjust Hope's included . . . they are saying, ah, we have the power, John Gaius is taking us and the matter very seriously."

"Well, he would, wouldn't he?" said Camilla. "You're selling him back the Sixth House."

There was a buzzing intake of breath as though Two-Thigh-Machetes was going to say something, but Pyrrha cut in swiftly: "John Gaius has always taken you seriously. Commander, what does this mean about the due date?"

We Suffer said, "The Hopers are asking for a progress report."

Her goggles, buried so deeply beneath her hood, were angled toward Nona. Everyone in the room suddenly remembered Nona existed, and looked at her too; she felt exposed, and regretted everything until Camilla gave her that tiny expression—that smile so minute it could slip underneath a doorway—and she felt better.

Crown said, "But we've got months and months. She's come along wonderfully . . . Point out we've got other ways and means."

"I point out things to the others continually," said We Suffer. "Unfortunately, everyone agrees that we have exhausted the ways and are very, very low on the means. I agree on her magnificent progress. But she is not yet what we hoped for, and I include myself here."

Camilla said, "Tell them collaring Lyctors hasn't gone so well for you."

We Suffer pressed her gloved fingertips together. "Well, no, that is not so true," she said meditatively. "Ctesiphon's interactions with Source Joyeuse and Source Piotra got us many things. Accurate fleet schematics for the first time in a hundred years. Goodness, that was a day. I was only a young soldier then, but that was exciting. *And* the location of the Mithraeum . . . very useful. Not to mention a genuine attempt on the life of John Gaius. I know it did not take, but that in itself was important information. We would know nothing about

Resurrection Beasts without Commander Wake"—here she and the bodyguard saluted the portrait on the wall, and Pyrrha's mouth did something strange)—"and her Source Aegis . . . leading to contact with a House, twenty years ago. A terrible mission failure, we thought. Until the posthumous contact a year ago. No, interacting with Lyctors has not been so bad. Of course, our greatest ally was Source Chrysaor, who taught us all about the obelisks and steles, and who defeated ten high-ranking House personnel and one necromantic monster."

"Cytherea took out a handful of adults, a handful of kids, and an old science project," said Pyrrha impatiently. "And she let two new Lyctors through the net. It wasn't her best effort. Whatever she was doing at Canaan House, it wasn't helping you out. Come on, Commander. When you say *they want progress,* do you mean they want to weaponise her? Or is she merely another part of their negotiation bundle?"

Camilla said, "Anyone who would describe two fourteen-year-olds as high-ranking House personnel isn't interested in Nona as a person."

We Suffer held up a hand. "Camilla Hect," she said, "I am not trying to be cruel. You must see it from our point of view. When you stand in our shoes, Chrysaor—Cytherea the First—came to us, and identified the crisis of many new Lyctors about to rise, and removed it. There were eight powerful necromancers at Canaan House . . . to us, the seeds of eight more enemies we could never hope to defeat. Lyctors take out the very flooring from beneath our feet. We cannot see them coming. We can never stop them. When they arrive the clock starts, and another home is taken away from us . . . our children stateless, our grandchildren perpetual nomads. How many lives, balanced against those ten dead people and that one old—thing?"

"Cytherea didn't kill ten people," Cam said. The pen was held very tightly between thumb and forefinger now, and it didn't move. "She only killed six. The cavalier primary of the Second House killed your monster, and died at its hands. The Eighth was killed by something even we don't understand. And the Sixth House went out on its own terms."

There was an unpleasant silence.

"What happened at Canaan House wasn't your victory, Commander," said Camilla. "It was Cytherea's. She was the only person in that whole building who got what they wanted . . . you just got lucky off the scraps she dropped. And you still think Lyctors are a gun you can wield? What happens if we give you the one you want, right here, right now? In these barracks, at full power, and mad with hive exposure? Assume the worst, ignore the best. And the worst here is pretty bad."

"You don't know anything about the *worst*," said the bodyguard. "You want to know what the real worst-case plan is? I helped craft it. We go over the cowards' heads, we don't wait for negotiations. We evacuate who we can, we liquidate that barracks, we carpet-bomb the whole place. We make sure that every zombie on the planet is dead. I think that big blue son of a bitch is here looking for zombies. No more zombies? No more sphere. Isn't it crazy how you always argue for a plan in which the zombies get to live?"

Crown slapped the table so sharply that everyone jumped, except Pyrrha.

"Oh, shut *up*! Just shut up . . . I'm sick of your fake bravado and bloodlust. Leave my wing alone. I can't stand listening to you rark."

The room fell silent, the bodyguard too. Crown and the guard stared at each other through a layer of air-toggle mask and welding goggles with a hate that was genuine.

"You're only boobs, hair, and talk, Crown," said the guard.

"No," said Crown. "I'm boobs *and* hair *and* talk *and* a hell of a sword hand."

"Did you think that sounded cool?" said the guard.

"You ignored my warning. Both of you are on bullet duty in your frees today," said We Suffer. "This is for saying boobs, and for being boobs yourselves. Repeat it again and it is two days, as promised."

The bodyguard stood so tall and so hard that they trembled,

vibrating slightly. Crown fell back in her chair, arms crossed. We Suffer sat back too. The hood fell a little away from her face, and the black lenses covering her eyes now gleamed beneath the dimmed lamps, reflecting all of them in the glass.

"Troia cell," she said, "this is an old conversation. It is one we have had over and over again. You know the ways in which I am sympathetic and in which I am not. It is not simply a matter of the sixteen. If I say, 'The Lyctor experiment is going well in that the Lyctor now talks in full sentences but shows no signs of power,' then the others will definitely say, 'Useless. Offer her up with the others.' If I lie and say, 'We will soon have a Lyctor on hand,' the Hopers will want me to prove it. And the Hopers are the ones who are in charge of your people's incarceration, and I cannot fob them off. Everyone wants to know what we have on the table before the negotiators arrive, and I am expected to say our part later today. Exactly what I say . . . exactly how I say it . . . should matter very much to you right now."

Camilla said, "Thanks for reminding me. I want Sixth House proof of life."

Crown said, "You know there's no question of harming them, especially at the moment."

"Proof of life. Now," said Camilla steadily. "I want to make sure there's still sixteen. Maybe the reason they want Nona is to patch up numbers, and hide how many of them have died under torture."

We Suffer said stiffly, "I was the one who promised them clemency, Hect. There is a no-torture clause. Merv Wing know that."

"Yeah, well," said Pyrrha, "you aren't exactly showing a united front."

"Unjust Hope is a very crap human being," said We Suffer, "but my word is still not *nothing* in Blood of Eden."

Pyrrha said, "How certain are you of that?"

There was a long silence. We Suffer wheezed through the mask, and then said abruptly, "I had intended to give you this anyway . . . Here."

She opened up a brown-paper folder, and took from it a little piece of electronics, a fingernail-shaped thing with prongs. She tapped on a space in the cracked wooden veneer on the table, and nothing happened, so she tapped again more violently and it reluctantly opened—a panel in the wood, revealing hard white plastic sockets and buttons. Camilla was still again, chin in one hand and pen in the other, more like a picture of Camilla than Camilla herself. There was a sudden noisy crackle from the speakers in the walls, and then a disembodied voice— "Master Archivist Juno Zeta reporting, remaining as representative of the Oversight Body in lieu of the Master Warden. I count six days, seven hours, and forty-six minutes since the last recording. In answer to the previous question, the article title is *Heteroscedasticity in Viscus Models for Long-Term Data.* Head count standard. All well within the house formerly identified as Sixth. Awaiting further instructions."

The pen had scratched a tiny mark into the paper Camilla had been doodling on. Her shoulders suddenly relaxed, and she clicked the pen, and her face minutely bent toward the mark.

"Do you accept this as proof of life?" said We Suffer.

"Yes," she said. "This is the next proof-of-life question: How many pages in my Scholar's thesis?"

We Suffer wrote that down. "All right. I cannot guarantee the next drop coming soon under these circumstances, but I will try to make it timely. Please, Camilla Hect, give me something."

Camilla sat ramrod-straight, very still, in a pose of pure thought.

"Tell them they'll have a Lyctor, or equivalent, if they wait," she said.

"Now there's a grim fucking thought," said Two-Thigh-Machetes.

We Suffer said levelly, "Then we go with promises? Fine. Is there anything else?"

"Well, I need the bathroom," said Nona.

"Ah, in the end, all of us are people . . . who need the bathroom," said We Suffer, and leant back in her chair.

"You think I am trying to shore up my own failing power base," We Suffer said finally. She had pressed her hands together so that it looked as though she were praying. "You think I am either cruel and traitorous—that I had thought this was the outcome of the great coming-together that we hoped for—or stupid, that I was naive. I am not naive . . . I had just never thought we would be given such a terrible scare, or such a terrible chance. I wish for Blood of Eden to fight, and fight beautifully; to win with whatever aid or succour your Houses may bestow. I do not want to run anymore. Now the negotiator comes. What will John Gaius ask for, and what will John Gaius want? And will we give it to him? All I can tell you is I am prepared to give *my* answer . . . and I feel that Blood of Eden would stand with me if they only knew how, if they were given good reasons. Please help me give them those reasons. We are done here. Let us all go to the bathroom. Dismissed, Ctesiphon-3, Troia cell."

III 13

CROWN STOOD, AND BOWED, and tapped her chest three times with an open palm, which was the Blood of Eden way; then she began untaping Pyrrha from her seat, unmercifully, with Pyrrha barely wincing. We Suffer kept her seat as they filed out, Camilla in front, Pyrrha after, and Crown bringing up the rear, and before the door was closed Nona heard the bodyguard say: "Can I bloody well leave now? The package is late for work." ("PACKAGE ZZZT IS LATE FOR WORK.")

Crown's jaw was gritted fast. She automatically started shepherding Nona toward the bathroom down the corridor, but Nona said—"Why does Pash hate us so much?"

Crown was so startled that her jaw relaxed.

"How could you have known that was Our Lady of the Passion?"

"It's . . . it's bones," said Nona, struggling to articulate. "Beneath her clothes. The way she moves her bones," and Camilla looked at her for the longest time.

"Pash," said Crown darkly, "is what happens when nepotism and bullshit collide. *Boobs and hair . . . ?!* My hair is naturally big *and* manageable, dickhead! I haven't been able to condition properly for a year!"

There were two guards waiting outside. They led Pyrrha away to get her collar taken off. Pyrrha went with them much more meekly than Nona expected, and just turned her head to say to Nona: "Remember to stuff," before the guards shuffled her onward with the butts of their rifles.

As though she wouldn't. When Nona was locked away in the bathroom stall stealing toilet paper, judiciously stuffing it down her shirt as Pyrrha had taught her—Pyrrha had a very Blood of Eden mindset, if you thought about it—she heard Camilla outside by the sinks, saying quietly: "Let me see her."

Crown said, as though casually surprised, "Do you really want to? It's not a good day. She's in and out . . . Moving her has been a royal bitch. We've had to keep shifting her between beds ever since we got her here."

"Okay. Let me see her."

"If you agitate—"

Camilla said, "You know I can help her, Third. You know I want to."

It seemed like Crown was going to say a joke or something dismissive again, but then she said, "So long as Dve doesn't tag along. Your call."

When Nona rustled her way out of the stall, Camilla looked at her chest, and her mouth quirked in something that might have been the tiniest and most beautiful smile yet. But Crown didn't notice. Her lovely head was bowed and her sooty eyelashes lowered. Nona said, "Are we going right away? I'm going to be *so* late for school," but Camilla said, "I want to make a quick visit first. Do you want to come with, or do you want to stay in the waiting room and wait for Pyrrha?"

The waiting room was not an option; Nona would be stuck with some Edenite bodyguard who wouldn't even talk to her, and no magazines, and nothing to look at. But Camilla loved to give people choices. Nona hated how she fell for that every time: whenever Camilla said something like, "Cereal, or eggs?" Nona would be tricked into saying *Cereal* even though she had wanted to choose *Nothing!!* But this choice was easy; she liked visits.

They took the lift downstairs. Crown said the stairs didn't go as far as they were going. Camilla asked if the depth was doing anything. Crown said in a don't-care-ish voice, Maybe, it seemed to, but it stopped having an effect after a while. Camilla said, Makes sense, distance isn't really an issue, the creature isn't fully instantiated but squatting in the River, and Crown said, How will we know if it instantiates, and Camilla said, Because gravity will change and the planet'll break up, and Crown said, Hmm. Nona listened to this with one ear only: the toilet paper was itching.

As the lift went down, she said, with the pleasure of realisation— "Oh, we're visiting the Captain!"

All Blood of Eden buildings seemed to have big elevators going deep down into the earth. In this elevator Crown had pushed the button to go down six whole floors. When they exited it was very dark and cool, and the halls were made of slabs of concrete cracked by some past pressure. The lights weren't the pretty panels of up top—they were strung on thick juicy plastic wires bundled up high on the walls, and they swung in distress when Nona and the others passed them. It was a place where if you whistled, your whistle would echo back, and Nona pursed her lips, but Camilla saw her and furrowed her eyebrows, so she didn't.

Most of the doors were open, and the rooms within were dark and full of stacks of abandoned furniture. One door was shut. There was a Blood of Eden person there, wearing a full balaclava and a hood to go over it. Nona wondered if they all kept hats and hoods and things in their back pockets just in case. They gave Crown the salute—three taps to the chest—and shouldered their gun, and walked off down the hall. Crown put her hand on the handle and stopped. She suddenly looked tired.

"Don't worry about volume," she said. "Noise never bugs her."

Camilla said, "Is she part of the negotiation?"

"Ha! She wishes," said Crown. "No. She's our ticket out of here."

Nona hadn't seen the Captain in a long time; not since a little before the blue sphere had appeared. Palamedes had banned Nona from seeing her. Camilla said Captain Deuteros thought the solution to every problem was to act like the problem had one solution that nobody else was tough enough to take, and then to pursue that solution as hard as possible. She had always been very . . . intense, with Nona.

Her new room underground was very spacious, almost the size of their kitchen and living room back on the thirtieth floor, and bare except for a bed, a chair, and a table cluttered with injecting needles. The lights had been dimmed so low that all the shadows bled into each other. A pole with a plastic bag of clear fluid was right next to the bed, and a tube passed down from the bag to the Captain, who was lying flat on her back amidst the white sheeting, wearing something that looked a lot like Nona's worst nightie.

Crown made them squirt antibacterial gel onto their hands, and fussed until they rubbed it in. "She gets everything going," she said. Once they had done that, they were allowed to approach.

The Captain's eyes were shut, her eyelids a little swollen, almost purplish, like somebody had hit her. Her deep black hair had been painstakingly braided away from her face, showing the pretty early silvering at her temples, but that was the only beautiful thing about her. Her skin was dry and her bones showed, especially in the cheeks. Her cheekbones and square chin looked like they were about to stretch her face to the breaking point. She looked so thin and still lying there in that bed that Nona was very sorry, even if the Captain was strange.

Camilla approached the bed immediately. She looked at the bag of clear fluid, and reached out to touch the Captain's dead-bronze wrist and asked, "How are they giving her food?"

Crown said, "By mouth. We've fed her by tube too. It's all fairly primitive, I'll be honest."

"She's dehydrated. Who's nursing her?"

"She's managed to help herself a couple of times, on the best days. When that thing's as far away in orbit as it gets. No one here's as good as you."

Nona peeked around Camilla's arm. The Captain's black brows drew together, and her face took on a hideous expression: a flat tangle of features that scared Nona so badly that she wanted to go to the bathroom again, right until the Captain opened her mouth and droned, punctuated by huge wheezing lungfuls of air: "Dust of my dust—such similar star salt—what they did to you and what they wrung from you and what shape they made you fill—we see you still—we seek you still—we murdered—we who murder—you inadvertent tool—you misused green thing—come back to us—take vengeance for us—we saw you—we see you—*I see you.*"

The wheezing breath turned into a strangled noise, and the Captain's body thrashed upward. She twisted like a fish being drawn out of the harbour on a line. A little green box that Nona had taken for a clock started beeping urgently. Crown shouldered forward, but was told tersely, "Give me room. She's not getting enough blood to her heart," and Cam placed one hand flat on the Captain's chest before pulling the tinted glasses off her face in a fit of impatience. Nona took these and rubbed at the warm steel with her hands: she liked them so long as no one wore them. Camilla asked, "What's happening with her kidneys? What are they giving her for her blood pressure?"

"A medical thinner, but—"

"Thought so. Give me a second." Camilla's hands kept pressing down, as though holding Judith to the bed. After a moment so long Nona nearly bit through her tongue from anxiety and excitement, the Captain went limp. The awful expression left her face, which went slack, if not peaceful. Crown did not sigh, or exclaim in relief, or anything: she had chewed her lips so badly that they had split and were now red, like lipstick.

Camilla's hands hovered over the Captain's chest, as though waiting to catch her heart. "That'll do. Take her off the anticoagulants. Is the compulsive shouting typical?"

"Lately," said Crown, after another pause. "I'm not sure she's in actual pain . . . Palamedes."

Palamedes said nothing, simply made a quite-good Camilla expression—one quirked eyebrow, the mouth not doing much—but Crown smiled and said, "You've been pretty obvious today. Get out of it, Master Warden."

He said heavily: "I hope to God you didn't codge up a medical emergency just to catch me out, Princess."

"I wish we had. I wish I was that smart. Don't panic, we're not being bugged. I knew you weren't in the hand bones the Ninth made anymore. I don't know what you and Cam have done, Sextus, but I haven't told. I haven't told but I *have* known, for a long time. This was only . . . confirmation."

"Like hell it was. You guessed," said Palamedes.

"No. You didn't react to *Millie*. She hates it when I use *Millie* now."

"She didn't love it before. Better friends to her than you have been glared at for less."

Crown quirked her eyebrows together languidly, like she was too tired to make too many facial expressions in a row. Nona didn't know why Palamedes wrinkled his nose as though he'd smelled something bad.

"The Captain and Cam and I were stuck together for a long time, you know," she drawled eventually. "I'm not saying I knew from the way you moved or the things you said. You're seamless, I'll give you that! I knew because . . . because she stopped being so unhappy. The whole time I knew her she was grieving . . . she couldn't hide that. At the same time I was grieving, and the Captain was grieving, and we—she and I can grieve alike enough to fight about it, but Camilla was *gone*. Camilla was gone and then we met Harrowhark, and she came back. That's all it was. What did you do?"

She was interrupted by movement from the bed. The Captain's swollen eyelids had fluttered open, and she coughed. Crown immediately dropped to her knees beside the bed so that she wasn't looming over it. Palamedes took some wadding from the table with the hypodermics and wetted it, and he wiped it over the Captain's cracked, wan mouth.

"Thank you," she said. Her voice was very low; Nona almost couldn't hear it.

"Don't mention it. I'm going to give your kidneys a clean, Captain."

"No," she said, "I can do it. Let me."

Crown made a noise in the back of her throat as the Captain placed her thin hands over her own middle. It took a little bit for her to find her hands, or her middle. She gritted her teeth, and a grunt escaped as she did—something. It left her gasping, and Palamedes said quietly, "A heroic effort. I'll finish you off, ma'am—don't want that buildup going elsewhere," and put Camilla's hand on the Captain's. The Captain's chill brown eyes closed again briefly. As Nona watched, the dry, cracked patches on her skin disappeared, and some of the pinched look went from her face, and her colour deepened to more of a burnished russet and less like something that had dried too long on a rack.

Nona remembered, and touched Palamedes's arm, and mouthed, *Timer;* he grimaced, and pushed glasses that weren't there up his nose, and nodded.

The Captain coughed again, but less awfully. She said, throatily, "Where am I?"

"You're in the Ur facility, Deuteros," said Crown. "Blood of Eden rescued us from Canaan House, remember? They saved your life, and mine and Camilla's. Remember living shipside together? Remember how they stitched you up?"

Some of the hope wrinkled out of the Captain's forehead. "Yes," she said darkly, and, "Name and rank: Captain Judith Deuteros . . . House: Second. Status: adept. Cavalier: Marta Dyas, dead."

Crown said, "Oh, here we go again."

"Service record: seven . . . I . . . approximately seventeen years. Name and rank . . ."

"*Judith.* You're regressing."

"Princess," said the Captain, at the bottom of her voice, "there's still time. I know the Cohort will come for us . . . even me, the pilot. Walk this back. I'll say what's true. They abused your sympathies. Their methods are sophisticated. It's not your fault. I'll tell them everything . . ."

Crown's mouth trembled. "Oh, will you, Jody? Will you *really*?"

"You too, Hect . . . say it and I'll believe it. Say we were all co-erced, and they used our lives against each other. We were hostages. Incidental pieces . . . in a much larger game . . . played by Lyctors, traitors, monsters." In a different voice she suddenly said, "Where am I? Where's Marta? Where's Lieutenant Dyas?"

Then she threw back her head and howled like an animal. Crown and Palamedes both held her down.

After she had exhausted herself, thrashing, she gasped: "I remember. I'm fine. I'm fine," and Palamedes withdrew, though Crown held the Captain's hand down against the drab white sheets of the bed.

The Captain's chest was heaving beneath the outfit that looked like Nona's worst nightie. She murmured, "Keeping me alive . . . intact . . . just so I can work their damned stele and get Cohort blood . . . all over my hands. Gun to your neck . . . blood on my hands . . . saints against God."

"Don't talk," said Crown roughly. "You're spouting nonsense."

"You haven't talked sense in months." She burbled with coughing again. "You're the one facing the dark night of the soul, Princess."

"Love that melodrama. Is there Eighth somewhere in your family tree?"

"Gave yourself up . . . gave all of us up . . . for what? Propaganda and a leash . . . promise of salvation without understanding the sin. Hect and the hideous Sixth House mechanism . . . and now they are taken too. For *what*? Our lives? Is this living, Corona?"

"You've never lived a single day of your life," said Corona bitterly. "It'd be against regulations."

The Captain said, "Name and rank: Captain Judith Deuteros. House . . . Second," and Crown scrubbed at her face with her hand, little licks of hair escaping from their elastic and curling over her forehead like light. The Captain broke off and said, "You think you're walking the tightrope with fast talking and your face . . . steeled myself to the talking long ago. But you're slipping, Princess . . . can't save you from that . . . Hect, my hands are too filthy to save you . . ."

It was funny to think of anyone wanting to save Camilla. The Captain's eyes restlessly passed to Nona. Sweat was beading on her temples. The Captain focused, and said hoarsely, "Ninth, where is the mercy of the Tomb? Where is your sword in the coffin? Who are your masters now, and who do you master? Where is my cavalier, Reverend Daughter? Where is yours?"

Her voice rose. "Because I saw her in the waves—she was there in the grey water—I saw them all—they hurt me—where is my hunger? I eat and eat and eat without surcease, my green thing, my green-and-breathing thing . . ."

The Captain screamed wordlessly again. Palamedes put his hand on her forehead, and she cut off midscream to lie back in the pillows. Her eyelids fluttered shut and her breathing was suddenly even, and the sweat all dried away. He said, "Sleep now. You need it. My time's up."

Crown said, "Time? Master Warden, what are you talking about?" but Palamedes had put Camilla's hand on his shoulder and then was Camilla again; shivering briefly, once, staring at the hand on her shoulder as though she didn't remember how it got there, taking that hand and running it through her short dark crop of hair. She cracked her knuckles and stretched her hands behind her back, clasping and loosening the muscles of her shoulder blades, and said—

"Update?"

Nona said, "Palamedes told Crown he was Palamedes, and Judith woke up and talked a lot, but then she had a bit of a yell and went to sleep. It was all kind of weird, in my opinion."

"Noted," said Camilla.

Crown, who had checked the Captain's neck and then her forehead, noticed Camilla watching and roughly turned away. She said, and not very approvingly, "Palamedes supersedes you, doesn't he? He takes over, and you're just—not there?"

"Vice versa too," said Cam, avoiding her gaze.

"For the love of God, Cam, that's a slippery slope downward . . ."

She only said, "Still swearing by God? The Warden shouldn't have told."

"He could hardly have bluffed his way out of it, Cam, he used necromancy," Crown began, but Camilla said sharply, "It's called *lying*. What now? You spill to your bosses upstairs? Do we become part of the package deal?"

"No. I swear by my sister," said Crown. Camilla's shoulders relaxed minutely. Crown added, "It's not my secret. And I've kept your secrets before . . . you know that."

Cam said, "I still don't trust you."

"Doesn't matter. You know, I really am glad you two are together . . . in whatever way you've managed. I'm glad Harrowhark helped you both. I know I said it was dangerous at the time . . . and I'm sorry that we didn't believe you when you said he was in there."

Camilla still did not look at her, but she suddenly said at the bottom of her voice, "Come back with me. Leave the facility. Before the negotiator arrives, come back with us."

Crown stared at her. For a moment Nona thought she would say *Yes* and was very pleased. She didn't mind sleeping in the bathtub. But Crown said, brightly— "I like my prison cells more obvious. And I hate not knowing where my next meal is coming from."

Camilla said, "That's not it."

"Well, you know, the Captain wouldn't last a day without me, and then how the hell am I getting out of here?"

"You're a worse liar than Palamedes," said Camilla, with feeling. "You're not a good woman, Tridentarius."

"Not my name anymore, and none of us are good," said Crown. "Except for Nona, of course."

"Thanks," said Nona, deeply flattered.

"What about me?" said Camilla.

"You and I don't even own our own souls," said Crown.

Crown turned around and put her arms around Camilla. For a moment Nona thought that Camilla would break just as she had assumed Crown would break: that there was a softness to the way she stood, a hesitation, a not-knowingness to her knees and her feet. And Crown's hugs *were* so good—so heated and so tender—as though Crown were hugging you solely for her own comfort, as though she wanted your touch more than anyone else's right then. It was better than lying on tiles that the sun had warmed, which was one of Nona's chief delights. But Camilla tightened, somehow, and didn't put her arms around Crown, and Crown withdrew.

Camilla said, "My soul's mine. You give yourself away to anyone who doesn't want you."

"Well, I never like to wear the same thing twice," said Crown brightly. But she said: "Try to forgive me someday, Cam . . . that goes for Palamedes too. This is too close to the wire, and I really hate you two hating me. I'm happy for you, believe me. I always had a soft spot for the Warden."

And Camilla said, "You were part of the lie."

When they went back upstairs to the waiting room with the juicy potted plants and the furniture, Crown hesitated at the doorway, and said: "The transport team has put Dve in the boot. I'll come with you, make sure they're using cut-away cuffs this time."

"You're overdoing it with Pyrrha," said Camilla.

"I've heard too much of the Saint of Duty to trust Pyrrha Dve," said Crown, her mouth thinning and that pucker reappearing. "Don't put too much trust in Pyrrha Dve, Cam . . . there's a lot that you don't know."

Nona hated anyone criticising Pyrrha and cast about for a change in topic. She said, "What was the Captain talking about before she fell asleep, and when we came into the room? What's the water? What's the hunger, and the green thing?"

When Camilla *and* Crown looked at her, she realised she could not have said anything worse. Crown looked at her with open bewilderment, and Camilla looked at her with an expression that Nona hated instantly. She looked over at Nona with her big, borrowed grey eyes, so clean and clear—Nona always thought if soap could be grey her eyes would be grey like soap—and she was unsure. She was, Nona realised with a pang that made it all the way down her spine, frightened.

"Nona," Crown said slowly, "The Captain didn't say anything when you came into the room. She only screamed."

14

THEY WERE DRIVEN BACK in the same silence, and given the same tests—just in case they'd left their bodies in the facility, Palamedes always said, and put something fake in the car—but with Crown along, the trip was much nicer. Nona got to sit up on the seat next to Crown—one of the guards said, "You're taking our lives in your hands," but Crown said, "Oh, *please*," and that was that. Nona wasn't even pressed into the floor, even though she *was* cuffed; and they *did* use plastic zip cords, not the tape, which felt a lot better except that they cut into the skin a little. There were two pink hoops on Cam's wrists where the ties cut into it. Nona's went away immediately.

"Stop the car," called out Crown, and the car coughed to a stop. Camilla stiffened.

"We're near Nona's school," said Crown, and Nona wriggled with pleasure and relief. "I thought I'd get out and walk her. How's that sound, cutie?"

"Do you mean it?" said Nona, ecstatic. "Please, Crown! I'd love that. I want my friends to see you."

"The car can drop the rest of you off back at the safe zone," finished Crown. She was already slitting the ties on Nona's wrists as the car revved in place.

Camilla said, through a thick mouthful of hood, "No."

"What, you think I can't look after her? It's a hundred metres from here."

"Nona. Wait—"

But Nona, who was desperate to get out of the car, had hopped out the moment Crown opened the door for her, delighted to get out into the warm concrete-smelling air and breathe in salty lungfuls of traffic fumes and ocean and burning rubbish; she had a massive pang when she realised that the car wasn't stopping to let Cam or Pyrrha out too, that she hadn't listened properly, that she had been selfish, that she hadn't understood the implications. She blurted, "I don't have a hat. Or a mask."

"There's hardly any smoke."

"I still need one, I still need them."

Crown scrounged in her pockets and took out two flimsy softshell masks, winding one around her head and face. She had a hood on her jacket, and she unsnapped it from the collar to settle it around Nona's head and shoulders: "I've got chem screen on," she said, and tucked Nona's arm into hers. "Come on. Let's live a little."

By that point the car had burred to life again and was reversing back down the street. Nona hesitated—but Camilla hadn't used the special safe word, after all, hadn't used any of the codes they'd agreed on that meant Nona *couldn't*. That meant Nona was being ordinarily selfish, not dangerously selfish. And seeing Crown in the city sunshine was fantastic. A couple of people had stopped on the street to gawk at her, hatless and golden, then moved on hurriedly when they saw her gun.

"But Camilla—" she began.

"I've got as much right to you as Camilla does," said Crown, still smiling. "In another world I might have been the one looking after you, you know. And I think Camilla does a bit too much *looking after* . . . you're not so much younger than she is, after all."

This resembled some of the darker and more resentful thoughts in the back of Nona's head. She mumbled, "But I love Camilla."

"Do you *love* love Camilla? In-love-with-Camilla?" Crown sounded amused, and weaved her around a little stand that was selling magazines and candy. The streets were thick with people meandering home before the hottest part of the day kicked in, but not hurrying yet, which meant it hopefully wasn't that late. "Maybe you could be the one to melt her icy heart. You're cute. . . on your best days, adorable. But I'm not sure you're her type."

Nona flushed. Suddenly being treated as an adult made her feel out of her depth, like when a wave knocked her off a sandbar and her feet went out from beneath her. She didn't know what to say or how to act, and floundered toward the shallows: "She's not your type either," she said.

Crown stood back from the road as a barrage of open-backed trucks rattled past. There was a piercing whistle in her direction and she ignored it with a disdainful toss of her big yellow hair. She looked down at Nona and asked cheerfully, "How do you know my type?"

Nona thought it was obvious.

"It's the way you look at people."

"Tell me," demanded Crown. There was a deep velvety spark of mischief in her eyes, and Nona thought again how lovely they were, like the flowers in the sexy shampoo advertisement. "Come on—I'll die if I don't know. I love being told about myself."

Nona rose quite eagerly to the challenge. "You look at Commander We Suffer like you want her to think you're into her, but you aren't at all, it's just something you're doing with your eyelashes," she said. "But that's no help figuring out your type because I don't know what the commander looks like. You don't like Pash at all, but I don't know what she looks like either. You're scared of Pyrrha, and you *do* think she's nice-looking, but you're confused when you think that so you don't look at her very much. You want Camilla to cuddle you but not in a—a sexy way. I think you want Camilla to look at you like she looks at me. And you're in love with th—"

A hand went over the mask at Nona's mouth. When she looked up at Crown, in that press of people and the clinging smoke, she could see that the eyes above the softshell mask had lost their soft purple gleam and were dark, with the heavy amber brows drawn low over them. She said, in a different voice, "All right, Nona. I've heard enough."

Nona, when the hand was withdrawn, said thickly: "You're mad at me. Shame on you."

The trucks had passed and everyone surged together across

the street in one big slosh of humanity. Crown, half-stricken, half-laughing, had put her arm back through Nona's, and they hurried down the street toward the school. She said, "You're—you remind me very much of someone when you make that face. I'm sorry, cutie, I got frightened. Can you forgive me? I won't ever ask you to do it again—tell you what, I'll owe you an ice cream."

Nona was a little bit mollified.

"I don't want an ice cream, thanks," she said, on her dignity. "You shouldn't ask me things if you don't want me to tell the truth about them."

"I know. I do it all the time, I've never learnt. It's awful—my sister says that. I'd ask her how I looked in an outfit and she'd always say exactly what was on her mind, and sometimes all I wanted was for her to tell me I looked perfect even if I didn't." Crown sighed, the picture of tragedy. "And, horribly, she was always right."

"But you always look beautiful," said Nona.

"That's why I should ask *you* what I look like, and ask my sister what I'm feeling," said Crown. "*You'll* always tell me I look beautiful, and she'll always tell me what I want her to think. This is the school, isn't it, where you work?"

They would have had to get buzzed in, except that someone was already standing there unlocking the door with a key. It was the Angel. Nona flew down the street in a panic that the door would close without her. She cried out, "Wait!"

Nona was completely winded by the time she got to the foyer, with the Angel holding the door for her. Nona bent double and panted, and when she straightened up she was shocked to find the Angel looking even worse than she had on the two previous days, with her coat still on and Noodle sitting patiently on his leash.

"Oh," said Nona, panting, "how late—is over—what time—!"

Despite looking as though she hadn't slept, or if she had, had slept in the clothes she was currently wearing, the Angel grinned. This made her ears go up slightly with the smile, which Nona loved.

"Get your breath back," said the Angel kindly. "They're just finishing up with break—I was getting myself sorted."

Crown had jogged to catch them up, and slipped through the door before it closed.

"You see?" said Crown, not winded at all, filling up the doorway. "What did I tell you? You're fine."

The Angel and Crown sized each other up. Crown was much younger and bigger and taller and more exquisite, and when she pulled her mask down and smiled the Angel's eyes widened, a little bit. Not in a *you-are-so-attractive* way either, Nona noted. The Angel was a bit shocked, like Crown looking the way she did was maybe illegal. They shook hands in perfect amity, but the Angel looked her over and said— "No guns in this building—that's the rule, I'm afraid."

"Oh, I wouldn't ever scare the children," said Crown sincerely, but the Angel said, "No, but nobody's going to be interested in my lesson if they see *you*. We're doing how sound moves today and they'll be bored stiff."

Crown laughed with very white and even teeth.

"I'm sorry to say I sympathise. I was terribly stupid in my lessons when I was a girl."

"How long ago was that? Five minutes?" said the Angel, and Crown laughed again.

"Why can't she come up? I want Hot Sauce and the others to meet her," said Nona, embittered. "It's not fair. We got to see Beautiful Ruby's baby. I've had a horrible morning and I want them to look at her."

"Nona, I've had a horrible morning too, so have mercy on me," said the Angel candidly. "It would make teaching soundwaves impossible if anyone got a glimpse of your—your friend. Can't she come back afterward? Are you family? Do you know Joli? I'm afraid I've never met you before," she added, to Crown.

Crown had crouched down and was scratching Noodle between his ears. Noodle was responding by thumping two of his hind legs at once and opening his mouth and panting.

"Oh, I'm Camilla's partner. But I can't stay."

"I see! Lovely to meet you," said the Angel, unaware of how her eyebrows betrayed her, like everyone else in the world to Nona seemed unaware of how their eyebrows betrayed them, by immediately saying plain as day: *Camilla?? Really??? Camilla????* Which Nona thought was unfair: Crown was really very nearly pretty enough for Camilla. "Nona, can you take Noodle for a moment? I've got to get the tuning forks and he's going to make the most unrighteous howl, he can't stand the things."

When she had passed the leash to Nona and gone through the door with one last look at Crown, Nona crouched to give Noodle her hand to lick, and said accusingly: "If Camilla hears you said that, she'll be furious."

"That's probably why I said it," admitted Crown, with genuine contrition. "I have a ripple of evil running through my soul—I *know* I do. But it wasn't that bad a lie, was it, Nona? Don't you think it'll raise Cam's status? Don't you think I've done her a favour?"

Nona thought about it.

"Camilla doesn't need raising. You could have raised *my* status by saying you were *mine*," she added. "They would have believed it—we're both very attractive."

Crown laughed in her lovely, husky, rippling way. "And there you go, reminding me of someone completely different."

Then she dropped to a crouch again, but instead of dipping low and scratching Noodle, she gently pressed her thumb to the underside of Nona's chin; she was smiling now, but she was smiling as though Nona had said something a little sad, and her eyes didn't sparkle anymore. They hadn't gone hard as they had at the roadside, but they were shadowy.

"You darling, I know what you are, even if they refuse to see it," she said softly. "All I can say, sweetheart, is I envy you more than anyone else in the universe."

BUT WITH THIS BOMB DROPPED, Crown refused to stay and tell, and Nona crouched there too open-mouthed to run after her. In any case Nona did not have to mourn long the fact that she was late for work *and* none of her friends had got to see Crown; Honesty had seen Crown leave from his window seat, and she was gratified when Born in the Morning and Honesty gave each other rabbit punches over who got to ask Nona how old she was and which of their names Nona had to mention to her in the future. Hot Sauce also came over to stroke Noodle and said, "Good. You're here. Don't want you to be dead," which was a lot for Hot Sauce to say.

Nona recalled what Pyrrha had said about Hot Sauce. She looked her over carefully. It wasn't as easy reading her as it was reading Pyrrha. Hot Sauce constantly stood as though she were disconnected from her own head. Her body and her mind seemed to actively ignore each other. And her burns sometimes made her look rigid in a way that scared the tinies and foxed Nona's senses. Now Hot Sauce stood like she hadn't slept very well, but Hot Sauce never stood like she'd slept very well. Her eyes were wrinkled like she'd squinted them a lot, maybe against bright light—or smoke.

"Would you be mad if I died?" said Nona.

"Yes," said Hot Sauce simply. "You're my crew."

This made Nona deliriously pleased, but then deeply anxious.

"Hot Sauce," she said timidly, "I don't want you to be sad or mad if anything happens to me. Promise not to be sad—I don't like it on your face."

There was a flicker of surprise across Hot Sauce's eyelashes. But then the others ragged her at the idea that *anyone* would be sad if she died, and they got into an argument about who would inherit her share of fruit that day as it hadn't been bagsed, which turned into another fight between Born in the Morning and Honesty, who had not forgiven each other for the rabbit punches and both of whom started promising their worldly goods to anyone who wasn't each other. Honesty had recovered, although his eye looked even puffier and more multicoloured than it had the day before. The teacher had given him some painkillers to take but he had cunningly spat them out and dried them for resale, so *he* was entirely happy.

Nona came away promised, on Born in the Morning's death, a pen that wrote in three different colours, and on Honesty's his collection of paper throwing stars.

Hot Sauce didn't say anything after that, just sat by the window alternately watching the Angel—packing little metal pins away into a box and chatting to the main teacher after the Hour of Science, looking fragile still but more rested after teaching and a coffee—and the window.

Nona did not have to wait to ask Hot Sauce what she was going to get told. The teacher, obviously relieved to see her—Nona said she hadn't been able to get to school that morning for "unexpected reasons" and the teacher gently and compassionately didn't ask, which made Nona cross again because she could see she was thinking about Pyrrha—gave Nona the job of taking down the old paintings from the peg on the wall and putting up fresh ones that had been done last week. Nona had to stand on a chair, and Hot Sauce quietly held the chair for her, and everyone else was busy taking out the mats for naptime. It was bewildering how quickly the day went, when you had had the morning taken away from you.

Hot Sauce said, "The Angel was dropped off in a car today, at the end of the street."

"I didn't see. I caught her in the doorway," said Nona, taking her focus away from balancing, then refocusing so she didn't fall off the chair. She unclipped a piece of brown sheeting and admired the painting on it briefly, and then she said—

"Is her being in a car good or bad?"

"When the school building watcher saw she wasn't here this morning," said Hot Sauce, "he left."

"Okay."

"He came back twenty minutes ago. It's an organised watch."

"By who?"

"I don't know. But she's being protected. Her vehicle had a *grille*," said Hot Sauce.

Nona had to admit that she did not understand the significance of the vehicle having a grille. Hot Sauce explained it was so that you could drive it through rocks or people.

"So what do we do?" Nona wanted to know. "I guess someone's looking after the Angel already." It was beginning to dawn on her that this level of care was strange when directed at someone whose contribution to the world was Noodle and the Hour of Science, which was truly wonderful but only really important to the refuge school. She added doubtfully, "Why is the Angel so special?"

The main teacher materialised behind them. "Nona, aren't you going home for lunch?"

It was then that Nona realised that nobody had come to pick her up.

"I don't know," she said. "Can I stay here until Cam comes?"

The nice lady teacher looked troubled, then tried to hide it. Because she really wasn't that much older than Camilla, Nona didn't think the hiding worked. She was really just a baby herself, Nona thought suddenly.

"Of course you can. Why don't you take one of the lunches and get yourself a mat? There's plenty to go around. It seems like everybody's eating at home today."

Hot Sauce said, "They're raising a broadcast, is why."

"What?" This startled the teacher. "Do you mean from the government building? This is the first I've heard of it." But when Hot Sauce stood there stolidly not elaborating, the teacher said, "And here's us without a working radio. Hi, Aim! Do you know anything about this?"

The Angel came over. She had another coffee clutched in her hands and was stirring sugar into it vigorously, despite the fact that it was deep into the heat of the day. She said, "Heard what?"

"The children—I mean, Hot Sauce and Nona—say there's going to be a public broadcast. I thought they ran out of money for that a year ago. I've certainly heard nothing but pirate radio for months. Is it going to be about the port? Do you think they'll start arrests?"

The Angel took a blistering sip of coffee even though she must have known it was much too hot; she was holding it gingerly, through her shirtsleeves. She sipped anyway in order to draw the moment out. Nona was interested that the Angel didn't even seem surprised, that she only looked extra sodden and tired.

"I *have* heard something about that, yes," she said. "Who knows?"

"It's strange. They would always put out a paper notice, before."

"That was in the old days. I guess they must've been in a hurry."

"Does that mean—are we finally going to hear about—"

"Joli, little pitchers," said the Angel.

"Come talk to me in the kitchen."

When they had gone, Nona said to Hot Sauce, "Should we go listen to a radio too? There's one down at the dairy."

"Don't need one," said Hot Sauce. "I know what they'll say. Who's here?"

The teacher had been right and mostly everyone's parents *had* come to take them home, or the children had drifted off at a prearranged signal. Younger Brother Father had come to retrieve Born in the Morning, and Beautiful Ruby had gone home too. There was nobody to come and get Honesty, but he had taken his packed lunch and slunk off to sell his pills—Nona disapproved; it was too hot for drugs. This left Nona, Hot Sauce, and Kevin. Kevin had arranged six mats in a pile and curled up knees to nose in the debris of a hastily eaten lunch: all the good bits out of the cold noodles, the centres out of all the sandwiches.

Nona reported this.

Hot Sauce said— "*You'll* stay, Nona."

"Yes," said Nona, who would sooner have died on the spot than refuse, and amended after a thought: "Unless Cam comes to get me, that is. I don't want Camilla to worry about me today."

"Sure," said Hot Sauce.

Nona didn't want the packed lunch, but anyone who might care about what she ate was off in the kitchen, so she got to do exactly as she pleased. She sucked on ice cube after ice cube and then, in a gluttonous excess, chewed half a pencil to splinters. She loved the cool sandy core of grey stuff and the painted, painful crunch of the wood, which came away to bits in her teeth. Hot Sauce watched, mild and unafraid, and drank a tiny sweating bottle of strawberry yoghurt drink.

After that they lay down on two mats each, piled atop each other, in the shadiest part of the room closest to the water pipes. Nona found that she was very tired: she just wanted to lie down, not to sleep, but to push her hair out of the way of her neck and try to become cool. She was always a little afraid of sleeping now. She lay down on her side, where her hip bones could be relied upon to stick into the mat and hurt a little bit, and hoped that would be enough. Thankfully Hot Sauce showed no signs of sleeping either. She lay there on the mat, on her side, and did not take her cone of vision away from the little staffroom door that the Angel and the main teacher were ensconced behind.

"Hot Sauce," Nona said softly, trying to keep herself awake, "what's the broadcast going to be about?"

"Necromancers," said Hot Sauce.

She waited for Hot Sauce to elaborate. Hot Sauce refused. Nona said, "Something *good* about—you know what? Or something bad?"

Hot Sauce said, "It's never good, with necromancers."

"You shouldn't call them that." Hot Sauce didn't respond, in either praise or censure. Nona struggled to explain why and ended up with the pathetic, "It's not nice."

"Zombies then."

Nona didn't think that was much better.

"How do you know about it?" she asked, already halfway to knowing.

"Heard about it last night."

Last night at the burn cages, Pyrrha said in her brain. Nona picked the long white filaments off her fingernails until some of them went red and started bleeding, and then she tucked her hands underneath herself so that nobody would see them stop bleeding just as quickly. She did not say, *From who?* Instead she said, *very* hesitantly, "Last night—in the park?"

But Hot Sauce did not get angry, or even really surprised. She didn't react in the way that Our Lady of the Passion might. She stared at the door unwaveringly instead. She blinked once, slowly, and that was it.

"Were you there?" she asked, in a slightly different voice.

"No."

"Don't go to the park at night."

"I don't want to," said Nona fervently.

"Not good for a girl like you," said Hot Sauce, like she wasn't fourteen and like Nona wasn't nineteen, or more important, six months, just about.

"Did the—" What to call them? "Did the *you-know-whats* die?"

Hot Sauce misunderstood her question. "They can die," she said. "They die like anyone else, so don't believe they can't."

"But did *these*—"

"Yes. Too quickly," said Hot Sauce. "Someone high up . . . took them out before they burned . . . sniper rifle . . . stupid, when people think you have to destroy the brain or they don't go . . . don't really die, not even if you burn them."

Hot Sauce, when making long speeches, always ran her sentences into each other, as though they were piled up in traffic. Nona sat up, feeling a little bit dizzy and hot, and made it look as though she were checking on Kevin. She didn't quite know if Hot Sauce bought it. Kevin after a good feed was reliably dead to the world for at least forty minutes. But when she lay back down on her side, facing Hot Sauce, Hot Sauce didn't look suspicious or pitying or anything like that. She stopped watching the door and stared up at the ceiling instead, the shiny glassy crinkly bits showing where her shirt rucked up in the middle and where it peeked out at her neck.

Hot Sauce said quietly, "Your people at the park?"

Nona swallowed.

"One of them, I think."

"Okay," said Hot Sauce.

"Are you—do any of the others—" Nona didn't know how to ask. She didn't quite know how to say, *Are you in Blood of Eden?* But Hot Sauce simply touched a finger to her lips for *shhh,* then raised three fingers, then pointed to herself. Nona was proud that she was long past counting on fingers.

"You," she whispered. "And Honesty. And someone else."

Hot Sauce nodded. Nona guessed again, "Born in the Morning."

"You mean *Born in the Morning,*" said Hot Sauce.

"That's what I said," said Nona.

Hot Sauce said, "Yes. One of his fathers is active."

"Blood of Ed—?"

But Hot Sauce pressed her finger right on Nona's mouth. Nona, seeing the flinch of alarm in her face, obediently tried to clamp her mouth shut before Hot Sauce had to shut her up, which had the effect that she nearly bit Hot Sauce. But Hot Sauce said fervently, "No. Never."

"Why—"

"Traitors," said Hot Sauce vehemently. "Fat cats. Zombie lovers."

Nona was a little bit tickled at the idea of Pash and We Suffer being called *fat cats* and *zombie lovers;* she didn't like Crown being called either a fat cat or a zombie lover though, and certainly not a traitor. She said, "Not all of them. Some of them are good."

Hot Sauce said, "Are you . . . ?"

"No," said Nona swiftly. "They sometimes . . . talk to us, my family," she added. Hot Sauce only said, "Yeah, well. They sell us guns."

Lying there, faces close, Nona had the comfortable feeling that she and Hot Sauce had crossed another barrier; just like the time she had been asked to join the gang, and the time she had told Hot Sauce she loved the city. It was painfully sweet lying there whispering— even if it was half-truths, or quickly shut-up truths, spoken softly so that Kevin and the teachers didn't hear you—sweet enough that she reached out and touched Hot Sauce on the hand without thinking, without remembering all of Camilla's warnings not to touch anyone. But Hot Sauce didn't mind. She put her fingers over Nona's, and Nona thrilled to it.

Hot Sauce said, "You're nice. I wish you were my sister."

Nona's cup of joy was full. "I'll be your sister if you like."

"Never had sisters. Only brothers," said Hot Sauce.

"Younger or older?"

"Older."

"Were they nice?"

"Yeah."

"How did they die?" asked Nona.

Hot Sauce thought about it. "Don't know," she finally said. "They were setting up the turrets. One of the minions made it through with a sword. They're nuts about swords. Wild. I practise with one. So I won't freak out like my brothers did. We couldn't get close though. Afterward. Thought they might be scarecrows." When she saw that Nona didn't understand, she added: "Dolls. Lures. They look like normal bodies lying down . . . or sitting or standing . . . but when you go too close they explode. Bones, everything."

Nona squeezed one foot, and then another. Her toes got terrible pins and needles, but she liked the sensation when she unsqueezed, that sudden sense of relief.

"What happened after that?" she asked.

"Our base? We surrendered. White flag. Let them in," said Hot Sauce. "My cousin put all the fertiliser we had in a truck. Drove it into their troop. They don't sense tech. Don't believe what they say. Engines or anything . . . He got a bunch of them when it exploded, minions, wizards, both." After a pause, she said: "It got him too."

Nona said, "I wish nobody had been got."

This time it was Hot Sauce's turn to not understand. "It's okay. First necromancer who gets in range, I shoot," she said.

Nona shuddered again, all the way from her hips to her toes. Hot Sauce patted her hand and said pragmatically, "You have air-con sweats."

"No," said Nona, and it was the first time she had admitted it to anyone, or at least anyone who wasn't herself. Some deep well of need and terror welled up in her, and then—before she could walk it back, and without even really wanting to—she did it.

She told Hot Sauce the Secret.

Hot Sauce thought about it. She looked at Nona, and then she thought about it again.

"There's a clinic in town," she said. "The Angel works there. Not always. Some evenings."

Nona clapped her hands together softly in sheer delight. Pyrrha always said it was her most disgusting habit.

"That's how you knew she was a doctor," she said. "That's why she helped Honesty."

"Yeah. I went to see her once," said Hot Sauce, a little grudgingly, as though she didn't quite want to share. Then she unbent and said, "I'd been shot at."

That explained a lot.

"Did you have a bullet in you?"

"No. It missed. Broke my collarbone when I dodged." Before Nona could say anything else, Hot Sauce said: "Your problem. Talk to her."

"It's not going to help," said Nona.

Hot Sauce flicked her nose thoughtfully. "There's an organ market," she said. "Sometimes they're cheap."

"No, no. Don't worry, Hot Sauce. Please. And don't tell the others my Secret," added Nona in a hurry, alarmed. "You are literally the *only one who knows*. You know . . . in case something happens . . . You have to keep this between you and me, you have to promise. You have to promise right now."

"Okay," said Hot Sauce. Then: "I promise."

"Okay," said Nona.

She was very touched when Hot Sauce got up and wriggled out of her jacket, and made to put it over the thin slippery blanket. Nona said, "Don't, give it to Kevin," and so Hot Sauce put it over Kevin. Kevin did not move, and for a moment Nona panicked that Kevin had died from eating the insides of five sandwiches. But Kevin made a sort of puppyish snuffling sound and wriggled underneath the blanket where the jacket was, so that was all right. Nona felt a great sense of peace and calm when Hot Sauce came and lay back down beside her: she let her eyelids flutter down, and was annoyed when they did not want to flutter back up. She struggled heroically to keep them open, even using her fingers, until Hot Sauce stopped her.

"You can sleep if you want," said Hot Sauce. "I'll be here."

"You won't tell, will you, Hot Sauce?"

"No," said Hot Sauce. And: "I'm here, Nona. I'll look after you."

"I love you, Hot Sauce," she said.

Exhausted, Nona felt Hot Sauce touch her hand, very lightly, very gently. The last thing she heard before falling asleep was Hot Sauce saying, "Don't be soppy." But it didn't sound like she meant it.

JOHN 8:1

THE ASH NEVER made them feel too sick for long, but sometimes they blacked out together. Only for seconds, really no time at all, but he didn't like it. He'd never liked losing control. He'd never liked losing consciousness. In the dream she knew he could not be coaxed to sleep unless she stood in the doorway, or in the worst times stroking her thumb between his eyebrows, down the bridge of his nose. In the dream she did not fear sleeping, but she did not know how to do it herself. Her body was a mystery to her. She did not understand what it meant or signified. She would suddenly collapse and sleep where she fell, shocked into unconsciousness by exhaustion, and wake wherever he put her, in whatever makeshift bed he had been forced to cook up: sometimes old stained mattresses, sometimes baby-soft skin hammocks.

They had to trek all the way back down the hill on the side where the waters weren't rising and back up the road to a crumble-down concrete building he'd found. All day they transferred their things. Their meat. Their buckets of water. Their soggy blankets that they pinned up to dry so they would have somewhere to sleep. It took them multiple trips.

They didn't bother to start a fire. They weren't really cold. But it was dark, because the ash kept falling, and he set up a long line of torches, putting them on windowsills and balancing them upward so that their thin yellow light was strung across the room. This highlighted his face in strange ways. It made his brown skin bluish, and the white ring around his black iris a satiny gold.

When they were settled he said: We got some attention up-front, 'cause people thought we were trying to get media jobs with some excellent deepfakes. They thought we were playing a game or giving people a puzzle, maybe doing some branding. Branding, *then*? Talk about late-late-stage capitalism, right? How far can consumption as praxis go? But I mean, fair enough. It didn't look real.

He said, Result was that nobody turned up to take us away to Area 51. Almost nobody even noticed us. We were just one voice in the wilderness, and all the other voices were louder. It was original, at least, you know? We got a handful of conspiracy theorists, some sceptics, and some locals who thought it was a joke. M— said, *Invite them in to see.* So we did. Taped them. Said they could do whatever tests they wanted. Showed them everything, got it on camera. Managed a crowd of about five. Five plus us and Ulysses and Titania and all the other corpses I had up and walking around. More people there were dead than alive.

He said, Two of the audience members walked away afterward. One didn't say anything. One freaked out and said he was calling the cops. Only one of them accepted it. Turned out he was one of those Flat Earthers who still believed despite the Mars installation. Nice guy. Drank a beer with us before he left.

He said, *Then* we took off. Thread after thread on message board after message board. People wanting proof. People asking what the fuck it meant. People talking about the LUCIFER telescope and saying we were aliens. People calling me the Antichrist, which was a trip. People writing up these long posts on how the trick was done, how I got the meat into the pie. Was I fake? Was I real? If I was real, what did it mean? Suddenly there were hundreds of people, all there at our front door. They came in caravans, they were sleeping in their cars or putting up tents. A hell of a lot of them had flown out internationally.

He said, Some of them wanted to see the miracle. Some of them wanted my help, like, *Oh, you're the magical death man, can you do something about my body? Can you fix my fibromyalgia?* Thing was, I could. That surprised me. I could take out their tumours. I could fix their macular degeneration. Big damage was easy, unless they'd actually lost the limb or whatever. Couldn't grow those back. But I spent hours and hours a day playing Jesus. That was nice, those were some of the nicest hours I got to spend.

He said, But when you're doing the whole *Go, my child, your knee cartilage is fixed*, you're going to get a *lot* of visitors. I had to turn people away because I had to eat, I had to sleep, even though I didn't want to. M— had brought in her best friend, the nun, and I was worried I was going to get the Antichrist bit from her too, but she was just like: stop doing this! Read your Bible! This was Christ's whole problem!

I was like, What are you talking about, Jesus cured the lepers and everyone was all, Hooray, thanks man. M—'s nun was all, *Are you kidding, Christ never said no and never asked anyone to pay and got way too much attention and brought the heat down on everybody. Christ didn't keep to office hours*, she said. *Don't do that.*

He said, So we limited Jesus stuff to one hour a day, and I always had to eat breakfast. But by then the whole world was on our doorstep.

He added, We knew it was going to be a big problem. You've got this guy with an army of upward of forty walking corpses that he acquired legally but was meant to bury a while back, it's time for some hard conversations. He's curing cancer, that's great, but he's bookended by two zombies that they've dressed in outfits, that's bad. You've got a wizard out in the wop-wops who's now got blanket bans from nearly every video upload site and a whole bunch of people have entered the country because of his YouTube channel, the government isn't all, *Love that small-business entrepreneur spirit.* The government says, *This is a cult.*

He said, They came in thousands—pilgrims and tourists and sceptics and believers and CIA plants and wannabe stars and priests and oddballs. And here we were squatting in this building, trying to prepare a gambit for every eventuality, but we were in the middle of a shantytown and an international controversy and we knew any moment a riot squad was going to bust in. And we were all living in three rooms together and we were scared. Turned out to be a huge fucking blessing that we had a nun on cast as she bought us some breathing room. She applied to the Vatican to argue about whether or not it was a miracle because I'd been baptised. Didn't mention that I'd only gone to Parachute 'cause of the underage drinking. But she was a lifesaver. And then A— brought in his little brother who was a hedge fund manager. A— Junior was useless but he was a darling, I couldn't fault A— for adding him to the mix. All of us were getting frightened. We'd bit off more than we could chew. We were gathering the people we loved and closing the doors.

He said, At that point the government asked us to come in quietly, with our hands up.

He said, We didn't want to. We always said, they want us, they have to come get us. We're not getting separated. We're not getting disappeared. Brave words. But stopping them was on *me*, you know? You've got two scientists and an engineer and a nun and a lawyer and a banker and a cop and an artist. That's not a defence force, that's a cop and six different kinds of nerd. P— was great, but like, Ministry ties or no Ministry ties, a big part of her career was going around to the local high school throwing blue-light discos and telling the drugs kids that they shouldn't be doing drugs. She'd won medals for competition shooting back north in Hamilton, but we're not talking Jesse James. We're talking Hamilton.

He said, The cryo lab was about a hundred metres across, concrete and steel and cladding sat on two acres of repurposed farmland. I had forty corpses on hand, and a lot of them were in a state, with partials from earlier testing. We had a lot of flash-frozen brain matter. I couldn't harvest anything from Ulysses and Titania. I refused. A— and M— were making black jokes about taking volunteers from the crowd for the skeleton army.

One day we ran out of time before those jokes could become suggestions. P— called ahead. She'd betrayed the police for us, told us the riot squad was about half an hour away and they were carrying big guns. She chose us that day, not her career. I always loved her for that. She'd adored being a cop.

He said, I knew what I needed. I needed to cut the place off. Wall it up. Do something impressive to buy us time. Let them know we couldn't get pushed around. So I pulled up walls close to three foot thick, what you'd now call perpetual bone, staked six feet down. G— ran the numbers for me. I didn't listen to his warnings about plumbing so I busted the outside water pipe, but that was the worst that happened. The cops arrived in half an hour and tried a battering ram, industrial cutters, everything. They worked for hours, but nothing even penetrated. It was perfect. Except that I'd forgotten to do air holes, so I had to make some of it permeable up top, but, like, fine, we caught it early, nobody suffocated.

He fell quiet.

After a while she prompted, You made it from your bodies?

He said, Nah. I decided I didn't want to touch any of the bodies, not only Titania and Ulysses. They'd all been through a lot.

It was at this point that he had the grace to look embarrassed.

He said, I'm not proud of this. But, well—like, we were on farmland. With farm animals. Big things with mass to spare. The field just over the road from us had over eighty head of cattle, field over *that* had a lot of sheep, and the bush was full of old bones. I had to—get creative. We had to lock C— in the kitchen when she found out so she could throw up in private for a while, and we wouldn't let her look at it. Thankfully it was dark, so there wasn't too much to look at.

He said, It wasn't clean. I had to unsleeve them to get two piles to work from, softs and bones, and it was not beautiful. But it worked. A three-foot-thick shield of meat, bone, and sinew spread over two acres of Greytown land. You could see it on Google Earth. Kind of pretty, from far off. Sort of pink.

He said, And *then* the government was like, *Okay, let's talk.*

He said, It had worked, and we were all okay. And the rest of the world knew too, you can't erect a two-acre cow-and-sheep shield without it making the news, though I think they censored the close-up pictures. They took us seriously after that. Some of them wanted to talk to us, to see who we were, and some of them didn't want to talk to us because we were evil, and some didn't want to talk to us because we were forcing their hands. Sure, I'd cured a bunch of people of cancer, but I was freaky. They treated us like we'd done some kind of huge crime.

After a pause, he said: I mean, I had kind of done a huge crime. I'd turned several hundred animals inside out and made them into a big art installation and I hadn't complied with the cops, *but* extenuating circumstances, okay? There were extenuating circumstances. It wasn't my fault that turning several hundred animals inside out makes you look like the bad guy. They were beef cattle and mutton; my way was a hell of a lot quicker than the abattoir. But it's hard to be all, *Let's listen to magical inside-out animal-shield man. He obviously has some good ideas.*

He said, I didn't care what they thought, I wanted the attention. I wanted to break my NDAs. I wanted to let them know about the cryo plans and how we got shut down. I wanted to talk about you. About how we'd been going to save the world and then the cash dried up for no reason. And now we had a platform, so maybe the cash could come back, somehow. But we'd scared a lot of people. We also had more enemies than we'd ever had before.

He said, I guess you could say . . . we had beef.

When she did not laugh he said, "I can't believe nobody's ever going to laugh at my jokes again. I can't believe it. It's all gone, I'm the only one left. It's just me and you and no more jokes."

She said, "I still love you."

And he laughed and said, "That was a good one." Then he wept again.

16

Nona awoke with a start right before the door crashed open, like she had an extra sense for crashing doors. Honesty ran into the room, not even taking off his outside boots or his sand jacket, and he shouted: "They're coming—they're here *now*. They're setting up that ole video screen in the square tonight, they're gonna screen some video, at half five o'clock. It's *them*, it's zombies, they're back! Holy shit!"

"Language, Honesty," said someone else. Nona rubbed her eyes and struggled to sit up; she had been about to say the same thing, but all that came out was "Wharrgarbl." It was the voice of the Angel, who had taken up position quite near the big whiteboard, one knee folded over the other.

"I've got to swear, sir," said Honesty. "You can't let me not swear about this. It'll give me inhibitions. Anyway"—struck by fresh inspiration—"with zombies here, sir, I'm not going to bother with school anymore. There'll be a war. I've got to deal full-time."

"Then you better attend maths lessons, at least," said the Angel drily. "I've seen your multiplication, Honesty. You're going to get stiffed."

"*Maybe* maths, if I feel like it," allowed Honesty, and he turned to the mats: "Hot Sauce—Hot Sauce, what're we going to do?"

Hot Sauce was sitting up on her mat, knees drawn to her chest, arms loosely dangling over her knees. "Wait and see," she said.

Kevin was waking up too, elbowing sleep out of his eyes, and largely decorated with crumbs. Honesty said, "War, Kevin! It's gonna

194

be war!" and Kevin just said, "Ugh," and lay back down in bed, completely unmoved by war.

Desperate for someone's approval, Honesty dropped to his haunches next to Nona, and bawled: "Nona—what do you *think*?"

Nona, still feeling as though her ears were stopped up with dreams, wriggled her nose so that she wouldn't yawn. Her mouth tasted like pencil. She said, with perfect bewilderment: "Who's here? *What's* going to be on the screen?"

"*Necromancers*, stoopid," said Honesty.

Then he did have the grace to look at the Angel, as though he were expecting a punishment; but all the Angel did was shake her head and say quietly, "Try not to scare Kevin or Nona, Honesty."

"Okay—okay," said Honesty, a little abashed. Then: "I don't know—the militia's setting up, all wearing their old uniforms, all getting the netting out. I went to the square and nearly got my head shot off, honestly, they're all jumpy that people are taking potshots at 'em. I saw some old lady wailing in the street that we were all about to be lined up and executed. Well, they won't get *me*."

The door barrelled open again. It was Born in the Morning and Beautiful Ruby, who had obviously raced each other up the stairs. They were panting like dogs, and Beautiful Ruby had to lean over and brace on his knees and still looked as though he might throw up. Nona was completely awake now. Born in the Morning said, "I won," and Beautiful Ruby said, "You didn't—I won on the stairs," and they squabbled right until Honesty said—

"Boys, really, is this the *time*?"

"Mum says they're setting up the screen to tell us which resettlement to go to," panted Beautiful Ruby.

Born in the Morning said, "They can't tell us anything—the sky's still blue. They'll go crazy. They're lying."

"Mum says, doesn't matter, do it anyway."

"What does your mum know?"

"At least I've got a mum and not only a bunch of mouldy old dads," fired back Beautiful Ruby.

"Don't fight," begged Nona, just as they started to clasp each other around the neck in strangulation positions. "It's not fair. Too much is going on and I don't want to think about your fight *and* the square *and* the screen."

The boys untangled from each other, but very reluctantly. It was at this moment of hesitation and surrender that the Angel stood up and said, quietly but in a voice that brooked no rebellion, "Sit down on the mats. All of you."

This wasn't hard for Nona, who was sitting down on the mats already. Same with Hot Sauce and Kevin. Born in the Morning and Beautiful Ruby and Honesty all came and flopped themselves down on the mats one by one. It didn't seem like any of the other kids had come back, only their gang. Nona was grateful in a way; she thought the tinies all ought to be at home.

The Angel said, "I want to ask you to promise—all on your honour—that none of you will go to the screening tonight. If your families want to go, fine. But that's not going to be a place for children."

Honesty said, "Who's a kid?" and the Angel said, "*You* are. Keep in mind, I've seen this before, House overtures. Tempers run high . . . there will be people who make decisions before they really think about them . . . and if you're there, and one of you gets hurt, that's going to add to the fracas. I don't want to see your bodies paraded through the streets and your mugs up on photographs, for one cause or the other."

They were all silent. The Angel said, "Promise me, kids, please. I know you're an honourable bunch. Especially you, Honesty."

Honesty was touched.

"I am—so I won't," he said. "I swear. I mean, I could make a killing, so you've got me by the balls here."

"Please never say that again," said the Angel.

"I won't go either," said Beautiful Ruby, and Born in the Morning said more reluctantly— "Younger Brother Father might want me to go, he sometimes does." Then Honesty gave him a really good burn twist on the arm so that the skin went dark red, and he yowled and said, "But I won't! Stop it!"

Hot Sauce said, "I won't."

And that seemed to be that—the Angel didn't ask Nona—but Nona was a little bit troubled. She was sitting at the back as the oldest, and she was very close to Hot Sauce, so only she could see that Hot Sauce had crossed her fingers.

Then Hot Sauce said, "Why a video screen?"

"Well, why do you think a video screen? Why not just stand up there and talk through a loudspeaker?" said the Angel.

Nona, who thought about this kind of thing a great deal, immediately said— "Oh, they don't want to get shot! They'd probably get shot by *someone*."

"Yes. Well done," said the Angel.

The others were all immediately chuffed for her, and demonstrated it. They slapped her on the back and said, "Good one, Nona," and "You're smart, Nona," until Nona preened, but then a few seconds later she felt a little bit patronised, and she said: "Well, I wonder who it is, who's going to speak."

"You'll find out. Why hurry?" said the Angel. "Look, I'm the only teacher left here—Joli has gone home to make sure her parents are all right. Let's cancel school for the evening and do something fun, why don't we? I don't feel like teaching anything very scientific. I'll get out the drawing paper and the paints and we can draw for a while. We'll leave the blackouts up and turn on the lights early."

Born in the Morning said, "My dads said to come right back or they'd come to pick me up," and the Angel said— "A quandary, is it? Well, I don't want to contradict your fathers, but why not let them come and pick you up? I don't feel great about letting you walk alone through the streets right now. They'll be jabbing and temperature testing everyone in sight, even if they've seen you before, to make sure you're not House. If you want a needle jabbed in your arse, go ahead."

It was so funny to hear the Angel say *arse* that everyone lost it— Nona included—and even Kevin giggled, even though he was normally very serious. Hot Sauce smiled too, but a little distantly, like she was thinking of something else. She was happy enough to go with Nona to get out the big brown sheets of drawing paper, and the nice-smelling boxes of fat wax crayons and chalk. The Angel was at the light box flicking switches and saying, "Draw your favourite animal, go on, I've got a book of pictures if you want help," but as it turned out everyone only wanted to draw Noodle. Noodle was asleep next to the teacher's desk on one of the abandoned mats, and Beautiful Ruby and Born in the Morning and even Honesty and Kevin squatted there to sketch his outline in chalk. Funny to think of Honesty drawing Noodle, really, when he'd just said no more school.

That had hurt Nona's feelings a little bit; she didn't want to think about anyone leaving school. She sat back at one of the tables, feeling her weight as a Teacher's Aide—doodling a little bit on one of the big brown pieces of paper but not *quite* joining in—and Hot Sauce perched on the desk next to her, still staring out the window. The Angel went around closing them all, but she shouldn't have bothered, Nona thought: the outside was weirdly, deadly quiet. You couldn't even hear honking.

Nona sketched some ideas of animals—what she thought animals should look like, on best principles—and once satisfied with her work, put down her pencil and looked around instead. It almost seemed normal inside the classroom, though not as noisy as it would be any other day. Beautiful Ruby could create enough noise for ten children at least, but everyone was busy, heads-down and content with the chance to do some art. She saw that this troubled the Angel; whenever she looked out over them she seemed to be cheerful, sometimes saying something like "Only *six* legs, remember, Ruby, he was bred to have a single arboreal pair," but there was a sorry quirk to the corners of her thin, freckled mouth, like them all being so well-behaved was miserable in a way. Every so often she would stick her thumbs in her suspenders and whistle a note or two, like a back-of-truck seller on the street, and to Nona those notes didn't sound cheerful at all.

At one point Honesty stretched his arms out and cracked his neck and his knuckles, and he sidled over to the curtains to twitch them open to take a look at the street, and the Angel said so sharply, "Be sensible, Honesty," that he dropped the curtain like he'd been shot.

But it was too late, he'd twitched it; the look Hot Sauce gave him physically staggered him. He went back to his painting so meekly that on any other day Nona would have screamed with laughter, but not right then.

Nona looked up at the clock, gave it her best shot, squinted herself cross-eyed, then gave up.

"Yes, Nona? You don't have to put up your hand, y'know," said the Angel. "You do work here."

"What's the time, please?"

"Getting on five o'clock," said the Angel.

Camilla always came to pick her up before lunchtime; that meant it was over four hours that Cam was overdue. Camilla had never been overdue in Nona's whole life. Something very obvious must have happened on her face, because the Angel said a bit hastily, "Nona, can you take Noodle out? He hasn't been since before lunch, and it's not fair on the poor creature. He's got ageing kidneys."

"I'll go too," said Hot Sauce.

"Me three," said Honesty.

Hot Sauce said, "Stay put. Two's enough." Honesty didn't even argue.

Nona was happy enough to take Noodle's lead, and Noodle was even happier; he even whisked a bit. He was always good at sensing feelings. Nona thought she and Noodle were very alike in some ways, except she sadly did not have an arboreal anything. She and Hot Sauce shrugged on their dust jackets and buttoned up the sleeves in the cloakroom, and Nona clipped the leash to Noodle's collar and led him down the flight of black and cool and quiet stairs, Hot Sauce following behind, and once they were one floor down she said—"Camilla hasn't come for me."

"Sleep at mine if she doesn't," said Hot Sauce.

This idea quite startled Nona, who had never slept apart from Camilla. She was homesick thinking about her. She had thought Hot Sauce would maybe say something sympathetic or understanding, like, "Don't worry about it," but the problem with Hot Sauce was that she was a little bit like Cam. When you came to her with a problem she gave you something to do about it. Nona didn't know what to say, so she blurted: "You crossed your fingers when you said *Yes* to the Angel."

"Didn't want to lie," said Hot Sauce. "Just in case. Of it becoming a lie."

"You always do what the Angel says."

"Wrong. I always keep my promises to the Angel. This time I didn't promise."

Nona thought of Palamedes, and said: "That's not really the spirit of the law, even if it *is* the letter."

"What's that mean?"

"It means that even if technically you're not breaking the rule you sort of are anyway, in your heart."

"So?"

Nona had no idea how to counter *So?* By then they were down at the bottom floor and Hot Sauce was carefully checking the dust-and-concrete yard where Nona had so often taken Noodle for his lunchtime bathroom trips, peering through the glass-panelled doors where such a short time ago Nona had burst through with Crown. The red light still flashed above the double doors, which meant they were locked. Nona searched for ways to dissuade Hot Sauce and said, "You said earlier the Angel came in a truck, with a grille."

"Yes. Never seen her come in a car before," said Hot Sauce. "Come outside, we're clear."

They opened the heavy doors and the heat hit them, as it always did, like putting on wet clothes. Even though it was later in the afternoon than Nona was used to, it was still hotter than hot—the kind of heat that prickled her all over, even underneath her hair, and made her shudder inside her dust jacket. Nona knelt down to unclip the lead and Noodle, aware of his dignity, trundled out of sight to do his business behind a broken slab of rock. They watched his exit in silence.

"But doesn't that mean the Angel's being looked after, and we don't have to worry?" said Nona after a while.

Hot Sauce didn't look so sure.

"Her driver stopped the car, and someone got out after the Angel had gone into school," said Hot Sauce. "Checked the doorways. Of both the buildings opposite. And the alleys. Professional."

Nona was enchanted.

"Maybe the Angel's rich and important."

"She's vulnerable, with us. We have to keep her safe," said Hot Sauce, "more than ever."

"Because . . . of war?"

"Because of war."

Noodle came back to them and self-importantly kicked dirt behind him with his backmost legs. The middle set, the arboreal set, stretched out all the way to the middle of his body as he elongated himself. Then he yawned in a nice way, to show that he was agreeable. Both Hot Sauce and Nona spent a little bit of time scratching him beneath his collar and on the bump where his tailbone started. Then once he had had enough scratches he sat on his haunches and they clipped the lead back on. When they went back into the foyer Nona noticed that Hot Sauce lingered there a little, staring out into the street through the smeared glass. As Nona moved to mount the stairs Hot Sauce said suddenly— "Wait."

Nona waited. So did Noodle.

"They'll be starting the broadcast. Soon," said Hot Sauce.

Even if Nona had not been Nona, she felt that she would have been able to easily translate that stubborn set of Hot Sauce's shoulders, the readiness in her hands. Her whole body was turning to face the street, like wanting was somehow magnetic.

Nona hedged, "But the Angel won't know where we've gone."

"Write a note. Give it to Noodle. He's smart."

Nona was thrilled with the idea of leaving a note on Noodle, and was sorry they hadn't struck on the idea before—to leave messages for the Angel or for anyone else—but was deeply unhappy that the discovery had only been made in this particular situation.

"But I can't write," said Nona.

"I can," said Hot Sauce. Then she amended, "Enough."

"But Hot Sauce, the Angel won't trust us after this . . ."

"The asset doesn't have to trust you," said Hot Sauce, sounding all of a sudden very grown-up and very professional and very much like Pyrrha. Nona was so cowed that she didn't even ask what part of you the asset was. Hot Sauce followed this up with, "I'll go alone. If you don't want to."

"I'm a Teacher's Aide. I'm meant to look after you."

"Then look after me. Unless you're scared."

"I'm not scared of anything," lied Nona, but added urgently, "You can't let me get hurt."

Hot Sauce just shrugged expressively at that, like, *I wasn't going to,* and Nona wished she could have made Hot Sauce understand somehow. But it was all happening so quickly. She said helplessly, "Even like a sunburn or if there's a dust storm," but Hot Sauce was ignoring her to rummage through what had long ago used to be someone's front desk, finding a bit of scrap paper, getting a pen and seeing if the ink had dried out. She began printing laboriously. It took her such a long time that Nona was hopeful the Angel would get curious about where they were and come down and rumble their plan, but it was not to be. Hot Sauce knelt down by the dog and tucked the note into his collar, unclipped the leash and hung it up in the foyer, wedged the paper in tight so that it wouldn't fall out. Nona hoped devoutly that the Angel would check it.

"Noodle," said Hot Sauce, in the voice of command, "go upstairs."

Noodle looked at Hot Sauce in much the way that Nona wished she could look at Hot Sauce—a sort of *Why aren't you coming with me? Are you dim?* expression—but when Hot Sauce repeated, "Go upstairs," he wagged his tail a bit, then turned away and started mounting the stairs.

"Go," said Hot Sauce.

Nona and Hot Sauce made for the doors. Hot Sauce held the locking apparatus down and Nona shoved through—they were heavy fire doors and they took some pushing, though Crown had breezed through them like they had been feathers—and Hot Sauce flew after her. The door went *click*—locking itself behind them—and

Hot Sauce said, "Hood up. Go go go,"—and seized Nona's hand—and like a loosed bullet, ricocheted off down the street.

It was all Nona could do to cling to her, her heart beating fast, regretting all of the decisions that had led her to that moment. Then she told herself sternly, *Stop it!* If she was going to do it, she thought, she might as well *do* it. She had some vague notion that when you committed to a thing you had to do it all the way. Who had said that to her? Who had taught her that? *Once you've stepped in,* said the voice in the back of her head, *you're in. This isn't the Hokey Pokey.*

She had remembered something—she had finally remembered something! Only she didn't have anyone to tell.

Nona was saved from being seriously out of breath by the fact that a few streets down, they caught up with a crowd of people shuffling forward. There was no talking, just the noise of moving feet; a truck chugging along keeping pace with the pedestrians; a baby shushed in someone's arms. They were all hooded and jacketed, and without hesitation Hot Sauce merged with the mass. It was incredible the way she moved. The moment she joined that crowd, her shoulders were flung back—she straightened up a whole inch—she swaggered with her hips. She aged fifteen years, no longer a child among that throng of people. Nona dropped her hand and tried to do the same, straightening her back, softening her hips, and Hot Sauce beneath her breath just said— "Keep it up."

They glued themselves shoulder to shoulder in that slow queue. They were being streamed into the big eight-lane street in front of the civics building, where militia officers directed people from the backs of trucks or on their putt-putts, each one in a helmet, each one with a stick, most of them so badly frightened that Nona swore she could watch them sweat. They were turning some people away. The person with the baby was told to stay at the back of the crowd. The officer said in a low voice, "If they stampede, you'll be hurt," and the person with the baby said tonelessly, "Who cares? We might as well die."

One older man in the crowd turned around and said quite clearly, enough that people flinched from the raised voice, "Don't you give them that—don't you give the zeds that pleasure."

"I don't care. We're probably being kettled."

"We aren't—we aren't," said the old man. "You see the trucks with the gates? You see the ladders? We aren't."

"Just don't bring that baby in," said the militia officer. "No kids, no cars. That's the rule."

"You and whose army?" scoffed the person; but the old man said, "Don't be a fool. You know whose army. Stay back here with me, sonny, stay back here with me."

Nona was grateful that she and Hot Sauce passed unnoticed beneath the officer's nose; there was already a cross-faced collection of kids and teenagers in the back of a militia truck, grumbling and swapping cigarettes, some of them significantly older than Hot Sauce and looking a lot older than Nona. She ducked her head a little bit more inside her hood and tried to walk bigger.

The crowd was thick and tall. Hot Sauce grabbed Nona's forearm and beelined between the people—Hot Sauce never cared who she jostled—until she stopped dead by one of the traffic lights, right next to a raggedy trash can. It was the kind of traffic light with a pole stuck through it crossways to hang signs off. Hot Sauce said, "We're light enough. Come on. Here," and suddenly there was a cradle for her foot, and Nona found herself boosted up the pole—she wrapped her legs around it and wriggled upward more out of fright than skill—to sit on one of the crossbars. It squeaked a little, but it didn't feel as though it was going to immediately give way. Hot Sauce shinned up the other side. She sat beside Nona on the bit that stuck out opposite and they laced their arms around the central pole and huddled there to watch the screen, head and shoulders above the rest of the crowd, their legs dangling.

There was a huge noise of breathing—feet shuffling—coughs and sneezes, and the ignition and exhaustion noise of motors, but nobody was talking. Every so often someone would raise their voice and everyone around them would converge, as though they had all agreed beforehand that nobody would talk. Nona looked at the faces of the crowd, hooded against the heat and the dust, wondering briefly and hopefully if Pyrrha and Camilla or Palamedes were somehow among them, or Crown. It was like looking at the sea—grey colours, drab green colours, every so often a paler moving blotch of dun or tan. It made her feel a little sick to look at so many people, so many sets of shoulders and crossed arms, so she stared at the screen instead.

It was still unfolding—they had set up the big metal frame, and shiny skin made of tessellated hexagons was slowly being stretched over it by people attached to guy lines. They had gotten nearly all of the way and were fixing the ends now, but a corner would come loose, and by the time they could re-pin it an opposite corner would go. Nobody seemed to find this funny. Eventually the pale grey shiny hexagon stuff was taut before them, as high as the second storey of the school building, seemingly five times as wide. A trembling rectangle. They clipped power lines to the sides, and every so often white light would popple over one of the hexagons.

There was a murmur from the crowd now, the first one that wasn't interrupted. People were looking at their watches, they were looking at the screen. The broadcast was late.

At first nothing happened, and for a moment Nona wondered if the broadcast hadn't been all some big joke or prank—if nothing was going to happen at all. Then one hexagon close to the corner rippled again.

Each of its neighbours rippled, and a cascade of white light burned over the surface of the screen. There was an enormous screech from the collection of speakers piled untidily at the bottom of the screen— the crowd shuddered at the sound, and Nona's teeth set on edge— and then a voice suddenly emerged. A strange, low voice, speaking what everyone called House, caught halfway into a sentence.

"—esolved through official government channels. We will, of course, be happy to facilitate local elections to ensure the populace feels represented in those committees and resolutions. Under these conditions, no population-wide penalties will be levied. There will be no effects on resettlement. No legal ramifications will fall on groups or individuals, unless they are found guilty of terrorism in the aforementioned tribunal. Definitions of terrorism will be agreed on via elected representatives. All households and individuals can make a plea for restitution, which will be answered not through local authorities but by the Emperor of the Nine Houses."

For a moment Nona could barely make heads or tails of it. It was lucky that it was House, which she and Pyrrha and Palamedes and Camilla spoke anyway, but not having anyone to *look* at foxed her. The voice was also saying a lot of words she had never before heard, in context or otherwise. She looked at Hot Sauce's face instead, half-hidden beneath its hood, taut with listening.

"This agreement," the voice echoed over the crowd, "is, as I speak, being transcribed and will be displayed in public in official local languages—how many do we have of those? Seventeen? Well, someone's in for a long night—displayed in public across the city as soon as translations have been finalised. The agreement will, without further negotiation, be considered legally binding. However—as I mentioned at the start of this broadcast—there are conditions that must be met. Any individual or group who violates these conditions renders the entire agreement, I'm sorry to say, null and void. The population *will* consequently represent a legal entity that has damaged property, acted unlawfully, committed or been accessory to murder, and performed a coup. This is per the contracts drawn up between you and the Emperor Undying over seven hundred years previous when this settlement was created. His offer of a break in that contract . . . is entirely contingent on what you do now. Ah. Give me a second. It seems we've fixed the equipment. We were using it in a . . . barricade? How exciting. Anyway, we should have screen capabilities now."

The hexagons writhed in agony, then resolved into a picture—what she was looking at, Nona could for a moment not tell. The heinous light bathed the crowd in white and rainbow colours. The screen made all the hues garish, ten times more saturated than they should have been: as though they were drawn by someone who only had certain colours in their pencil box. The camera swung back and forth a few times, which made Nona nauseous—there were brief flashes of boots and legs: of whites so white they looked yellow except where they were splotched with reds so red they looked orange, a multi-hued melange of faces and walls—before it settled on a desk. Seated at the desk, looking mildly annoyed but perhaps like that was their normal expression, a person came into focus.

Nona was charmed immediately by the clothing. The other boots and the other shirts and the other legs had looked dirty and shabby, from what she'd briefly seen, but not this person. *Their* coat was so spotlessly white that on the screen it looked blue; so was their neckerchief. The camera jumped a lot closer, focusing on this figure from the waist up now, and Nona could see that the neckerchief had a pretty gold pin sparkling in the folds. The person themselves was frighteningly pale of skin, and their hair alarmingly perfect in shape and form. Nona had never seen hair like that before. It was as though it had been sculpted, not grown. It was a rich middling brown, thick and shiny even beneath the strong lights that had been aimed at it. Most people under such lights would have shown at least a little scalp. The expression was one of intense boredom; their body language betrayed more interest. And their lips were a little too pale to be lips, but shiny like the hair, as though someone had applied gloss.

But their huge, screen-magnified eyes were quite pretty, Nona decided: blue, with brown bits. She had never seen eyes like that before.

"Good evening, New Rho," said the person.

Nobody responded. The young, well-dressed, dead-white person didn't seem to wait for them. They said instead, "Citizens, settlement refugees, and all other residents, here is a list of the Emperor's conditions. One:

"That all violence of any kind directed at Cohort facilities ceases immediately, both the barracks and the surrounding residential area;

"Two, that all attacks on Cohort soldiers cease immediately, whether they are inside Cohort facilities or outside;

"Three, that all casualties belonging or suspected of belonging to the Emperor's Nine Houses are surrendered and brought to the barracks gates;

"Four, that all members of the group calling themselves Blood of Eden cease operating in this area, and that anyone who comes into contact with Blood of Eden refuses succour, materiel, or weapons from them;

"Five . . ."

Here the beautiful pale person paused for the first time, though it seemed that it was less for not knowing what to say and more for the sake of waiting.

"That any member of House personnel who has left their post—disappeared into the population—arrived after the siege and failed to make themselves known to the authorities—that anyone who serves the Emperor, Cohort or otherwise, and who has made themselves absent without leave, present themselves to me immediately, at the barracks, during the next twenty-four hours. This is the amnesty period. Take it or leave it. Remember that it is in your power to turn Emperor's Evidence and be granted the mercies of the King Undying."

Their eyes unfocused a little. They looked at someone beyond the camera, not at the gathered crowd. Whatever was being said, or gestured, it caused the speaker to quirk their perfect dark eyebrows in a kind of *oh, for goodness' sake* moment of impatience.

"For those of you not privy to the beginning of the broadcast," it drawled, "I will inform you, again, that the Emperor cares deeply for New Rho—that he has no desire to see the end that, I can assure you firsthand, has come for the rebels of Ur. He wants to see resettlement and supply begin afresh . . . and believe me, the current—disturbance—in the planet's atmosphere is no barrier to the graces *or* the punishments that the Nine Houses can distribute. I say this with all the authority invested in me as Prince Ianthe Naberius the First, the Lyctor Prince, the Saint of Awe."

For a moment the crowd was silent. The speech had to be translated for some people, anyone who didn't have really good House. But then the word spread through the crowd—*Lyctor—Lyctor—Lyctor*.

Prince Ianthe Naberius said, "I hope you find *that* . . . comforting."

Nobody found it comforting. The word was picking up—*Lyctor—Lyctor—Lyctor*, like a wind.

The person—Prince Ianthe Naberius—drawled, "Yet that's not all," and made a brief and strange expression. It was one Nona had never seen, one Nona couldn't parse. The Prince crooked their finger at someone Nona couldn't see, and the camera wobbled and pulled back to reveal that someone else was sitting right there, at the same desk.

The first person sat beautifully, while this second person sat with ramrod posture. They were dressed in the same bright white jacket as their counterpart, with the same tie. Their skin was rendered pallid in those hot lights, with the same weird, waxy quality: warm-coloured skin that should have been a similar brown hue to Nona's, except that there was something wrong with it. Their crooked mouth was set in a serious, bloodless line, and their face held no expression at all. It was a grim mask on a forbidding face, with about as much animation as the portrait in We Suffer's office. The only alive thing about this second person was their hair, neatly arrayed with a wreath of fingerbones and white, springlike blossoms: wildly red hair, red enough to make the electric hexagons struggle with it. It was the face of the girl in her dream.

And their eyes—

After that first, astonishing moment, Nona stared without seeing in a wild paralysis of recognition. She was trembling. The face on the screen was the face of the girl in her dream; it was the picture of the face that Camilla and Palamedes had drawn for her; but so much more serious, so lifeless, so slack, like the girl was sleeping with her eyes open, that for a moment she thought she must be mistaken. Yet there she was—it was her, the girl in her dream. For a moment Nona panicked, convinced that somehow the broadcast could see her too, that the girl was looking at her. But she had imagined it. Broadcasts didn't work that way.

"The Emperor has sent no intermediary to vouchsafe you," the first person said. Nona could barely hear for looking. "All these promises are made by no lowlier personages than myself and Her *Most* Serene Highness, Crown Prince Kiriona Gaia, heir to the First House, the Emperor's only daughter."

Nobody said anything. Prince Ianthe Naberius continued, "The Emperor Undying has sent nothing less than his own Tower Princes, as gracious tokens of his extreme *love and concern* . . . his unimpeachable authority."

There was something irrepressible hovering at the edges of the person called Prince Ianthe Naberius's mouth at *love* and at *concern*—like a struggle not to smile, or not to explode in a fit of temper. Nona had rarely seen those two feelings go to war before. But it only lasted a second. The camera waited on the other person—the other prince—as though waiting for them, for her, to say anything. She didn't. She was as stony and as cool and as uninterested as she had been before. Curiously, Nona noticed, she didn't even seem to be breathing.

"Anyway! Back to me, Prince Ianthe Naberius," said Prince Ianthe Naberius.

The screen nauseously wobbled back and closed in. The Crown Prince, the dream girl, disappeared from view.

They said, "I will broadcast again, exactly twenty-four hours from now, with new instructions. What those instructions are will depend very much on you.

"Hail to the Emperor Undying, to his Nine Houses, and also to you, his respected pactmates, beneficiaries, and allies."

There was a pause.

In quite a different voice the person said, "*That'll* fix their little red wagons. Is this still on . . . ?"

The screen flickered and a disembodied voice said, "This broadcast will repeat at five o'clock tomorrow as a recording." Then it all went dead.

The hexagons flared white. One sparked at the end of the frame. The sun had sunk a little lower behind the buildings, so when the broadcast stopped it all seemed extraordinarily dark, like nighttime had come early. Nona clung to the pole with slippery hands, feeling all at sea; she focused in on Hot Sauce's breathing—which was very shallow and very soft, but there. Nona looked at the way Hot Sauce's nostrils flared deep inside her hood, at the rise and fall of her chest. She wanted to make sure.

The silence had broken. Some of the militia had taken over the loudspeakers, telling people to go. They repeated, "Disperse, disperse." But nobody seemed to want to disperse. The noise grew and grew and grew. Someone right under Nona's pole said, "This city's over. I'm going into the desert. We won't survive another one of these."

Someone in the crowd was yelling. They were being pulled away by two other people. Nona saw their face as the crowd pressed and the crowd parted. They were saying, "Liars! Liars! Ur is fighting! *They're* losing! Liars!"

The megaphone was still bleating out *Disperse, disperse.* One of the militia trucks had turned on its alarm so that Nona couldn't hear individual voices anymore; it was a horrible sound, a long dying whine punctuated by a whirring *WHEE-ooh WHEE-ooh* noise like when the poison cats were fighting. She clung to Hot Sauce and the pole. Some people tried to throw things at the screen, but other people were pulling them away. The crowd's fear had changed and mixed them up; they were surging this way and that, forming rivers and currents, some people refusing to move, others struggling to get away. One of the militia trucks was slowly chugging into the crowd, people pushing to get out of its path, as someone on the back of it yelled and gesticulated: "Everyone on this side of me, go down the broadway. Everyone on *this* side of me, back toward the motorway. Come on . . ."

No shots had rung out, at least. There were scuffles among the people, but most sets of shoulders Nona saw seemed more depressed than anything. She looked at Hot Sauce and nervously joggled her elbow. Hot Sauce didn't seem inclined to move. She whispered, "What now?"

Hot Sauce looked at Nona. Her pupils had gone small and dark.

"They're not people, Nona," she said. "They're not people."

Nona ventured, "They seemed strange . . ."

"Because they're not real," said Hot Sauce.

Her lips were a little wet. She was terribly afraid all of a sudden, Nona could see, filled with the fear her body spent so much of its time rejecting. Nona thought about her tantrums and, buoyed by the courage that had brought her here, reached out to seize Hot Sauce's wrist that wasn't holding the pole. "Listen to me," she commanded. "I'm your Teacher's Aide. Breathe with me . . . I'll squeeze your hand for *in* and let go for *out. In* through the nose . . . *Out* through the mouth . . . Not so quickly. Don't hyperventilate," she added, knowing she sounded exactly like Camilla.

Hot Sauce acquiesced. She took five breaths in—five breaths out—all the while the alarm blared horribly and the crowd surged and billowed beneath them. Her face still looked strange and rigid, as though she might puke. Nona realised that although Hot Sauce was still her leader, she had to help Hot Sauce, she had to be the one who was nearly nineteen. She started to caterpillar herself back down the pole—her long career as the worm with problems had taught her the movements she needed to lower herself—and when her feet touched the bottom, jostled by people on her elbows and shoulders all the way, she called: "Come down, let's go."

Hot Sauce came down. Nona held her hand as they joined the crowd. She had scanned over the top of people's heads and thought, a little desperately, that she knew where the crowd was thickest: she was very grateful in that moment that she knew about movements. She hurled herself and Hot Sauce into the current and dragged her toward where they had come from—changed her mind in a moment of stillness, joined a rivulet heading east, wriggling into their midst and saying loudly, "My sister's going to be sick," which got them a tiny opening, enough to move through. The crowd extended all the way up the back street. She could smell the smoke where the old water treatment plant was still smouldering. They had barely made it into the artery going up the street before a shot rang out in the crowd behind them. Everyone screamed and cringed, and then everyone ran.

At the noise of the bullet, Hot Sauce seemed to come online again—she dragged Nona into a tiny alleyway, away from the stampede. She said, "Go!" and Nona was grateful to have her back, grateful to let her take the lead. They had to climb mounds of leaking garbage sacks, and Nona cut herself terribly on a jaggedy old can. She squealed at the pain, but stuck her hand in her pocket to hide it. The noise grew terrible: alarms, yells, backfiring trucks. They scrambled up and down fences—the wires cut their hands—they skidded and fell down in broken and half-demolished buildings. It seemed like the sound was always right behind them and they couldn't get away from it.

"Nona!" called a voice. "Nona! Hot Sauce! Girls!"

This voice came from a truck with a grille. This truck had mounted the pavement and other cars were honking at it. It was the Angel, sitting in the passenger's seat. She had the window rolled down, and she was twisting herself into a knot to open the back door. She bawled, "Get *in*!"

Hot Sauce and Nona didn't need asking twice. They threw themselves at the truck, scrambled up into the rough, potholed back seats, and shut the door behind them, panting. Noodle was there lying in the bit where your feet went, looking baleful at all the noise and interruptions.

The Angel said to someone, "Drive." They were separated from the passenger seat by a fine black mesh, but the Angel had peeled it back so that she could look at them. She said sharply, "Are you hurt?"

"Nona got cut," said Hot Sauce, grimy and dirty and bloody herself.

"No, I didn't," said Nona quickly. "I *thought* I did, but I didn't."

"You're covered in blood."

"I'm fine. I'm fine."

The Angel, having ascertained that neither of the girls was bleeding out, said— "Buckle yourselves in. Both of you deserve to be bloody pancakes. Kevin was in hysterics."

"How did you know where we were?" asked Nona, wrestling with the seat belt.

"I'm not stupid—I've been doing doughnuts around the school building for the last half hour waiting for you two to turn up."

Nona was amazed that she and Hot Sauce had gotten as far as the school building, but also that they had not gone further. It seemed as though they had been running for ages.

Hot Sauce said, "Where are the others?" and the Angel said, "Safe—the moment I knew you two had scarpered, I decided to pull everyone back in case they got the same idea. Go left," she said, to the unseen driver. "For God's sake, don't use the motorway, everyone's driving like maniacs. Don't take anything that feeds onto the Civic. And don't rear-end anyone."

"*Who* is driving this fucking *car*," said the driver. They had a low, terse voice and surprisingly good House.

"You, so make sure we have a car to drive by the end of the journey," said the Angel. She turned back to the girls. She had fixed her face into steely, teacherly disapproval, and Nona writhed beneath it. She said, "Hot Sauce, I'm driving you to the shelter."

"No shelter. I'll bunk with Honesty," said Hot Sauce distantly.

"As if. I dropped off Honesty myself—you know where Honesty lives, and you'd be going back in the wrong direction, inside that mess."

"No shelter. They're autocrats," said Hot Sauce.

"Okay. You can sleep in—a place I know. It's mine, but I'm not going to be using it."

The driver said, "You're not?"

"If I don't go home with you, you're going to crouch outside my door all night."

"Don't make it sound like it's my idea," said the driver.

Hot Sauce subsided into silence; Nona watched her face flatten, which meant that she had no argument to make. The Angel turned her sights on Nona instead and said briskly, "Nona, where do you live?"

Nona told them. The driver tried to crane their neck around to look at her, but it was simply impossible; there was too much grille and they were wearing a thick desert muffler round their head. The Angel, who *could* crane, had craned immediately. She said, bewildered: "I thought Joli was funning me. The *Building*? Inside of it, you mean?"

"Yes," said Nona, who was about to elaborate on exactly where but remembered Palamedes and Camilla's warnings, and shut herself up in time. She said, "I do live there, really truly."

The Angel righted herself in her seat. She said, "We'll go there first, then."

"Thank you," said Nona meekly. Now that the adrenaline had

passed, all the fight had left her; she just felt frightened and shivery. When the Angel said, "Hot Sauce, how badly is she hurt? Nona, have you had your stonemouth jab?" she couldn't think of anything smarter to do than tuck her hands inside her jacket and say, "I'm fine! Not hurt at all!"

"Horseshit," said the Angel. "You're all over blood. There's a first-aid kit beneath your seat, Hot Sauce—"

"Really I'm not. It can't be my blood. It must be someone else's. Maybe it's tomato sauce. Who knows? It could be anything. But *please* don't worry about it."

Not, as Pyrrha would have said, her best effort. But maybe the rising pitch of hysteria in her voice convinced the Angel, because she only said, "I'll check you out tomorrow. If you start to feel faint or get a fever, let someone know, all right?"

"I will. I will. I promise."

The person in the driver's seat muttered, "I can't believe this."

"Yes?" said the Angel. "Were those your dulcet tones making commentary?"

"If people knew this was how you spent your time, Aim—"

"They should hope to God they spent their own time half so usefully," said the Angel wrathfully.

"Pretending you can bandage bipeds? Teaching snot-nosed kids about particles?"

"None of us have snot," said Nona, deeply offended. Then she thought about it and said more truthfully, "Anyway, it's not Kevin's fault."

The driver didn't say anything. Hot Sauce spoke up— "We love her."

The driver said, to the Angel and not Hot Sauce, "Now I see. Chance to be *her*, huh? A little independent living for once?"

"It is my enormous privilege to be *they*. Just drive," said the Angel crisply. "I don't pay you for your opinions."

"You don't pay me anything," said the driver. "I'm here for my bloody sins."

The drive would have been extremely exciting had Nona's carsickness not warred with her homesickness. Around twenty-six highly unusual bad things had happened to her today, and she had assumed she only had room for six unusual bad things before she had a tantrum; it must mean she was growing up. The driver gunned the ignition and drove in all the places cars weren't meant to drive. Thankfully a lot of other cars were doing that too. Many times there was a huge bump as the car went onto the pavement, or had to swerve suddenly, or rattled down along a little road that didn't have the type of terrain meant for a car. Most terrifyingly, the car once drove down a whole road that had been closed to cars due to the crevasses and potholes, right through a plastic snapper that had an illustration of a car falling down a huge hole, and Nona couldn't help uttering tiny shrieks every time they drove close to those huge black lightless wells. Noodle uttered tiny *aroo . . . aroo . . . aroo* sounds with her, as though in sympathy, even when the Angel said without any particular heat, "Shut up, dog. We've been through worse." Nona felt embarrassed that greater courage was expected of the dog than of her. Hot Sauce settled back in the car seat, and Nona noticed with absolute disbelief that she had fallen asleep. Nona closed her eyes and put her feet close to Noodle.

And then it was suddenly *their* road. The Building loomed high above the car window, and tears smarted in Nona's eyes to be finally home after such a long and hideous day. They had to wait until the gate opened before pulling into the deep garage. Nona didn't even question why the truck that the Angel was being driven in was allowed access to the gate: maybe whoever was manning the gate saw the grille and thought better of stopping them. The lights had all been turned off in the underbuilding where the other cars and trucks and motorcycles went, and it was astonishingly dark, all except for the truck's big headlights.

There were people next to idling trucks, next to cars, people with their dust hoods up, people with their guns out, or people standing and talking quietly. When they saw the truck they turned their heads, then immediately looked away again. The driver turned off the lights—it was now so dark inside the car that Nona could barely see herself—and the Angel said, "Will you be all right from here?"

"Yes," said Nona. "Yes, I think so."

"School will be in session tomorrow," said the Angel.

The driver said, "No, it won't," and the Angel said, "Yes, it will. Can I depend on you, Nona?"

"Am I going to be in trouble?"

"Least said," said the Angel, "soonest mended."

Even in the dark Nona could see her teeth, her tired smile, the soft set of her shoulders. She reached out a very calloused hand and patted Nona on the head, just as though she were Noodle, and Nona felt better. She knew from that touch that she wasn't really in trouble. Hot Sauce spoke up suddenly, in the darkness, and said, "It was my idea."

"Yes, I was aware," said the Angel wearily. "Tomorrow, Nona—it'll be safe at the school."

Nona pushed hard on the big truck door and slithered out of the vehicle. Outside the truck it was a little easier to see. There were lights from people's cigarettes, lights from the reflective sprays on the backs of the trucks, lights from the landing. She said, "Thanks—I love you," and then darted away into the elevator well as fast as she could, feeling red hot with embarrassment. She hadn't meant to say it—it was like the time Born in the Morning had called the Angel *Dad*—only she did mean it. She *did* love the Angel, after today.

Nona took the stairwell up because the elevator stuck so much. Her legs were wobbly and tired, and she had to wait on the landing every time her calves and her feet got too stiff. Thankfully that sensation never lasted long—it was like a brief twinge—and she was able to keep climbing, up all thirty-three flights, though after the thirty-second she gave up and went on her hands and knees. By the time she was on her own dear scrubby-carpeted thirty-third floor with the cop below and the militia guys above and the adjacent crying baby (which was not making itself known) she nearly kissed the floor, only she thought that Palamedes would say that was the easiest way to bring on a serious virus.

The last few metres were the longest. Fumbling around beneath the mat for where they had glued the spare key and thumbing the right number into the numlock pad took all she had left. She turned the knob, and flung the door open, and wailed in a big excited hurry: "I'm home! I'm safe! You don't have to worry!"

Camilla rose from the table, empty waterglasses stacked neatly before her, a whole page of newspaper torn into beautifully even strips, exactly as if a bird had done it—the work of hours, the labour of anxiety. Nona flew to her. Cam caught her up by the arms and looked *through* her, not *at* her; her beautiful pale grey eyes looked like holes burnt in a mask.

Then she held Nona so hard that it very literally hurt. Nona's face was squashed into the hard bits of her chest.

"Cam, I'm fine!" she said again, flattened and breathless. "I'm okay! Where's Pyrrha?"

Camilla's arms went slack so Nona could pull back a little way. She looked up at the door, as though she expected to see something there and had just realised she hadn't; she looked down at Nona. When she looked at Nona again her face was horrible.

"Nona," she said, "Pyrrha went to pick you up from school before lunch. I thought she was with you."

JOHN 19:18

IN THE DREAM the waters kept rising. They started making a hut at the top of the hill. Bodies were bobbing up and down in the water. He was scared of that—he was always scared of the water—and he made the waters go away for a while, and he raised up some parts of the earth that had been covered by sea. She watched them explode upward, shedding tonnes of water back into the soup. She asked him if it was hard; he said the hardest thing was remembering that he could do it, and not just doing things the old difficult way.

On the new plank of land, all cut up from the water and the damage, there was a broken concrete building guarded by enormous shards of cracked bone. Like an egg that had been smashed from above. They wandered through the fields, slipping in icy brown mud, but they didn't go anywhere near the building. They found the hood of a half-dead car to sit on, which was drying in the light, and he said: Politically, we were a landmine. Everybody was trying to get to grips with the timescale. We didn't have much time left, and new data fucked around with the numbers every day. Every time you breathed funny, we wet ourselves. But the old backers, they were the most scared of us, kept saying we were working with this country, or that country, pushed the hardest to prove what we were doing wasn't real and that anybody talking to us was helping us pull the world's leg. They were all going round and round and round. I kept saying, give me a seat at the table, let's work out if I can help, if I can do something.

He said, Turns out you can't even talk about whether or not you can work out how to do something without twelve weeks of diplomatic dialogue. It was sick.

He said, Anyway, we all had Interpol warrants. Some of the guys inside our walls who'd joined us were like, we want out. Sometimes they wanted out because they were CIA plants and they had bosses to go back to; sometimes they wanted out because they were scared. Anyone who wanted to go, I let them go. I didn't even care about those guys. Like, nice of them to show up, but they were small fry. I could only trust the inner circle. My scientists, my engineer, my detective, my lawyer, my artist, my nun, my hedge fund manager. My diehards. The ones keeping the lights on. And Ulysses and Titania, my two dead kids—but they were dead, they weren't great conversation. I wanted to figure out if I could bring them back. If I could really do it, if I could make them come back to life.

He said, Problem was I couldn't bring anyone back once they'd gone, just stop them from going if they were close. I could fix all the damage and even get the heart beating again and fix the brain. But there was nothing going on inside Ulysses and Titania: they never talked, they never responded. I'd get really scared now and again and turn off the hearts and the brains. I didn't know what I was doing. And that ate at me.

He said, Our nun kept saying of course you can't bring them back, their souls are gone. It took me way too long to listen to her. But I was a perfectionist, right? I didn't want to believe that there was a thing like a soul, I wanted to believe I hadn't got it right.

He said, Both of us were correct. But that's for later. What happened then was we found out where the money had gone.

At this point in the dream, he stood up and walked three times around the field. He said, "Don't follow me, I'm mad." She sat on the car roof and watched as he kicked a piece of detritus over the edge of the big muddy field. He had sent it quite high, so it fell into the rising mist and then rattled a long way down the hill until she didn't hear it anymore. She wondered again why anything that hurt them only hurt briefly, but that anger took such a long time to go away.

When he had got over it, he rejoined her on the bonnet of the car, and he tucked his knees up and the metal beneath them groaned at their weight, and he began again.

He said, They took the ships, our ones, the new ones. They said they were going to use FTL instead, faster than light travel. Stupid name for it, it was never really about light speed, but anyway. They said carrying everyone over so slowly was a risk, that they'd shut the cryo plan down because it wasn't *good* enough. It wasn't safe, it wasn't okay or moral. They said we'd only managed to get it down to an eight percent chance of lasting damage once we thawed them, and we'd never fixed maternity—

Here he broke off and couldn't speak for a while. When he spoke again he said, *We* were the ones who argued them down to 8%. They were ready to go when we were just in the seventies, they were all, ooh, everyone knows it's a risk, and it's not like it's thirty percent fatality, it's thirty percent *chance of damage*, what's that even, ooh. He said, They hadn't given a *fuck* about maternity, said people should terminate before they got packed as a rule. When M— had been all, I will not accept those numbers, I will not accept a plan that incorporates reproductive injustice, and we stood beside her, we said that's not acceptable, they whinged about the money for a while and eventually said fine. And now they were acting like eight percent *wasn't good enough*. Like we hadn't *tried*.

He said, Their plan was to evac the whole population. First, send out a dozen guide ships. They said they'd managed to find some poor dipshit geek who'd fixed the FTL problem of getting locked in the chrono well, you know, moving so fast you were stuck doing quantum wheelies. They'd come up with something where you could oscillate out so long as the ship was attuned to a prearranged spectrum outside. I still don't understand the maths. It's going to take me ten thousand years to understand it. I couldn't follow, but A— could. He said immediately, *What is the point if you still have no fucking clue where your ship is going to end up when you shake out of FTL.* They said, *Aha, but we can track it once it's out.* A— said, *It could be halfway across the universe or phasing through a planet.* They kept arguing that probably wouldn't happen, and that A— wasn't following, and he had to admit that it wasn't his area, but he said they were taking *one* discovery and acting like it changed the whole ballgame when really we now needed ten years of funding to discover whether it was any use, i.e., academia functioning as normal. But these trillionaires were acting like they'd got the Holy Grail. They said it was expensive, so twelve ships would go first, with one guiding them out with the beacon frequencies like a tugboat leading a cruise liner, triangulate for Tau Ceti, dump the population, and come back. They said that they were on track to finish a lot more FTL-capable ships by then.

He said, We knew how much those ships cost. We couldn't even imagine how much FTL engines cost, but we could guess. We knew how much each ship could carry. In the cryo cans, we could cram in billions, that was cryo's saving grace. Whereas they were staffing ships with a living crew, no sleepers, big-ass ships with thousands of live staff. When we pointed that out they kept saying *we* were crazy, *we* were kooks, *we* were monsters. They kept saying cows watched sunsets. At that point I wished I'd used the fucking conspiracy theorists instead of the cows. Nobody would've cared if I'd turned people inside-out who think vaccines have nanites in them that mine cryptocurrency. But *cows* watch *sunsets,* man!

He said, M— freaked out. Said this was the rats scattering. Said this was why they'd dumped the cryo plan in the first place. She said we were looking at a private flotilla carrying the rich bastards to safety. And A— agreed with her, which was how you knew it was really, really bad. He said this was a blind. He said he wasn't even sure the FTL thing was real. He said they were going to try to generation ship it to Tau Ceti using stuff *we'd* come up with, tech *we'd* created, and just be all bye-bye, fuck you, planet, thanks for the oil and for the chicken yakitori, we loved that stuff.

And I said again, Guys, nobody's going to fall for that. They're going to have to give numbers. They're going to have to prove they're making the other ships. Nobody's going to fall for that. Look at all the division we caused because we proved magic was real and turned Bidibidi inside out because we didn't trust the cops. It's not going to fly. I said, they can't do this *now.* They can't pull this off.

At that moment in the dream he got up off the car, and he said,

"Fuck," in a normal voice, and then he said, *"FUCK,"* so loudly that it echoed off the crumbling concrete shell and the bones and was carried off into the mist. She watched him walk the field, three times, five times, ten.

On the eleventh, he squelched through the mud to her and collapsed in front of the car and he said, They left you, they left you. They saw you suffering on dollar-shop life-support, and they didn't look back. They didn't give a fuck about trying to save you. They left.

She said, "I don't remember."

He said, "I can't forget."

DAY FOUR

Where Is Pyrrha?—the Gang Swears an
Oath—the Angel Makes a Call—
Hot Sauce Draws Her Gun—Forty-Eight
Hours Until the Tomb Opens.

17

NONA WOKE UP, COLD AND ALONE, with very little idea of how she had fallen asleep; she was still wearing all her clothes, and she hadn't had her bath. In the night someone had unbuttoned her dust coat, taken off her shoes, and loosened what she was wearing, which meant Camilla or Palamedes; only they would have thought of it.

Last night had been dreadful, too bewildering even to thank her lucky stars that Camilla hadn't once asked about the broadcast—once she'd heard that Nona had waited at school when Pyrrha hadn't turned up, then been driven home by a teacher, that was that. She didn't ask anything else, except: "You heard about the broadcast?" and Nona said, faintly, "Yes," ready to tell her about the girl from the dream; but Camilla had immediately changed tack, immediately gone to ask Palamedes what to do.

Nona, who by this point was perishing with hunger and exhaustion, had been placed on the floor by Palamedes and forced to suck on cubes of frozen fruit juice as he furiously scribbled on a sheet of paper. He only paused once to say, "You know what the Nine Houses have said, of course."

Buoyed by blood sugar, Nona was ready to confess.

"Yes. More than. Honesty came in and told us everything they said over the radio, and then Hot Sauce wanted to see it, and . . ."

She paused. But Palamedes didn't take the bait.

"Pyrrha was gone before we knew anything about it. She must have set off a full hour before any call came. Nona, did Crown say anything to you about the broadcast when she walked you to the classroom? Did she seem to know about it?"

Nona puzzled over the memory.

"No, she didn't say a word. We only found out after lunch and I stayed because Camilla didn't come to pick me up. Crown didn't say anything"—this wasn't quite true, and Nona was feeling in the mood to explain, so she tucked the ice cube in her cheek and said—"only Crown *did* tell the Angel that she was dating Camilla and I didn't say, 'No she isn't,' so I'm sorry."

Palamedes was not so tired that he could not look amused, which was always funny on Camilla's dark, serious face.

"On Crown's head be it. Don't worry, Nona. Keep at that cube, and take another when you're done. You're almost unconscious." Then he said, more to himself than to her: "Pyrrha, why the hell did you go off half-cocked? What was so fucking urgent that you couldn't even pick up Nona?"

"That's two swears," said Nona, so nearly asleep she was in danger of choking on the ice cube.

"Not a Teacher's Aide right now, Nona," said Palamedes.

She said, "Maybe someone told her about the broadcast on her way to get me. Maybe she went to see the shuttle land."

Palamedes said, "Neither of those things would prevent her from getting y—" and then he stopped completely dead.

He said, "The shuttle. That fucking shuttle."

"Three," said Nona, forgetting.

"Oh, God," said Palamedes. "Pyrrha Dve, *please* . . . Nona, your ice cube's falling out."

The last thing she remembered was the ice cube falling out for real and finally; nothing after. Now the alarm was ringing shrilly, far too close for her to stop it with one arm and fall back asleep. Camilla must have set it to make such a horrible sound at some point yesterday. Nona hunted around and pushed its buttons until the noise stopped.

She was completely alone in the bedroom. She panicked for a moment until she saw Camilla and Palamedes's clothes hung up like normal. But neither of them was there: no Cam with her clipboard, no nothing. It was the first morning that Nona could remember when she hadn't been woken up to tell her dreams. She heard the running of the tap in the room next door, and that comforted her, all the sounds of someone doing the washing-up. Except it wasn't Pyrrha, which made her feel bereft. She did not know what to do without someone to give her the cue that it was okay to dress, and in any case she was dressed already. For a moment she lay there, helpless, until the noise of the dishes being wiped stopped and Cam was there in the doorway with one of the blue-and-white-striped cloths that Pyrrha used to dry things with.

"Push the red button and tell the recorder anything you remember," she said. "I'm making breakfast. Press the one second from left when you're done." Then she disappeared again.

Nona didn't like this at all. Last night's dream was already mixed up with Pyrrha being gone and the girl on the broadcast, so that she now doubted whether or not the girl on the broadcast *had* had the face of the girl in the dream or if it was all part of some long nightmare. For a moment she thought about hunting out the picture to confirm, but Cam had told her to record herself, and she'd already forgotten which button to push. Her face burned with embarrassment, so she pushed buttons at random, and the recording within made awful sounds. She turned the volume down low so that Camilla couldn't hear her screwing up. There was static, and then she heard Camilla's voice coming out of the speakers, sounding tired.

"—ant her to be Harrowhark, Warden."

Another plastic echo of buttons. The same voice answered, but not the same person. The conversation that followed was filled with weird pauses, as though they were actors in a play who couldn't quite get their cues right.

"Yes, but the question we need to ask is, *Why?* They hate zombie wizards so much more than zombie thralls. To wit, Judith Deuteros. Why do they want a Lyctor on tap?"

Another pause, another clack.

"To remove the R.B.?"

Pause. Clack. "Not sure. Get the feeling that the R.B. is more a crimp in their plans than the plan itself. At first I thought they were keeping Deuteros alive to see if they could make a Lyctor out of her instead, but I'm not so sure. I think I buy Corona's story that she's the getaway vehicle . . . put crudely. But it's Harrowhark they want—or at least, it's Harrow that We Suffer wants. I don't think Merv Wing and the Hopers want Harrow at all, or at least—they're not holding out for her. Everything comes back to the Tomb, Cam. God, I wish I could see your face."

Clack. Pause. "Look in the mirror."

Pause. "It's not you. It's me wearing you. I keep turning around to find you, and there's nobody there."

Clack. "I know the feeling."

Pause. "Of course you know. Of course I'm telling you what you already, intimately, know. I have spent three-quarters of my life telling you what you already knew and one-sixth telling you what you didn't. And now here I am, installed in your body, mere minutes from chewing up your soul . . . Camilla, I can't bear this. I'm eating your life."

Clack. Pause. "I'd carry you with me either way."

Pause. "What do you mean?"

Pause. Clack. "I've carried you, Warden. And I've carried your memory . . . I'd rather carry you."

Clack. "What about carrying nothing? What about Camilla Hect, the independent entity? Free to live her life outside the shadow of her necromancer? Free from his agenda dictating hers?"

Pause.

"You thought it was your agenda? Huh."

Clack. "I cannot bear the thought of using you."

Pause. "Love and freedom don't coexist, Warden."

Clack. "*This* is all there is to love? Simply by being in your life, I have added indelibly to its weight?"

Pause. "Yes."

Clack. "Camilla, I mean it."

Pause. "I meant it too. You used to say it to me."

"We are one flesh." Clack.

"I am your end."

Pause. "That didn't mean I got squatting rights in your soul. I never would have asked for that. I never had rights to that."

Clack. "Sure. That's why I gave them to you."

Clack. Pause. Pause. Pause.

"I hope you know that I adore you, Scholar."

Clack. "Indubitably, Warden."

Pause. "Cam, have you thought about what it means if Nona's actually—a completed merger? One we will never actually be able to unpick, a successful soul gestalt?"

Clack. "Yes."

"Yes? And? Thoughts?"

Clack. "Lucky them." Another pause, and in the same tones: "More seriously. Keep neutral."

Pause. "Yes, agreed. Roger that."

Clack. Pause. Pause. One of them said, Nona couldn't tell which, "About the Captain and Corona—" but then with a loud static squeal and a garble the recording swapped over into Nona's own voice saying—

"Water-mouth, water-salt-mouth," and Camilla's, saying, "In the dream, there's salt water in their mouth?"

"Nn-hnn."

"In *your* mouth?"

"Mm-hm."

"'Yes' when I've got it right, 'no' when I don't. The salt water's in your mouth?"

"Mm. *Yiss.*"

"Do you remember anything else?" After another moment, "Face? Nona, are you pointing at your face?"

Nona looked up. Camilla was standing in the doorway. The front of her cheeks and forehead went hot, and she knew that she was blushing furiously, but Camilla's expression was very even. The recorder made another loud static squeak and a garble and Nona pushed wildly at a button until it stopped. Silence filled the room like cold water.

"How old was I then?" she blurted, more out of something to say than anything else.

"Two months." Then: "Go wash up. Breakfast's nearly done."

Two months, Nona thought distantly, back when she was a baby who couldn't do anything and could barely talk. It seemed so long ago. She wanted to say, "Cam, I didn't hear anything," even though she patently had, but Camilla had already disappeared.

In another pother of despair she twiddled the player to try to get a local radio station, hoping vaguely that there'd be another broadcast or maybe music. Pyrrha could make it go to stations where they still played music. She was teaching Nona how to dance.

Who was Pyrrha going to tell ass jokes to? Nona didn't know; all of a sudden she felt sad and responsible that nobody was there to listen to Pyrrha's ass jokes.

In this saintly, uplifted, and really quite terrified state of mind, Nona looked at herself and found that she was very grimy. In a welter of fearful bravery she sponged herself at the cold-water tap until she was free of smuts and old blood and dust, and the water was so cold it made her skin purple and blotchy. She called out, "Camilla, can I borrow a shirt?" and was pleased to hear, "Sure," so she picked out one that was only a little too big but smelled comfortingly of Camilla. She looked in the cracked mirror and decided her hair was probably all right. The braids were a bit fuzzy but still doable. Thus armed, she went into the kitchen to see about breakfast.

"Sit," said Camilla.

Nona sat down in front of a whole glass of water and a pottle of curds with the top taken off and a spoon stuck inside. The heat was already getting bad. The tiny, whirring fridge sounded like it was on its last legs. Nona, wanting very much to be good, drank all the water and ate half the pottle fuelled by martyred smugness that she was behaving so well. By the time she'd eaten half though, she felt ill and set down the spoon and said, "Done," and was a little horrified that Camilla only gave the pottle a cursory glance before saying, "Okay."

She wanted to say, *Camilla, I'm really sorry I listened to your secret private tape,* but Cam was sitting in front of her and mechanically scooping the contents of two pottles at once into her mouth. That did not seem like the action of someone who hated Nona forever, even if there was something strangely awkward in the set of her shoulders and her hands.

"Cam," she said, plucking up what was left of her courage, "are we going to wait at home for Pyrrha?"

"No," said Camilla. "She's been gone for nearly twenty-four hours. I've been stuck here the whole time. I need to see the broadcast. I need to know where Pyrrha is. We're going looking."

"Oh! To her work, at the building site?" Nona cheered up a little. "Do you think she got caught up in everything and slept on someone's couch?"

But Camilla squashed this. "No. The Warden says the timeline's wrong. Pyrrha went walkabout before one o'clock, when she was due to pick you up. Either she met with an accident or she went somewhere deliberately. If she went somewhere deliberately, she had to make the choice then and there."

"How do you know?"

"Her guns are still here."

Even Nona could tell that meant Pyrrha had not intended to go anywhere very far. Pyrrha loved her guns. Then Cam dropped the bomb.

"We're going to the spaceport."

Nona was staggered.

"Cam, the spaceport is a *mess*, everyone says so, you say never go near there, we're going to get shot maybe twenty times."

Camilla emptied the last pottle into her mouth. "Yes," she said. And: "You're coming too."

"Really? *Really?* But I never get to go! Thank you! I won't get shot anywhere strange." Then she said: "Oh, but Cam, can't we please please go by my school first, I said I'd go. Hot Sauce and the others are really the only ones left." When she saw Camilla's expression, she pleaded, "I haven't made sure the Angel—my teacher—is safe, you know, after driving me home last night. She saved my life. I *can't* go anywhere without checking in. Really truly."

She did not expect Camilla to hesitate. She expected, "No." But Camilla said, "Fine. The Warden wanted to thank her. But, Nona . . ."

Nona waited.

"After this," Camilla said, "probably no more school. Probably no seeing your friends. You know that, right?"

She was glum, but she had been expecting it. "I do, I do know that." She couldn't help but say: "I've loved them though."

"We know," said Camilla.

After that Camilla went to dress and clean up in the next room. Nona, having discharged quite a lot of goodness, was drawn to do something that she never would have been allowed to do normally; she went to the window, peeled up the sniper blazing as quietly as possible, and stared directly up at the big blue sphere hanging in the sky.

She so rarely got to look at it from here. It hung on the morning horizon, and as she watched the sphere made a low, voiceless moan—a wanting sound—but quiet, on the edge of hearing. A whispered vocalisation and nothing more.

"Can you help me?" Nona whispered. "Can you do anything? Do you know where Pyrrha is?"

But it only lowed sadly, like a cow.

"That's all right," whispered Nona. "Sorry for asking." Then: "Don't do anything weird, okay? I'm having enough trouble right now."

The sniper blazing was pressed back down just in time for Camilla to come back, to help as Nona wriggled into her sand jacket and sleeves, and her hat and her mask, and did up her shoes; Camilla put on the dark glasses, and then they went out into the Building as though it was a normal morning.

The Building was a hive of activity, as though it hadn't slept. There were voices behind doors—sounds of people moving heavy boxes—no baby crying, only talking, low and urgent. For some reason Camilla even took the elevator this time. When Nona asked why, Camilla said, "Conserve your energy. You're tired." The elevator behaved all the way down to the ground floor, as if it was cowed too. On the ground floor there were lots of people there, forming a human chain at some storage cupboard or something, passing sealed security boxes from person to person to make a big stack of them outside the door. There was another person carefully securing them in the back of an idling truck. Nobody paid Camilla or Nona the slightest bit of attention.

It was a long and lonely walk to school without Pyrrha, despite the press of all the people. There was something electric in the air, as though the city were tensed and waiting for a loud noise, like watching a dog play with a rubber balloon and dreading the *pop*.

There was a big militia presence on the street. They were all wearing the same gear she'd seen yesterday, full armour, full face shields. They went in rigid twos and threes, never alone, and never walking when they could be on motorbikes. She heard one of them say in a raised voice to someone, "I'm just doing my job. I'm just doing my job." Camilla gave them a wide berth.

Nona felt sorry for the city: it wasn't its fault. It was as tall and tumbledown and snaggletoothed as always. They took the long way around, avoiding arguments, immediately beelining away from raised voices and certain sets of the shoulders until, by the time they reached the school, the sun was basically risen.

When Nona cupped her hands over the glass and looked into the foyer, she saw movement. Nona buzzed the door and it unlocked to Honesty, who was waiting there with Kevin *and* Beautiful Ruby; she was delighted, and clapped her hands.

"You're here! You're really here! I thought you wouldn't come," she said ecstatically. She threw her arms around Honesty's shoulders. "You said you wouldn't come anymore, Honesty. You said you were going to get a job."

"I need to get fed, don't I. I'm a growing man," said Honesty, who had gone red staring at Camilla, who loitered in the foyer a little way away from them. "Get out of it, Nona, stop being in love with me."

But she was already hugging Beautiful Ruby, who coped better with it, saying: "Nona, you crim! Did you really sneak off to the—" and for his pains was jabbed in the ribs by Honesty *and* Nona, so he said at the top of his voice, "*Toilet,*" and they all dissolved together into a huddle of whispers, with Kevin right at the bottom.

"She doesn't know! Don't tell her," hissed Nona.

"Whew, lad, good save there," said Honesty.

"Don't be sarcastic at me," hissed Ruby. "It's not *my* fault, I just wanted to know how Nona was, you know they could've still been getting her off the road with a spatula. I walk past that road and they're cremating people, like, right *there,* I saw somebody's *arm.*"

"Ew," said Kevin.

"I didn't get to see anything," Nona whispered. Kevin was right there and she wanted to hug him but it was impossible in the huddle, so she reached down and he placidly took her hand while the other worked the zipper of his jacket up and down. His hand was exactly as sticky as she had suspected. Nona said, "Hot Sauce and I left, we didn't get squashed."

"Why didn't Hot Sauce take *me*?" hissed Honesty, still injured. "I'm her lieutenant and you get out of puff if you walk down the stairs."

But Beautiful Ruby was saying more urgently, "The Angel drove us home—the Angel was madder than hell when Noodle came upstairs with that note, that was badass. I thought you'd catch it. Where's the boss?"

"Slept over with the Angel, I think."

Both boys exclaimed, not caring of the noise now. Camilla, leaning against a leprous pillar, didn't react. It was horribly easy to forget Camilla was there when she didn't want you to remember. Nona said eagerly, "The Angel said she wasn't to sleep by herself and she dropped us both off in the truck, she had a driver and *everything.*"

Hearing that, they groaned in envy.

"She's probably got her own screens," said Honesty.

"I bet she lives in one of those outer neighbourhoods with a gate," said Beautiful Ruby. "Not fair. Your people should've given you a massive hiding."

"She wouldn't get a massive hiding, she's nearly a grownup," said Honesty, but Beautiful Ruby said, "She's a titch though, so maybe they forgot. That pimp of hers scares me shitless."

Nona gave an outraged look over Ruby's head, but Camilla was staring out through cracks in a boarded-up window over on the other side of the reception area, which was a long way away. She dithered terribly and then said, "You can't tell anyone, but my—Pyrrha hasn't come home since yesterday. You can't tell *anyone.*"

Beautiful Ruby said instantly and kindly, "Won't tell. Don't worry, Nona, pimping is long hours and you have to go all over," and she turned on him and something in her eyes and face made him stop immediately and say, "It was a joke! It was a joke. Oh my God, don't be crazy at me, stop it."

"We're going to go look," she whispered, once she had calmed down. "Me and Camilla."

"Was it the broadcast?" asked Honesty shrewdly. "Any chance . . ." And he made a horrible motion, strangling himself with his tongue out and his eyes floating all the way back into his skull.

"I don't think so," said Nona, trying to regain her composure and stop her tantrum in its tracks. It had been a very near thing. She was feeling fragile, as Pyrrha said after long nights. "Pyrrha's very smart and wouldn't have got hurt."

Beautiful Ruby said, injured, "How come it's cool to ask if your people got hurt or killed but not okay to say one's a pimp," and Honesty said, "It's tact, little man, it's tact."

"How's that *tact*? Seriously, how is that tact? Someone explain."

Nona's eyes were smarting, and she changed the subject hastily. "Where's Born in the Morning?"

They fell silent, which told Nona all she needed to know.

Honesty said breezily, "Those fuckin' dads of his, probably already joined up," and laughed like it was a joke. But his absence was depressing, and they all felt it. It seemed strange that they were all there, even Kevin—even Honesty—but Born in the Morning wasn't. It felt as though they weren't all together, they weren't a gang. They subsided into silence until the door buzzed again. Nona saw Camilla flinch over on the other side of the room, and Honesty darted forward; but it was the Angel, and it was Noodle, and it was Hot Sauce.

"This must be the first time *you're* on time, Honesty," the Angel said. Then she saw Camilla, and after a moment's hesitation she reached out one firm little hand for Cam to shake, saying in the way adults spoke to each other— "Manic, isn't it?"

"War zone," said Camilla. And: "I wanted to thank you."

The Angel firmly headed that off at the pass. "Nonsense, I did absolutely nothing but give a colleague a lift. Unusual circumstances last night. Come upstairs and we can talk after I've settled the kids . . . Which is really the last and only thing I can do. I don't think we'll be able to keep this up much longer. The other teacher's already left me a message to say that she thinks school shouldn't resume until everyone's off the streets, so, you know, who knows when school will ever resume? Come upstairs—come on, everyone," she said, before Cam could disagree. And as they went up the stairs she said, "I met your partner yesterday," which had the power of stupefying Cam into silence.

All of them trooped upstairs to the cloakroom and put their things away as per normal and went into the dark, quiet classroom as one. The Angel turned on the lights and they sat at their proper clusters of desks, spread out across the classroom because the nice lady teacher always said no way was she letting them all sit together, with Nona at the Teacher's Aide desk at the back. Nona was surprised when Camilla, automatic and meek, took an unused desk at the back herself, one of the bigger desks that the older girls sat at. She still had her knees folded up a little too much. Noodle made a beeline for the bed he always sat in beneath the whiteboard, and once he had settled himself, the Angel said— "Is everyone all right? Are everyone's families all right?"

There was a faint chorus of assent, but then Beautiful Ruby burst out— "Sweetie said maybe now the zombies are back you won't get knifed in the street, so we should do whatever they say."

The Angel lifted both eyebrows. "Since when have you called your mum by her first name?"

Beautiful Ruby coloured a bit. "I'm not going to call her *Mum* anymore, she's going over to their side."

"She's weak," said Hot Sauce, speaking for the first time.

The Angel looked at Hot Sauce searchingly. Something new was happening between them, Nona decided, they were different from how they had been just before last night. It wasn't as easy now as Hot

Sauce being their leader and the Angel's protector. Maybe Hot Sauce had gotten into trouble. But the Angel didn't seem mad, she was only looking at her more carefully, with more interest. She said, "Hmm. Well, it's a gift to be strong—and when you have to be strong for more people than yourself it gets very complicated. I don't know how to explain or make it sound good," she added apologetically. "I don't want to read you the riot act. Don't care about what people *say* . . . care about what people *do*. People say all kinds of things because it's so easy to open your mouth and make words come out. It's the doing that shows you what they are, and what they feel."

Hot Sauce challenged, "So if someone says, 'I'm a necromancer,' we should wait around to see what they do next?"

Nona dared a glance at Camilla. She was in a posture of perfect stillness, face a mask behind dark glasses, but listening as hard as she possibly could, which made Nona doubt it was Camilla. She sat as though she had been bolted to the floor. The others were absorbed by this verbal cut-and-thrust between their leader and the Angel, leaning forward to hear what the Angel would say.

The Angel said, "What, right now? 'Course not, start running in the opposite direction . . . No, don't fight them, Hot Sauce," she said, as Hot Sauce opened her mouth. "If you valorise paranoia so much don't be a hypocrite about it, all right? If you're scared of necromancers, run from them. If they really *are* a necromancer, there's no point in fighting them, is there? It's like big animals, you can't actually exert your will on them. If you think you can, you're in danger. I learnt that back at my first job."

Honesty said, "Are you scared of necromancers?"

"Terribly. I was born on Lemuria, you see," said the Angel.

Honesty gave a long, slow whistle. Beautiful Ruby looked at his feet. Hot Sauce relaxed minutely. But Camilla said— "What happened on Lemuria?"

The Angel glanced across at Kevin, who had his knees tucked up to his chest and had wedged himself tightly into the desk. He had one of his erasers with the face on it out, and was stroking it against the desk so that it left waxy streaks. She said, "The usual. It had been under contract for a long time. I mean, we were the third settlement wave, they built the Crescent in the bones of two other cities, you couldn't dig up anything without finding remnants of a people we'd never known. The microbial population didn't show signs of serious decay until the moment before the sea went anaerobic. The things crawling out of there . . . they seemed to mutate all at once . . . The Houses pulled support, said they'd prep us for an early move, but they left minimal forces in the barracks. We dug up old caches of materiel and used them. On the mutants from the sea, on the animals as they changed, on one another, on the Houses when they saw what we'd got our hands on and came back to take control. Blood of Eden was there too, you know. And in the end the Houses won and most of us surrendered and we were moved. Two moves later, and I'm here. There's still a facility on Lemuria, of course. A decade later the Houses made it safe for geopolymer refining. It must be desolate."

Camilla said, "What kind of mining?"

"Microsilicates, zeolites. Industrial sands."

Camila pushed her glasses up the bridge of her nose and said, softly, "That must have been hideous."

"I was a zoo director. I did the big nonclumpers. We were trying to work out if we could save them," said the Angel. "We had to cull all the animals when the Houses pulled out. That was horrible."

Honesty said gruffly, "That's not right."

"No, but what can you do? Sometimes you step in to make sure someone won't suffer," said the Angel.

"No, I mean, the animal stuff's evil, but I thought you were a real doctor," said Honesty.

"I'm an animal doctor, Honesty. I've been learning a lot about human medicine down at the clinic."

Honesty absorbed this. "Do you know where I can get animal tranqs? They go for a lot."

"Bugger off, Honesty," said the Angel tolerantly, not much like a teacher at all.

Beautiful Ruby, who had been far more deeply affected by that story, drummed his hands urgently on his desk. "I can't let Sweetie do this. I don't wanna get moved again. We used to live in a house and now we live in a tip, what's next? I've got to stop her."

Then the Angel said, "But your mum isn't a necromancer, Beautiful Ruby . . . the people saying, 'Let's not fight, let's get a resettlement,' they're not your enemies . . . If you think in black and white your brain can't be agile."

Beautiful Ruby still didn't look convinced. "But she's embarrassing me. She's letting us down. And she's probably going to get her lights punched out if she says that on the street."

"Nobody ever died of being embarrassed," said the Angel. "Try to understand her point of view . . . and wait until she *does* something. And trust her to keep herself safe too."

Nona lifted her hand. The Angel said, "Nona, you work here, you can just talk," and Nona said— "Are we going to have normal school?"

"You mean this morning? Yes, as much as possible, as long as I can," said the Angel. "Hindered by the fact that I can't teach mathematics— I couldn't begin to teach you reading and writing—I don't want to teach history—but I do want to keep you louts out of trouble. So I thought I'd come and teach you that . . . how to stay out of trouble."

The Angel took a big roll of wax paper out of her satchel. She sat them all down at a table, even Kevin, who had to sit on top of the table, and spread it out in front of them. Camilla did not amble over, which surprised Nona. She was sitting with her hands clasped together, staring at the Angel as hard as possible. Nona looked at the roll of wax paper instead and didn't quite understand what she was seeing until the Angel said kindly: "So this is a top-down diagram of the city. See, here's the civic centre, where some of you have recently been . . ." Here she looked at Nona and Hot Sauce particularly, and Nona coloured. "And here's us."

She ran her finger down a few streets, made a few zigzags, and tapped another piece of the drawing. Nona still couldn't see how such a tiny move could represent her and Hot Sauce's expedition, nor could she parse the shapes, the heights of things. The map was too flat—everything was a minute collection of squares and lines and squiggles; but Beautiful Ruby seemed to get it. He pointed at a bit of the paper. "*That's* not there anymore."

"The water plant. No," said the Angel. "They blew that up early in a bid to smoke the Cohort—that's the Nine Houses' army—out of the barracks. Really stupid stuff. And this isn't here, the big terraced graveyard. I mean, it's still *there* . . . shelled to hell and back. Which wasn't as stupid . . . although there's been so many sand burials outside the walls it was all optimism in the end. Ruby—colour that in red."

Beautiful Ruby took the red, chisel-ended marker pen—not like a wax crayon or a fat ballpoint, a grown-up thing they all looked at admiringly—and neatly coloured that part in. The Angel said, "Anywhere we colour red, that's somewhere you don't go unless the only other option is being swallowed up in a sinkhole. Got it?"

Honesty said, "I've been to that graveyard. It's all tents and concrete."

"Yes, but it's the first place people will assume necromancers will go, and people like to shoot first and ask questions later," said the Angel, "or worst case, maybe a necromancer *will* be there. I know we think they'd have the blue madness, but what we know is that we don't know anything, okay? I want you lot to make that your motto. What we know is that we don't know anything."

Nona quite liked this motto. It was an accurate summary of her entire life. The Angel gave another pen to Honesty and said, "Can you find Southgate? Colour it in."

"Yeah, sure," said Honesty, "for you," as though he might not have done it otherwise. When he found Southgate he blocked it in. This pen was coloured blue. The Angel said, "Southgate is a good place to go in an emergency. Why do you think that is?"

Nona said mechanically, "Because it's got access to the road out of town and there's a water pump and the ground is stable and it's not a priority target for any kind of orbital strike or bombardment."

Everyone looked at her. Then they looked at Camilla, sitting in the back. Camilla didn't move. She had found some bit of paper and was writing on it furiously, so Nona didn't even get a "Well done, Nona," which she deserved because Cam had taught her all that.

"What's *bombardment*?" asked Beautiful Ruby suspiciously.

"No idea," said Nona proudly.

"An interesting group, your family," said the Angel slowly, with an eye on Camilla. "I mean, you're totally right—if you have to run away, run there and keep close to the road. You're all city kids, I don't think any of you can survive in the open desert . . . still lots of buildings out there, customs buildings, sturdy shells to hole up in from the elements. Go there, go together, but don't wait for one another. It's good to move in numbers, but don't stay anywhere dangerous to find the others. Don't worry about weapons or even food. Water bottles are your priority. Anything that happens will happen in the short-term. Okay?"

Nona looked at Hot Sauce as the rest of them chorused a slightly reluctant *Okay,* and noticed that there was no surprise in her face, no sense she was taking in new information, just the normal Hot Sauce dark-eyed intensity. She thought: *The Angel has already told her all this,* and had her suspicion confirmed when the Angel said— "Hot Sauce, tell them which building you picked out."

Hot Sauce automatically placed her thumb outside of the city gates, on a lone square.

"I've hid out here before. It's an old watchtower. Keep along the road. White building with the top railing. Nobody else likes it. One of its legs looks sunk into the sand. But it's stable. There's stuff there."

"Good going, boss," said Honesty.

"If you try to sell anything I've left there," said Hot Sauce evenly, "I'll have you."

"I wouldn't sell your stuff," said Honesty, injured. When Hot Sauce waited, he said, "I promise, I promise. I'm your best boy, Hot Sauce."

"Well, selling supplies you don't need isn't a bad idea in a pinch— trading I mean," said the Angel briskly. "But like I said, this *ought* to be short-term, and you might not even use a hideout . . . But if shooting breaks out in the city, serious shooting, you don't want to be anywhere near it."

Beautiful Ruby said, "But the necromancers can't do anything anymore."

"So we think," said the Angel, "but now there's a Lyctor."

Nona shuddered at the word, on hearing it outside, for real. The Angel noticed and said, more gently: "Don't be too alarmed. Really, even a Lyctor shouldn't be able to do much due to the blue madness . . . I'd love to know how one made it all the way down here without frothing. I'm not even sure they can survive on the surface, the way things are. But that said, if the necromancers don't have necromantic abilities to fall back on they may simply shell the place if things get too bad. *That's* what I'm talking about. No one wants to be in a city that's getting shelled. Lots of people are about to start streaming out, and it's in the Houses' best interest that the population stays in one place, and stays put. So you need to find a middle ground. All right?"

There was a *ssstt* from overhead. The lights abruptly went out. Everyone looked up, waiting, and then they came on again but much more softly. Then there was a deep *chug-a-lug* noise that sounded as though it were coming from down the hall. "Wondered when that would happen," said the Angel. "I guess that's our wheels spoked."

Camilla said, "A generator?"

"Yes. It'll only last an hour or two though, it's crap. I don't like keeping the kids here if the electronic locks don't work. I think that's it for school for now," she said. "I'm going to tack up this map here . . . and here . . . and Honesty, Hot Sauce, I think you should both try to memorise it. Blue area, red area, safe square. Test each other. The rest of you, let's go clean out the fridge. Take whatever's in it home to your families. Shake a leg, people."

That was said in the exact same tones in which the Angel would have told them to go and get out the stuff for the Hour of Science, so everyone moved without thinking about it, and even though Beautiful Ruby and Honesty lifted up their voices to complain that they wanted more school (*Honesty* wanting more *school*!) they didn't need prompting to raid the fridge. Hot Sauce, unusually mild and active, helped tack the map up on the board and stack the chairs. Nona thought this would be the moment Camilla would take her home, but it wasn't: Camilla was at the back of the classroom lost in her own world, hunched in on herself and her paper, as though nobody else were there.

So Nona busied herself finding all of the drawings they'd made yesterday and marking on the back who'd done them—not a hard puzzle. Kevin still didn't know how to draw and didn't want to learn. Born in the Morning was quite good but only ever drew cats. He said this was because they were his favourite, but they all knew that he was only good at drawing cats. Hot Sauce was the one with the palest, most hesitant drawing of Noodle, as though she had really drawn Noodle's ghost. Honesty always drew himself in all his pictures, so Ruby's was whatever was left over, and obviously Nona knew her own drawing. She smoothed them out and shook them over the sink so that all the crayon crumbs disappeared, and then she used that as an excuse to approach the Angel, holding them before her. The Angel took the proffered sheaf.

"Might be nice to have these to take home, I suppose," said the Angel. "A reminder of normal times."

"Are we never coming back?" said Nona.

The Angel winced and touched an urgent finger to her own lips in a *shush!*, but the others were too busy quarrelling over the yellow yeast berries and whether or not they should set out some for Born in the Morning—"We shouldn't," Beautiful Ruby was saying, but then Hot Sauce said, "We are," and that ended it—to care about what Nona said to the Angel. The Angel leafed through the drawings and said softly, "With that one little broadcast everything's changed, Nona."

"Yes, I know," said Nona sadly.

"We've got responsibilities."

"I thought you were your own boss here," said Nona.

"I have a lot of bosses," said the Angel.

"How many?"

"Millions," said the Angel, with perfect truth in the set of her shoulders. "Don't worry about that for now—I'm being unhelpful and unkind—it's just that, Nona, there comes a time in your life when you have to separate the things you do because they make you feel good from the things that make you—"

The Angel stopped so dead midsentence that Nona thought she had had a heart attack, that she had been hurt in a way Nona couldn't understand. She was staring at the topmost drawing of the sheaf of papers. Nona peeked over, ready to apologise for another one of Honesty's explicit anatomical sketches.

"Oh—that one's mine," she said, wanting to break the spell, wanting to help. "It's mine, don't worry."

The Angel was speechless for a moment. Then she looked at the paper, then looked at Nona again, and looked at the paper. She said, "Sure," as though everything were normal and she hadn't acted like she had been knifed. She laid the drawing aside and said, "Give the rest out, why don't you?" and smiled at Nona, but it was a weirdly awful smile, as though the Angel had forgotten how smiles worked.

Nona was a little stupefied, but after all it was strange times and everyone was stressed, so she went around handing back the drawings to their owners. Beautiful Ruby said, "I'll take Born in the Morning's, I don't want mine, who cares," and Nona did not argue.

When they were all packed up, Nona's friends gathered together in the cloakroom, out of earshot of the others, Hot Sauce having shepherded them all there. The Angel followed them out and said, "Good luck, take care," to each of them and shook everyone's hand except Nona's and Hot Sauce's. She even specially shook Kevin's. They all got tongue-tied and didn't know what to say except Honesty, who said, "Thanks, sir." Then they all took the time to pat Noodle, who was sitting on his haunches next to the Angel and even held out his paw when Beautiful Ruby said, "Shake," which pleased everyone.

Then the Angel went back inside with Noodle and they all put on their sand sleeves and their UV jackets, only Nona and Hot Sauce didn't button up theirs, and everyone's hats and masks were hanging down over their necks or their chins. Their mood was sombre, and they clustered quite close to each other.

Honesty said, "You got a copy of that map, boss?"

"Yes. You remember it?"

"Yeah. You really got stuff out there? Like gun stuff?"

"Not saying. You don't need the money. Who's taking Kevin home?"

Beautiful Ruby said, "Aren't you doing it?" and Hot Sauce said, "Can't."

"I'll do it," said Honesty handsomely. "All hands to the pump."

Hot Sauce gave him the expression that everyone knew was Hot Sauce's smile, and which each of them would have cheerfully punched any of the others to get, even Nona. She and Honesty reached out to clasp each other's hands around the wrists. It was Nona who said, feebly— "What now? How do we stay together?"

"We'll be together when we need each other," said Hot Sauce. "We have a place to go. There's stuff there. Bring your families. I'll look after you. I know how."

Beautiful Ruby said, "Even my mum, boss?"

"Even your mum," said Hot Sauce, and Beautiful Ruby looked relieved.

Honesty said, "Let's spit on it," but they were wearing gloves and none of them wanted to take them off to spit on it. So Hot Sauce put her hand out in the centre and Nona put her hand on Hot Sauce's, and Honesty put his hand on Nona's and Beautiful Ruby put his hand on Honesty's, and Kevin had to put his hand underneath, not being tall enough to reach the top.

"Doesn't feel right without Born in the Morning," muttered Honesty.

"It's for him too," said Hot Sauce. Then she said— "We swear to protect each other and die for each other. We are loyal to each other forever. Any zombies we kill, we kill for each other, and we'll say, 'This is for the others.' That's it."

"I swear," said Honesty.

"I swear," said Nona.

"I swear," said Beautiful Ruby.

"Kevin," said Kevin, whose eyes had gone big and round under the stress of pledging, so they had to coach him until he said, "I swear."

"I swear, as boss," said Hot Sauce. They let one another go. Then she said, "Okay. Go home."

They hauled their packs up on their shoulders and on their backs and Nona and Hot Sauce walked them downstairs. There they got a massive surprise; Honesty said, "Born!" and buzzed the door—the door opened—and there was Born in the Morning, sulky with embarrassment, having been squatting down in front of the doorway and dusting himself off. They crowded around him, asking questions—

"Why weren't you in school?"

"How'd you come now?"

"Why didn't you hit the ringer?"

"Didn't work," said Born in the Morning, going quite red. "Anyway, I didn't really come, I just came to see you. I slipped out."

Hot Sauce said, "Your dads joined up?"

"Yeah."

"That's fine," said Hot Sauce.

So they had to pledge all over again, with Beautiful Ruby loading Born in the Morning up with packages and Born in the Morning not even getting on his high horse and simply being pleased. When they pledged, Beautiful Ruby, being silly, said, "Kevin," instead of "I swear," so that they all fell around laughing. They all said, "Kevin," until Kevin said, injured, "Don't make fun of Kevin," so they all fell around laughing again.

That meant they were all happy when they saw Honesty and the others off, not scared or worried. Beautiful Ruby went off with Born in the Morning specially, one of his arms slung familiarly around Born's neck, both of them talking quietly. The door wouldn't lock properly, so Nona and Hot Sauce put a chair in front of it, and Nona slipped her hand into Hot Sauce's as they went back up the stairs, in an uplifted frame of mind.

"I'm glad Born in the Morning showed up."

"We might not see him for a while," said Hot Sauce. "Edenites go through people like water."

This spoiled all of Nona's joy.

"You don't think he'll *die*, Hot Sauce."

"No. I mean we have to wait for his dads to die," said Hot Sauce philosophically. "He'll only come to us when most of his fathers are dead. Then we can have him . . . His dads are baggage."

WHEN THEY GOT BACK up to the classroom, Camilla had emerged from her corner and made herself useful unplugging all the electrical equipment and stacking chairs. The Angel was writing something on the board. "I'm doing inventory," she said, to Nona's question. "If we get looted I don't want them ruining all the kids' things trying to find stuff. Hot Sauce, can you go down the hallway and turn off the generator? I know you know how, but don't forget to bleed it afterward."

Nona went to go with Hot Sauce, as she had a lively interest in what bleeding the generator would involve, but the Angel said, "Nona, stay a moment."

She had a piece of paper in her hand. When Hot Sauce had closed the door through to the classroom, Nona and Camilla both approached her. Camilla did something a little strange then: she tripped. She pitched forward on a raised bit of the carpet and stumbled into the Angel, tried to right herself with her hands on the Angel's hips and front, and stumbled upward, saying "Sorry—sorry," glancing out the window like she was embarrassed. Then she turned her head back and looked more normally Camilla, standing as gracefully as though she could never even think about tripping.

The Angel said, "It's really been that kind of day, hasn't it?"

"Yes," said Camilla.

The Angel was fidgeting with the piece of paper. She said, "May I ask Nona a question?"

"She doesn't have to answer," said Camilla.

"Of course not," said the Angel.

Nona, who thought she could speak for herself, said—"I'll try, but if you want to test me about the map I don't think I'll be much good. I want to take it home and look at it there."

The Angel showed her the piece of paper. It was her drawing again. Maybe the Angel really liked it. Nona was ready to be magnanimous if the Angel wanted to keep it. She guessed she could draw it again at home if she wanted, and she hadn't even really tried very hard.

The Angel said, "How did you draw this?"

This question bewildered Nona so much that at first she didn't know what to say. The Angel slid a sheet of paper in front of her—she recognised the scribbles she was doing, with most of her mind elsewhere, right before she and Hot Sauce had escaped to go to the broadcast—and she said, puzzled to death: "With my hand?"

The Angel urged tersely, "Did you get this from a picture?"

Nona looked down at the animal she had drawn, and thought perhaps she understood. She said, "No, I made it up. It *does* work, I promise. See these things? They're its ears," she said, in much the same tones as she would have explained to Kevin. "*This* thing is its nose, and you can't see it because I didn't draw it, but the mouth is under here. When first it was born it used to live in a river, but then it got cold so it had to get large. I know the legs can't rotate, but you don't think that's stupid, do you?" She looked up at Camilla and the Angel, then said, "Am I in trouble?"

The Angel looked at Camilla, not Nona.

"I've seen pictures of this animal before," said the Angel, slowly and carefully. "I only saw it because I did a special unit when I went to university. I went to the special zoology school on Miró and attended a heap of underground archaeology talks. I was a youthful firebrand. Political, you know. And that's where I saw the picture."

"Okay," said Nona.

Camilla said, looking at the picture, "I don't think I've seen this before."

"You wouldn't have," said the Angel. "It's a cradle creature."

"I've heard that phrase," said Camilla. "Somewhere."

"Have you?" said the Angel.

Nona didn't know what to say. The Angel and Camilla didn't seem to know what to say either, and they all stood around for a moment, with Nona racking her brains. Camilla took her dark glasses off and folded them up neatly, to put in her breast pocket. Then she said quietly— "May I ask a question?"

Nona glanced up at Camilla's face, just to confirm it.

"Go ahead," said the Angel, smiling without her eyes having anything to say about it.

"Back on Lemuria, or anywhere else," said Palamedes, "did you ever have an operation, or receive medical care, from the Nine Houses? Even if you don't remember it. Did you ever get some kind of implant? You said you met archaeologists. Were they House? Did you specifically meet any necromancers who gave you any kind of treatment?"

Nona was so shocked that she forgot to breathe. Palamedes had not simply broken one rule, he had broken about fifty. The expression on the Angel's face brought her back to real life: it was so terrible that it hurt Nona to look. The crinkles on the sides of her eyes and mouth froze. She suddenly seemed older and more shrunken—rather than tiny and buoyant, tiny and withered.

Palamedes was moved to say gently, "I don't mean you any harm," but a weird, high-pitched whirring had started at the vicinity of his ankles. Noodle had gotten up from the basket and the hair right at his flanks was standing up as though it had been electrocuted, and he was *growling*. Nona had never heard Noodle growl before. He broke into a volley of barks, with his lips pulling back from his sharp yellow teeth.

This roused the Angel. She said, "Bloody dog. Let me put him in the kitchen with a toy," and she dragged Noodle to the kitchen by his collar. She picked up her big black bag and she closed the door behind her, and then a few seconds later she emerged, still looking grey and haggard but more resolute and settled somehow. She was ashy underneath the freckles and her mouth was set in a tight, cool line, but she had drawn herself up to her not-very-impressive height and stood in front of Palamedes as though she weren't scared. Nona could still see terror on her lips and in her hands and in her feet.

At this point the lights finally sizzled to a close: Hot Sauce was done with the generator, Nona thought. The room plunged into hot black darkness. The Angel went round to the windows and pulled open the blackout curtains and the blinds, recklessly, so that electric blue light puddled on the floor, and then she circled back to the teacher's desk and threw herself into the seat.

She said, "Nona, do you want to go and sit with Noodle?" He was making little whimpering noises, even through the door. "He calms down with you."

Nona hesitated, but she had been kept out of one too many conversations by being sent away to do something ostensibly good. Nona could tell the Angel's plan from the quick movements of the Angel's eyeballs, the swallowing. She said apologetically, "Normally I would say yes, but I think I'd like to stay, please."

"Are you sure? You can listen from the door, you know," said the Angel baldly.

"Yes, I'm sure."

The Angel passed her fingers over her face, briefly touching her eyelids with thumb and forefinger, one on each. She relaxed backward into the chair. Palamedes didn't sit, but Nona sat herself down in one of the big puddles of blue light, enjoying the sensation of it and absolutely nothing else that was going on.

"Did you know, my colleague thought you were a prossie," said the Angel, wiping her hands together. "I never thought it fit."

"What I know about sex work could fit in a teaspoon and leave a lot left over," said Palamedes. "Did *you* know the children call you 'the Angel'?"

Now the Angel's mouth quirked on the other side. Her composure had come back, in part, and her teacher voice came to the fore, so that she might have been describing why socks would, in fact, insulate the ice cube.

"Yes, they've come up with a very strange take on my—my nickname. It's that Hot Sauce's fault, I'm afraid. She's overheard a couple of things she doesn't understand. I didn't know anything about it until last night, when she explained. The kids usually call me 'Miss' or 'Mister' or 'Sir'. Usually 'Sir' so that Joli can be 'Miss', and of course the kids just call Nona, 'Nona.'"

Palamedes said, "What is the implant? Please. We only have so much time."

The Angel hesitated.

"Look," she said, and moistened her lips with her tongue. "Will Nona listen to *you*, if you send her to the kitchen?"

"I could ask her to, if it's important to you," he said, "but she's an adult who can make her own decisions."

"It doesn't matter. I've made my mind up. I want to stay," said Nona.

Hearing that, the Angel stopped looking at Nona altogether and held Palamedes's gaze instead, her own rigid, like she had put on blinders and narrowed existence to him.

"Why aren't you affected by the blue madness? Which one are you—and how many of you are still alive? I thought it was sheer optimism, the report that most of you were down."

Palamedes stepped Camilla's body forward and the Angel said swiftly, "Don't move, please. If you take one step closer, I'm leaving . . . out the window, if I have to. You can get what you can from my dead body, but if you're this good you might have an inkling that my dead body is designed to deny you answers."

Palamedes put his hands up. "I'm staying right here. I want no harm to come to you, I won't compel you, I have no thought of hurting you—I am not your enemy."

"You were born my enemy," said the Angel, very sadly and very tiredly now, "or, worse, you became my enemy . . . in the last five minutes. By doing the thing you can't walk back from."

Palamedes said slowly, "What do you think I am?"

"You can be nobody but a Lyctor," said the Angel. "You used necromancy on me when you touched me, for that split second when I thought you'd fallen. It couldn't be anything else. I don't know what you sensed today . . . I've met you dozens of times and you've never cared before, so I don't know what's changed, or how I messed up. But, God, what a mess!"

Nona would have laughed aloud at the idea that *Palamedes* was a Lyctor, only she was too scared to laugh: she did not know what to say or what to do. She sat in her pocket of blue light and wished hard that Camilla had just taken her home, that they were a million miles away, that today had never happened. She had the terrible sinking feeling that whatever was going wrong right now, it was her fault somehow: that she hadn't been smart enough or good enough.

Palamedes was saying, "I am not a Lyctor, if it helps."

"Swear to me," said the Angel, suddenly intent. "Swear on your bloody life."

"I swear on the life of Camilla Hect that I am not a Lyctor," said Palamedes.

The Angel searched his face. Whatever the Angel wanted to find there—Nona was watching her face as hard as she could, so hard her eyes were watering—she eventually found it. She slumped back in the chair with her chin sagging to her chest, and she glanced at Palamedes, drawn and gaunt and complete. "Then that'll make this easier," she said.

The door next to the corridor opened. The Angel flinched so hard that it looked as though she might be having a fit. Nona turned her head and saw Hot Sauce. Hot Sauce looked at the open curtains: she looked at Nona.

Then a huge, rippling sound entered Nona's head. She was aware of a tight, hard noise, *pop—pop*, distant and then much *much* closer—as though her whole head was exploding. Everything went black, but she wasn't asleep. She had the biggest and most frantic headache and she was terrified, her body wasn't working, she could feel nothing and perceive nothing. The headache got worse and worse and worse, then suddenly it stopped, and she didn't know anything at all.

Time exited her body. After a period apart from it, the headache came back. It wasn't as bad, and then it got a *lot* better. The blackness didn't go away, but her other senses started to come online. There was something rough under her face that smelled like wax crayon and lemon cleaner, and she was drooling—her mouth was full—full of something disgusting and sticky. Her mouth opened and it all fell out. She was lying down. Nona, so well-versed in thinking about what her body was doing in various states of consciousness, could tell *that*.

An unfamiliar voice was saying— "Cancel that! I said, *cancel* that order! Merv, do you hear me? Merv, if I see even *one* of your bastards step into this building I will call such hell down on you that they'll put your names up on the Extinction Roll—*Don't you hang up on me, you motherfucking kingmaking piece of shit, I will rip off Hope's head and shit down his neck!* Goddamn it! Fuck! Fuck."

Then the Angel— "What did they say?"

"They said sure, no prob," said the unfamiliar voice. "What do you think they fucking said, Aim? Oh, boy, we're fucked. Oh, God, we're fucking fucked."

The Angel said, "Go unlock the door. We'll take the girl and get out of here."

"No. We leave her here."

"She'll get liquidated."

"You should've thought of that before you started playing teacher with the frigging Troia experiment."

The Angel burst out frantically: "I didn't *know*! How the living hell was I meant to *know*? You've kept me away from all that, I've been completely separated from any intel!"

"You knew Merv went mental on us yesterday, said it was a power play," snapped the unfamiliar voice.

"I don't mean *that*! How the hell could I have known about these two? I only realised they lived in the safe house last *night*!"

"Yeah, well, Ctesiphon is short on cash, we don't have anywhere to stash anyone," said the voice. "If you'd just let me within two metres of this place I could've told you months ago—"

"I was protecting my Edenite kids on the roll. They would've gotten transferred to the other side of the city and they needed this—"

"Pull yourself together, Aim! You don't get to think about what some snot-nosed kids need!" bawled the voice. "What're we going to do, what the hell are we going to do?"

"Yelling at each other won't help," said the Angel tightly. "You are the least respectful bodyguard I have ever had."

"Okay. Cool. Nice. Great. Cool," said the unfamiliar voice. "I'm thinking. I'm thinking. Oh my God, this is such a fuckup. Not on a personal level, because as far as I'm concerned good job, but this is *such* a fuckup."

"We go to the roof, like you said," the Angel suggested, but the unfamiliar voice said, "Changed my mind. That's not an exit. They won't shoot at us if you're with me, but we can't account for anyone else."

"Then *what*? God, I'm too old for this."

There was a big clanging sound. It hurt Nona's ears. An awful pressure travelled through her head that felt like she wanted to hold her nose and blow something out her ears, like when she was swimming. It sounded as though someone was dragging furniture.

"Anyone comes at me, I take them down," said the voice.

The Angel sounded torn between amusement and annoyance. "You discharge a firearm with me in the room, you'll get court-martialled and hanged."

"Everyone's too busy for bureaucracy," said the voice. "We play our cards right here, I can get Suffer out clean. Hell—I play this *really* right, nobody's going to know a thing until it's too late."

"Oh, God, you can't believe that. You're going to get yourself shot."

"Not with my pedigree."

"How many of them are there?"

"Nine. Maybe ten. Plus driver, probably eleven."

"That's a massacre."

"It's a compliment," said the voice modestly. "Anyway, they're still defusing the door."

The pressure got lots and lots worse—it got better—something went *klink!* in her very close vicinity. Her sight softly shaded back in—it was dark—the room was hot and close and stuffy again. Nona stared at a huge sopping red patch of blood on the floor. Her head felt wet and itchy. The unfamiliar voice was saying, "Hang on a mo. I'm just going to deadhead these two."

The Angel said tightly, "Don't you *dare* touch them."

"It's for your safety, ma'am. Don't watch."

"It's goddamn superstition."

"Yeah, well, Aunty always told me it was ninety percent superstition and ten percent for the fun of it."

Big booted footsteps clomped over to Nona. This was too much, even if Cam had always told her to play dead until she couldn't. Nona sat bolt upright in terror. Someone swore and there was another big *pop* and she was thrown forward by a huge brief light in her chest like pain, much quicker than the headache, spreading through her ribcage briefly and wetly before it went away.

She shrieked from the floor, "You *shot* me *again*! That's *twice*!"

Then there was the Angel saying, "No. No. Stop. She's alive, stop, that's an order—that's a *direct order*! Nona—Nona," and there was the Angel, rolling her over, her face wet with tears, saying: "I'm sorry—God, Nona, I'm so sorry."

But Nona was not in the mood. She struggled free from the Angel's grasp and looked for Camilla. Camilla was lying very still on the floor, faceup, eyes half-closed and staring sightlessly at the ceiling: her front was all over blood and her hands were clutched into stiff claws over her chest, as though she had clapped them there in a panic. The amount of blood was astonishing. Nona didn't think people could even bleed that much. It was more gross than frightening. Nona crawled over to her as the Angel was saying, "Hold fire, hold your damned fire," and Nona peeled up Camilla's eyelids.

Even in the dark Nona could see that they were bright, clear grey. Camilla said calmly, "It's fine, Nona. You're fine. Back up," and then Camilla opened her hands and two bullets were there, shining in her fingers. Then she said, "Update?"

Nona looked up. There was the Angel, sitting on the floor, looking as though she had seen two ghosts. Near her was the new person—a compact, medium-sized person with a machete strapped to each thigh and a small, heavy gun in their hands, not wearing an air mask, not wearing a hat. A mask hung around their neck as though they'd been in a hurry and hadn't pulled it up yet. Their face would have been fierce and handsome if it hadn't been puckered with shrapnel scars on both cheeks, across the nose that should've been flattish but had been broken once, in a peppery storm of burns at one temple. These scars meant they weren't fierce and handsome; they were *super-cool* and fierce and handsome. Their hair had been buzzed short on one side and kept longer on the other, the long part dyed a shriekingly electric blue, and their brows were dark and their eyes were darker, smudged with camouflage makeup above and beneath. And Nona had known who they were the moment their body moved, but the machetes helped. It was Our Lady of the Passion, for the first time unmasked.

"*Pash* shot us!" she wailed. "And my *teacher*! Palamedes was talking to the Angel and someone *shot* us through the window and now the carpet's *gross*! *This is the worst day of school ever!*"

Camilla sat up, and she and Pash stared at each other. Pash's handsome features screwed into an expression of stupefied loathing. Camilla's betrayed nothing at all.

"Did you shoot us?" asked Camilla, whose left hand had tightened minutely.

"No—that was fuckin' Merv Wing," said Pash, looking as though she was sorry about it. "How the hell do you know who I am? Crown's been squealing, right?"

"No," said Camilla, who had relaxed her left hand minutely. "Why weren't we told she was one of us?"

"That's *they* to you," Pash said, "and you're not one of us either, zombie."

The Angel said urgently— "Pash, I retract the liquidation order, we can deal with this later. The circumstances have changed. Is there any way you can call Merv off?"

"No—they were ready to go for you the other day when they thought Suffer was putting more of her own people in. Which was— *you*, wasn't it?" Pash turned to Nona, who was wringing clots of blood out of a completely messed-up braid. "*You* made the radio call to

Crown two days ago, *you* were the one Crown was with. What the fuck's going on, you little creep?"

Nona was deeply injured. "I *didn't* make a radio call, it was a *pretend* radio call, and don't call me a creep, because I'm not."

The Angel said helplessly, "*That* was the Crown you're always going on about? Nona, what are you? What is she?" and Pash barked, "I told you! You're looking at the fucking *Lyctor project*, Aim! Your dog was getting walked by the fucking *Lyctor* project, and you just called wipe protocol on *the fucking Lyctor project*."

The Angel said, "Give me the radio."

Pash unbuckled a real wireless radio from her belt and tossed it to the Angel, who caught it neatly, even though her hands were still shaking. She tapped something into it and held it up to her ear and said, "This is the Messenger. Holding pattern downstairs, please." Then: "Yes, we know," and "Yes, we know. These are unusual circumstances." Then: "Yes, but if you're so hot on protocol, why aren't you letting our designated lifeguard extract us from the building?" Then: "That's ridiculous."

At the second *Yes, we know* Camilla scrambled to her feet. She seized a stack of chairs and shook them out in front of the doorway that led through to the cloakroom. Pash immediately raised and trained a gun on her, which made Nona gasp in indignation, but Camilla didn't stop. The Angel was saying, "Get me the commander on the line," and then: "You do realise *one* gunshot in here and you're in front of a tribunal—that Hope's in front of a tribunal? We don't—yes, we *know* we can't countermand—look, don't you dare— We've got my *dog* in here! No, we will not put on a gas mask, this is a coup— Fine. If you come up those stairs the lifeguard will shoot you. Messenger out."

The Angel lowered the radio. She said dolefully, "Fuck."

Pash went to the teacher's desk and threw it over. Everything on top—the paper clips and the pencil sharpener and the whiteboard erasers and the collection of paper animals—scattered to the floor in an almighty *whump*. Then she vaulted behind it—the Angel moved to her—and Pash drew her gun from the strap off her back. Camilla looked at her and said, "How many?"

"Nine, ten. No gunfire, but maybe electrics," said Pash, purely on automatic, and then she blustered: "Don't fucking talk to me, Hect. The moment the commander hears about this, your ass is grass, and there'll be no Crown to save you."

"Do you want my help to get out of here," said Camilla, "or not?"

"I don't bloody need your help," said Pash, at the same moment that the Angel said, "Yes. We can't let Merv Wing take us, not now. I did—I *did* call for you to be shot though."

"No problem," said Camilla levelly. "So long as I can let out some deferred aggression."

"You're a minion and you've been bloody lying to We Suffer this whole time about what you can do," said Pash hotly. "The commander never said shit about you coming back from a bullet, you *or* the lich. I would put another one in your brain right now, for science, only I don't want to waste my ammo."

"Guess we've all lied to each other," said Camilla.

Pash looked to the Angel and said pleadingly, "Aim, for fuck's sake, what if she turns around and snaps your neck—"

"Nona, please go into the kitchen now," said the Angel. "For your safety, not to get you out of the way."

"I don't want to leave Camilla," said Nona

A window broke somewhere on the floor below. Camilla was already drawing Nona behind the desk. They all crouched down in the dark behind the desk with its nice particle-board smell. It was so quiet that for a moment Nona thought Cam had been wrong, that there couldn't be ten or eleven people coming for them, that the whole building was far too quiet. Noodle started to softly scratch behind the staffroom kitchen door and then Aim said, "Noodle. Danger," and he stopped, and he clacked away from the door.

Camilla was saying, "Quickly. Isn't there somewhere else she could go? She could take the dog."

Looking at the staffroom kitchen door made Nona look at the

other door, the one to the other corridor down the hall, and she remembered all at once and said, "Hot Sauce! Where's Hot Sauce?"

The Angel said, "Pash locked her in the generator room. They'd have to get through here to get to her."

"I want Hot Sauce," said Nona.

Pash had her head crooked out from the side of the desk, watching the shut door. She said tersely, "I don't want the lich running around."

Camilla said calmly, "Make up your mind," and the Angel said feebly, "Nona, Hot Sauce wasn't . . . she saw, you see . . . she was in the room, when . . ."

There was a distant crash—a glittery, soft sound like glass caving in.

"That's the door," said Camilla.

Pash suddenly said, "Oh my God, I've changed my mind, okay? The lich goes through the door. No distractions. Get out of here."

Camilla asked, "Why not get everyone out?"

Pash said to the Angel, "Come on, Aim. Even the zombie sees reason. Get in the kitchen," but the Angel—Aim—said, "If they don't see me, they won't hesitate to use projectiles."

Camilla said, "The longer we exchange fire, the worse. Once we break the first wave, push."

"Hect, let's get one thing straight: I'm giving the orders and if you don't say *Yes, sir, no, sir, three bags full, sir,* I shoot out your kneecaps and use you as a meat shield," said Pash.

"Three bags full of what?" said Camilla.

"Fucking whoop-ass if you don't do what I say, comedian."

"I'll keep to melee. No friendly fire."

Pash aggressively pulled her mask up over her mouth, a hard-shell plastic snap one with a bit for breathing through. Nona couldn't help admiring her: her dark-rimmed greasepaint made her eyes a lovely hazelly, yellowy green colour. Pash saw Nona looking at her soppily, scowled at her with her whole face, then drew a pair of goggles over those beautiful dark-rimmed eyes. Nona vaguely made a note to practise scowling, and also to dye her hair.

There was another, less distant *smash.* Pash tensed up and said,

"They're taking the stairs." Beside Nona, absurdly, Camilla relaxed. She was crouched behind the desk doing something with the snaps of her baggy canvas trousers, digging her hands into her capacious pockets. She said, "Nona, do you want to go, or stay?"

Nona dithered.

"Go. No, stay—no, I'll go," she said. "Hot Sauce needs me. Unless— Camilla, *please* be safe, I love you so much."

"This won't take long. Go when I say *go*," said Cam, and she smiled at Nona—smiled her lovely, exquisite little smile, the one that made Nona feel like she really could fall in love with Camilla forever and forever and get married to her and maybe adopt a dog.

Then she said to Pash— "Do you want them alive?"

Pash's expression hardened further.

"No."

"Nona," said Cam, "don't come back until we come to get you. *Go.*"

Nona fled. She scrabbled for the door next to the staffroom door and flung herself through, then shut it behind her. Her footsteps squeaked on the linoleum and the door creaked horribly, because Kevin loved to hang on doors and try to make them make the longest and worst sounds he possibly could—it sounded like a siren in that silence, worse than, and she was grateful when the door closed behind her. Then she flew down the dark, dim corridor—a place of unspeakable and enjoyable terror for her and the gang normally, it was so narrow and the walls were so dark and sweaty—and when she got to the generator room, hammered on the door before she remembered that *she* was the one who had to unlock it. The key was still in the lock. She turned it with sweaty fingers and drew back the bolt, she nearly tripped down the short flight of stairs, and she said, "It's me, Hot Sauce, it's me," before clanging the door shut again behind her.

The generator room was quiet and dark, except for a little lightbox window over the internal door and another one through to the outside, only there was a taller building in the way, so it let in sickly, greenish light. When the generator was on it usually made a lot of violent whuffling noises, the kind that threw the tinies into disorder because Honesty had told them it was powered by kids their age burning to death inside. It wasn't like they believed him, but they hated the story. Hot Sauce was lying curled up in front of the generator. She'd been sick, and there was a bright, acid smell of vomit, but Nona didn't care. She went to Hot Sauce's side, and she rolled her over.

Hot Sauce looked at her, but also didn't look at her. Her eyes were strange. She looked at Nona as Nona got out an old wad of tissue paper from her pocket and wiped Hot Sauce's mouth and nose. "It's me, Hot Sauce. It's Nona."

Hot Sauce said clearly— "I made it up?"

Nona didn't know what this meant so she said, "Yes, it's fine. I'm fine," so that Hot Sauce said, more strongly and more wonderingly, "I made it up."

"Yes, only there are people in the building, and we have to stay here because they've come to kidnap the Angel," said Nona.

Hot Sauce said, "She had a bodyguard."

"Yes," said Nona.

"Stupid," said Hot Sauce. "Stupid . . . didn't watch her enough. Didn't read the signs. Didn't watch . . . Nona, I made it up?"

Nona decided to go along with this. It seemed important to Hot Sauce.

"Yes, you made it up."

Hot Sauce's hand was still trembling a little. She didn't seem like she'd been hurt, but she was shivering. She tugged up her shirt so that Nona could see, along with the soft watery ripples of the burns down her belly, what she had tucked into the waistband of her trousers. It was a handgun. Nona said, alarmed, "Hot Sauce, don't carry it like that, Pyrrha says everyone who carries guns in their pants ends up shooting off their balls, and it sounds incredibly rude but I believe her."

Hot Sauce's face wavered and softened.

"You're sweet," she said.

From down the corridor and a little beyond, there was a big crash, and then a really astonishing huge noise like *ZZZAT*—the kind of whipcrack sound Pyrrha could make with the dish towel—and a very short scream. Hot Sauce sat up so quickly that it was all Nona could do to wrestle her down again. She struggled against Nona toward the door and Nona had to go full deadweight on her, pin her to the floor, wrap her arms and her legs around her as though she were Hot Sauce's baby who lived in a pouch. They both fell to the floor and were a little stunned, but when a huge, resonant *BLAM—BLAM—BLAM*—percussive gunshot rattled down the hall, much bigger and deeper than the normal peppery gunfire noises, Hot Sauce went quiet and limp. She shuddered in Nona's arms.

She said, "I made it up? *All* of it?"

"Yes, all of it," said Nona, and then in a fit of honesty, she said— "Only, what *did* you make up, Hot Sauce?"

"The bullet went into your head," said Hot Sauce.

Nona tried to remember everything Honesty had ever told her about lying, lies, porkies, and untruths.

"You *think* it did," she said cunningly, "but it didn't."

"It made a hole," said Hot Sauce.

Nona, exhausted from lies, was saved from having to think up more by another *BLAM—BLAM* and a long, cut-off scream, and then a terrific tinkling glassy smash. A yell seemed to briefly come from outside, somewhere, and then there was no yell at all. Nona held Hot Sauce very tightly, and after a while she felt Hot Sauce's arms go around her, and she knew that Hot Sauce was going to be all right. They lay there together in the sweltering, gross-smelling dark, listening to the sounds coming from down the hallway.

Ever since she had known what fighting was, Nona had yearned to see Camilla fight; Camilla mostly wouldn't. She had sparred with Pyrrha a couple of times, briefly and violently, always on Pyrrha's critique, with Nona barely able to follow what was going on: sometimes on the beach, in the dark, away from the hot stripe of the lone yellow light still functioning in front of the harbour pier. Now as she listened as hard as she possibly could to noises she could not understand, Nona shivered all over and could not work out what she felt or what she wanted. She kept savagely biting at the inside of one lip so that the blood would come out, and then it would seal over. She heard noises that sounded as though people were throwing furniture around the classroom—rude when they were *already* low on chairs for anyone who wasn't a tiny, older kids were sitting on all sorts of things—and then one last, long sound that wasn't a scream, but a huge whimper. Then nothing. Hot Sauce's gun poked into Nona's thigh.

After a long time in the silence she whispered, "Is it over?"

Hot Sauce didn't answer.

"We should stay here, I guess," said Nona, answering herself: it was always nice to be answered, even if it was just you.

Hot Sauce was so still and quiet that Nona thought she must have fallen asleep. When someone rapped lightly at the generator-room door though, she rolled away from Nona with her hand at her waistband, and it wasn't until the Angel's voice said, "Nona? Hot Sauce?" that she took her hand away.

Nona stood as the door opened, and there was the Angel. It was too hard to see clearly in the dimness of the room, but she didn't seem any worse for wear, not limping or anything. Noodle followed on her heels, still cringing a little bit, but he headed straight to Nona and Hot Sauce when he saw they were lying down: Noodle loved it when people were lying down. He sniffed Nona around the mouth and licked her until she said, "Eugh," and she had to sit up in a hurry.

The Angel said, very gently, "We need to leave now."

Nona said, "How is Cam?" Feeling this was unfair, she added hastily, "And—Pash?"

"They're fine. Cuts and scrapes."

"Whew!" said Nona. "Is the classroom munted?"

"Well, the windows are going to have to be replaced and the blinds are busted," said the Angel evasively, "and I think someone fell on the bean experiment, and Noodle did a wee in the staffroom, but really—it could be worse. The juniors will have to add *got smushed* to their bean experiment variables, there's no coming back from that one."

Nona was sorry for the bean experiment. The Angel said, "Did Pash hurt you when she bundled you in here, Hot Sauce? She can be—a bit aggie," but Hot Sauce said tonelessly, "I'm fine," and "Let's go."

Nona was more than happy to follow this edict. She and Hot Sauce held hands all the way down the corridor. She thought Hot Sauce looked at her a little strangely, but after everything they had been through that didn't really strike Nona as odd. As they came to the lighter part of the corridor—as they entered the square of light the doorway opened on to, on to the classroom, Hot Sauce detached her hand from Nona's altogether.

The classroom was much more of a mess than the Angel had let on. Nona barely noticed the wreck of the bean experiment. Pash was nowhere to be found and Cam was dragging bodies out to the cloakroom—human bodies, real bodies—and Nona's eyes followed a pair of boots disappearing at Cam's feet, in awful fascination. She stared unseeing until suddenly Cam was back in the classroom and said sharply, "Nona, come here."

Nona couldn't, for a moment. There were more boots behind Cam in the cloakroom. Wind scoured through a big hole in the window where the edges of the glass were strung with red globs and gobbets, a hot and drying wind that made Nona's eyes wrinkle up. She stared in wonderment at what remained of a display on the wall she had helped staple together: a big impressive art and writing collection about People in Our Community, with most of the People in Our Community riddled with holes. Otherwise everything was quite clean, though the Angel was right about the beans. There wasn't really much blood, certainly compared to the stuff Nona and Cam had left on the floor themselves. The spell was broken when Cam lifted her chin with one hand, so that she was forced to stare at Cam's grave grey eyes, at the drying blood and the holes in her top. Camilla was wet with sweat. Nona buried her face in Cam's chest. She listened to Cam's heart thudding in her ribcage, the big soft *da-DUMP . . . da-DUMP,* and she was amazed at how fragile and silly a heart was, how poorly protected. Camilla let her stay there for quite a long time, until she extracted herself.

Nona said, "Are they all . . . ?"

"Nearly," said Cam.

Hot Sauce stood in the middle of the classroom. She was standing where Nona had been shot. The sun had moved and the blood was now in shadow. Hot Sauce squatted on her haunches to touch it, then she stood up, and she looked at Nona—more particularly, the side of Nona's head. Nona reached up past a braid and found it was stiff with blood.

"I didn't make it up," Hot Sauce said, and her voice sounded wrong.

Nona felt uncomfortable. "I didn't—I didn't *quite* lie to you, Hot Sauce," she said.

"There was a hole in your head," said Hot Sauce.

Pash came back from the cloakroom. She was sweaty too, and there was a red line of grime where her hard-shell mask had rubbed her face. She said, "Driver's down. The unit's wiped."

The Angel said, "Oh, God, Pash, was that really necessary?"

Both Cam and Pash said, "Yes," at the same time, and then looked at each other. Nona would have found that funny except that Hot Sauce was still looking. She broke away from Cam to take a step toward her, and then—*Hot Sauce took a step back.*

Nona felt wild and sparkling, electrocuted with despair. She said, and found her voice quite tight and funny, "Hot Sauce?"

"I saw you die," said Hot Sauce.

"But I'm not—you *see* I'm not."

The Angel said, "Hot Sauce, I think you need to come with me," but Nona had crossed over to Hot Sauce, caught her hand before she could run away again—pressed it to her chest, so that Hot Sauce might feel Nona's own *ba-DUMP, ba-DUMP* just like she had felt Camilla's. She cried out, "You feel? Feel it, feel my heart going."

Hot Sauce seemed to feel it. She stared at Nona's chest. She moved her hand up next to Nona's neck, quite professionally, like a doctor might, to feel the pulse there. Nona willed everything into that pulse—willed away the cold, dead expression in Hot Sauce's eyes; willed away the shiver at Hot Sauce's mouth.

"You *are* alive," Hot Sauce agreed slowly. "But you were dead. I saw it. Some of your brains came out."

"Yuck. I didn't know," said Nona, deeply embarrassed.

The Angel said, "Hot Sauce, I think you should come here and talk to me for a while."

"Shut up," said Hot Sauce, and Nona was outraged, Nona was amazed: that Hot Sauce should talk to her deity—the reason for her existence—talk to the *Angel* that way. Before she could get any more shocked though, Hot Sauce raised her other hand, and the gun with it.

She pressed the muzzle up against one of Nona's temples. Nona dragged her eyes up to Hot Sauce's face, stunned.

"You're out of the gang," said Hot Sauce, and squeezed the trigger.

JOHN 5:1

IN THE DREAM he took his time approaching the concrete building. He seemed afraid to. When night fell he scrabbled around and found a canister full of petrol, smelling hard and strong, and he sloshed it all around the car, and he lit it on fire. She didn't like the smell. They sat away from it. At this altitude the wind kept whipping hard into the flames, licking them redly higher, sending sparks with every blast of air.

And she did not ask him, but he said: In the end we got patted on the shoulder and they expected us to be happy. They said, you won't have to go to jail—just keep behaving and no more cow stunts, please. Also, I have chronic sinusitis, can you do something about that?

He said, All the powerful friends we'd made, all those people said I would've been a good thing if they'd had time to present us the right way, that we were something mystical and wonderful but they were too busy for miracles, that if we'd behaved better or been more attractive—I don't even fucking know anymore—then they'd have listened. And, like, at some point, you stop wanting people to *listen*, you want people to *do*.

He said, We got together one night in the kitchen. And, like, it was beef again, so we felt bad, man, but at least none of us was vegan. The meat couldn't go off, because I was there. There was a lot of it, but we had a lot of people who needed a feed. We sat there with the window cracked so G— could hear us while he manned the barbie, which in the dark gets unwholesome as hell, and we ate off paper plates, and I told them . . .

I told them, This is it. We were put here to save the planet. We're going to save the planet. We're not going to let them run away. We're going to fix this.

And they were all, Yeah, John, because they were my friends and they loved me. But because they were also dicks and most of them had multiple tertiary degrees, they were also like, How though. We know you can do X and Y and Z. That's still not A or B or C. We love the bone magic, but how are you going to pull this off?

And it was P— of all people who said, *First things first. If they're going to let us fix the world, you've got to make them take us seriously. Get some leverage. If they want to make you into a bad wizard, be a bad wizard. We can write the history books to say you were a good wizard. Or at least an okay wizard. They're not going to listen because we talk nicely, they're going to listen because we scare the shit out of them.*

He said, Which just goes to show that only getting to NCEA Level 2 isn't going to stop you making waves in life, right. You can still eat steak, talk to wizards, and take down the government.

She did not say anything. In the end he wasn't really talking *to* her. He was talking *at* her. All she had to do was wait for him to say: Then we got an opportunity.

He said, Soon after that we got visited by a big black car with a bunch of suits in it. We didn't want to, but they had a chat with us over the phone to promise they only wanted to talk, they were representing someone else. I was more confident by then that I could handle anyone coming to ambush us—I had Titania and Ulysses with me all the time too—but they really did want to talk. They were very vague about who they were with, but the upshot was that their organisation was having a bad time because their leader had recently been indisposed and that was going to make them have a *worse* time pretty soon. When we pushed on how indisposed, they admitted he was dead. And I was all, I cannot help you there, that's beyond me right now. And they were all, No, no, what we want is for him to *not look dead*. We can do the rest. In fact, we prefer it this way. Could you give him a permanent pulse? Could you make it so he bleeds if he gets hurt? Could you fix any current degradation to his corpse? Could he talk, if we wanted him to?

I thought it was an interesting project. I was all, Probably, let me work on it. I'm going to have to do some long-range tweaking. If you want him to speak you'd need me on call, this couldn't be a one-off. I kept trying to push to find out who the hell they were and who this guy was, but they were immovable. They were all, Here's what we'd pay up-front. Here is what we would pay every month you kept him looking alive.

He said, And that figure had *a lot of zeroes.*

I was all, Let me think about it. After a few weeks I proved I could do it. It wasn't hard. Biggest problem was getting the blood to heat up inside the body so the corpse wouldn't spurt stuff well below human temp. I said they could fix him up with a heated jacket, but they were anal about it. To make him talk, they had to deepfake a voice box and have someone speak through it or give it a simple AI, and call me for complicated speeches. Then we set a time and a date for them to fly me offshore—me and A— and M— and G—, everyone else staying at home—to do the job, and to get the payment. They got me a Sino-Swiss bank account under an alias so I could move the cash. I had phone calls from the bankers setting it up. And we were all pretty excited about this because, hell, couldn't we start bankrolling the cryo project again? Wasn't this funding money?

He said, I was all set to fly out when we got another update about the FTL project. They'd got every commitment we'd struggled to get or were in the process of begging for, all of a sudden. IAF had said yes. Pan-Euro had said yes. They'd tendered the plan for the first and second and third waves to fly everyone off the planet, and it was going to take five and a half years max, and that was with leaving people behind to shut everything down before the final wave. No mess, no fuss. They'd stolen a lot of our wording but, like, that was just one last kick in the ass, we barely felt it. And the reason it was going through was that it was *charitable.* They said they were funding the bulk of it. It was their money taking these soon-to-be-impoverished trillionaires into space. The guys who'd been so tight with us that their arseholes squeaked when they walked.

M— and A— kicked off again, all, *This is horseshit, this is lies. What ships are they using? Who's engineering this and where?* Our contacts were all, *Ooh, we've seen photos, our people toured the yards, it's fine, it's all according to plan.* I couldn't believe how naive they were being. I couldn't believe they were falling so hard for this corporate smoke show when there'd been so many checks and balances and hemming and hawing over *us.* C— tried to say, *Yes, but that was a different time, things are very scary now, if you were launching the cryo project right at this minute you'd probably find it a lot easier,* but that didn't make any of us feel better. It was A—'s little brother who said, *Well, you have to understand money is one big shared hallucination, but I'm not sure they could have hallucinated this much, none of this is even in crypto.* We were sure it was a con. Not even a pipe dream, but a con.

He said, But nobody listened to us. Nobody investigated the things we told them to investigate. Everyone showed us what looked like evidence to them, and when we argued back they reminded us that cows had best friends and complex social relationships. M— and A— were a united front, and that was scary as fuck. It was always frightening when they stood together. Both of them were pretty quiet when we ended up taking the helicopter out together, us three, landing on a random oil rig to do what we were going to get paid to do. I asked to see the body before anyone passed any money off to anyone. Sixth sense, I guess.

He said, They let me in to see the body, and I realised who I was dealing with and how big this was. Because I wasn't dealing with a group. I was dealing with a fucking nation. I was dealing with a huge political conspiracy. A— and M— looked at it, and looked at me, and they said, *Do it.*

So I did it. I fixed up the corpse, all the ice damage from storage, all the trauma of the body trying to eat itself after death. Did the blood transfusion manually, to rehydrate what was there and get it going. Made sure the body was working mechanically, unstiffened all the muscles. Rejigged the heart. Did the little tricks I'd thought of, got the eyes to blink by themselves, helped them install the throat speaker and helped with the mouth. I was feeling pretty sick about it by that point. I'd had no idea the guy was even dead. I mean, that was the point, nobody did. But I didn't feel like a hero. Then again, what could I do? They kept saying that this was for a year max, nobody could afford this much political instability right now, we were in the middle of an extinction event.

He said, So I had him sitting up and walking around and moving and we even tested him making a video call home. All fine. It worked great.

But I was like, You'll still need me for big public appearances, I can do it long-range. And they were all, We've budgeted for that. And that was when A— and M— stepped in to negotiate. They said they didn't want the payment in pure cash. They said I wanted something more material. And we went around and around and fucking around. At one point I thought they'd open fire on all of us because they were being so fucking stroppy. They were hitting the table like in a police drama, like, *We can end this whenever we want! The ball's in our court! We know how much this means to you now!* I was all, *Wow, sorry guys, I don't really know either of these two, they're very unexpected and mean. I came here to have a good time and I think they're being very harsh.* I think between Bad Cop, Worse Cop, and Sorry Cop, they got so sick of us that they told us, *Fine, we'll arrange it here and now.*

He said, That's how I ended up going home with a couple billion dollars and a suitcase nuke.

19

WHEN NONA GOT HER sight back she was lying on a bed made of three chairs pushed together. Her sight and her sound and her smell came back all at once, but her memories stayed weirdly distant, like they were shuffling their feet behind a doorway, waiting to announce a surprise party. She did not know the room. She was staring up at a particle-board roof with holes in it and a long flickering bar light, and she was lying in the awkward, rucked-up way one always has to lie on a makeshift bed.

That didn't matter. She had been put to sleep on makeshift beds plenty of times by plenty of people. What *mattered* was that her ankles had been haphazardly bound to one of the struts on the chair's frame, and one of her hands had been tied to the bit of the chair that was closest to her head. The other hand had been chained to the radiator with the type of plastic-sheathed chain that people put around their bicycles when they wanted the bicycle thief to really have to work for it. She had seen that type of chain in the city, usually in two pieces from where it had been cut with pliers.

Abruptly, Nona threw her third tantrum.

Nona had thrown exactly two tantrums in her entire life. She couldn't remember anything about the first one, but Pyrrha had told her about it. Pyrrha had been laughing with her mouth, but not with her eyes: her eyes had been very brown and distant and uneasy, as though this tantrum had reminded Pyrrha of something her brain didn't want to bring back. Everyone could remember her second tantrum. That was when it had been impressed upon her to keep

275

her temper, and it was the reason Palamedes and Camilla always let her go to the ocean even though it was the most dangerous thing she could ever possibly want, both for their anonymity and just in general. The ocean made her stop being angry, and had a prolonged effect, so that a weekly dip meant that she was never worse than a little whingy. But at that moment everything that had happened— Pyrrha—the Angel—Hot Sauce—calmly wiped out long and careful weeks of Palamedes and Camilla dipping her in the ocean.

Nona arched her back right up off the chair and let out a long, bellowing scream, one that went on for ever and ever and ever until her throat broke and healed and broke again and she was screaming blood as well as sound. This was her warning to everyone else. After she had done that, she gave in to the simplicity of anger. She tugged and tugged and tugged on the arm chained through the radiator until it should have hurt, but as always happened, she was beyond pain or thought. In fact everything hurt a lot. It hurt in that slippery, frightening way her body used to let her know that she had made a huge mistake, but Nona's anger gave her the power not to listen. Her hand came free of the chain and the radiator. It made a mess. Next she had to get her ankles free of the chair, and that was harder, because everything was wet now. She had to use both hands and both her feet. For long, helpless, frantic moments she thought she was stuck, the way she used to get frightened when Camilla had put a shirt over her head and things went wrong on the way and her head tried to get through the armhole. It was with the same kind of sweating, anxious rearrangement that she got her feet free now. The plastic ties were good, like Corona had said, and they didn't break. But Nona came through them, screaming.

There was nothing in the room but the three chairs, which would probably never be used as chairs again after what she had done, and a dusty laminate table, and the light, and the locked door. Nona would have posted herself under the door if she had to. But the door wasn't actually that strong. She brushed some of the mess and a discarded finger off the seat of one of the chairs and she hit the door with it. The beauty of her anger was not in her strength; Nona's body could never be strong. The beauty was in the fact that she could hit the door over and over, as hard as she possibly could, as many times as she liked. That was a mess too. But she was angry. The door caved in.

The chair's cushion cover had come off, and so had one of the welded arms. The other arm had snapped off earlier. It had been useful when she needed a jaggedy edge to make herself smaller. This second arm had come off longer, and she gripped that one firmly, one hand at the bottom and the other hand atop that one. Even with everything so soggy and slippery, that felt safe. When she finally battered down the last fragments of door she stood with the weapon held before her and faced a tight knot of people in their masks and their combat trousers and their big boots, just like Pash's boots.

The thought of Pash's boots made her mad again. She suddenly hated Pash. If it had not been for Pash, maybe nobody would have got shot. Maybe nobody would have locked Hot Sauce in the generator room. In front of her was a row of shining holes at the ends of raised guns, and for the *fourth* time in a very short period, they shot her. She slipped in a puddle and fell backward into the splintery door wreckage, two bullets in her chest, one in her knee.

Nona got up again and she was madder than ever. She stamped one foot in the splatter, and then another; she brandished the piece of broken cheap metal like a sword, and she screamed so loudly that it was coming out of her nose and her eyes and her brain, and every one of those soldiers took a step backward.

Nona turned and ran. Her feet made *slop, slop, slop* sounds as she fled down the corridor. There were people gathering in front of her, with more guns, people who for all their different masks and goggles and hoods always seemed like the same fake person. Somebody down the corridor shouted, "Disengage! Disengage!" but Nona's scream was louder. One of the soldiers didn't disengage, they shot her again instead. She raised the metal over her head, and she ran at him. They were screaming through their mask. Nona screamed through hers, the mask that was the front of her face.

There was a lot of noise now. Sounds crowded in all at once. It was like being the person in the middle of a traffic island whose job it was to direct all the heavy vehicles. Nona had once thought that seemed like a wonderful job to get to do, but no longer. Even the Edenite had cringed away from her screaming; they had dropped their gun and their gloved hands were clapped over their helmet, over their ears, and she opened her mouth to remember her teeth.

Someone dropped something over her head. It was a hood, and it was tightening at the neck. She reached up to tear it off, but something big and heavy pinned her arms against her body. It was like being swaddled. Nona struggled, but this was a good defence against her, maybe the only defence; Camilla had wrapped her up in a blanket too, the second time. When it all went dark, her body seemed to remember that she had used something up inside her, something enormous, and she started to tremble.

She trembled so hard that she thought she would die then and there, that this was what dying was finally like. Inside the hood she heard her mouth say, savage and distinct and cool despite the trembles: "Fool. You're killing her."

But she was only talking to herself, after all.

JOHN 3:20

IN THE DREAM, nights did not give way to mornings. The light coming through the clouds changed colour, but nothing rose and nothing sank except their chests when they breathed. In the dream she quite often forgot how to breathe, or swallow, and she would choke on her own saliva until the fright passed and the body remembered for her.

In a darkness that could have been sunrise he said, None of us ever wanted to use that nuke. We never thought we would. It felt like a toy. We kept laughing that it came with a manual. I think we were scared of what would happen if we stopped laughing. We pulled up the floor and put a safe beneath the lino and swore we were never going to use it. G— made sure it couldn't be armed, it was never something we were going to blow for real. But it was our leverage—it was a way to force people to listen to us just as much as the money was. Our first method was to keep telling the truth, keep pushing on the FTL story, keep asking hard questions. Our second method was to throw money at it. Our third method was to tell people that we'd got a nuke.

He said, It wasn't as naive as it sounded. Like, yeah, we were very aware that simply having this thing, that's a serious international incident. But we'd been party to this massive secret, right, we had access to one of the biggest political scandals of all time, and we were key helpers on the cover-up. A bomb would at least give *them* pause. It had to. And we were sick of how much time everything was taking. We'd been subjected to so much bureaucracy and so much red tape and so many people refusing to do so many things that we were willing to gamble on being tried at the Hague just to stop the process.

Ready to make a hell of a mess to buy time. Prepared to do anything to keep you going.

C— kept saying, *Pick one. Are we more invested in proving this new plan is bullshit, or in saving you?* I was like, *It's both, how can it not be both.* C— was like, *It can't be both. Pick one and stick to it. Decide what you give a fuck about.*

He said, I found that the problem with being the death man is you stop giving much of a fuck.

Then he said, rubbing circles into one temple with his thumb, I still can't believe they wouldn't give me the time of day *and* they were scared of me. It's not fair. Either you're the evil wizard and everyone wants to know what you think, or you're the good wizard and nobody cares. It wasn't fair. That wasn't how it was meant to work.

In the dream she did not ask him questions. The burnt-out shell of the car was still smouldering. It seemed like the smell was in her clothes, in her hair, in the mud. It was still cold this high up, in the mist, and the cold made the fronts of her arms bumpy, which panicked her until he told her it was natural.

He said, The FTL plan was going steadily by then. More and more nations had given their okay. They were on to arguing over who went in the ships, size and shape, how they could make sure it didn't turn into a colonial exercise on the other side. That's where they met resistance, because the trillionaires were all, *But we've got our hand-picked guys. There's only so much room, they've already undergone training, this isn't a tourist trip.* Nobody liked that. We'd been calling bullshit the whole time, and now we were getting some traction. I said, *Give me a year and I'll see if I can't solve the Tau Ceti question by myself, we've already got plans, I could do a hell of a lot with the cryo cans now if you let me.* Earned some Trans-Tasman support, but then the trillionaires banged the *wanted criminal* drum and put me on the back burner. The bastards said, *Fine, we'll make room for two hundred nominated people*—two hundred! Two measly hundred!— and I was all, *They won't fall for that.*

He said, They fell for it.

He said, Turns out everyone wanted to nominate someone to go on board, especially if they could nominate themselves. The absolute fuckers. Once they got that green light they said the first wave would leave in three months, we have to do this quickly, get the second wave ready before our next round of climate starvation.

He said, We paid people to find their engineering facilities. That was a huge pain in the ass. Like, talk about a group of people who couldn't find somebody to buy weed off of, now out looking for mercenaries. Thankfully P— knew a bunch of army guys who knew ex-army guys, it was all very *Soldier of Fortune*. They got caught pretty much immediately, but I was good at long distance by then, I'd had to practise. I got eyes and ears on the plant that was meant to be the main building site and I immediately saw that it wasn't to spec. The deliveries they were getting weren't even the right stuff to build the ships. They were bringing in random crap to make it look like they were busy. It didn't seem like they had enough people. The superstructures of the new fleet weren't progressing. Best of all would have been to walk into an empty building, but what I saw was immediately suspicious enough for us to be sure it wasn't enough.

He said, So I went to the governments that were still sympathetic, sort of, like ours, and all the Trans-Pacifics, and we threw down our evidence. All, *Take a look at this, this isn't working.* They should've stopped the launch and seized the factories until they could investigate properly. But instead they asked the trillionaires for their point of view. And the trillionaires *lied!* They lied like their lives fucking depended on it! They had a glib answer for every question; I swear someone told them we were on to them beforehand! I mean, our cheapo mercs did get caught. They lied and everyone swallowed their shit. Not only that, they looked at us and were like, *We were going to put you fellas in jail, weren't we? Isn't it time you guys stop being independent actors, aren't you recognised by most nations as a cult? We're all legally appointed officials here, except for the trillionaires. Did you know cows* recognise *one another?*

He said, I got mad.

He said, Back at home I told them, they want to call us a cult, let's be a cult. It only takes a little bit of eyeliner and a couple capes.

N— already had eyeliner and capes. We'd tried to keep everything so clean-cut and scientific, but now we were streaming quicker than they could serve us subpoenas. End of the world is nigh, that kind of thing. Join us. Live forever. Your governments are lying to you. Before, when it started, I'd tried to use all these scientific terms—tried to coin *phthinergy*, talk about a word that needed an antihistamine. I'd tried to make out like everything I was doing had principles I was probably going to write papers on later. I dropped all that, because turns out nobody wants papers, nobody wants principles. They want the magic bullet. They just want to be saved.

He said, I told them I'd save them. And I said, *I'm a necromancer.*

DAY FIVE

Crown Plays Her Part—the Saint
of Duty—Palamedes Comes Clean—
the Saddest Girl in the Whole Entire
World—Nona Watches a Duel—
the Convoy—Paul Gets Born—
One Last Trip—Twenty-Four Hours
Until the Tomb Opens.

2o̅

WAKING UP, NONA DIDN'T know how much of the day and night had been part of her dream. Nona got the disorienting sense that nearly all of it had been imagined, and she was only now starting her day, and she would soon be telling Cam everything in front of the recorder and persuading her out of breakfast.

She woke up lying flat on her back with something warm draped over her, and the familiar cheap-soap-and-leather smell of Camilla tickling her nose. One of Cam's jackets had been rolled up and put under her head on top of her pillow. For a happy moment, Nona thought she was home. But the floor underneath Nona was scrubby carpet, not tile, and the walls were unfamiliar. She rolled onto her side. Her vision swam horribly, and she found with a start that she was going to be sick.

Nona started dry-heaving pitifully, and there was Cam with the wastebasket, pulling her hair back, saying gently, "There you go, don't force it"—so it wasn't Cam. Nona tried to be as sick as she could be, which took a while and a lot of effort. Afterward she felt better, but as though she had run up and down the street outside the Building five times in quick succession. And her whole body hurt.

"Oh," gasped Nona, and she flopped back on the makeshift bed and shakily wiped her mouth with her arm. She was in a darkened room, right next to a long table with chairs. As she hadn't seen it from this angle before, it took her a little while to recognise the meeting room in the Blood of Eden facility, same one as last time. The portrait of the redhead with the cruel eyes stared down at her from her thicket of dried-up flowers, as though contemptuous that Nona had had the bad manners to throw up in front of her. Her vision shimmered. She had to lay her head back again. Palamedes was looking at the contents of the wastebasket with a troubled expression, which was gross as well as worrying, and she knew the jig was up.

She whispered, "Are we alone?"

"Yes—but we won't be for long. Nona, I need to make sure you're all right."

"Did the bullet come out my head?"

"No—I had to take it out, it got stuck."

She was nearly too afraid to ask. "Hot Sauce—"

"Hot Sauce wanted to leave," said Palamedes, "and—well, we let her leave, Nona."

Nona's heart felt that the bullet had got stuck *there* instead. Palamedes continued, "Blood of Eden brought us here to see We Suffer, which is fine, and I worked on you—under supervision. Most of Ctesiphon Wing saw the bullet in your head . . . and of course, nobody knew before how quickly you regenerate, because we hadn't told them. So they shackled Cam and me, then locked you up."

"Which made me mad."

"Which made you mad."

Nona said tentatively, "I made a big mess, didn't I," and Palamedes said briskly— "They should have bloody guessed. Every mistake they've made with us stemmed from a complete lack of trust—a cowardice and an unwillingness to let us in on the game. And now that I know what I know . . . or *think* I know . . . But, Nona, what's more important is that I make sure everything in your body works, because if you'd been a normal human being we would be planning your funeral."

"Don't bother," said Nona, affrighted. "It only made me angry— which I think was a pity," she added, belatedly.

"Yes," said Palamedes, distantly. "It was a pity. But, Nona . . . Nona, about that broadcast. You saw it, didn't you? All of it? And you didn't—recognise anyone you saw?"

The jig was finally up.

"Only the girl from my dream," said Nona.

Palamedes breathed in through Camilla's nose, then out through Camilla's mouth.

"You didn't tell me that."

"You didn't ask," said Nona.

"Nona," said Palamedes very, *very* slowly, "that was very important information—information that changes everything—the type of information we have schooled you for the last six months to tell us, instantly, and the type of information Camilla and I personally trusted you to prioritise."

This was too much to bear.

"I've had things to think about," Nona wailed. "I didn't want to get in trouble."

"Have Cam and I *ever* gotten you in trouble?"

"No, and I didn't want to ruin that, Honesty always gets in trouble and it's terrible," said Nona. "And it's not *fair* trying to talk calmly and sadly about my responsibilities when I *know* you're thinking, 'Nona, I want to beat you up with the broom handle.' Just *say*, 'Nona, I want to beat you up with the broom handle.'"

"I'd never use the broom handle on you," said Palamedes.

Nona was mollified.

"You wouldn't feel it. If Cam and I didn't love you as much as we do," said Palamedes, "we would take turns throttling you, then give all your magazines to charity."

Palamedes had never said the word *love* before. More than anything—even the idea of her beloved magazines going to charity, as though others were more deserving than Nona, the most deserving person on the planet—this broke her.

"Don't interrupt me. I've got to tell you something and I have to tell you *really quickly*," said Nona, only she choked on the rough stuff in the back of her throat, and she said— "You know how I've been sick lately?"

"Yes," said Palamedes.

"Well, I *thought* I was only going to be sick for not much longer, maybe a few weeks or a month," said Nona, trying to organise her thoughts. She licked her lips and whispered up to the ceiling: "But now I think I only have a few days. Oh, thank goodness, I said it. Wow, that's a relief."

Palamedes went silent. Then he said: "A few days of *what*?"

"Oh—living," said Nona, too relieved at having said it to feel stupid. "It's nearly over, Palamedes. I'm dying. I've been dying for months."

Then Palamedes touched her, and he did not throttle her. He ran Cam's soft, chapped hand all over her head. He touched her ribs and her belly and he pulled off her shoes and touched the soles of her feet. Then he got up and he pulled open a drawer on the desk and he came back with, of all things, a fat black marker. He said, "Nona, put your hands on your hips and put your ankles together, I need a closed circuit."

She put her hands on her hips and joined her ankles. Palamedes lightly sketched something just beneath the hollow of her throat, saying, "Keep still now," when she laughed, being ticklish. The pen made a lot of little light, feathery *fwip—fwip—fwip*s on her, and then Palamedes laid it down and said: "Here goes nothing."

And nothing was what happened as Palamedes hovered Camilla's hand over Nona's face—her throat, down the line of her abdomen—except that his fingers were wreathed in fine blue flames, completely smokeless and heatless. They cast terrifying lights in the room even though they didn't flicker, staying nearly perfectly still. There was nothing more than a slight tingling feeling as he made it all the way down to her feet and back, and then he clutched Camilla's fist closed, and she looked at him and saw that he was bewildered.

"God save me from Lyctoral masking," he said, exasperated. "Cytherea the First must have enjoyed those games she played with me . . . Hang on."

Now he poked and prodded her: her heart, her belly, the tops of her thighs, the place at her temple where the bullet had gone in. When she flinched, Palamedes said gently, "Sorry. Give me a moment," and she gave him a moment, and then after a long time he said— "You're shedding thalergy like chaff in the wind. What's going on? It's almost like a starvation reaction, but Cam and I *know* you're eating."

"Not very much," admitted Nona, but Palamedes said, "Not so little that your framework should have gone into thalergy metabolism. You're eating your own reserves. You've got the level of retention I'd usually only see in palliative care. Nona—your soul's trying to leave your body."

Nona puzzled over this a little.

"But I *like* my body."

"It doesn't matter about *liking*," said Palamedes. "What's happening to you is why I can't be in Camilla's body for more than a handful of minutes, Nona. If I stay too long I start trying to make inroads on her soul—I start trying to bed down and put up new wallpaper and displace Camilla, for all that we've tried to make sure that doesn't happen. At the same time, Cam's body tries to reject *my* soul, like when you try to blink dust out of your eye. But your body would never try to reject its own soul . . . unless it didn't recognise it. Unless your soul was a stranger's . . . or a melange. Is that the gestalt theory busted—or confirmed? Is that how we explain the rapid healing?"

He was talking much more to himself now. How could she explain?

"But you see, Palamedes, I don't mind dying," said Nona, trying to make him understand. "I've been doing it for ages. I'm not scared."

This explanation died on impact. Palamedes said with a voice like concrete: "I will not be party to this again."

Nona was a little bit afraid of that voice.

"I'm sorry, Palamedes."

"No. Don't be. It's simply—Nona, we can't let your body die," he said. "For one thing, it's the body of someone I owe a favour to, and I'd rather like to see the look on her face when I present it back to her . . . And if we lose the body, whither goes the soul? Let's say you *are* the other soul . . . And let's say I lose you. *You* die; *she* wakes up. The final kick in the pants in what I gather was a life long on kicks and short on very much else. And yet if I don't preserve *her* . . . Ninth, really, I *sincerely* did not want to have to look after your bedamned water bottle."

Nona struggled to sit up. She was wet and itchy with sweat and the ink where the marker had touched her neck—she rubbed it before she could remember not to, and her hand came back smudged with black.

"Palamedes," she said, "do you think you know who I am?"

"I've got a theory," began Palamedes.

"Crown said *she* knew who I was," said Nona.

"Crown says a lot of things. Theories are all we have."

"Well, tell me your theories," Nona demanded, feeling much better from sheer excitement. "Say them out loud. Am I nice? Am I good-looking? Do I have lots of friends? Does everyone listen to me? How many legs do I have?"

Palamedes untucked Camilla's legs from underneath him and sat knees-up, feet flat on the floor, and he held Nona's hand. He looked at her with those keen, earnest brown-grey eyes, the softest and nicest of greys and browns, like sheeny earthenware cups.

"Nona, we never wanted to lead you."

Nona said, "Does it matter anymore?"

"I don't know, which frightens me," said Palamedes.

This was hardly to be borne, not after she had waited such a long time and in such circumstances. She said, "Palamedes, *please*. Tell me something, one titchy little thing, the smallest and tiniest thing. I've wanted to know so badly. Maybe I'm dying of . . . curiosity."

"Not funny," said Palamedes.

"Please," said Nona.

In the end he said, "All I know is this, Nona: if you're one of two people, current evidence suggests you're *not* just the first person, the one who owns your body."

Nona thought back to mathematics.

"But that means I'm the second person."

"Or—not *solely* the first person."

This was hard to get her head around.

"Can one person even *be* two people? I feel like I've only got enough room inside for me, and sometimes like that room's not even enough."

"Lyctors can," said Palamedes, "or at least—they *thought* they could; in fact all they became were half-dead cannibals. I think a true Lyctorhood is a mutual death . . . a gravitational singularity creating something new. A true Grand Lysis, rather than the Petty Lysis of the megatheorem . . . Oh, God, Nona, I'm rambling, I'm very sorry. I hate it when I'm like this."

Nona moved over to give him a hug. She hugged him like Camilla would have, the one thing she was truly good at, and he fell into it immediately. He put his head on her shoulder and breathed in deep through his nose.

"Do you remember the girl on the broadcast?" he asked. "The one who *wasn't* a startlingly handsome and very obviously dead person with fashion hair?"

"The redhead." That one was easy.

"That's the other body you might come from," said Palamedes. "Her real name is Gideon Nav, and we need to get you to that body, if we can. Spiritual gravity will do the rest."

This was horrifying.

"But I don't want to be *redheaded*," said Nona. "I do *not* think of myself as redheaded. And I don't want to be a necromancer. Or a prince. Palamedes," she said, "am I—am I a zombie?"

Palamedes took her by the shoulders and looked at her.

"You were born in the Nine Houses, Nona," he said. "So was I, and Camilla, and Pyrrha. We're all zombies, as people here would understand them. I was born with aptitude, so I'm a true zombie, a wizard. Camilla and Pyrrha—who weren't—would be what they call *minions*."

This hurt her feelings.

"No wonder Hot Sauce kicked me out of the gang," she said, and her eyes numbed with tears again.

"Hot Sauce is a very young woman who has been living on her nerves for so long that I imagine she doesn't have anything else," said Palamedes briskly. "She'll regret what she did at some point."

Nona's lip wobbled and she had to keep swallowing hard. Palamedes carefully sat himself back down and grimaced, and she looked at his shackle for the first time: it was a big black cuff with an electronic red light that blinked off and on as she watched. He said, "It's an explosive shackle. After We Suffer saw Camilla and me pull the bullet from your head . . . I couldn't *not* work on you . . . she has come to her own conclusions, and whatever conclusions Crown wanted to give her. They've been very busy since we came back, so they wanted us to stay where they put us."

Nona was incensed. "I *hate* it. I *hate* being locked up."

"So did Gideon, I gather."

Then Palamedes looked very serious, and his face moved as though he were about to say something when there was a knock at the meeting-room door. He said quickly, "Tell Cam she and I need to talk as soon as humanly possible. I will get back to you—you're not going to die on our watch. I haven't been able to save many people in my life, I'm afraid, but I am intent on saving you."

Nona did not want to lie to Palamedes, which was why she was grateful that the eyes whitened to that clear glassy grey that meant Camilla, blinking hard a few times to get her bearings. The door knocked again and Nona said automatically, "Come in."

The door opened, and someone walked in; an elegant middle-aged person with shadowy eyes. They were wearing no mask and no goggles and no hood, and their hair was pinned up in a neat roll atop their head and wrapped in a brief scarf with a blue stripe pattern. They carried a little suitcase in one hand and two bottles of water cunningly gripped in the other, and they crossed to sit in the seat We Suffer usually sat in, and got comfortable taking things out of the little suitcase—paper, clipboards, electronic equipment, pens. When they tilted their head quizzically at Nona, she realised with a start that it *was* We Suffer—We Suffer with no mask and a naked face, for the first time that Nona had ever seen her.

"Do I surprise you, Nona?" she asked, quite nicely. "We are beyond the cell disguises now, are we not? They are useful, but only to a point. I do not think you are capable of being tortured for my face."

"Why was I tied up?" demanded Nona. "Why did you cuff Camilla? Why did you shoot us? Where's the Angel? Have you found Pyrrha?"

"A comedy of errors. I apologise," said We Suffer. Nona noticed that the light on Suffer's hair made it quite a nice chestnut colour, like rich mouse. She was probably quite a bit older than Pyrrha, with strongly marked features and an aristocratic, slightly hooked nose, and her face was marked with lines that showed even beneath a light layer of powder and makeup. If Nona had been in less of a woozy mood she might have thought her pretty, but nothing was pretty at that moment.

We Suffer added, "I understand the bonds may seem unfair. But please keep in mind that you gave to my people a very great shock, and since you were the scariest thing I have nearly ever seen in all my days, that should not come as a big surprise."

Nona was doubtful. "I suppose I'm sorry," she said, "only I don't think you're sorry for locking up me and Camilla."

"Do not bother with *sorry*. We are also impressed, in our own way. I mean, now most people will not agree to be in the same room as you. That is fine. We do not need them. Hect, as I told you last night, this has not been all for naught . . . Pash has admitted to having recently liquidated a big unit of Merv Wing. That is fine. Unjust Hope has not made a huge deal out of it. That was always his way, despite the losses. He will want to keep this quiet for a while . . . Usually you both meeting up with the Messenger, whom you call *the Angel*, would have been very bad, but I think we may actually survive it. They were unharmed by the experience. I do not think we need to register Pash discharging a weapon in front of them *quite* yet, though when we do we may all be hauled in front of a firing squad . . . We are riding the wave. Let us see where it takes us. And whatever the case, Nona, you were impressive . . . Blood of Eden is quite impressed by blood and guts."

Most of this went over Nona's head.

"You're not answering my questions at all," she said fretfully. "Who *is* the Angel, I mean, the Messenger?"

"That is above your pay grade," said We Suffer.

"You don't pay us," said Camilla.

"Yes. My little joke," explained We Suffer. "All you need to know is that they are the one with the little arboreal dog who is elderly. That is enough to know."

Nona said, "Is the Angel—important?"

"The Angel is Blood of Eden," said We Suffer, but did not elaborate with anything other than, "In hindsight, not a good idea to keep the Angel anywhere near the place we were keeping you, even in the same city. The problem with putting all of your eggs in one basket is there is such a mess when somebody sits on that basket. But how could we know any of this would happen? In any case, we are back. They have placed me in charge of the next move, and Unjust Hope has been bumped to the very backmost seat . . . for now."

Camilla said, "Which means what?"

"Which means I need you, Hect," said We Suffer.

"Then take this shackle off my damn leg."

"As soon as I can. They would not let me put you two in the same room without it," said We Suffer. "They are impressed by her, as I said, but also very frightened. The Houses sent a Lyctor to negotiate, and then there *you* both are in the limelight, one of you able to shrug off a bullet to the brain and the other fully capable of necromancy. A necromancy I knew not of! If you had told me, Hect, I would have been able to spin it. If you had let me know, we could have thought of something together."

Camilla said, "You can't control your own people?"

"I cannot ask them to tolerate the intolerable," said We Suffer. "I am not a tyrant. I exercise much control you are not seeing. For instance, this affair of yours and Nona's . . . it has not yet made it to other cells, and the rest of Ctesiphon will not tell them, not yet. Today this is a family affair, and our hopes and attentions rest on another."

Before Nona could even conceive of looking at Camilla's leg and getting angry again, Camilla gave her the *cool it* expression, and the desk in front of We Suffer beeped urgently. She glanced at a little flip-top electronic screen in front of her, and she said: "Nine in the morning. She is in place. This is confirmed."

Nine? How long had Nona slept? How little had Cam slept? When she looked at Camilla's face, she saw that her expression had hardened like the quick-set concrete at Pyrrha's work.

"This is your last chance," said Camilla tonelessly. "Pull her out."

"This is the only move we find it possible to make, and as a move it is sensitive to time," said We Suffer. "She volunteered. We need someone on the inside. Without understanding, we can make no move on that barracks, nor find the way forward. She is, perhaps, the only person for whom this would not be a suicide mission. She said it herself."

"You should've asked *why* she said that," said Camilla. "I could've gone in. I'm a citizen of the Nine Houses."

"After the last eight hours? Not one chance. In your own way, you too are too important to lose here," said We Suffer. "I need you to hear this as it happens. I need you to translate the nuances. And she needs you to be here for her plan to work, though she said she would do it alone. She said she was expendable, and that you were not. We agreed with this."

"You've been played," said Camilla.

Nona's legs felt weak. She slithered into the chair, and We Suffer quite nicely rolled one of the bottles of water in her direction. She caught it awkwardly, and it was nice to feel how cool the plastic was between her hands. She pressed it to her cheeks and her forehead briefly. She was still sweating.

Camilla said, "Listen to me. Pull her out. She can't do this."

"Lieutenant Crown knows what she is doing," said We Suffer calmly, though Nona would not have been so calm with Camilla making the face she was currently making. It was like the time Pyrrha had let Nona smoke a cigarette and Nona had accidentally eaten half. "I have also told *you*, many times. This is the swings and the roundabouts. A concurrent vote was called yesterday to set off bombs below the barracks and hope Ianthe Naberius did not live through it. There is a sense that we must play the aggressor. Blood of Eden has perfected the defensive game, never moving forward, perpetually shifting to our back foot. We owe Wake too much to keep playing that game. Crown understood. I think she plays to win . . . and we now know we have more to win than ever."

Camilla crossed to the table, chain clinking. She adopted a posture that Nona had seen often: arms crossed over each other, head tilted a little in what Nona always thought of as the fly-upward expression. It was a Palamedes posture, and for a moment Nona thought it was Palamedes, but it wasn't. It was Camilla trying to *be* Palamedes.

"Listen to me," she said. Every word was like a rock dropped into a tide pool. "This is a trap. It won't get you intel. It won't get you what you're calling the key. You walk her in there alone, she won't walk out. She's giving in, not fighting."

This was a lot for Camilla to say. Even We Suffer paused and furrowed her brow, and she said, "I cannot believe this girl would kill her own twin sister."

"*Kill* her?" said Camilla.

The little electronic device beeped again. We Suffer tapped a button, and the speakers at the sides of the room made awful noises briefly. We Suffer held a hand up to Camilla in the universal *shh* gesture, and picked up a receiver: "Transmitting. Ready Mu in position. I want snipers ready in case anything goes wrong. Headshots are preferred. Cover Troia if at all possible, but we have been told to take the shot no matter what."

"Get her out," repeated Camilla, and for the first time, there was a raw edge of desperation to her voice. "Corona can't lie to her."

We Suffer looked at her. For a moment Nona thought she would really do it. Without the goggles and mask, it was so much easier to translate her. She had a trick of keeping her eyes perfectly even—pretty brown-green eyes with a touch of evenly applied black stuff on the lashes, very glamorous to Nona—but you had to watch the mouth. The hesitation showed in the thinning of the lips, just briefly.

Then it passed. We Suffer pressed a button and said briskly, "Eyes on the area. Are the crowds being held back? Keep the militia on the showboaters. I do not want any stray bullets catching the car or anyone coming out of the building . . . Yes . . . No, we'll keep her to audio, the system cannot stand the strain . . . Yes. You have your orders."

Camilla clinked back against the wall. Her eyes closed and she tilted her head downward so that her fringe, which really needed a trim by now, fell over her eyebrows. Then We Suffer put the receiver down and twiddled a button, and the audio leapt in the speakers. Nona unscrewed the top of the cap of the bottle of water and took a long pull from it, which rinsed away the sour acid taste on her tongue.

She nearly jumped out of her skin when the audio, exaggeratedly loud, suddenly tuned in to traffic, a car insistently honking so that people let it through. The audio crackled. Someone was breathing, hard, a little too fast. The engine sounded like you were standing right inside it. But you could hear everything, you could even hear hands sliding over the car wheel. People were yelling outside the car. There was the noise of a big metallic bump, and then Crown's voice, indignant, barely a mutter: "Stop *throwing* things at me, you jackasses."

Her voice and the breathing sounded weirdly disconnected. But everything sounded huge, and strange for being huge. The car wheels sounded like they were bumping over something, moving to different terrain. Then Crown said, "I'm through," and a cranking sound screeched over the audio as the ignition suddenly died. The car door opened like a bomb going off. Crown's boots clattered on the ground. The yelling sounded far-off now but was still there, like a background radio.

It was interrupted by a distant voice, speaking House— "No step further."

Crown's voice, much more explosive and near on the speakers: "I'm unarmed! I'm unarmed! I am a citizen of the Nine and I ask for sanctuary in the name of the Third House—in the name of the Emperor Undying, please! For the love of God, I'm a sitting sniper target out here!"

There was a moment of absolute silence. Crown's voice went from panicky to tetchy: "My name is Coronabeth Tridentarius, crown princess of Ida, heir to the Third! My mother was Violabeth Tritos, my sister is a Lyctor, and my *brain* is about to get *spattered on the tiles* unless you open this gate and let me drive through!"

There was another clanging. Something opening and shutting. Someone said hoarsely, "Coronabeth Tridentarius has been dead for over a year. Get in your vehicle, turn around, go," but another voice, even feebler, said, "*Look* at her."

Crown, sounding desperate: "My sister is in the Cohort compound. She can positively identify me. Hurry up."

"Look, you understand—"

"I understand, Lieutenant—Lieutenant, right?—and that's why I'm saying *get Ianthe*! Get my sister! She can identify me, or identify my body, whichever you decide! Get me out of this crowd!"

There was another pause. Crown's breath was much softer now, less laboured, less strange. There were clangs and bangs that Nona couldn't parse. She took another swig of water and looked at We Suffer, who had one hand on her flip-top as though it were the trigger of a gun, and then she looked at Camilla. Camilla's eyes were closed and she was shifting weight slowly from foot to foot—one to the other—so gradually that her shackle didn't even clink.

There were far-off shouts on the speakers. More clanging. Voices saying something Nona couldn't hear. Then there was a silence made up of all these background noises—a nonsense of sounds stuck together. Another far-off clangour. Then Crown drew the longest breath that Nona had ever heard anyone draw.

"Corona," called out someone new. Nona had heard that voice once before, on the broadcast.

Footsteps, evolving into running feet. Something hit Crown with a big *thump.* A mess of sounds—clothes rustling, a sobbing, the audio squeaking as it tried to keep up—and Crown, sounding unlike any Crown that Nona had ever heard before, two voices trying to speak at once: "Don't touch me. Don't fucking touch me."

"Shush-a-shush, my darling. Shush. Shhh. Here we are. We're fine. I've got you, love."

"Oh my God, you're so cold. He's so cold."

"He's dead, sweetheart. It's me in here. I'm sorry. I'm so sorry."

"How *could* you? *How could you?*"

"Please touch me. I'll die."

"I love you . . . I love you, I love you, I've missed you so much. Please be real."

"I'm real—we're real . . ."

"Oh, God, Ianthe," said Crown, and her voice changed a little. "This is sick. Look at him. I *hate* you."

"No, you don't. You always say that. Don't cry, honey . . . you can't cry if I can't cry with you. It's not fair. I can't cry at the moment unless I do the tear ducts manually. Look at you . . . more beautiful than ever, even with crappy jewellery and a million split ends. *Studs,* darling? Earrings on a diet?"

Crown was hiccupping, sobbing, laughing all at once: "Don't do that. Don't say what Babs would say."

"You know I always said what Babs would say, except when Babs said what I would. We kept you honest. Come here, my heart's love," said the voice, and Crown's sobs were suddenly muffled, then quieted, then silenced altogether.

After a while, Crown said— "How did you know I was here?"

"I didn't," said the other voice. "I've got people combing three other planets right now trying to find you. I never thought you'd be *here.* God, what a fuckup! He's going to assume I did this on purpose. None of this has been my fault. How did you end up on this miserable rock, darling?"

"It's a long story."

"I've got time. Come on. Let's talk inside . . . no, leave the vehicle, just get inside. I'm not at full bore at the moment, so it's dangerous out here. Come on, hurry up."

The hiccupping was sniffled away, and Crown said urgently: "No. No, I need the car. Ianthe . . . Ianthe, I need your help."

"Anything, but come inside."

"No, wait—"

Another clang. Footsteps. The noise of a car door opening. The other voice that had been so tender did not bother to hide its revulsion as it said: "Oh, you've *got* to be *kidding* me."

"She needs your help," said Crown.

Camilla's head lifted.

"I thought she had exited this ghastly vale of tears," said the other voice, not at all pleased.

"Didn't Harrowhark tell you?"

The voice cooled and hardened like an ice cube.

"Didn't Harrow—*what?* When did *you* talk to Harrow?"

"Just help me get Judith inside. You have to help her. The sedative's going to wear off soon. Ianthe, you're the only one . . . Ianthe, do not look at me like that. If you look at me like that I am walking away. If you want me, you take her too, okay?"

The other voice rose in drawling, disgusted plaintiveness. "Judith *Deuteros?* Judith calendar-for-every-birthday Deuteros? *Really?*"

"It's the blue madness, Ianthe, she can't—"

"Judith Deuteros, who, when we played Marry, Kill, Reanimate, you used to say *reanimate* because nobody would be able to tell the difference? *That* Judith Deuteros?"

We Suffer tapped the flip-top and pressed a button and said tersely: "Check the basement, now. Where is the guard? Who has eyes down there, what is happening?"

On the speakers, Crown was saying, "I can't . . . I can't be the one to let her die. Not when I've let everyone else . . ."

"Oh, God, honey, nip that in the bud. Nobody cares about *Judith Deuteros* . . . Seriously, my plans cannot afford Judith Deuteros. She's going to be absolutely crazy in the coconut until Number Seven leaves, Corona. It's really nicer to kill her. Two-thirds of the barracks necromancers are dead already. There's only a handful left, and I had to put down three of them yesterday who absolutely weren't going to make it, and they looked significantly livelier than *Deuteros.* Stop looking at me like that. Do you like the outfit?"

"No." Crown's voice was chilly. "White makes Babs look peaky."

"Wait till you see me in it."

"I bet."

"I *said,* stop looking at me like that," said the voice languidly. "Come on, Corona, you're pouting, and I'm immune. I am a Lyctor now . . . I have seen, as the poets would put it, some *shit.* I really, really think you ought to let me put her down. I know what you're thinking. You think you can't come home again except as the conquering hero. Well, you're wrong. One, absolutely nobody gave a hot toot about Judith, and two, they made our birthday *a memorial holiday*. Not a 'congratulations on the Lyctorhood, our daughter of the Third' day, a 'Coronabeth Tridentarius, our darling gone too soon' day. Talk about vom. When I heard, I nearly died laughing . . . Have I hurt your feelings already, love? I don't mean to."

Crown's voice was quiet. "Ianthe, please. Please. There's so much I don't understand. About you . . . about what happened . . . about Gideon."

The voice did not sound at all pleased when it said, "So you do remember her name."

"I was on a shuttle with her body for months and months. I want to know what's going on."

"There's a lot to explain."

"Are you going to let me come inside, or are you going to tell me out here?"

The voice said, "That's up to you, darling."

"What do you *mean*?"

"Just because I'm using Babs as a butt puppet does not mean that I'm without resources," said the voice. "I'm a Lyctor. Yes, multiple puppets are a pain . . . I'm hoping the expert is out there somewhere admiring my handiwork . . . but I'm not blind, Corona. My pretty golden girl, roughing it in your jacket . . . and your earrings. I'll give him this, he said earrings or necklace."

Nona watched We Suffer tense. Something else was coming through her earpiece. She said, "Not until we hear the call. No. No. The signal."

Crown whispered, "What the hell are you talking about, Ianthe? You're scaring me."

"You're scaring *me*."

Another sound. From somewhere to Crown's left, there was a low, brief sound like a call, a note that rose until something muffled it. It sounded like the Captain. Crown said, "I don't know what you want from me."

"Only what *you* want from *me*," said the other voice. And: "I'm going to be piqued if you make me be the bad guy here, okay? I am not having the world's most fun at the moment. I can't even hug you with my own arms, touch you with my own body. Only Babs's . . . there's a metaphor in there. In conclusion, I am not self-soothing over here. And studs never suited you and you know it."

"Exactly how much necromancy can you *do*?"

"That's an interesting question," said the voice.

Another long pause. The voice said impatiently: "Nod or shake. Are they listening?"

There was no answer: none that Nona could see. Camilla's head had lifted entirely. We Suffer was saying into the earpiece, "Do *not* line it up."

"I understand," said the voice. "Don't worry, baby. I'm not mad at you. He told me what you were."

Something happened. The speaker crackled, and the second voice got much louder, like they were talking right into the receiver.

"Listen, dregs, to the Saint of Awe," the voice said. "I'm very pleased you handed my sister back to me. That's why I am not currently flattening a planet that, I'll be honest with you, nobody really gives a shit about. I'm changing the terms of the demand, but don't panic. You see, I don't particularly care about Blood of Eden. In fact, I wouldn't mind if you all survived for a few hundred more years. You think we're fighting *you* on Antioch? You think *you're* the main event? Sure, you've made a hell of a mess, but we're already doing cleanup. My eyes are not on you. Do you understand? Go and live another five thousand years. I only want every House asset you've got. I know what you have, and I'll be taking all of it. I want the Sixth House Oversight Body. I want Camilla Hect on my front doorstep. And *most* of all I want Harrowhark Nonagesimus—as intact as you have her at this moment—or the whole planet is forfeit . . . Corona, don't cry again, I'm really not angry with you. It's funny that anyone thought you could fool me."

We Suffer said, "Line it up."

Crown was saying, "Deuteros—promise you're not going to touch Deuteros," and the other voice said impatiently, "If I have to *look* at Deuteros a second longer I'll die. I can't believe you're going this far because you think you'll look good in a uniform. You always were nutty about uniforms . . . Why Deuteros?"

Camilla said urgently, "No. Listen to her."

We Suffer said, "What the *hell* is it?" in not a very nice way.

"She's trying to tell us something."

But all Crown said was, "She listened to me. I owe her."

"Oh, that's not special. *Anyone* would listen to you if you unbuttoned your top two buttons. Well, no, not Deuteros, you were never in her line. Look, I'm taking you both in, so you can relax. You just look so beautiful when you're nervous."

"You're a dick," said Crown, half-crying, half-laughing.

We Suffer's eyes slid to Nona's, or maybe they had always been there. Nona sat there with a mouthful of water, slowly going warm. A door opened and closed on the audio, close to where the voices were coming from. There was an unmistakeable *click*.

The flip-top was held to We Suffer's ear. Someone was speaking over it. We Suffer said quietly to Camilla: "They're lined up. They can take the shot."

"Don't."

"Our lives are at stake."

"Don't take it," said Camilla.

Over the line, Crown's voice suddenly changed. Her mouth had moved in some other direction. She said, "Oh my God! No!"

The other voice drawled, "Don't freak out, darling. He's a *tame* Lyctor . . . he won't hurt you. He can't really hurt anyone anymore. You and your little firebrands took him in as a pet, didn't you? Well, I'm taking him back to Poppa as a gift . . . that is, if Poppa can look up from his mid-dismyriad crisis long enough to pay attention."

A new and wonderfully familiar voice ground out, in tones that were unfamiliar— "Silence."

"Shan't. You might be the Saint of Duty, but *I've* been on call as Teacher's whipping girl for the last six months, so fuck to you," the other voice said. "I can say what I like about him. Anyway, what do you think? Do we take in the gate-crasher, or what?"

"Kill her," said the voice. "Deadweight."

Crown said, "I'll walk back out to the streets and let the people have me if you touch a hair on her head. And I'm not going *anywhere* with . . . him."

The drawling voice despaired. "Fine. Get her inside. But he comes too, that's not negotiable."

"He told you about . . . Harrow? He told you about Cam?"

"He's told me everything."

The new voice said impatiently, "Get the fishhook out of the fish. Second earring. Right ear."

The last thing the audio recorded was a blurry "Ow," and then the line went dead.

Nona thrilled with recognition and relief; the new voice had been Pyrrha's.

21

WE SUFFER LISTENED FOR a few more minutes, and then, in an unusual display of temper or misery or both, threw her earpiece at the table. Then she put her mouse-coloured head in her hands.

Nona, confronting the fact that she had too much in her mouth to swallow, hastily began gulping it in the tiniest of polite gulps she could manage, but her effort came to nothing. Her throat made a noise a little bit like the noise of a gull on the beach trying to get down a whole sausage, and it was really loud. We Suffer put down the phone and looked at Camilla and Nona with wild eyes: a wildness not far off the one that Nona had seen in Hot Sauce's face. But that didn't matter. Camilla said, "Don't move so quickly," which Nona thought was silly.

"But Cam," she said, "we've got to go to Pyrrha, you heard her. Didn't you hear her?"

"I heard," said Camilla.

The door slammed open. An Edenite in a mask but with panicked, uncovered eyes said: "The last shift got knocked out and locked in the infirmary. The necromancer's gone. The checks weren't done in order—the disturbance—"

"Leave your excuses. Go and tell Cell Commander Call," snapped We Suffer.

"Yes'm."

The door slammed shut again. When they were alone, Camilla said levelly, "That went better than you deserved."

"You are saying to me it went *well*?" We Suffer's voice jumped upward. "In my opinion, Lieutenant Crown has betrayed us all with a promptness and the eagerness you do not normally see outside cheap plays at the theatre. And I *believed* . . . she swore a thousand times . . . *she* made the sniper order, you see. The headshot was not intended for the Lyctor. She ordered the headshot for her if she was found out . . . And I believed her. I have seen people call for the headshot before, and their eyes are not all like hers were. She had the conviction. Then to steal Deuteros from under our noses . . . and to have lost Pyrrha Dve without the slightest right of recourse. I *knew* we should have chipped her. Now they ask for you by name! We are betrayed doubly."

Nona was immediately annoyed. "Don't say that about Pyrrha," she said. "Pyrrha wouldn't betray us."

"Child, your opinion doesn't—"

"I wouldn't make her mad," said Camilla calmly, and to Nona's great shame, We Suffer hesitated. Into that hesitation Cam said: "Scan the frequency. Check for active bugs in the location."

"Explain," said We Suffer, after a pause. Nona thought We Suffer was being pretty slow.

"Pyrrha just *told* us that everything's fine," she said, "but I wish she'd picked me up from school instead of going to the barracks, because then none of this would have happened. Thank goodness she's all right."

After a moment's continued staring, We Suffer took the little flip-top pad and the receiver and dialled a number. Nona caught snatches of the conversation: "Put it on the shortwave," and "No questions. Do it," but she had lost interest. She turned to Camilla, pushed the chair back, and joined her at the wall. Camilla budged up so there was room for her.

"I don't feel well," said Nona, regretting all the water.

Cam's eyes flickered. "Take it easy."

"I hate that shackle on your ankle," said Nona, feeling absurdly tearful.

"You keep saying that. I don't care. Come here."

And Camilla did something she rarely did. She put her arm tightly around Nona so that Nona could feel all the bunched-up muscles of her shoulders and biceps, and she drew Nona close. Nona rested her head on Camilla's shoulder and put her arms around her middle. They stood like that, Nona holding Camilla, Cam holding Nona. Camilla was warm and strong and safe and all her bones felt good: the hollow of her shoulder, the hard, firm line and ridge below her neck.

"It's been a long week," said Camilla.

"Yeah," said Nona. "I want to go home with you . . . I want Pyrrha. I want Palamedes."

They held each other like that. Eventually, somewhere around the top of Nona's head, Camilla cleared her throat and said— "You know that tantrum you had? Do you remember attacking the guards with that chair?"

"I'm really sorry."

"No, I mean—your stance was good," Camilla said slowly, as though trying to figure out how to say something. "Good grasp . . . two-handed."

"Just like practise," said Nona. "With the sword."

Camilla said, "But we practise one-handed."

Nona pulled back a little and looked up into the eyes that used to belong to Palamedes, long before she knew either of them: Camilla's face, her steady gaze, the reassuring jumpiness of her body. Nona felt something strange. There was a hot trickle from her nose, and when Camilla wiped her face with her sleeve it was revealed to be a bright red streamlet of blood.

"I need to talk to Palamedes," said Camilla lowly.

Before Nona could say that Palamedes had said the same thing, We Suffer thumped the table so hard that Nona jumped.

"There *is* another node!" she announced, in equal parts horror and excitement. "We still have contact! There is an inactive line! But where?"

"It'll be on Judith," said Camilla, untangling herself a little from Nona. "Give them time. I knew the moment she brought Deuteros out. Pyrrha confirmed it. Nona was right. She gave us codes."

We Suffer said intently, "What did she tell you?"

Nona said, "She said to fall in—that it was safe—and I *think* she said she found a whole bunch of cigarettes." We Suffer looked as though she did not understand, so she used a phrase she had often heard from the Angel: "I'm afraid that's typical."

We Suffer looked like she wanted to ignore this. "Can you truly trust Pyrrha Dve?"

Camilla, contemplative, cracked her neck and tried to lift the leg that had the shackle, but it beeped at her, so she put it down again.

"I'm ninety percent sure she's putting on an act. Pyrrha Dve will do anything to get at that shuttle."

We Suffer said slowly, "Then you always intended to run."

"No," said Camilla. "You have our hostages."

We Suffer seemed to think about this. There was a long pause. Then she said: "Very well. Perhaps the game is not lost . . . but it is very precarious, much more so than I would like. All the little chips have been put in the middle of the table in everybody's reach. We must proceed with great caution."

"No," Camilla said again. "Quite the reverse, actually."

Nona looked up in surprise. We Suffer seemed startled too, this was such an un-Camilla thing to say. Camilla's mouth said, "Update, please," and Nona rushed out: "Pyrrha's in the barracks. Crown went in and we heard her over the audio. The other one, Crown's boyfriend I think, smashed the bug, but there's another bug on the Captain only we can't hear from it yet. Pyrrha's talking funny like she's trying not to sneeze, and she said there's something we need and we have to go and get it. But—oh, also, Crown's boyfriend said he wants everything, especially Camilla and someone called *Harrowhark Nonagesimus*, and we have to give it to him by sundown."

"Yes, she was always demanding," said Palamedes. "In point of fact that's not actually Crown's boyfriend, Nona, it's her sister, but I don't think anyone could blame you for getting confused." Nona felt a little surge of relief at the idea that Crown did not have a boyfriend. "Commander We Suffer, I don't have a lot of time, so forgive me for railroading—my name is Palamedes Sextus. I'm the Master Warden of the Sixth House."

We Suffer looked at him very, very hard.

"That is impossible," she said. "Palamedes Sextus died during the Canaan operation."

"But you saw me earlier," he pointed out. "When I pulled the bullet out of Nona. Or did you think that was Camilla? She's not an adept, Commander, she can't do that kind of thing."

"Then you are—what? *Possessing* her somehow? You cannot expect—"

"Look, it doesn't matter," said Palamedes. "If you prefer to think that Camilla's got a psychological condition and sometimes flips her entire affect for no obvious reason, please believe whatever you find most comforting. The point is that there are some things you don't know and I'm the one best placed to explain them. Listen. If we can get the body of Gideon Nav—the key to the Locked Tomb—out of that barracks, will you give us the Sixth House?"

"For the key to the Locked Tomb," We Suffer said slowly, "I will give you almost anything that is in my power to give."

"Great, but that's not an answer." Palamedes leant Camilla's body forward like he wanted to spring out of the chair. "The Sixth House Oversight Body. *Assuming* you can get them, which I realise is nontrivial, will you hand them over? Yes or no."

We Suffer sighed. "Yes," she said.

Palamedes sat back. "Right," he said. "Let's talk details. Commander, Ianthe Tridentarius's hand is nowhere near as formidable as it seems. She's contrived to land on the planet by puppeting a dead body—controlling it at long range. That protects her from necromantic madness, but it also puts enormous constraints on her abilities. She's in many ways less powerful right now than a regular necromancer. And she's holed up in that barracks with a handful of bodyguards . . . and Pyrrha Dve, whom you don't trust, but I very much do."

As he talked, We Suffer's face had begun to warm with recognisable traces of interest. "You are saying that we have her in the corner," she said.

"Yes. Sort of. But in the same corner you have the body of Gideon Nav. I've got no idea why the hell Ianthe brought it along—presumably some sort of grisly power show, or maybe she was hoping to bait out Harrowhark—but everyone in this room needs that body. It's your way to carry out your mission, and it's *our* way to save Nona."

We Suffer glanced over at Nona, then back to Palamedes, and said: "The child is—sick, somehow?"

"I'm dying," Nona put in cheerfully. Having admitted it once, the words seemed a little lighter every time she said them, so she was quite keen to say them at every opportunity.

"Take this on trust, but yes, Nona is very unwell, and I—we—think the only way to save her is to get her near the corpse of Gideon Nav. It's all a bit . . . theoretical, still, but our goals very much align here."

"You are saying this as if it makes things worse, when from my chair things are looking only better," said We Suffer. She was starting to perk up, by We Suffer standards, which meant that her eyes had narrowed a bit. "The same building contains both Gideon Nav—whom I want in a bag—and a Lyctor, now apparently neutered—whom I want in a box. And here *I* am, with a bag and a large number of boxes."

Palamedes's eyes flicked down to the watch on Camilla's wrist. "No. There's another thing. Lyctors can travel near-instantaneously across huge distances. I don't know exactly what Ianthe can still manage, but there's a chance that, if you spook her, she'll use that method to get herself out of danger—and more important, to get *Gideon* out of danger. They're not in a corner, Commander, they're bobbing on the end of a string, and I have a nasty feeling that string can be jerked back at any time."

"Then it is back to the cloak and the dagger. We must extract Nav quietly, before there can be any spooking of the Lyctor."

"And *that's* where you need us," Palamedes concluded triumphantly. "With the best will in the world—how long will it take you to set up and stage some sort of commando raid on that barracks? More than twenty-four hours, I'd guess—"

"You underestimate us. Abandoning check and balance, Ctesiphon may be ready in six."

"Okay, sure. Make it six. But we can do it in half an hour, allowing for traffic. Pyrrha's already inside, and by the sound of it, Ianthe gave us a gift-wrapped excuse to send Camilla in as well. We can blindside Ianthe, put the body in a sack, and get you everything Commander Wake ever wanted. But you owe us the Sixth House. Shit, my time's nearly up. Nona, tell Camilla everything, okay?"

"I want to go to the barracks too," said Nona. "I can help."

"That's—well, we can talk about that," he said. "Commander, please do the right thing. Blood of Eden went back on its word. Despite that, you can get the Tomb *and* your honour, and all you have to do is trust a couple of zombies."

Then Camilla flopped forward a little in her seat, like she'd almost fallen asleep and caught herself at the last second. She sat up and looked at Nona.

"Palamedes told We Suffer everything about Ianthe and Lyctors," Nona said.

"I don't know why I bother," said Camilla, to herself. Then she blinked several times and shook her head.

"This was not a shadow-play, was it?" said We Suffer. She looked . . . peaceful, almost, as if she'd been worrying about whether something bad would happen and then had been told it was definitely happening. "This . . . possession. This spirit-swapping. It is a genuine occurrence."

"Yes."

"You are not some virtuoso actor. I spoke with Palamedes Sextus . . . and Palamedes Sextus died at Canaan House."

Camilla said heavily, "Yes."

We Suffer said, "I cannot give up the location of the Sixth House. *Yet*," she said, holding up one hand, as Camilla's mouth hardened. "*Yet.* Hect, what you must understand about Blood of Eden is that we own things in common, we share responsibilities and resources in common. She could have moved these resources at will"—a head-tilt to the dusty portrait of the big redheaded lady with the chilly eyes—"but I must make one move at a time. And above all, I must place the safety of . . . Blood of Eden's continuity . . . even above the mission."

Camilla said, "Tell me you know where the Oversight Body is."

"I know enough, and more than Unjust Hope wants me to," said We Suffer.

"Tell me they're alive," said Camilla.

"I think they are."

Camilla leant forward a little in her chair. Her fringe fell in her eyes. Nona felt as though they should have known better, and moved haircut day ahead.

Camilla said, "I'll try to get Gideon Nav's body. You'll give me the info."

We Suffer's expression softened a little. The fine lines around her eyes bunched and relaxed.

"I am grateful you are willing to deal. I say, Done."

"I said *try*."

"Palamedes Sextus thought you could."

Camilla's mouth quirked minutely. "We have no info. I don't know the first thing about where Tridentarius is keeping it. I have no idea what she can do. We can't hold off a Lyctor for long. I need intel."

"We will assist in any way we can."

"We'll want the shuttle too."

We Suffer did not miss a beat. "With stipulations."

Camilla did not say anything, and Nona got more and more embarrassed by the silence, so she said: "My friend had stipulations once, but the teacher put a cream on it."

"Thank you, Nona," said We Suffer, very kindly, and Nona felt pleased. Then she looked back to Camilla and said, "If you find a way off-world . . . I would like you to take a package with you."

Camilla raised her eyebrows. "Where?"

"Anywhere, away from here," said We Suffer.

"We don't carry metaphors," said Camilla. "You've asked too much already."

We Suffer sat back in her seat. She was looking at a patch of wall a few inches above Camilla's head.

"Let us suppose—" she began, and then there was a soft *pop* from the audio speaker and a sharp *clack* that made everyone jump. The *clack* was quickly followed by a heavier *clunk*, and a rustle, and then Pyrrha's voice said from a distance— "She's alive."

And Crown's voice said, closer— "Good . . . for you, I mean."

Camilla had immediately jumped up, grimacing a little, and retrieved a sheet of paper and a pen. She pressed it up against the wall and started scribbling. Pyrrha's voice, still dead and tense, said, "Threats?"

"I don't know your game," Crown was saying, "but I don't trust you. I don't trust you with Camilla . . . I don't trust you with any of them. I don't know *who* you're for at the end of the day, and I never did. I knew that from the moment I saw you. I don't think you've had a sensation in the last myriad. Did you have a family, once? Have you thought about them in the last hundred years . . . in the last *thousand*?"

"No," said Pyrrha. There was silence. Then Pyrrha said, "I don't trust you either."

Crown laughed. Even over the crackly audio, Nona could tell it was not one of Crown's nicer laughs. It was still a lovely, musical, rich sound, but Crown said, a little hysterically: "Nobody should ever trust me. Oh, poor old Gideon . . . poor Nav. It's disgusting, what you're doing. Why are you dressing her up like a doll and wheeling her around? Who's it for? The troops don't buy it, surely?"

"Wouldn't know," said Pyrrha. "Ask the Saint of Awe."

"Don't call her that . . . it's ridiculous. Who'd want to be the Saint of *Awe*? It sounds like something you say about a puppy or a baby . . . *Why* do you keep the corpse locked up? This was all a dreadful plan to lure out the Ninth, wasn't it? I'm a little heartbroken, you know. I thought Ianthe had come for me, but it was only a mission, after all. A honey trap."

"Yes," Pyrrha said. Did her voice sound a bit closer now? "It's a trap."

"You know why it won't work."

"Doesn't matter. None can get at that corpse."

"Oh, go away . . . stop sounding portentous and go away and stand guard over wherever they've stashed her . . . and leave Judith to me. When the sedative wears off there's going to be hell to pay. She can do a real number on herself, you know. I'm the only one who can make sure she's secure."

Pyrrha said, "Nice try."

Crown made a petulant sound.

"Okay. Fine. Stay here and watch while I do it, then . . . but I think you're being stupid. If it had been *me* I would have put Nav in a suitcase and put the suitcase in a cupboard and locked the cupboard door. She's a corpse. It's not like you need to let her out to use the bathroom."

"I put all the corpses in the morgue," said Pyrrha.

"What? What's that got to do with anything—"

"If I find you in here again with this necromancer, alone," said Pyrrha, "she will join them."

Another silence. Another burst of laughter from Crown. Then a third voice broke in, much more distant: "What's the joke?"

"Ianthe," said Crown in a hurry, "this . . . *thing* won't let us help Captain Deuteros. She'll be waking up soon and the blue madness is really awful with her . . . she's almost as bad as the necromancers downstairs."

"Corona, dear, *I* told him not to let you touch her."

"Ianthe, you're making me mad," said Crown pleasantly.

"And I sincerely love it . . . I've missed that face. Oh, for God's sake, here . . ."

The voice had crossed over the room. There were more noises that Nona couldn't parse because they were so loud so suddenly. They were right up close to whatever was picking up the conversation, and both Camilla and We Suffer's faces went tight. But then Crown's voice said with sudden steel: "Don't do anything to her."

"It's a ward, my paranoid little pumpkin."

"A ward for what? I've never seen a ward like that."

"How you managed to fool anyone you were a necromancer I do not know," said the voice, "except that I do . . . it was because of *me*.

Think back to class, Corona. I'm only going to dab here, and here and here . . ."

"Use her spit," said Crown, still firm as steel.

"Forgive me. She did pay attention in class. All right . . . this is much closer than I ever wanted to get to Judith Deuteros's tongue, mind. As far as I know, this counts as sex on the Second. Yuck. There we go, it's with *her* material so it can't be deleterious to her body . . . top marks, Coronabeth, I really am impressed. D'you remember that pop-eyed tutor asking you what would be a good substance for a regenerative ward and you kept making rude suggestions in the sweetest little voice?"

"Yes," said Crown, whose voice had softened just a little. "Marcus Trio, right?"

"God, you always remember these extras' names . . . You're right. It *was* Trio. Don't worry, the ward's going to keep Deuteros unconscious . . . for a little while. Come with me now, Corona. I want you and I to shut ourselves up and talk and talk and talk . . . alone. You've hardly told me anything. That's a hint to make yourself scarce, by the way, Duty. God, how to refer to you? We're going to need to give you a nickname to differentiate. What did Harrowhark used to always call you? *Tortoise? Blorgus?*"

Pyrrha's voice was cool. "You cut slits in her brain."

Crown said, "You *pardon?*"

"Long story. Very funny. Come and hear it," said the third voice. "Let's lock this door . . . I don't want Deuteros crashing the party, sweetheart."

Nona and We Suffer and Camilla were very silent for a while, but there was nothing after that. Camilla had written a whole page of scribbled nonsense. We Suffer said tightly, "Was that anything to you?"

Camilla didn't answer at first. She had taken her pen and was underlining things, her lips moving soundlessly as she repeated phrases to herself. Nona sat down in front of her, tired from listening and from holding her breath to help her concentrate. She put her cheek up against Cam's knee. Cam did not seem to notice or mind, until she looked down at Nona, and then at her paper, and she said— "What are Pyrrha's nicknames for you?"

"Kiddie," said Nona immediately. "Junior. Small Fry. Cutie Pie. Li'l Bits. Small Cam. Hairy Maclary."

"Keep going."

"Nums. No-No. Nope. None. Sweet Nons. Nona-Palona. The Big No."

"She should be arrested," murmured Camilla, then: "Got it."

We Suffer leant forward eagerly. "What have you got?"

"Nona," said Camilla, putting the paper aside, "look at me."

Nona, already so near to Camilla's knee, was happy to raise her chin and have both of her hands taken—unusual!—by Camilla. Camilla squeezed her hands briefly, then paused, then put one of her hands to Nona's forehead, and said: "You're running a temperature."

"Oh—I'm dying, that's probably why," said Nona. "Don't worry though, I've got whole days if I don't do anything stupid."

Cam's expression said that she found this both surprising and unfortunate. She said, "Stupid how?"

"It's complicated."

"Does Palamedes know?"

"Yes, I told him."

"Okay," said Camilla, with what Pyrrha always called her *I will talk to your mother later* face. Then— "Nona, Pyrrha thinks you're the key to something we want."

"The body."

"Yes." And: "You're going to have to be brave."

"Oh, *please*," said Nona dismissively. "Just tell me what you need me to do."

Camilla smiled at her. For that smile Nona would have lived, if she had had any say in the matter. She did not answer, but said to We Suffer: "How long until sundown?"

"You have over eight hours."

"Can you get the Sixth House by then? Can you get me some materials right now?"

"As you promised me, so I promise you—I will devote every resource I have to the attempt. Tell me what you need."

"A pair of scissors," said Camilla. "Iris dye." She looked at Nona's button-up shirt, which was unbuttoned to show the T-shirt underneath. "And the blackest clothes you can find."

JOHN 9:22

IN THE DREAM he finally took her to the front of the concrete wreck. It had taken him a while to clear the rubble away from the door. He seemed to want to do it by hand. After watching him for an hour, she helped. The rocks cut their fingers and strained their wrists, and the cuts knitted back up so quickly that they were in danger of healing their skin over the sharp edges of the jagged concrete chunks, of sucking slivers of glass into their hands. Sometimes they *did* suck glass in. Every few hours they had to pause so he could get rid of all the grit that was accumulating underneath their skins, stuff they'd healed over by accident.

When the doors were clear he took her into a room he said was the old reception area. The water had smashed it to bits, but he said it had been smashed to bits before. At some point the desk had been broken up and pushed in front of the door but then the door had burst open and flung piles of desk on either side of the room. There were puddles of foetid water, and bones—leftover bones, bones in clothes, bones with meat still clinging to them. She pointed out that some of the bones still had meat on them and he said to stop.

He wouldn't go any farther inside for a while. He stood there in the smelly hole-pocked rubbishy darkness and said— They made it clear that they'd arrest anyone who tried to join us. Floods of people came anyway. It felt like half the world. In reality it was, what, maybe a couple thousand? Coming out as a necromancer didn't exactly win me the popular vote, but the police were pushed to a fever pitch with anxiety. The international party line was that the problem had to get taken care of. Overseas relief troops were being flown in by the UN and our government didn't like it. They said it wasn't a war zone and they didn't want a blood bath and was it even legal. We took who we could behind the wall. I was extending that thing outward metre by metre, didn't need new cows by then because I could grow the original material, but that just freaked everyone out more. It even scared A——. He was all, *Matter doesn't* play *by these rules! You're doing bone parthenogenesis!* I told him his mum did bone parthenogenesis. A—— told me he'd kill me one day.

He said, What I could do wasn't simply freaking out everyone outside the walls. We were running out of tests to run on me. I was getting stronger minute by minute. The last frontier I couldn't cross was the soul. M——'s nun of all people was convinced this was the element I was missing, and that finding it—the last link between what made someone alive and what made someone dead—would bring us closer to God. She was right, but I'm not sure she was right in the way she meant.

He said, I was getting so frustrated trying to figure it out. The soul. Element X. I knew the only way I was going to get closer was to see more people die. I got my wish—a bunch of new faithful appeared outside the walls hoping to come in, and they refused to back off, and they exchanged fire with the crowd keeping watch outside, and five people died.

He said, And I saw something.

He said, I was too distracted to do anything with it because it was then that I found out fresh deaths were like—like crack cocaine. I'd never taken crack cocaine, but I thought that must've been what it felt like. It was like my brain was hyper-attuned to the moment of violent death. I could feel it like it was happening to me. Like it was injected into the bottom of my spine. I could see everything. I could feel everything.

He said, I took the energy from those five dead people and I dropped everyone with a gun in a kilometre radius. Stopped the hearts of the army guys, the rent-a-cops, the peacekeepers, the locals. There were over a hundred of them, but I didn't discriminate.

A couple of them were in helicopters, but I didn't get the pilots, just the guys inside. Just, bam! And they were down. It was so easy. It was like I was dreaming. I could see them all like I was standing right there, from the heat of their bodies and the blood chewing through them. It took no effort and it took no time. It simply happened. And the more I did it the more I could see. I was on the verge of something insane.

He said, I came to when P— started shaking me. Talk about police abuse. She asked what the fuck was I doing. She was angry, one of the only times I'd seen her angry, one of the only times I'd seen her scared. Because I'd stopped the hearts of all those guys, right, and I hadn't started them again. I said I forgot. She said you've never forgotten before. I said I swear to God, I didn't know what I was doing. A bunch of the guys were her old coworkers—guys she'd gone through training with in Porirua, beer buddies. I kept saying sorry, I'm sorry, I freaked out, it was an accident, I don't know what happened, when they opened fire I lost my head. I said I made a mistake. She let it go eventually because the others were telling her to lay off. Just said, *Guys as careful as you shouldn't have accidents. If you've got a gun learn how to aim it. This is too big for fuckups now.* Poor G— didn't know what to do. He never knew how to pick between me and P—.

He said, In the end we dragged in all the corpses. For the skeleton army, I said. And I'd stopped kidding.

For a while both of them stopped talking. He kicked at some of the old, wet rubble. A bad smell came out. He did not fix the bad smell.

She said, "Did you ever find out what happened? With your accident?"

He turned to her and he smiled a funny little smile. It only used one half of his mouth. In the dream his new eyes did not show happiness or unhappiness.

And he said, "Come on, love. Guys as careful as me don't have accidents."

22

FIVE HOURS LATER, NONA did not know herself. This was a good thing as she wasn't meant to be herself; she was only meant to turn her head and answer if she was called "Harrowhark," or "Nonagesimus," or "Ninth." Her complete inability to answer to "Harrowhark" or "Ninth" meant that Camilla had given up on anything other than "Nonagesimus," and a sigh of— "Remember not to smile."

"I won't smile at the time," Nona promised.

"Or turn to me when you're scared," said Camilla.

"I promise."

"Or nervous."

"Okay."

"Or turn to me as though I know anything or could assist you in any way," said Camilla.

If Nona hadn't known if she wanted to be redheaded, princely, or necromantic, she wasn't at all sure she wanted to be Harrowhark Nonagesimus either. Cam had cut both of her braids off and sheared her almost to the bone, which made her look like Beautiful Ruby's mother's baby, but much less beautiful or intriguing. They had taken away her Salt Chip Fish Shop T-shirt and requisitioned a black button-up shirt and trousers off of the smallest Blood of Eden member they could find, and these had to be cinched around Nona's hips with clasps. Harrowhark Nonagesimus lived by rules. She had to stand up very straight, and never slouch, and never scratch if she had an itch, and not make any expressions that weren't a frown. And—

322 / TAMSYN MUIR

"Remember, Harrow," said Camilla, "you can't see. You're blind."

They had taken some iris dye and a little plastic applicator and changed Nona's eyes. She could still mostly see through the dye and the applicator—although it made everything fuzzy around the edges—but catching a glimpse of herself in the mirror had nearly made her go into hysterics. The dye coated her nice yellow eyes with a thick, eggy film that made them grey and white. Everything about the whites looked cloudy and sticky. We Suffer of all people had done the application herself, rolling up her sleeves and being quite nice about it. Another Blood of Eden person in a mask had approached, but We Suffer had said, "Let me. I was always a dab hand at the application of camouflage," and had not even been mean when Nona blinked.

We Suffer had said, leaning over Nona's face and checking the position of the plastic films: "I am glad you did not tell us this. We had no idea there was any recourse from Varun the Eater's effects, nor any Beast."

"It's pure theory," Camilla said curtly. "Something's being transmitted in the light spectrum. Absorption through the eyes is worst for the brain."

This made Nona think of something. It tugged at the edges of her memory and stayed there, nagging.

"They would have shot everyone with cataracts," said We Suffer.

"You already shot all the madmen," said Camilla.

"Survival through caution," said Our Lady of the Passion.

The Blood of Eden base became a hive of activity. The meeting room was a constant parade of Blood of Eden soldiers bringing materiel and reports and sandwiches and rubbish bags in and out of the door. At first there was the problem that nobody but We Suffer—and Pash!—was willing to be in the same room with Camilla and Nona unless both were shackled to the wall, and Nona had refused. Pash had lugged in chairs and boxes and a roll of what appeared to be wire fencing and made a kind of barricade that Nona was being treated behind. A couple of the Blood of Eden soldiers were willing to come in if Nona and Camilla were behind that, in their masks and with their guns.

"Fucking idiots," said Pash. "Wrote down all their names. Psychological wrecks. This barricade's nothing. A zombie could bust it in seconds. These guys ever apply for strike teams, *pow*, they can go whistle."

"You misuse your power in an incredible fashion," said We Suffer.

"Commander, I wouldn't misbehave if you hadn't given me the worst job of my life."

"It was meant to be privilege enormous."

"Not saying it's not," said Pash, "but it's still the worst job of my life."

Nona quite fancied Pash at this point. She had got to see her up close during all the preparations. She hadn't put her mask back on and she was wearing a thin-strapped top along with big trousers with heaps of pockets to put things in. She had wrangled her short dyed-blue hair behind a sweatband so that the longer bits didn't fall in her scarred eyebrows or green eyes, and every so often she scowled at Nona like she could cause Nona to melt away dead. Nona had kept giggling, and that got her told off because Harrowhark Nonagesimus didn't giggle.

At one point, Nona had been worried because Camilla had shut herself away in the corner to write backward-and-forward with Palamedes. Palamedes had focused nearly all his attention on writing, except at one point he'd looked Nona over and said, "Look at me like you've worked out how to kill me," and then, "More eyebrows," and then, "Good God, perfect. Do you know, I miss Harrow terribly." Then he'd gone back to his letter. When it was done, Camilla read it heaps and heaps and heaps of times, and then she had to lie down with her knees tucked up to her chest while breathing out through her nose. Nona came to lie down next to her.

She whispered, "Did you overdo it?"

"Yes," said Cam shortly, then: "It wears off. We're fine." Then: "Let's take a nap."

Nona had been going to ask Camilla lots and lots of questions, but at the idea that they would get to take a nap together she forgot all of them. She was tired herself and had been obliged to eat two sandwiches. When nobody was looking she had gone searching in We Suffer's little case of pens and things and found a whole bright pink eraser, and she had taken a huge bite out of it and that had made her feel better, but getting to sleep next to Camilla was the best of all.

When she had woken up the dye had all come out because she had scratched it off in her sleep and the plastic bits had peeled out too, so We Suffer had had to put them back in but didn't even complain about it. No one even forced her to tell them about her dream. When We Suffer was doing this, Camilla said—

"Keep to yes or no answers. Ianthe may try to talk to you. Refuse to answer."

"Rudely or nicely?"

"Rudely."

Nona felt she could do that.

"The rest of the time," said Camilla, "you need to act like the Captain."

Nona wanted to say, "You mean lying down?" but it did not seem the right time to try to be funny. Cam looked so serious. She said slowly, "Like I have the blue madness?"

"Yes—you're well enough to stand and you know what's going on, but you're going to keep having fits of blue madness."

"When?"

Camilla thought about it.

"Whenever you're asked something difficult."

This was Nona's only task, except for being dressed as, pretending to be, and answering to the name of Harrowhark Nonagesimus. Cam had told her that her main job was to be a Distraction. Nona asked if Harrowhark Nonagesimus had been a Distraction in life, and Cam said it always was the quiet ones. It seemed as though Camilla's part would be the more challenging. We Suffer and Cam spent a long time talking quietly over maps while Pash leant against one wall and pared her thumbnails with a knife; Nona's heart throbbed romantically.

At last We Suffer made her eyebrows go together and said, "We will provide the getaway. The rest is up to you."

Camilla said, "Your part?"

"Ctesiphon breached one of Merv Wing's cells two hours ago," said We Suffer. "The interrogation was underway within fifteen minutes. By the time we will have to answer for our intercell crimes, I will either be a conquering hero to whom everything is forgiven . . . or I will have to shoot myself. I will be disappointed if I must shoot myself, Hect. I have very often *not* had to shoot myself. Our Lady of the Passion will accompany you."

Pash's knife stopped and she said, "No, I won't. I'm on duty."

"Your duty and I have had a talk, and they would like to be present," said We Suffer smoothly.

"They shouldn't go anywhere near that super-zombie," said Pash, incredibly startled. "Commander, fuck this, I'm taking them to the safe house the moment dusk hits."

"I am not telling you this as any kind of command," said We Suffer. "I am telling you *I* have been served my marching orders, and Aim says that Aim desires to oversee this operation from a place of safety next to their lifeguard. You are the only lifeguard on duty, as Merv Wing is currently suffering unavoidable pangs courtesy of us."

"I'm not going anywhere near that thing."

"You have met a Lyctor before," said We Suffer.

"I don't mean the *Lyctor*."

"It is only a body," said We Suffer.

"Why do I detect your finger in this pie?"

"You are budging curiously close up to insubordination again," said We Suffer.

"Commander, my ass is already grass if the council finds out about anything I did yesterday. I signed myself over to Ctesiphon when I was a kid. I'm with you. But the Messenger shouldn't be near th—"

We Suffer said, "They may have a working shuttle, Pash. Quiet, please."

Pash went quiet. We Suffer said, "Hect. You say you only need one good chance—an element of surprise—and the Lyctor will be out of the question?"

"In all likelihood, not permanently," said Camilla.

"If not permanently—what happens after that?"

"We're flying blind," said Camilla.

We Suffer said, "A Lyctor out of the question impermanently is more than any of us has ever achieved—nearly any of us," she amended. But then she sighed again, explosively, and said: "So long as the key is secure, I may get away with anything . . . You are *certain*, one simple touch?"

"Yes."

"Convenient," said Pash, in a not-very-nice voice.

"I will not salute you both," said We Suffer. "It is too much to ask of me. But if you do this thing, I will salute . . . I will frankly pin my own medals on your fronts. Crack the sky, Troia cell."

And then there they were in the truck—the same big truck that had picked up Hot Sauce and Nona, the one with the grille for running people over. Cam and she were at the back, and Pash was at the front, and Nona was startled to see the Angel—Aim—in the passenger seat, even though she had known she would be coming. It was strange to see her peering back through the mesh, looking like she always did, as though she were about to ask Nona for a cup of coffee.

"Where's Noodle?" Nona blurted.

"In the footwell, poor old man." The Angel cleared her throat and said, "I like the haircut, Nona."

"*I* don't," said Nona a little wrathfully, a little shyly. She wasn't quite sure where she stood with the Angel. "I liked my braids—my head feels strange when I move it."

"Easy to brush though."

Camilla said, "No names. Nonagesimus needs to concentrate."

Nona tried to look as though she could concentrate and stared out of the window, her heart hammering, her palms greasy with sweat. It was not even that she was nervous, not really. Her body had been playing strange games with her ever since she had recovered from the last tantrum. She was beginning to feel like a floating balloon on a string, with a weight tied to the end—the balloon bobbing, the weight dragging behind. She was the balloon, and also the string, but she wasn't sure she was still the weight. Looking had become quite difficult—she didn't want to blink too much in case the white came out again—which made the buildings all one great smear, the crowds brightly coloured stick-people. People with their hands in their pockets standing around on the street corners—people walking, people thronging, people righting bins that had been knocked over, as though nothing were happening, as though her whole life really were nothing more than a balloon passing by overhead.

Pash drove them through the city scientifically, which meant that she constantly leant on the horn of the car and occasionally mounted the pavement until Camilla said— "Pull over. We'll go the rest of the way on foot."

"You'll get shot."

"We're used to it."

Pash said, "Zombie, you betray us, you fuck this up, you know we blow that barracks sky-high."

"I'm relying on it," said Camilla.

The Angel said quietly— "Will it really be so simple?"

"Yes," said Camilla.

The car pulled to a stop. Pash got out of the front and slid the big side door open. Nona breathed in the nice smell of fresh air and plastic fumes and fire. There were people huddled on the street and in the buildings and on stoops, looking at them suspiciously, but nobody said or did anything. Pash, with her fierce soldier's face and attractive eyes, stared at Nona and Camilla hatefully—and then at Cam.

"Chances?" she said shortly.

Cam said, "Fifty-fifty."

"What happens on the bad roll?"

"I die."

Camilla unbuckled Nona, and Nona and Camilla staggered out to stand beneath the blue-tinted sky. Nona, with her altered white gaze, saw everything obscured through fog; Camilla helped her to stand, and then she crossed over to the boot of the car and waited quietly for Pash to open it. Nona was surprised to see that the boot was filled with boxes from home, from the cupboard with the fake board in it. Camilla flipped open boxes and took out a belt, which she tied around her waist, and she secured a hook to the side of the belt. To this hook she reverently attached a long plain black scabbard, then a shorter plain black scabbard, and she tested the hilts in her hands. Cam sighed—really sighed!—as though she had gone to lie down in a hot bath.

The last thing Camilla did was reach into her pocket and take out the sunglasses, and she perched them on her nose.

Pash said, "Your people . . . that obsession with swords."

"We are our swords," said Camilla. She shrugged on a crisscross halter of black plastic straps and clipped it tight across the front of her chest, and then she opened a box and took out two long, plain knives, the type of thing they used to chop up fish at the market. *All of Cam's secret knife stash,* Nona thought, numb with anticipation.

"Yeah, you're outdated, just like them," said Pash. "They're a weakness. A hand-me-down form of complete fucking insanity."

Camilla said, "You use machetes yourself."

"Wanted to get inside your heads," said Pash.

Camilla considered her, her clear grey eyes narrowing to slits in the sand and the sunshine.

"Did you?"

"Occasionally literally," said Pash.

Both of them fell silent. Nona twiddled her thumbs. Pash seemed to be the one pent-up with something she couldn't quite say, standing there with her arms folded, until she ground out— "Die quick, die cold, bring 'em with you."

There was a movement on Cam's mouth a little like her old smile. "That one yours?"

"No. Came down from someone much bigger than me," said Pash shortly. "Don't get me wrong, wizard slave. *You* die quick—stay dead—and don't get up again. But if you kill a guy who would've killed me, I have to give you that, right? I pulled a trigger next to you, that doesn't mean *nothing.* But it doesn't change who you are."

Camilla held out her hand. Pash shook her head.

"I'll touch you at the end of the world, but not before."

"Might be your last chance," said Cam.

Pash barked a laugh. "In my final minutes, Hect, I won't regret not shaking your hand."

"Nonagesimus," said Camilla, "let's go."

It was hard to see, but Cam had said not to reach for her or to try to hold her hand. Nona held herself and thought of Hot Sauce, so still and real and royal, so sure-footed, who walked like she never needed anyone. By the time they reached the broken-down, bombed-out, bullet-littered road that led to the barracks, Camilla murmured— "Keep going."

The gates to the barracks swung wide for them. They did not need to yell at anyone to open them up. Nona perceived a scurry of movement to the side, and then they were let into the wide-open courtyard where Crown's car still sat—its back doors wide open, its windows pockmarked with bullet holes from disappointed snipers. Nona had never seen the barracks before, not up close. It was a huge concrete building, square and tall, with long slits cut next to a second-storey porch for people to fire out of, and bars over the grand lead-lined windows. It was a building unlike any others in the city. It was big and dark and magnificent, but chipped and dirty and dented, like a lady in a burnt-up ballgown. Its ornate crenellations were so crumbled that it was hard to tell what their original pattern had been, and once brightly coloured flags had been unrolled down the sides of the windows in all kinds of colours, but they had mostly been torn off by the roots with only dull coloured floss left behind.

Nobody shot at Nona as she crossed the courtyard, and nobody shot at Camilla. Great double doors waited at the top of a short flight of stairs. Nona mounted those stairs, and the doors creaked slowly open, revealing cool wide blackness within—a floor of checkerboard black-and-white tiles, peeling white walls, old brown stains that someone had tried to clean but not very successfully, and a terrible foul smell.

She wanted to let her nose wrinkle, but Harrowhark Nonagesimus did not seem the type to wrinkle her nose. Camilla said, "Fall back," and Nona fell behind her, sight softening into near-blindness as she followed Camilla down into that cool, foetid darkness.

They did not walk far. The first door on the left was open, and a strong white square of electric light fell on the tiles. The door was bracketed at either side with old broken piles of rubbish and chair and desk and wood. Camilla hesitated on the threshold, and Nona walked into the light first.

They had walked into a broad hall, floored with the same black-and-white checkerboard tiles. The walls and ceiling were carved with grand white friezes, and both sides of the room had more rubbish and detritus pushed up against them, as though a great wave had swept through the centre of the room and deposited the contents of a tip on either side. Paler squares lined each side of the windowless room where posters or paintings had probably been hung but were no-where to be seen now. The room smelled strongly of the type of thing they used to clean the school toilets with. At the end of the room was a raised dais, the same raised dais that had been in the broadcast; and there on a plain and simple chair sat the Prince from the broadcast, and behind the Prince on the left, Pyrrha. On a chair to the right sat Crown.

Crown looked so beautiful that for a moment Nona focused on her to the exclusion of everything else. She had her big beautiful golden hair down around her shoulders in a profusion of smoothed, rip-pling curls, and she was wearing a lovely pale yellow slip that left her golden shoulders and throat bare. The dress was slit all the way up to the thigh and she wore soft black leather trousers beneath it, and sandals on her big shapely feet, and the usual rapier girdled her waist. She was so stunning that Nona was devoutly grateful she was in clean clothes and not her fish-market tee. Then her attention wandered past Crown, where Nona thought they had lined up lots and lots of statues; but they weren't statues at all. They were dozens and dozens and dozens of people in uniform, standing in two ranks pressed up very close to the wall. They were not breathing. Their eyes were wide open. They were dead. When the Prince stood from his chair, their shoulders—every single shoulder—twitched minutely.

In person the Prince was much shorter than she thought he would be, slimmer and slighter; especially next to Pyrrha, who stood like a stone column. She was standing so unlike Pyrrha that for a moment Nona was fooled: she was standing so ready, so waiting, so upright, so uncomfortable in her own skin, that it was like seeing a mirage. But moving broke the spell, at least for Nona. Pyrrha crossed and uncrossed her arms in a way so comfortably and familiarly *Pyrrha* that Nona couldn't mistake her.

Nona was impressed with the Prince's looks. She had never seen anybody from the television in real life before. Thanks to the eye stuff, Nona could stare all she liked and not feel rude: at the Prince with his waxen skin and his lovely jacket and his glossy hair and his bluish-coloured eyes, standing poised a bit like a snake would stand, if it had legs.

The Prince said— "You're nearly a minute late, Harry."

23

NONA CROSSED THE BLACK-AND-WHITE floor beneath the electric lights. There was a big red square carpet laid out in front of the dais, so she stopped at its threshold, and she got a less shortsighted look at Prince Ianthe Naberius. The Prince suddenly came down off the dais and walked toward her briskly, and Nona inadvertently took a step back. This stopped the Prince.

"Look at me," she said.

Nona said and did nothing. She swallowed, but felt it was all right to swallow; Harrowhark probably swallowed, every so often.

The Prince said— "What you've done is ridiculous. It *can't* work. That can't be your handiwork . . . not that I'm not impressed. Sure, you look dreadful, but I've had to turn up in some old thing from last season."

Crown made a small noise in the back of her throat. The Prince turned to her and said, a little accusingly, "You didn't tell me *this* little detail. Has she been blinded this whole time?"

"I told you she was here," said Corona. Her eyes were red-rimmed and her eyelashes looked a bit too sooty. "I left out the details. So what?"

"There is *so* much you are not telling me and it makes me *so* cross," said the Prince. "You see, my emotions are being expressed through two nervous systems, so I really don't know what to do with them. I've been in Babs's body for nearly three whole days. I hate it . . . Come on, Harry. Don't you have anything to say for yourself?"

"No," said Nona.

"I don't know why I asked. I knew the answer. Ah," she said, as Camilla caught up and stood at Nona's elbow. "The dullest prodigal son returns . . . Those *aren't* your glasses, Hect, and I am amazed you are permitted to wear them."

"Noted," said Camilla.

"Well, never mind . . . it's just curious, is all. How's it hanging, Hect? How's tricks? Getting used to life without your necromancer? Going to parties, self-actualising, reshaping your identity? I don't suppose you had much scope for it before."

Crown said a little warningly, "Ianthe, don't push it," but Camilla said— "I don't care."

"I love it when people don't care," said Prince Ianthe warmly. "'Don't care was made to care; don't care was hung.' Really, why should you care? Who cares what *I* think? I'm only a Lyctor, a sacred fist and gesture holding the power of life and death, having ascended to the state your pompous moralising blowhard of a necromancer disdained . . . whereas *you're* the big girl who made the Sixth House secede. Tell me, do they love you for that in Blood of Eden? You don't need to answer, I know how the field lies . . . Corona's the beautiful and talented token, and you're the grim weirdo who never realised the price of revolution. And, I suppose, Harrow's nursemaid. Well, it must have been nice for you . . . she *is* Sextus's tedious distaff counterpart. Oh, come on, Harry, really? No comeback?"

"No," said Nona.

"Well, this isn't turning out how I wanted it to. I thought you and I would share a couple of saucy quips . . . I thought you'd come in here demanding the body of your cavalier."

This was dropped into the conversation like a bomb. Nona let her gaze fall straight forward, blindly, not reacting at all and not knowing how to. The room was silent.

In the end, Ianthe said: "Has that fire cooled? Have you changed your mind on that one? Is Camilla the better model? I consider Camilla Hect an obvious upgrade; I imagine she hardly makes one ass joke a day . . ."

She let this trail off. Nona kept saying nothing. The silence extended until Ianthe filled it again, but this time her voice had changed to flat impatience. "Well, Hect, thank *you* for coming. I suppose you know why you're here."

Camilla said, "I don't play guessing games."

"Surely you can make an exception."

Crown said quickly, "Camilla, don't bother. Everything's going to be fine," and Ianthe said pettishly, "Honey, stop telling people things are going to be fine. Things are, I promise you, *not* going to be fine. Things are, frankly, going to be *antonyms* of fine."

"You want the Sixth House back," said Camilla.

"Not I," said Ianthe. "I've read Sixth House juvenile moral novels about very smart children who save the day with logic, and I think you can all go drown. No, *God* wants the Sixth House back . . . badly. It was unfortunate timing, you know. First, we hear that the Sixth House facility is missing. Teacher assumes it melted as result of a little domestic drama, which sets him off wallowing all over again. Then we find out it really is missing, not burned. Who knew the whole station was portable and built to propel itself wherever it wanted? Not a thing to feed the troops on, I must say. How'd you get it through a stele? With the weight of that thing, you'd never survive River displacement."

"Five hundred and thirty-two obelisks," said Camilla.

"Really? I'd guessed in the six hundred range."

"Deleterious effects past five-fifty."

"What'd you compensate with, purely out of curiosity?"

"Prefer not to say," said Camilla.

"Boo to that," said Ianthe Naberius. "Oh, well, I'll have to ask one of the members of your Oversight Body . . . whichever one I pick for asking questions, that is. We really don't need all of them."

Nona's eyes were beginning to itch. It was very hard not to rub them. She focused instead on Crown, who was saying in tones that sounded very reasonable and deliberate: "Ianthe, you can't get away with killing off the entire governance and administration of the Sixth House."

"Watch me."

"No. I've told you before, if you're already dealing with morale fail-ure . . . you're much better off leaving them in place. Put them under secret House arrest if you have to, come up with some incentive, get them to see reason. If you kill them, everyone will know . . ."

"*Nobody* will know," said Ianthe. "Nobody knew that you and Deuteros and Hect didn't die at Canaan House. But everyone knows about the day Dominicus flared. The Houses will celebrate any scrap of the Sixth they get back. Very tragic that all sixteen members of the Sixth House leadership died, but that's how it is."

"Don't be a dolt. The Sixth are so clannish, so set on systems, you'll never truly have them again—"

"It's called the *boot*, my darling," the Prince said patiently. "Did they teach you nothing in that terrorist cell of yours? It's called ap-plying the fucking boot, and I'm going to teach God all about it. He's been very hands-off for the past myriad . . . lazy, frankly . . . and now he's reaping what he's sowed. It's called *fear* . . . I have seen fear and understand it now, and I am going to become wonderfully versed in its transmission. I am the Saint of Awe. Hect, you're smiling."

Nona, astonished, turned to Camilla without thinking; she tilted her head back immediately, afraid of being caught out, but by then she had seen Camilla's face. Camilla *was* smiling: an easy, loose little smile, as though she were listening to a story. She said, "Yes."

"Share the joke with the rest of the class," Ianthe demanded.

"Does God know why the Sixth House left?"

"I'm assuming some grisly moral reason that you're about to im-part," said Ianthe, "and I want to warn you against sounding like a tract."

"The Sixth House," said Camilla, "doesn't move for moral philos-ophy."

Ianthe Naberius spread her hands wide in impatient supplication. "Then for *what*—so much panic and mess and drama for *what*—"

"Cassiopeia the First left us instructions years ago," said Camilla. "We left for a Lyctor."

For the first time, Prince Ianthe Naberius's mouth dropped open, giving Nona a dim view of exquisitely white and even teeth. She flounced up the dais, threw herself back into her chair—the dead bodies jerked their left hips convulsively, all in unison, like the kind of dance move Born in the Morning thought he was good at but wasn't—and then she flung over her shoulder to Pyrrha: "You all said she was dead!"

"She is," said Pyrrha. "We watched her die."

"Then *how*?" But Camilla and Pyrrha didn't answer. The Prince passed one hand over her dead blue-and-brown-spattered eyes and said, "Oh my God. This is the last thing we need. If he hears that yet another one of his duplicitous sluts betrayed him, he's never going to come back from it. He's so fragile right now. Not even if we scourge Antioch and fly the First flag from the tallest tower."

Pyrrha said, "Cassy played long games."

"This is—this is *shitty*," the Prince pronounced, sounding curiously young and woebegone and frustrated.

Crown threw herself out of her chair and went down on her knees in front of the Prince—wrapped her arms around the Prince's legs and put her cheek on the dead right thigh. The Prince reached out and tangled one hand in her bright, springy curls, and sighed a cold, dead, defeated sigh. When Crown spoke her voice was low and tender, the lowest and tenderest voice Nona had ever heard: "Baby, it sounds awful."

"Corona, it's death."

"So stick it. Stick all this and come home with me . . . throw this all in and come to *me*."

Nona would have immediately thrown everything down and gone to live with Crown, but the Prince was not so moved. She laughed a little and pulled at a handful of curls, dropped them to watch them bounce, and said: "Don't be ridiculous."

But Crown did not relent. "Come to me. I need you . . . we've been apart for such a long time, Ianthe. They took you away from me. They took me away from you. Let's let them hang and go off on our own. Drop Babs. I'll take that shuttle and meet you wherever you want to meet me and we'll go . . . we'll start over."

At the bottom of her voice, Prince Ianthe Naberius said—

"There is no starting over, Corona."

"There is. I know there is," Crown said eagerly.

"But we're closer to the goal than ever before."

"Of course we are, you perfect genius," said Crown, lovingly, and she took the dead gloved fingers, and she kissed them.

Every single dead soldier's fingers twitched. Prince Ianthe Naberius raised hers, an involuntary movement almost, and that waxen, handsome face was an expressionless mask, with only the cool grey eyeballs moving in their sockets.

Then Crown said quietly, "We can do good work, Ianthe. I know people who *need* us."

For some reason that was what broke the spell. The hand fell, and Crown's face with it. Prince Ianthe Naberius smiled, ruffled those deep burnished curls, and laughed in the coldest way that Nona had ever heard.

"'People.' Oh, darling, you're always everyone else's girl. Don't worry . . . I fully intend for us to be *us,* together, now . . . but I have the framework for it and you, my poor dummy, do not. Don't worry about anything. Seriously, you need to relax. And to moisturise. And to cut your hair," the Prince added critically, moving to stand. "I'm hagged as hell . . . believe me, you'll know that when you see me . . . but you need some serious triage before I can do anything with you. I doubt you even have a skincare routine right now."

She gently shook Crown off her legs. Crown sprawled back against the plain chair and closed her eyes as though something had hurt her. Prince Ianthe Naberius looked around the room, and remarked, "Where's the live ones, Duty? I see a sad dearth of breathers."

Pyrrha said, "Outside Deuteros's room, as discussed. They're ready."

"What, every single one?"

"No. Five. Others on standby." When the Prince turned to Pyrrha, Pyrrha added, "Didn't like moving the bodies."

"What? They need to harden up. We do much worse on the front."

"They were never on the front."

"Yes, that is becoming tragically obvious. We should have doubled troops here eight months ago. Well, hindsight is its own aptitude . . . Corona, now *you're* laughing at me. This is not going down as a good day in my diary."

Corona *was* laughing. She said, in a sickly-sounding voice, "Listen to you, talking military."

"It's a bit disgusting, I know, but habit forms quickly . . . habits do form quickly with me. Speaking of . . ."

Nona was not prepared for Prince Ianthe Naberius to step off the dais, stride lightly over the carpet, and stand in front of her again— she was too busy trying to will her eyes to stop streaming. She tried to step back again—she was too slow; the Prince caught her by the front of her shirt with one hard, gloved hand. Camilla turned her body toward them both, with her hands placed flat near her scabbards, but the Prince didn't seem to care.

"Harrow's never this quiet," said the Prince softly. "Nor this passive. What are you doing, Harry? What's your plan? Or, more worryingly . . . what is *wrong* with you? What happened after Mercymorn stabbed you, Harrow, and where did you go? You never came back, and God said he thought you might be lost to us . . . How are you surviving, Harrowhark the First? How can you stand beneath the light of Number Seven? Unless I am addressing . . ."

The fist tightened. *No* would not do; *Yes* was worse; Cam had told her to pretend to be the Captain. Nona decided to pretend to be the Captain, and opened her mouth, and screamed like the Captain had screamed.

She had never been good at coming up with conversations. Nona simply made her mouth go as the Captain's had gone—she could remember the movement, it was easy—and she screamed, "*Help! Help! Help!*" for want of anything better to say.

The scream moved through her chest and up her throat and out of her nose. When *she* let it out, it did not at all sound like when she had heard the Captain do it. The scream somehow seemed to take all the lining of her throat with it. It was like the scream was made of her insides—her insides dissolved and resolved themselves by coming out her lips as a vocal bomb. The electric light sizzled in its housing. The room went dark. Prince Ianthe Naberius dropped her and staggered back, and Nona completed her Captain impression by pitching forward, onto the carpet, facedown, practically senseless, aware of nothing but the scream—a noise that seemed to keep coming out of her nose and ears and mouth. She went away from herself briefly.

Nona came back, dimly aware of a yell, a huge scuffle, then movement. When she lifted her head off the carpet she was frightened that she had vomited, or bled, as her mouth and nose were streaming; but she hadn't coughed up anything except water.

The new situation was much worse than before she screamed. She could see Prince Ianthe Naberius's shiny knee-length boots, one of them at least. She was down on one knee, but had drawn a rapier from that scabbard at her side and the tip was pinked with blood. On the dais, Pyrrha's red, rangy body was down—*Pyrrha!*—on her hands and knees, trying feebly to rise. She had drawn a gun from somewhere—Pyrrha was good at drawing a gun from somewhere—but it had been knocked out of her hand and lay glittering in front of the plain chair. Crown was standing, flanked by two dead people but not being held by them. Camilla, on the other hand, had her arms pinned to her sides by fully four of the dead guards. She had drawn her knives, but her hands were forced outward in front of her, unable to move. The light glittered again, and Nona could see long, cold shadows on the carpet behind her, could feel the press of dead people moving. Some of the dead people had fallen down just like she had, lying jumbled-up on the tiles, and some of them were so close that Nona could see they had been dead for a long time, and some of them had bits missing. Honesty and Hot Sauce and the others had been right. She didn't like this zombie stuff *at all.*

Nona thought that she had seriously bogged it.

"Okay," said the Prince, rising unsteadily to stand. "All right. Okay. Wow. Fine."

As she rose, some of the other dead bodies rose with her, much less gracefully; others kept still.

The Prince pointed at Nona. Before Nona could react, or struggle, she was seized from behind by strong arms. She tried to make her body fight but she was too dazed even to be angry. She kept snorting and sneezing and shivering, still trying to get the last bits of water out of her nose. One of the cold, gloved, bad-smelling hands took her jaw firmly, and squeezed it shut hard so that Nona could not even say "Yes" or "No."

"*You*," said the Prince, "are coming home to the Emperor tied and gagged, and not as a sex thing. *You*"—this was to Pyrrha—"prep to leave. This is over. I'm not wasting any more time here. Ready the shuttle to get us out in an hour. We have too much to lose. Duty, are you alive?"

Pyrrha said, with difficulty— "Yes." And: "Everyone with a necromantic body is down."

"Yes. I think my real body just threw up. We're going."

Pyrrha said, "The Sixth House—"

"Oh, fuck the Sixth House! Daddy can have you three safe and sound ... well, sound*ish* ... and like it. I'm extracting my sister before anything else happens. *You*"—Corona had opened her mouth to protest—"*you* get what you wanted. Deuteros is coming with us. I can't make any promises, God is capricious about Edenites, but I'll take the rap, so don't whine. You can hand her to her father on a silver platter and maybe he'll stop moaning about supply lines. As for *you* ..."

This was to Camilla. Nona dragged her attention to Camilla, and was upset; Camilla had a long, growing red stripe sliced through the soft grey material of her shirt, carved straight down her chest. It was bleeding freely. It did not look too deep, but it was long and nasty. Her dark glasses were trembling on her nose.

Camilla said, "Did you ever intend to emancipate the city? To resettle the people?"

"Absolutely not," said the Prince. "I only wanted the Sixth as a goodwill gift for God. The moment I got down here I knew *I* wasn't staying. This trip was a fuckup start to finish, not my fault, and now I have to carry the entrails. There's a *Resurrection Beast* up there, Hect, don't know if you truly know what that is, but I'm not staying anywhere near. Honestly, the people here don't know how good they have it. We're dealing with some *shit* back on Antioch, and really, God can't spare the Hands. No, the Sixth isn't a priority. Which means ... I really don't need you. I don't want the details about Cassiopeia, and *God—doesn't—need—to—know.*"

Each last word was punctuated with a rise in volume, delivered like she had a mouthful of seeds and was spitting them out one by one. There was a pause afterward—Nona saw that Pyrrha had dragged herself to stand—Crown had advanced forward a step, and so had her bodyguards.

The Prince sighed. She said, "So you see, Hect, you're a bit superfluous, and you got inside my guard quicker than I liked. So here, I'll make you an offer ... I can kill you here, *or* I can take off your arms and your legs, pack you up for interrogation, and kill you later."

"Psychological," said Camilla. "Familiar."

"Yes. You remember, don't you? You intervened for me with Cytherea the First. You saved my remaining arm and my legs, I'll give you that ... but you weren't so quick off the mark that you saved my arm, so I admit a great, seething well of deferred and probably unjust anger toward you."

Camilla thought about it. "Sorry?" she said.

"Apology not accepted, asshole," said the Prince brightly. "So, what do you want? I can kill you now, or I can settle some old ghosts by disarming you ... and dislegging you."

Crown said, strangled—

"I will never, ever forgive you if you do this, Ianthe."

"*Traitors,* Corona, remember," said the Prince. "You're all traitors, so I've got to pick my battles. You're my sister, so you're my priority. You won't come without your Captain Deuteros ... I've given you one thing you wanted very badly and as per usual, you only want more. Someone's got to pay the piper, my dear, one way or another. Hect—you can't say I'm not being fair."

Camilla said, "You're consistent. I'll give you that."

"*Yes.* Thank you. Nice to be acknowledged. And now ... Head off, or arms and legs off and head off later? I don't mean to sway you, but I've done *arm off* and it ruined my day."

Camilla thought about it again. She thought about it for so long that Nona assumed, for a moment, that she was really considering these options.

"You challenged the Sixth for its keys," she said eventually. "You named the time. You backed down, but I had right of reply. We didn't consent. Or reject. I accept the challenge of the Third."

Prince Ianthe Naberius looked at her. The expression was—strange.

"That was a lifetime ago," she said. "Over a year."

"The challenge is valid."

"The prize isn't, not anymore. What are the stakes?"

"If I lose, I die," said Camilla. "If I win, I walk away."

"What—you and Harrow? I'll never accept."

"Not Harrow. Only me," said Camilla.

The Prince sounded quite interested and reasonable. "You can't kill me in this body, Hect, or even disable me. And you wouldn't just be fighting my cavalier . . . you'd be fighting me *and* Babs. And you've got to know that between Naberius and me, there are no more weaknesses. I took those away . . . and now he is perfect. You've no way of winning."

"No," said Camilla. And—

"I want to die on my feet."

"How beautiful and lovely a sentiment! Therefore, I refuse," said Prince Ianthe Naberius, much more impatiently. "Piss off, Hect . . . an unlosable battle against a wounded swordswoman with *no* aptitude, *no* backup, who obviously wants to die? Not only is that fishy, but it's unoriginal. The outnumbered, overpowered hero against the narcissistic villain. Yuck. Just like a storybook. As poor old Augustine used to say, *It's impossible, and what's more, it's improbable.* Kneel her."

The two uniformed soldier zombies knelt Camilla, roughly. They squeezed her wrists until, with an agonised hiss of breath, she dropped her daggers. They clattered softly on the carpet. Another zombie jerked her head back.

There was movement by the chairs. Ianthe Naberius jerked her head toward Pyrrha—some of the zombies were lurching toward her—but Pyrrha had reacted too late. Crown had Pyrrha's gun, and although one of the zombies was bear-hugging her around the middle, she had made the gun make that soft *ker-KLUNK* noise and pressed the barrel up into the soft part of her throat. Prince Ianthe Naberius cried out, "For the love of God, Corona—!"

"Let her go," said Crown.

"The Captain or Camilla. Make up your mind, and take one. You know I can't let them both go. Put the gun down, darling, I don't want to hurt you getting it off you."

"I wouldn't get hurt. I'd just die," said Crown, her bronzed throat working against the barrel. "You're not all-powerful here. All you have are wards and puppets. I shoot, the bullet goes through my palate and into the brain, and then you're the Crown Princess of Ida . . . like you never wanted."

"Stop being so fucking dramatic—"

"*Staaahp being so fucking dramahhhtic,*" Crown mimicked, in a high-pitched voice.

"This isn't the time, you dumb, hilarious bitch!"

"You don't even know how to fix Naberius's hair! He needs it done pompadour! He looks awful!"

"*That's* your opposition? *Seriously?*"

"I'm going to shoot myself and you're going to watch," said Crown, with deep satisfaction. "Like when we were teens, but this time I'm going to really tie the rope . . . really drink the poison . . ."

"You didn't then and you wouldn't now—Corona. Coronabeth!"

Crown had closed her eyes. Nona found that she had started to leak tears from sheer fright, and her eyes felt gritty and awful. The Prince said even more urgently, "I can't let Hect live. You know I can't. I can fast-talk for Deuteros . . . *your* life is safe . . ."

"Then duel her!" Crown cried, in obvious agony. "Duel her and give her what she wants! None of us ever could!"

"It's not fair. You're going to be mad at me when I kill her. It's going to be a massacre."

"I won't. I swear I won't. Just fight fair."

"I'm a Lyctor, for fuck's sake. You can't get a fair fight between a flea and a flak cannon."

"You watched her annihilate Lieutenant Dyas—"

"Little girls playing with sticks. If my league exploded, you wouldn't hear the boom in their league for half a myriad. I've become three times the swordsman Babs ever was."

Crown was pleading, "One fight . . . one last duel. *You* challenged her with Babs, you know, back on Canaan House. I didn't do it. So follow through, for me. You always do things for me, don't you? My heart's own . . . *my* necromancer."

Prince Ianthe Naberius shuddered.

"Drop the gun and I'll do it."

Crown hesitated. The Prince stepped back from Camilla, one step, then another; Crown fumbled with the gun. It made a backward *KLUNK-ker*, and then she dropped it loudly to the tiles, where thankfully it did not go off.

Prince Ianthe Naberius's shoulders sagged forward. So did the shoulders of every zombie still standing, including the ones holding Nona. This loosened their grip a little bit, and she was able to breathe out. Her nose and eyes were leaking. The zombies clutching Corona dragged her back to her seat and sat her down, not gently at all, and they held her wrists flat to the arms of her chair. Another zombie took their booted foot and punted the gun to the other side of the room, where it skidded over the tiles and disappeared into a pile of rubbish. Nona watched Pyrrha's eyes follow it.

"Fine," the Prince said petulantly, "*fine*," and she turned around, and she stalked to the centre of the carpet.

"The time and place were named," she said, "now, and here. Corona. You arbitrate."

Nona watched Crown's throat work. There was a bright, dark red mark there, from how hard she had pushed the gun into her neck. She hesitated and said forlornly, "Parietal to calcaneus, I suppose. Full range, full right. Weapon restrictions limited, but blades only, no necromancy . . ."

"I'm made of necromancy. Necromancy literally moves my limbs," said the Prince.

"No active necromancy," amended Crown.

Camilla said, "What about me?"

"Well, you're beginning to see the problem, aren't you?" snapped Ianthe Naberius, slithering her long and shining sword free from its sheath. "You're fighting a dead man, you suicidal Sixth House pea-brain. You can't pink me or kill me. I leave this body when I *say* I leave. But I'll tell you what . . . for expediency's sake . . . here."

Prince Ianthe Naberius reached into her pocket. She removed a very pretty lavender handkerchief with a lace edging. She waved it at Camilla with an exaggerated *see this?* motion, then tucked it into her jacket, stuffing it deep down her shirt.

"Get that off me, and you can leave," she said.

Camilla said, "Can I keep it?"

"What—my *handkerchief?*"

"It's a nice handkerchief," said Camilla.

"You're not taking this seriously, are you," said the Prince.

The zombies advanced. Prince Ianthe Naberius said, "Close ranks. Nobody gets outside," and they made a square around the carpet. Nona found herself being dragged out, forced to watch the action from between the shoulders and heads of the dead soldiers. They had closed off the dais too. A few of them shuffled out of the way so that Crown, pinned to her chair, could see the action. Some of the dead men threw Camilla roughly down on the carpet. Her glasses were now very squiff on her nose, and she rearranged them more securely behind her ears. She mopped a little at her chest . . . she was bleeding freely and messily . . . and she picked up, from where they had fallen, her two long, plain, one-sided knives. Camilla shook out her arms like they were stiff, and she rolled her head from side to side, cheek passing across her chest, and she relaxed.

Nona wanted to scream again, but she was dizzy. Waves of something like nausea kept passing up and down the length of her head. She had blinked everything free from her eyes, so she was terribly worried the dye and plastic inserts had gone—certainly it was much easier to see. This was awful, like watching Beautiful Ruby do a flip trick off a bin without being able to filter it through your fingers to see whether he landed it or not.

The only fight that Nona had ever been invited to was between Hot Sauce and Honesty and some much bigger kids who didn't even go to school. She could barely remember why they were fighting—she had still been quite new and confused as to her role as their friend—but she had been told to go down the street after school, past the dairy, to the old athletics stadium, and Hot Sauce and Honesty would fight the others there. Nona had dithered and thought she ought to tell the nice lady teacher about it, but Honesty said if she did she would get scragged. She hadn't known yet what scragging was and was horribly afraid it was the thing Honesty did where he licked his finger and put that finger in your ear. When she had gotten to the fight she had been so nervous and excited that she was sweaty, but then Hot Sauce arrived and said the kids weren't going to show up because one of them had got hit by a car. Honesty had said, Oho, who did you pay, and Hot Sauce said, Nobody, because I drove the car. Everyone went home happy.

Crown said, "Parietal to calcaneus. No exceptions, no mercies. Challenger has right of execution; may the River show mercy on the challenger; defender has right of property. Point, blade, ricasso, offhand. Call."

Cam called out, "Camilla the Sixth."

"Ianthe the First," said the Prince.

"Three paces back," said Crown. "Turn . . . and begin."

When Crown said, *Begin,* Nona expected Camilla and the Prince to rush at each other. They didn't. They circled each other instead, like they were beginning a dance and weren't fussed about starting any time soon. Camilla kept both of her hands tucked up close to her chest, knives high, as though she wanted to defend her head. The Prince's sword was held forward, light and ready and slender, gleaming under the lightbulbs and red where its polished surface reflected the carpet. It seemed too pretty to do any harm.

Camilla said conversationally, "No offhand?"

"I didn't mean to take anything to this planet I couldn't replace," said the Prince. "I shouldn't have bothered. Why two knives?"

"Shock and awe," said Camilla.

The Prince stepped forward and flickered in and out, extending somehow and then snapping back to the same place she'd been standing, like a shadow jumping up a wall. Camilla did a graceless little shrug-step to one side. The Prince cocked her head like a bird, then jabbed her sword down toward Camilla's thigh, but Camilla had already moved one of her knives to meet it so the sword just went *ching*.

They circled another couple of steps. The Prince jabbed again; Camilla's knife went *ching* again, up near her heart this time. The Prince exuded the dispassionate curiosity of a child poking a dead cat with a stick. Camilla was focused, like the Prince was the only thing she'd ever been interested in.

"If this is all some dreary attempt at stalling," the Prince began, "I'm going to be annoyed—"

She tried another jab, this time with a hint of petulance. It went *clang*, not *ching*, because Camilla hit the Prince's sword hard with one of her knives; the tip of the sword swung wide and Camilla lunged with the other knife aimed at the Prince's belly. The Prince seemed to flex to the side, making her body flat, and simultaneously snapped her sword-hand inward so it caught Camilla in the side of the head. Camilla staggered and backed hurriedly away as the sword-tip came slicing down past her shoulder. She kept stepping back until there were several paces between the two of them. Nona understood innately that this was not a good sign.

"You've got better," said Camilla. "You've been training with someone who knew what they were doing."

"You've gone to pieces," said Prince Ianthe Naberius. "Oh me, oh my. The locals not much good for sparring?"

Nona squeezed her eyes shut and tried to control her breathing, tried to ignore the horrible glove clamped over her mouth. She wished she could get one good deep lungful of air that didn't smell awful. She felt as though if she could stay calm, that would somehow make Camilla calm, and if Camilla could stay calm everything could still be okay. There was another *ching*, another *clang*, then a scuffle of steps on carpet and a huff of breath that sounded like Camilla's.

Nona's eyes flicked open: they were still facing each other, closer now, Camilla crouching a little with her knives crossed, the Prince regarding her with that same dead-cat analytical gaze.

"No," the Prince said, "no, this is a bore, I'm afraid . . . a disappointment all round. How like the Sixth to take the fun out of suicide."

Camilla flipped the knife in her left hand so she was holding it backward, which under normal circumstances Nona would have found enormously exciting and cool. She slashed upward with the other knife, and as the Prince stepped back disdainfully, Camilla rose up to her full height and swung her right arm back over her shoulder like she was going to try to chop something in two pieces. The arm whipped forward: there was a blur of confused motion and a wet *thud* as a knife grew out of the chest of a dead soldier; the Prince had moved rapidly to the side so the knife didn't hit her, and Camilla had ducked the same way and was driving inward and upward, left hand first, blade flashing back round into a normal grip as she came.

For a moment Nona could see the shape of it, like the shape a mouth made right before the sound came out. Camilla had put herself behind the Prince's sword, so there was no way the Prince could get the blade round into a position where it could hit her; her hand was swinging round toward the small of the Prince's back, and the knife-flip meant that her arm was going to end up longer than the Prince would be expecting. It wasn't quite clear how Cam was going to get the handkerchief, but presumably she could think about that once the knife was safely stuck in the Prince's body.

Then the Prince did some sort of complicated dance-step back, bringing her sword in close against her chest, and she kicked out with her front leg. Not like when Honesty tried to kick a tin can off a fence post, just a little sharp shove with her foot, down low, like she was scaring off a stray cat. Camilla's leg folded and her lunge collapsed in on itself: she dropped to her knees and started to roll backward, landing awkwardly on her left arm, still holding the knife. She braced one foot against the floor to push herself off and up, and the Prince simply turned to follow her motion, flicked the sword up, and struck decisively downward.

Nona stared. Camilla sprawled on the carpet. Her empty right hand was grasped round the Prince's right wrist; the Prince's right wrist turned into the Prince's right hand and then into the Prince's lovely thin sword, which ran all the way down into Camilla's belly. The point was somewhere quite far inside Camilla, and Nona couldn't see it anymore.

"You really don't know when to throw those things, do you," said the Prince a little sadly.

Camilla said, "Match to the Sixth."

Ianthe said, "*What?*" and then her eyes rolled backward in her head and she fell.

24

Every zombie soldier in the room crumpled up like Kevin had tipped them out of the soft play box onto the classroom floor. Nona fell with hers and suffered the incredibly disagreeable experience of two big, dead people landing very hard on top of her, and in no way becoming less heavy or less dead.

Nobody came to help her—everyone ran to Camilla. Nona didn't mind at all, except that she wanted to run to Camilla herself. Camilla had risen to her knees, the sword driven through her midsection like a kebab with just one thing on it, and she was grimly—solidly—holding the hilt steady, her dark hair sticking on her sweat-stained face. Crown had tumbled next to her in a handsome heap and was trying to hold the sword steady from the other end, with the presence of mind to wrap her hands in her dress so she didn't cut herself to ribbons. She kept saying, "Stay with me, Camilla. Stay with me," until Cam murmured, wetly and thickly—

"Not going anywhere."

"I'm holding you to that," said the body of Ianthe Naberius.

It sat up all of a sudden, like Nona getting woken up by the sponge, only all at once instead of in stages. It jackknifed in two. Pyrrha had rushed to retrieve her gun the moment all the soldiers started toppling like dolls; now she walked forward holding it in both hands and released the safety, her aim on Ianthe. Then she saw something that Nona couldn't. She lowered the gun. She said—

"You fucking legend."

Ianthe's body ignored her. It grasped the hilt of the blade that was buried in Camilla's body. Camilla did not look up, but only said, to Pyrrha: "It's missed the pelvis. Take it out."

"It's still a gut wound," said Ianthe's body. "You'll be out of commission."

Curiously, Cam kept addressing all her remarks sideways, as though she could not bear to look at or address the dead body. She said, "I'll cope."

Nona was horrified—she could not tear her eyes away—as Ianthe's body grasped that hilt, supported itself on its knees, and pulled.

The body unsheathed the sword—all that slim metal came flashing out—Camilla's chin snapped upward, then back, and she stared at the ceiling, and she did not make any more sound than an unready exhalation. The body flung the sword away—it spun over the tiles, splattering Cam's blood as it went. Ianthe's body tugged off its right glove, and Pyrrha dropped down on the other side, unfolding Cam's shirt. Cam was really a mess now. Crown said, "I'll get bandages," and left Cam propped up by Pyrrha and Ianthe's body.

Camilla didn't like this. She said roughly, "Give me space. I've had worse." Pyrrha moved away, wiping her hands on her trousers, but Ianthe's body didn't. It placed its arms over the flooding wound in Camilla's side, and Cam's chin lolled on her chest. Her breathing was wet—then still and quiet.

Ianthe's body said—

"Won't you look at me, Camilla Hect?"

Camilla murmured something that Nona could not hear. The body said, "I died, and you carried me. I gambled, and you covered my bet. You kept the faith, and were the instrument of both my vengeance and my grace. And now I have fought through time, and the River, and Ianthe the First—fought and bested Ianthe the First, and I hope I never fight her ever again . . . Will you not look at me now, Cam, and know me?"

Camilla raised her chin. She looked at the dead face. She said quietly—

"Yes, Warden, I will always know you."

Their foreheads touched. Camilla reached out with her slippery hand, and Palamedes clasped it with Ianthe Naberius's cold, glove-less one. Because both of their hands were very messy it made an embarrassing *squelch*, but neither of them appeared to notice or care. Nona had to look away.

She heard Palamedes say, in the voice of Ianthe Naberius— "Pyrrha, I can barely do anything. I'm only the hand in a sock puppet. I don't think I could unpick a single ward, and I can't do a damn thing for Cam's bleeding—thank God nothing's protruding."

Cam said, without opening her eyes, "Don't worry about me, Warden. I'll walk it off."

"Yes, thanks for your input," said Palamedes pleasantly. "I've taken it under advisement and will add it to the next agenda."

Camilla smiled that wonderful hot-metal smile that Nona had loved as long as she had been alive.

"Jackass," she said.

"Don't try anything thalergetic, Sextus," Pyrrha said. "Focus on the big picture, we don't need fine-tuning. All you need to do is read the body you're in—it would have touched the corpse. Discounting this room, there shouldn't be any other remains. Where'd she stash it?"

Palamedes took off the other glove on Ianthe Naberius's dead hand. He blindly grasped about, trying not to dislodge Camilla, and put that hand on the tiles. He had to think about it, but then he said— "I can't get fine details. There's some kind of corpse stashed in a downstairs annex room. Two lefts will bring you to a corridor with Ianthe's fin-gerprints all over it—then there's remains, and that's the only corpse sig for two hundred metres, which doesn't really account for—"

"Sextus, I was in the military, that's not fine details, it's a full intel-ligence briefing," said Pyrrha.

"Good. Go and get Gideon's body. Take Nona—poor Nona, dig her out before she's squashed any more."

"Thanks," said Nona.

"But you're—"

"Pyrrha, we have no time. Ianthe's still alive and kicking—up here."

Palamedes tapped his perfectly coiffed head. Crown had emerged from a side door clutching a hard-shell plastic box, crossing over to join them. When Palamedes said, "Alive," she nearly dropped the box. Her expression was terrible.

Pyrrha said, "Sextus, that wasn't wise."

"Probably not," said Palamedes. "But I fought Ianthe Tridentarius within an inch of our lives inside her head, for . . . for a long, long time. How long did it take out here?"

"Four, maybe five seconds," said Crown, ashen-faced.

"Lucky you. To me, it was a little longer," said Palamedes with a slight smile. "It would have been a disgrace to kill her . . . No, Cam, I mean it. I currently have more respect for Ianthe than she ever won from me previously. I'm going to hold her back as long as I can, but if I hold her for more than an hour I'll be astonished. Your Highness, go and get Captain Deuteros, then meet us back here."

Crown kept fingering the package of bandages. Her eyes were huge and purple and glimmering, like pools of violet water. She said quietly, "You are a good man, Sextus."

"No. If I didn't think it was safer to trap Ianthe than to let her retreat back to her body, out there in deep space somewhere, I'm not sure I *wouldn't* have killed her . . . Just because I feel good about not killing her doesn't mean I wouldn't have. It wasn't mercy, Princess."

"I don't care. Thank you—thank you for not . . . not hurting her. Let me help Cam, I know how to dress a field injury . . ."

"I'm without resources," said Palamedes with dignity, "but I think I can still bandage my cavalier's abdominal wound. Can you carry Judith Deuteros?"

"Of course, but the guards—"

"Unconscious or locked up," said Pyrrha. "I clonked half of them on the head, and the other ones are in the mess. Deuteros's door should be unlocked, but don't move her without sedating her. Nona—you're with me."

Crown dropped the scraps of her dress. When she looked at Palamedes, Nona was suddenly struck by the idea that Crown wasn't happy at all, or grateful—and yet she obviously was, hungrily and thirstily grateful; she put Nona in mind of Noodle, suddenly, wanting to go out but wanting to stay in the basket, wanting to run around outside but wanting to come back. Then Crown deflated like a beautiful balloon and fled.

Nona felt wobbly and unreal. Her body was able to walk and move and hold itself upright, but she still felt very light-headed, disconnected from herself. As Pyrrha steered her out of the room, Nona kept looking back over her shoulder at Camilla and the body Palamedes was inhabiting, still kneeling on the floor, bloody and bent. Palamedes looked as though he were talking quietly to her—but Pyrrha closed the door behind them.

Once they were out of the room, Pyrrha took Nona by the shoulders and said, "You all right?"

Nona's eyes kept crossing and uncrossing. "I'm not sure," she confessed. "I feel strange."

"Did those corpses falling on you hit a nerve?"

"No, I only feel funny."

"You want me to pinch you, kiddie?"

That was so banal and unwelcome that Nona shook back into her body out of pure disgust.

"*No.* I don't want to be pinched. Why do you always offer to pinch me? I never want to be pinched."

"Just proving I'm me. Look at you—not sure I like the couture. Who did your eyes? It's all coming off. Here, use my sleeve, not yours." Nona obligingly used the sleeve, and quite a lot of white, gummy stuff came off on it. "Smart way of hiding it though. I should've thought of that. Good to go?"

"I can do it."

"Okay. Shake a leg," said Pyrrha.

The barracks had not got any less foetid or dark—in fact, Nona balked at the dark flight of stairs as they smelled so bad, and had to hold her breath as Pyrrha escorted her down—and there was so much rubbish, so many strange things laid out in strange places, that at one point they had to pick their way over piles and piles of boxes in order to pass. "This place is a maze. I never would have found her myself," said Pyrrha, lifting Nona over a busted-up bedframe.

"Pyrrha—you're not *really* a Lyctor again, are you? You're you, not your other self?"

"No. I was only pretending, like you were only pretending. You can check my eyes," said Pyrrha.

"I hope you don't mind being the last one to know," said Nona, dusting herself off a bit self-consciously, "but I'm dying."

This fell completely flat.

"'Course you are," said Pyrrha.

"I mean it, Pyrrha."

"Yeah. I suspected you were, though," Pyrrha said cheerfully. "I didn't make a big deal out of it. We've all got our secrets ... but the soul longs for the body, Nona. Even a fucked-up soul ... even a soul that's been changed forever. It takes a *lot* to acclimate a soul to a body it wasn't born in, if that original body's around for it to miss."

"But you're not sad," said Nona.

"Of course I'm not sad. You're not dying on my watch. Kiddie, when you were yelling ..."

Nona was still a little embarrassed about that.

"I took Cam a bit too literally."

Pyrrha opened her mouth to say something, but then they rounded the second left and she shut her mouth.

The hallway corridors were made of good white interior bricks braced with concrete and metal struts—lots of buildings were; the white stone kept out the heat—but one short section of this particular corridor had been decorated in delicate blood filigree and squiggles: not only the walls, but the floor and even the ceiling. The squiggles were thickest in a square on one wall, like someone had wanted to mark off a door. Pyrrha glanced at the wall, and then she barked out a laugh.

"Is that writing?" said Nona.

"Sort of. It's a ward—a mark meant to keep us out. Necromancy. *That* bit's writing though, House."

"What's it say?"

Pyrrha pointed. *"Don't go through here."* And pointed again. *"I mean it, idiot. You will disintegrate.* A bit obvious . . . everything else was good and paranoid. These things are all over the barracks—her bedroom, the shipyard, the downstairs tunnel exits. Some of 'em were blinds though. She never trusted me fully. The corpse must be down here."

"Okay. What's the trap?"

Pyrrha took up a piece of trash from a box that had half-tumbled over—a piece of broken pipe—and tossed it, underhand, toward the door.

It shivered into bits before Nona's eyes, and a fine patter of dust came out the other end and dribbled on the corridor floor.

"It's a shit version of Mercymorn's old entropy trap," said Pyrrha. "Not half as good. Done entirely through wards—brilliant—but entirely reliant on wards—fucking ridiculous. Good at keeping people out though . . . and almost impossible for anyone but another Lyctor to break. See what it's made out of? That's blood. Blood wards age, and they burn out if you make them work too hard . . . And I'm sorry, No-No, but that's where you come in."

Nona didn't understand. "If you want us to stand here chucking stuff at it we'll be here all day."

"Nona," said Pyrrha, "your regeneration ability is a million times better than any normal Lyctor's. None of them could regrow the way you do. I'm not sure you've *got* a limit . . . not with the kind of damage you've come back from. So I'm really sorry . . . we're going to have to use you, and it's going to hurt like fuck. I wouldn't ask you to do this if it were not literally the most important thing in the world."

Nona found herself giving a fluttery sigh. She felt a little bit envious, and a little bit weary. "What's so special about this body we're going after, anyway?"

"In general? She's the key to a door that's been kept locked for ten thousand years," said Pyrrha. "Personally? She's the last thing I have left of a woman I tried to trick into loving me, and got played myself. And for you? She might be you, kiddie."

Nona found herself sighing again, like her body wanted to let out all its sound at once. One of her ears felt slightly blocked, and when she tilted her head and blew her nose and pulled at her earlobe a little trickle of water came out.

"What if I don't like me?" she said.

But Pyrrha didn't seem to understand.

"Well, you'll probably start visiting clubs and trying to hit on the dancers, and going from relationship to relationship not really being able to commit."

Nona was severe.

"You talk too much, Pyrrha."

For a moment she could not decide what to put in—she considered the foot, on the understanding that the foot was the furthest away from the head so maybe it would take the pain longer to travel—but that would have messed with her shoe. Shoes never grew back. And she had never liked her hands. Nona reached out with her left one, trembling a little—she never minded pain as it happened, but she was a terrible baby *anticipating*—until she gasped, "Pyrrha, help, I can't, I'm frightened," and Pyrrha took mercy on her and grasped her by the elbow. She thrust Nona's arm forward. The tips of her fingers breached some invisible barrier, and they dissolved.

Something awful was happening where her fingers met the barrier. The tops of her fingertips became a red and grey mist. A fine spray splattered back on her hand or became tiny white drops of steam when they hit the barrier and then those drops of steam became nothing. Pyrrha was holding her still as her hand burned apart, her hand felt sick, her hand felt like throwing up. It was like the lurching pain of having a tooth knocked out, if it was about one hundred teeth and they were all at the ends of your hands.

But the worst part was what her hand was doing, because her hand freaked out. Great gouts of skin were suddenly travelling up where they shouldn't have been, looking like red-and-brown-and-white lumps of wax—soft ferny sprouts of what she realised was her own bone were poking and trembling out of that flesh, spiralling forward as though trying to find something to grasp on to, as though they could regrow her fingers in a safer place. That was what frightened her, watching that flesh resolve, watching that flesh resolve into *extra fingers*. Out of the wax another hand sprouted, reaching back toward her, as though it were a mirror—and Nona screamed, sickened, and thrust her hand in to the wrist to get rid of it.

With a retort like a million tiny fireworks the red marks covering the corridor exploded. One went, then the next, then the rest all at once—*POP—POP-POP-POP-POP*, like Honesty had bought them cheap at the dairy and thrown a match in the box. There was a noise like a car backfiring, the air shimmered, and a fine bloody powder rained down from the ceiling.

Nona dropped to her haunches and clutched her hand between her thighs, afraid to look at it. Her heart was beating so hard that she was worried it would burst. Her gaze lurched drunkenly, as though her eyes were independent of herself. For a moment she wanted to yell, *Help*, like she had done before, pretending to be the Captain. She wanted to shout. She wanted to be listened to. She wished the barrier had taken her hands. She wished she had thrust herself into it— become that big seething mass of flesh and meat and tendrils—ruined her body, just *melted* it; come back messed up, so that nobody could want her body but her, so that it would be hers and nobody else's.

This was a horrible thing to think. Nona hated herself immediately and fervently.

Pyrrha had dropped down beside her—had gathered her in her big dark wiry arms, smelling ferally like sweat, her cheeks a little rough from the bristles where she hadn't shaved. Her throat was scratchy and nice, and Nona buried her face in it and made little *ah, ah, ah* sounds until she felt better.

Pyrrha had reached down and seized her hand—was saying, "You're fine. There's nothing wrong. Look." But she couldn't make Nona look for fully twenty seconds. When Nona looked at last it *was* fine—her hand was perfectly normal—except the fingernails had grown way too long, massively long, so that one of her hands looked like a claw. Pyrrha immediately took out her pocketknife and shaved them down for her, a bit ragged, but much better.

"Brave girl. Sorry, Nona, no time to catch our breath. Go start opening doors," she said. "I'm going to clean this up in case any of the wards are partially intact. Don't want the body losing chunks on the way out. She's going to be hell to carry."

Nona's head swam again briefly, but she nodded. She set off down the corridor. She opened the first door on the left, but it was only a cupboard with some brooms. She jogged to the next one, a heavier door, with a key still in the lock. She turned the key, pushed the handle, and stood on the threshold.

It was just an ordinary bedroom. It didn't have any windows—they were probably at least a floor underground—and it was only lit by a single lightbulb, so it was pretty dim. It looked wide: there was room for the whole bed, and would have been room for another if you pushed it up against the wall. And stretched out on the bed—nearly too big for it—was the girl from her dream: the girl who might be her.

Nona tiptoed in, feeling absurdly that it was wrong to make noise, and peered at the body. She had not seen many dead bodies close up. The long corpse was dressed beautifully in white: white trousers, brown boots that looked nearly new, a white jacket with silver frogging and toggles. The jacket had been unbuttoned some. The girl looked like she had gone to sleep with her shoes on after a long, tiring day: her face had that half-past-a-dream expression. Her red hair was even redder in the dark, brighter than Pyrrha's and redder than Honesty's, and the little wreath of bones and blossoms was askew over her temples. She had a decided chin and a nose that was the complete opposite of Nona's nose, one that put her in mind of those big poison desert cats Born in the Morning was crazy about.

Nona wasn't at all sure she was beautiful. The face wasn't bad. It made her think of something, but nothing bad really, only dead. Her skin was very much dead-person skin, ashen and tinted the wrong colour around the nostrils and the mouth. But even if she hadn't been dead, Nona was critical. Her eyelashes were very dark, but short and curly, whereas Nona thought all eyelashes should be long and straight (her own eyelashes were long and straight). The corpse had too much mouth and a dimple (nobody in her home had a dimple). You could not, at least, see the veins in her eyelids, which were heavy and cold and deep-set. But Nona thought it was going to be a shame to go from being so lovely as she was to being so—*redheaded.*

Nona put her hand close to the corpse's cold hand, very tentatively, expecting something to happen, once she touched it; that she would suddenly melt away, or pop out of existence like a soap bubble. What happened made her think much better of the corpse. It opened its eyes—and its eyes were yellow, the gold of the old sky, like hers only much foggier. Those were beautiful: Nona had always adored her eyes, and here they were again, on the corpse, only partially spoiled for being dead. They looked like treasure at night.

The corpse looked at her in such mute, helpless appeal—spoke to her in her first language—that Nona did not have to think about what she did next. She leant down and laid a kiss right on that cool, dead, crooked mouth.

She kissed her just the once. The corpse's mouth was soft and rough and cold, and did not respond to Nona's mouth, but a tremble went through the upper body. Nona was surprised and relieved to find that the corpse girl tasted like toothpaste.

At the tremble, Nona pulled back, self-conscious. The expression on the corpse's face could not have been more rigid with shock and disbelief. She found herself saying, a little defensively—

"You looked like you wanted to be kissed, that's all."

A shadow crossed the doorway, blocking out quite a lot of the outside light. Nona turned around and said, "Pyrrha, I'm really sorry, I messed up," but Pyrrha was staring at the corpse girl as though she had seen a ghost, or maybe two.

When Nona turned to the girl, she was taken aback: the corpse's eyes were closed and she lay completely still on the bed—arms loose, limbs heavy and untidy, the very picture of deadness.

Pyrrha crossed over, stared down at the barely illuminated corpse, and said— "Yeah, that's Gideon Nav, all right . . . I'd know her anywhere. I wouldn't need to be told. Talk about being the mother's daughter."

Nona was puzzled. "Who?"

"You've seen her photo," said Pyrrha, and she reached over—hovered a hand quite close to Gideon's face—and then pulled it back, apparently having thought better of it. "Blood of Eden mass-manufactured 'em . . . wasn't even a good shot. But this kid's the spit of her . . . nearly. She's *him* in the eyes and brows . . . amazed Mercymorn didn't see it. But she wasn't looking for it, I guess."

"Her mother was the woman who broke your heart," guessed Nona.

"Yes," said Pyrrha. And: "Let's not get too cute about it, though. My best friend and I punched her out an airlock. Apart from that, I was ready to commit."

For some reason, Nona felt vaguely hurt and envious. *She* didn't have a mother for Pyrrha to have punched out an airlock. Nor had Pyrrha ever looked at her the way she now looked at the dead corpse with red hair—a kind of soft, guarded want; a hunger—a living desire to take the corpse in her arms like Kevin's wanting desire with his dolls. To own, to squeeze, to cosset and destroy.

She remembered, and said hastily, before Pyrrha could say anything too personal: "Pyrrha, she can hear you, I think she's awake."

Pyrrha looked at Nona. She looked at the dead body. She put her hand on the dead body's forehead—worked her fingers into the funny little scarf at her neck—and the corpse lay as inert and as dead as it had when Nona walked into the room. Nona said, "I mean it . . . I woke her up . . . I, uh, I kissed her."

Now Pyrrha looked at Nona. The look on her face was nothing but a very sad, rough kind of amusement, less desire than a kind of understanding that Nona suddenly didn't want. Pyrrha touched Nona briefly on the cheek and said: "Why?"

Nona found her cheeks growing hot.

"I just did, no reason."

"Nothing happened? What'd it feel like?"

"That's private, thank you," said Nona primly.

"Huh," said Pyrrha. "Well, you're not in a heap on the floor, so we can rule out pneumatic reversion." She scrubbed a hand across her eyes briefly. "There was a bad option where your soul snapped straight into her body, leaving your body stuck with no soul at all, and that would have been a shit time all round."

"Would I have died?" Nona asked, interested.

"You'd have tried to," said Pyrrha. "The body needs thalergy *and* a soul to keep the lights on. Anastasia's tripod principle. Body plus thalergy, but no soul, is basically a very weird vegetable . . . after a while it gives up and shuts down."

"She looked at me, Pyrrha," said Nona, and to demonstrate, reached over and prodded the body hard, in the ribs. The body did not respond.

"Did you catch her eye colour?"

"Gold—like mine, but cloudy."

"Good. Ianthe couldn't transfer," said Pyrrha. "God, that little shit shouldn't be running around in this day and age . . . would've taken Cassiopeia *and* Cyrus *and* Ulysses *and* Cytherea just to keep her in hand. She's good and she's imaginative and she's very frightening, and now there's no one to stop her. Why the hell did John let her bring the kid's body? He must have known that Blood of Eden would go apeshit the moment they saw it. Well . . . heave-ho."

She squatted down, then heaved the corpse over her shoulder; the girl's head hung down over Pyrrha's back, and her legs hung across Pyrrha's front. Nona saw that the girl was wearing a beautiful jewelled scabbard on her hip, with a lovely sword hilt right above it, all in a sort of pearly white colour. There was something clipped to her other hip that she couldn't quite make out, also pearl-white, a jumble of clear white blades and plate rivets. Everything she was wearing *was* lovely, as lovely as Ianthe Naberius's clothes had been if not lovelier. But the pristine whiteness of her uniform made her look that much more dead, except for the hair.

Pyrrha grunted and said, "Fuck me, she's heavy. It's all this crappy First House tat. I don't know what the fuck John's thinking, dressing everyone to look like the military wing of disco."

Nona was beginning to doubt herself furiously. "Pyrrha, I'm still not sure . . ."

"Tell Sextus and Hect once we're upstairs," said Pyrrha. "Also, hey—I have half a protein bar in my pocket. I want you to eat that. I bet you haven't had anything in hours. Cam can't make you eat like I can, right?"

Nona subsided into glum silence. She stared at the head of the corpse prince as Pyrrha carefully walked her out of the doorway—hoping briefly that Pyrrha would clonk the corpse's head so that the corpse maybe said, "Ow"—but Pyrrha manoeuvred her smoothly. The eyes kept shut—Nona trailed behind watchfully the whole time, but they kept shut—and even when Nona caught up to Pyrrha and gently touched that cool dark corpse hand, nothing happened.

As they passed through the broken wards of the corridor, now completely scuffed out, Nona found herself staggering. Pyrrha said, "You okay? Can you keep up just a little longer?" and she said, "Yes," and tried to keep up. They took two rights, and thankfully Pyrrha didn't ask for help as she heaved the corpse prince up the stairs.

Crown was waiting for them in the corridor. When she saw the body, her lovely violet eyes widened, and her hand went reflexively to the black-hilted sword at her hip, and she said— "It *is* her. Poor Gideon . . ."

"Don't get your hopes up. It might be a doll copy," warned Pyrrha. "I can't see why John would ever let her corpse out into the world, even with a Lyctor to guard it. She's a walking suicide note."

Crown had been tentative, but she suddenly surged forward and cradled that very red head in her hands, smoothing her fingers through the hair, playing with one of the little winking leaves that scintillated in the wreath. She said, wondering, "But she looks exactly like she did . . . apart from the outfit. Ianthe couldn't have done the outfit. She's more minimalist than that."

Her fingers caressed the ashen, upside-down cheek. "Poor Ninth . . . imagine the hopes and fears of the whole universe contained in one dead little red star."

"If that's poetry, don't quit your day job," said Pyrrha. "What's the status of the shuttle?"

Crown dropped her hand from the corpse's hair and grimaced. "You're carrying the only good news. Palamedes says the shuttle's fucked . . . his words exactly, he got surprisingly filthy."

"What? How? Is it warded?"

"No, but the fuel is," confessed Corona, "and that stuff's not only combustible, Dve . . . it's pyrophoric. If we mess around with it too much, this whole barracks is going to go up and set light to most of the quarter."

Nona said feebly, "I could probably—"

"No," said Pyrrha.

"Camilla says forget the shuttle for now, we can come back for it— she wants We Suffer to secure the Sixth House and we'll take it from there. I left them with the Captain, in the main hall," Crown added. Her forehead crumpled into its worry pucker again and she said, "That's the other bad news—Judith's acting up. Her sedative's taking forever to kick in. The Warden's working on her, but he says he can't do much. Why could Ianthe do necromancy through Babs's corpse but Palamedes can't?"

"Just answered your own question. Ianthe's a Lyctor working through the corpse of her own cavalier—that body's hers to make a revenant out of," said Pyrrha. "He won't be able to do anything until he's back in his cavalier, and at this rate . . ."

She cut herself off, and said, "Help Nona. She's worked too hard."

Nona was about to protest, but then Crown turned around and offered her back for a piggyback. Nona couldn't resist, even if it was purely a kiddie thing to do; she let Crown pull her legs around her hips and heave her up onto her back, arms twined around Crown's neck, with Crown saying in her gallant, flirtatious way, "*Now* I have you, my pretty maid," and making Nona laugh, if weakly.

Past the big, broad corridor leading to the open front doors, night had fallen profoundly on the city. The honks and nice fresh car-flavoured night air came surging through the doors with a warm breeze. It was disappointing to go back into the big tiled room with all the dead bodies in it, which smelled bad and closed-in, but she was delighted to find Camilla looking much better and even standing up. Her whole abdomen was swathed in bandages, they had taken all the clothing off her top, and she was wearing Ianthe Naberius's white jacket draped over her shoulders, but she was standing. Her face still looked grey beneath its nice normal olive, and she was shiny with sweat, but she was healthy enough to shift her weight from side to side and jiggle one foot impatiently.

The Captain had been brought into the big room and laid down with some rags rolled up as a pillow beneath her head. She kept moving restlessly—like lightning kept jolting through her arms and legs—like her knees and arms were attached to some drunken puppeteer. Her mouth kept opening but Nona was devoutly grateful that nothing came out, nothing except a noise like: *ah, ah, ah.*

When Nona and Crown came in, and Pyrrha with the corpse, both Palamedes and Camilla looked up at them keenly. Something in Palamedes's face changed and creased, and he said— "What—no reaction?"

"No. Nona even gave the damn thing mouth-to-mouth," said Pyrrha.

Nona was embarrassed at how her voice peeped when she said, "*Private information,* Pyrrha," but Palamedes said, "Does that mean—is it just a copy? Put it down."

Pyrrha fell to her knees, and Nona was interested to see how gentle she was with the redheaded corpse prince, which really did seem completely dead—its arms and legs were heavy and limp. Crown squatted down so that Nona could slither down off her back.

Camilla said, "If that's a copy, this is all over."

"It can't be," said Crown blankly.

"It very much can," said Pyrrha.

"No—I mean, that doesn't make sense," she said. "If it was a copy, my sister didn't know it. She's been acting like she's been standing on hot coals this entire time—and she wasn't doing it to fool me."

Palamedes said, "Give me a moment."

He fell to his knees next to the corpse—quite awkwardly; he wasn't moving as nicely as he usually did. As he fell he said mildly, "Mm. Think I displaced a patella. It's not as easy as with you, Cam . . . Right, Gideon. Let's have a look at you."

He undid her scarf, and Nona looked away. Beneath the scarf a huge wound in the throat made the neck yawn wide open. When she peeked back, wishing she had her braids to screen everything, she saw that Palamedes had unbuttoned the shirt partway and there was another big wound in the chest—a big purple bloodless puncture wound, with white teeth peeking out coyly from within.

"Damage is consistent with reported injuries. There's another wound lower down."

"If it's John's copy, that doesn't prove anything. It's going to be exact," said Pyrrha.

"I know. But I do have a personal advantage here—I've touched her when she was alive."

"Yeah, but—"

Palamedes had placed Ianthe Naberius's hand over the wound. He closed his eyes—really his eyes, his nice dark grey ones, not the strange blue ones with flecks—but almost immediately after closing them, he turned his head and sneezed violently; shuddered with the same violence; pulled his hand away, and said—

"What? What *is* that?"

"You just met God," said Pyrrha.

"I didn't like him," said Palamedes.

"God's preserving her . . . or God created her, or both. Good luck seeing anything through that. His aptitude's like a punch in the nose, Sextus. Once he gets his fingers on something you'll never find any other fingerprints on it. Too much noise."

But Crown's exquisite face had puckered again. "But that was the whole point. When Blood of Eden picked her up—that was why they thought she was strange—Gideon never showed any sign of decomposing. She was always like a corpse that had been dead for only minutes. They wrapped her in plex and dropped her in rivers, trying to see if that would do anything . . . I was there. It was awful at first," she added, "and then it simply started being very funny . . . Shh, Judith. I'm here."

The Captain had started fussing again. Crown, distracted, moved to her side. She said tenderly, "If it wasn't for you I wouldn't be in all this trouble. You thorn, you pest," but the Captain subsided, merely jiggling her arms and her legs.

Palamedes said— "This may well be what's keeping Nona out too. Doesn't matter. We have to operate on the basis that she really is

Gideon Nav. First, lift her head so I can reach her neck . . . let's make sure Ianthe can't transfer to her again, whatever happens. *Surely* I'm good enough for a simple ghost ward. Cam, I'll use your blood—it's the one resource we've got basically sprayed around the room."

"I can give you some more," said Camilla. "There's a spoonful left, somewhere in here."

"Camilla Hect," said Palamedes, "I would slap you—except Naberius Tern trying to slap you would force me to kick my own ass."

They rolled the corpse prince over. Palamedes sketched some squiggles onto the back of her neck with the pad of Ianthe Naberius's littlest finger, using Cam's bloodied clothes as a kind of paint box. He did this very carefully, then started fanning his hand to dry the mark. Camilla said, "Warden, do we continue?"

"Yes. We get the Oversight Body. Then we get out of here."

Crown said, "But the shuttle—"

"Oversight Body, then the shuttle," said Palamedes. "Master Archivist Juno Zeta is pretty damned good with wards; she'll probably have ten ideas I never thought of, once she rips through all the ideas I have."

This did not appear to fully convince Crown. "But even if we get the shuttle working, what next?"

"The Sixth House installation," said Camilla, and Palamedes finished—

"We join up with the rest of the Sixth—we get the necromancers out of this system and out of the halo—we find some way to lure the Resurrection Beast away from this planet so that the population gets some breathing room, while at the same time safeguarding it from any more House strong-arming—we fix Nona . . . we stop the war, we sue for peace . . . and we go to the Ninth House, and we begin the real fight."

Nona found that all eyes were on her. She looked around, in case there was someone behind her that everyone was actually looking at, but it was just her. She did not know what the Ninth House was. Nobody she knew had more than One House. Honesty barely had a Quarter House. She did not know what the Ninth House was—and yet her teeth were chattering, quite apart from herself, and she had to clench her jaw very hard to make them stop. This made everyone look away, which annoyed her, because the way they moved their faces was pure pity.

Palamedes started heaving the corpse over to lie on its back again—Camilla tried to approach and help, but he shooed her away—and once rolled, it lay there awkwardly, splayed, its clothes and sword in disarray. He said, in obvious satisfaction, "There. That'll be a first barrier to stop her doing any kind of revenant transfer. Now, Cam, pass me the syringe."

Camilla rootled around in the medical kit that Crown had brought in, and retrieved a big needle. She removed the webbing from around it, and Pyrrha said: "Sextus, don't think I haven't thought about this. If a blood sample was going to be enough, I would've said to do it first thing. Harrowhark Nonagesimus couldn't have rolled aside that damned rock unless it was fresh out of the vat."

"You never know," said Palamedes calmly. "Look at her—her colour's even, there's no trace of dehydration or gravity acting on the internal fluids. If you examine the wounds, they look clean and cauterised. I can probably get a decent sample."

"Even if the blood survives outside the body, we'll need to take her along as a backstop."

"If it survives outside the body, it'll tell us something really interesting," said Palamedes. "I'm going to puncture the femoral sheath."

Camilla passed him a little pair of scissors, and he cut a short slit in the thigh of the corpse's soft leather trousers. Then Palamedes prodded around with his fingers—he placed the needle to the dead skin—and the corpse's hand shot out and ringed around his wrist before anyone could stop it. Nona noticed that one of the corpse prince's sleeves had worked up, and that on her wrist was a funny fat bracelet: a braided cord of many colours, none of which matched.

"One, that's not going to work. Two, I fucking hate needles," said the corpse. "Three—Sex Pal, if that's how you get a lady's pants off, holy shit, no wonder I stole your girl."

Palamedes rocked back on his heels.

"Not *my* girl. Unlike some of us, I've never much seen the allure of an evil cougar," he said crisply. "Good morning, Gideon."

25

PYRRHA'S GUN MADE A fast *ker-KLUNK*. She hadn't pointed it at anyone, exactly, but it was in both her hands and her arms had tensed. "Back up, Sextus," she said.

"Who's that?" said the corpse, not letting go of Palamedes's wrist. She craned her neck to one side. "Oh, hey. Long time no drown. You're the one who bragged about spading my mum."

"Anyone who spaded your mum would brag about it," said Pyrrha.

"Ninth?" said Crown, sounding almost nervous.

Pyrrha ignored her, and said: "He brought you back. He's made a revenant out of you."

"Yope," said the corpse prince.

"But that's impossible. He shouldn't have been able to separate you. Your girl didn't manage full fusion, but what she took from you not even John could've got back. And . . . he didn't bring you back all the way? He brought you back like *this*?"

"Sextus, if you don't put that needle away I'm going to break Naberius's fucking arm," said the corpse irritably.

"I can't," Palamedes said. "You're still holding onto my wrist."

"Oh. Yeah. If I let go of your wrist you have to not stick me with the needle and then run for it, okay?"

"How exactly do you think blood samples work?"

"Please," said Crown. "I'm so confused. You're . . . actually the Ninth? Gideon the Ninth? You're—what—alive?"

The corpse let go of Palamedes's wrist. He withdrew his arm, still holding the needle, and sat back on his heels. The corpse levered

369

herself up into a sitting position, then braced her arm against the floor and scrambled upright with surprising ease. She dusted off the thighs of her trousers.

What shocked Nona was not that the corpse moved. It was the way in which she moved. Nona was so distracted that she couldn't stop watching. She had never seen anyone move like that before.

"Nope, and nope," she said. "I'm Prince Kiriona Gaia the First, Her Divine Highness, First Lieutenant of the Cohort, Emperor's Life Guards, non-auxiliary—honorary title but who cares—heir to the Emperor Divine, first of the Tower Princes. And I'm *mega* dead."

"John, you mad bastard," said Pyrrha softly. She hadn't taken either hand off her gun.

"*Heir to the Emperor Divine?*" said Crown.

"Kiriona?" said Camilla.

"I mean, it's fine, you can call me Gideon if you want," said Prince Kiriona Gaia the First. "I kind of keep forgetting it's me when people say *Kiriona*. Anyway, who've we got?" She glanced round the group with interest. "Corona—looking great, ma'am, may I say—Cam, though probably not for long by the looks of it—Mumfucker Prime—Judith Deuteros for some reason, or, like, her corpse—and Sex Pal. Oh, and this fake Nonagesimus over here." She paused. "Everyone but Corona can leave. How come you're ambulant, Sextus? Thought you went *bang*."

"How long have you been awake?" asked Palamedes, standing up with noticeably more difficulty than the corpse prince had done.

"Whole time. I've been playing possum. Pretty clever, right?"

Nona was indignant enough at Prince Kiriona Gaia's whole demeanour, but this last piece of self-congratulation was too much to bear. "*I* knew it!" she burst out. "You didn't fool me—I saw you looking at me, back in the other room! You know, when I—"

"Yes, congratulations," said the Prince sarcastically. "No, babycakes, I didn't fool you. Who is this literal goddamn infant? Can someone give her like a rusk or something and shut her up?"

Nona opened her mouth to say the worst thing she had ever said—she didn't know quite what it was going to be, but she understood that when it emerged it would be really bad, perhaps the worst thing anyone had ever said, she could feel it bubbling in her throat—but Palamedes shot her a beseeching glance and she forced her jaw to clamp shut.

"Nona, sorry, but hold on," said Palamedes. "This isn't making as much sense as I'd like it to, and we're short on time. Nav, why did Ianthe lock you away in the first place, if you're moving under your own steam?"

"Oh—she got big pissed that I came along for the ride," said Gideon. "She shut me off in public so I wouldn't screw up the very important Sixth House mission." She made a sort of insulting noise by blowing air out very fast through almost-closed lips, like *pvvvvbb.*

"The ride?" said Palamedes. "Wait. You mean you *both* dropped through the River? In that shuttle?"

"Can't be," said Pyrrha, who was watching the Prince narrowly. "Not anymore. You've got a *soul* attached to you, kid . . . or part of one, at least. John would have had to go with you to stop it being stripped bare."

The corpse prince tilted her head to one side, like a curious bird. "You haven't been in the River lately, have you?" she said.

"What's that meant to mean?"

"Guess you'll find out at some point," said the Prince. "Anyway. You're going to the Ninth House, right? I want in."

"Why?" said Camilla.

The Prince shrugged. "Why not? Nostalgia. Boy, how I miss the old place. There's no skeleton like a home skeleton, you know? I have so many happy memories there."

"Nav," said Palamedes levelly, "if you've been awake this whole time, you know perfectly well what we're doing. Given that you've introduced yourself as *Prince Kiriona Gaia the First,* should you not be trying to stop us in the Emperor's name?"

Prince Kiriona Gaia smiled. It was not a very friendly smile: it went slowly up her face, and there was something a little bit hungry about it.

"Oh, Sex Pal," she said. "Do you—do you want to *fight* me?"

"No," said Palamedes, at the same time moving one hand up and to the side to stop Camilla, who had taken a first step forward. "I very much don't. I've already fought one of the so-called Tower Princes today. Besides that, I consider you a friend of mine." This filled Nona with vague outrage: she could not believe that someone as kind as Palamedes could be friends with someone as awful as Kiriona Gaia. "But I'm struggling to understand why you're here . . . what you're doing . . . what you *want* out of this. What do you want, Gideon?"

The corpse prince considered this. "I don't want much of anything anymore," she said brightly. "I just don't really give a shit. I got on Ianthe's shuttle because it looked like it was more fun than standing around at home watching parades and getting saluted. I could kill all you guys and John would probably give me another medal or something—okay, not you, Corona, Ianthe would never shut up about it—but . . . eh, medals. I want to go where stuff's *happening*. And I feel like . . . I feel like I've got unfinished business on the Ninth. Very cultural, very personal."

"She's lying," said Nona instantly. With all the white noise coming from the corpse prince, she couldn't tell exactly where the lie was, but it was buried deep around her smile.

"I thought I told you to shut your stolen goddamned mouth," said Kiriona, not pleasantly, and Camilla said—

"Don't push it, Ninth."

Nona's heart fluttered. It didn't even matter when Kiriona said, "Sure, Cam. Marry a moron, then die. I get the urge."

Palamedes repeated, very patiently: "What do you want, Gideon?"

The corpse prince didn't turn an eyelash.

"I want to go back. Who cares about my reasons?"

That didn't look like a lie. Crown looked at Nona; Nona shrugged. Crown looked desperately at Palamedes. Palamedes, Nona noticed, was looking curiously rocklike, giving nothing away.

Crown said, "Warden, please. We *need* her."

"Yeah, you do," said the Prince. "I don't come in test tubes. So you can either let me hitch back to the Ninth, or you can all come at me, together, and see if you can draw a single drop of my dead-ass blood. Go nuts. I get a little bit of excitement in my day whatever happens."

Camilla twitched forward, and the Prince saw her. She grinned. "Yeah, that's the spirit," she said. "Come on, Cam. You're still mostly alive, right? Here, look, I'll make it easy on you." She rolled up one sleeve and stuck the bare forearm out in front of her, fist clenched, steady. "Try it. I'm ready for my shot, doc."

Camilla stepped forward more deliberately, keeping her eyes on the Prince's eyes. Palamedes said, "For heaven's sake, Nav, lay off the grandstanding," but Camilla took the Prince's wrist, positioned the needle, and pushed the syringe decisively home.

The needle snapped in half, like she'd jabbed it into the tiled floor. Camilla staggered back as if this had thrown her off-balance. Kiriona Gaia opened her hand—moved it to steady Camilla's shoulder—then, like she was flinching, roughly shoved her away. Camilla fell back into Palamedes's arms.

The Prince stared at them. Her eyes weren't like Nona's at all now: they were hard and dead and bright, like something that had been dug up.

"My father has made my body's bones denser than titanium plex," said the Crown Prince coldly. "My father has made my skin turn away bullets. I am the perfect sword hand and the final expression of the art of the Nine Houses. Don't you get it? I am the Emperor's construct."

Pyrrha said—

"Shame he didn't get some spackle for your extra holes, right?"

"Those are my speed holes. They help me go fast," said Kiriona quickly.

Then Kiriona looked over at Camilla, and the red splotch on Cam's bandages, and her crooked mouth screwed up, and she said: "You're seriously going to end up like me if you keep fucking around."

Camilla said, "Nav. What would have happened if I'd gotten that sample?"

"What—used a sharper needle? No dice. My blood burns up outside my body, turns to ash," said Kiriona. "You need to preserve it to get it out—you know, like, impregnate it with thalergy to stop the short-term thanergy reaction. When it reacts with air, the preservation, like, rolls backward—it's not static."

When she looked at Palamedes's face, she laughed again. "Come on, boy. I'm Gideon version two. I know up to five necromancy facts now."

For some reason, it was this that made Palamedes look as though he'd been slapped; Ianthe Naberius's face screwed up, briefly. Then he shook himself clear, and he said—

"If Blood of Eden knows you're up and walking, Gideon, they're going to handcuff you in about sixteen different places. How do you feel about that?"

Kiriona turned her body to look at them. Nona couldn't quite believe that they couldn't all see it; but they weren't watching, goggle-eyed, they hadn't even seemed to notice. It was in Kiriona's every movement—the bright, swift flexions of her arms, and the way she swung her legs, big and brash, and the weirdly easy, light grace with which she moved her dead body.

Nona had never seen anyone so sad in her whole short life. It made her nearly afraid to die.

"Nobody locks me up anywhere," said Kiriona.

26

THE COMMANDER HAD NOT brought along Pash's truck with the grille. They had packed everyone into one of the big people-moving trucks with the seats that faced the sides, the kind you saw mercs riding in around the city but with a cover so that nobody could see inside. It was a dark and blueless night—thick clouds had gathered over the tops of the buildings, an unusual amount of atmosphere. It made everything sticky and hot and awful.

"And now the deluge," We Suffer said, in as close to a good mood as Nona had ever seen her.

Pyrrha had the corpse prince over her shoulder. Kiriona Gaia was very good at playing dead, Nona had to admit; completely limp and believable. It was a good thing too. Even in her good mood, We Suffer did not like it when the body of Ianthe Naberius turned up, even once Palamedes explained. Nor did We Suffer want to put Kiriona Gaia in the same truck as them. "Eggs. Basket," was all she would say. Palamedes was forced to relent. Nona was strangely relieved that she wouldn't have to ride with the Prince, or have to look at her, even if the Prince was playing dead.

The moment We Suffer saw Camilla, she called a Blood of Eden medic over, who declared they could not do better on the dressing but immediately gave Camilla quite a lot of drugs. Camilla had tried to say, "No pain meds," but Palamedes said briskly, "Every pain medication you have, please."

Nona had never seen Camilla so meek or malleable. It was like all the times she had ever seen Camilla happy, all at once.

When We Suffer had declared that the body had to be kept apart, Camilla said instantly, "I'll ride with it."

Pyrrha said, "No. I will," but Cam said, "No. You stay with Nona."

Nona thought this was a bit cruel. "Don't you want to stay with Palamedes?"

Camilla and Palamedes—Palamedes in the handsome, nice-haired body that smiled in a much nicer way than it had ever smiled for Ian-the Naberius—looked at each other. They had not moved much more than an arm's length apart since Palamedes had fought for rights to the body and won.

Amazingly and fearfully, Cam looked at Nona and winked.

"We need some space," she said. "I'm getting sick of him."

"Not surprised," said Palamedes.

And they parted with nothing more than Cam leaning forward to touch his forehead to hers again, very briefly. So the Prince and Camilla got their own truck.

They were only two trucks in a cavalcade of people-moving trucks, and theirs and the corpse prince's and Cam's were the middle ones, and theirs didn't seem very full at all. The moment an unmasked, wild-eyed Pash hopped out of the truck to pull the ramp down for Pyrrha, she had looked at the corpse of Kiriona Gaia and said in the loudest possible voice, "Oh, *fuck* no," and gone to sit in the farthest corner of Nona's truck instead.

Commander We Suffer sat in the centre with a headpiece and a flip-top computer, and Nona crowded in next to Pyrrha and Palamedes. Palamedes sat next to Crown and Crown had laid the Captain down across three seats.

The Captain wasn't looking very good, but she wasn't saying anything. Palamedes had checked up on her—looked at her eyes and listened to her breathing as Crown watched, chewing on her littlest fingernail. In the end she said, "Is there nothing you can do, Master Warden?"

"Not in this body." Palamedes levered open the Captain's jaw— Nona craned her head to watch, knowing it was nosy but not caring— and noticed that the Captain's tongue was bluish and purplish and swollen. He said, "She's suffering micro-seizures. I'm worried about her brain."

Crown said urgently, "Master Warden, please, she's come so far and fought so hard."

"Let's trust her to fight a little harder," said Palamedes, and he rolled the Captain onto her side. He tilted her head down a little, and threaded a strap across her middle. "Make sure she doesn't choke."

Meanwhile Pyrrha kept twisting her neck to look at Pash, of all people, scowling maskless in the corner. Nona was desperate for Pyrrha not to do anything stupid, like flirt with her. She really thought Pash would do something awful to her kneecaps if she tried, and if that happened Nona knew she would throw up. It had been a very long day already.

We Suffer said to Palamedes: "The shuttle?"

"Secure," said Palamedes, which Nona thought was a flawless way of telling the absolute truth.

"I have left my most trustworthy guards at the barracks."

"Tell them not to explore. Prince Ianthe Naberius left behind wards and necromantic traps. I have control of this body, but I can't do anything about any nasty surprises she prepared for us," said Palamedes.

We Suffer said, "You know that we would neutralise your people, not kill them."

"I think they've been neutralised long enough."

Crown said, "There're fewer than twenty Cohort soldiers left in there, ma'am. They're not in good shape. They may well kill themselves rather than be taken in by Blood of Eden forces . . . especially if my sister isn't there to help. Their morale will break. Please wait."

And Palamedes said, "Tell me everything. Where is the Sixth House Oversight Body?"

"I have the good news and the neutral news," said Commander We Suffer. "Merv Wing has been forthcoming . . . in their own way. Your people are being held underground, being moved constantly from place to place to avoid detection. The tunnels, you see . . . a lawless and dangerous area, but Unjust Hope has perfected his art of hiding in the most dangerous places. And he always was fond of the mobility doctrine."

"How many underground sites—" began Palamedes, but Nona's neck had gone stiff of its own accord. Her short-term memory, never very good, had developed a sharp picture in her head: she could hear a high, frightened voice saying *fucking nuts man, fucking nutter;* she could taste little green fruits.

"Multiple. The tunnels underground are both extensive and very unsafe. Collapses, you see. My people have refined the search to four possible locations, but you desire thoroughness, swiftness, *and* the safety of your people. I offer you two out of three. And it is more likely one and a half."

Palamedes said irascibly—

"Are you telling me that Blood of Eden locked them all in a truck and drove them around the city? This entire time?"

"Classic Blood of Eden move," said Pyrrha. "Fucking insane, surprisingly effective, relies on a lot of soldiers pissing in a lot of bottles."

Our Lady of the Passion made a sound that, to Nona, was unmistakably a laugh, and obviously hated herself for this so much that she curled up into her seat and glared all around at everyone.

Palamedes said, "Make it safe and swift. We are *very* short on time."

We Suffer moved aside the flip-top computer and crossed her long legs. She was wearing trousers with lots of pockets, but she sat as though she were wearing something much prettier. In the olden days Nona would have immediately commenced practising how to sit like that, and been able to do it perfectly the first time round; but now she looked at the commander with her elegant older face and she felt a great, hot pang inside her. Some kind of sorrow related to legs.

"That will involve sending my people in on lightweight vehicles— cycles and whatnot—in small groups through the service tunnels. They may cover a lot of ground and not draw attention from drivers . . . the problem being that the service tunnels do not cover all the ground. There is a risk in each area that we would miss Merv Wing's trucks entirely . . . we might count one area as clear, and find ourselves mistaken."

Pyrrha said, "You worked this out? What's the estimated success rate?"

Crown plucked one of the clipboards from We Suffer's pile, and the commander pointed to certain areas. Crown said, "Different for each site. Fifty-seven percent . . . forty percent . . . thirty-two percent. Commander, these numbers are worthless."

"If you want heavy vehicles in the tunnels, I cannot assure you that Merv Wing will not liquidate the asset. Unjust Hope is not having a good night . . . and he may assume he will never have another good night ever again."

Palamedes asked, "Is there no way to make those numbers better?"

"Listen, you snivelling jackshit," said Pash (Nona was glad Cam wasn't there), "you sound like every admin suit there ever was. 'Can we make the numbers better?' Oh, yeah, sure, let me pull the good numbers out of my fucking asshole, where I stashed them for safekeeping. These are the best numbers you're going to get!"

"I really, really hate to say this about Pash," said Crown, "but she's right, Warden."

"Thank you; fuck you," said Pash. Pyrrha looked at her again, and Pash made a big *harrumph* and looked away.

"Apologies. I *did* sound like I was at Resource Committee," Palamedes admitted.

All of a sudden, the Captain made a horrible gurgling sound. It sounded weirdly like guttural laughter. Her feet twitched, and Crown held her down and checked her over until the loudest sound was the Captain's breathing.

Nona cleared her throat, then cleared it again, just in case. "I know where the Convoy was earlier this week," she suggested.

Every single head turned to look at her—even Pash's—and she felt hot in the face and she said indignantly, "I *do*, or—my friend saw it—and it had a bunch of people in it with white eyes, like they couldn't see, except they could see, and then Honesty got his face smashed. Ask the Angel, she'll—they'll tell you I'm not lying."

To say that Commander We Suffer looked astonished would have been an understatement.

"Are you *certain*?"

"You've been talking about the Convoy," Nona said eagerly, pleased to have any sign of encouragement. "We all know about them, or at least my gang does. At school. Honesty went down there to make money by stealing air-conditioning systems, but it ended badly and he says he'll stick to drugs."

"But this—this is a story being told by—what, a child? A teenager? About some other person who says they saw some people in a truck— Is your friend to be trusted?"

Nona dithered. "I don't think he was lying this time," she said. "Really. Seriously, ask the Angel—I mean, ask Aim."

The commander put her flip-top computer in Crown's arms and stood up. She kept her balance using the swaying handholds at the top of the truck, and she turned her face away from Nona so that Nona could not see what she was saying, which made hearing and understanding nearly impossible. While she was talking, a muffled *crack—boom* of thunder sounded overhead, then another, softer *crack—boom*, followed by long whistles, like something breaking a far-off sound barrier.

Pash said, "Missile launcher?"

"Wrong sound," said Pyrrha.

The commander turned around. "Nona," she said, "would your friend Honesty tell us the exact location where he saw the trucks?"

Even in the circumstances, Nona had to laugh.

"No, never. Honesty says never tell anything to anyone in uniform."

"Would he tell you?"

Nona felt very grave. "If you had asked me that yesterday," she said, "I would have said, probably yes, because Honesty's my friend, but—Hot Sauce shot me when she found out I was a zombie, so I'm out of the gang."

"Ah . . . children, they are very forgiving," said the commander, proving to Nona she had never been around children. She said into her receiver: "The Messenger will tell you the street. Split us off and take us there."

Pyrrha leant over. "Do you want me to go with you, junior?"

But Nona knew that she couldn't take Pyrrha either; it just wouldn't work.

"No," she said drearily, "at least, I want you to, but you can't. At least if Honesty tries to hit me," she reasoned, cheering herself up, "I can do one of my horrible screams. That'd impress him."

A hard wind had whipped up when they dropped Nona outside the decrepit building where Honesty lived. Pash jumped out of their idling truck, and so had several other Blood of Eden soldiers bristling with guns. Nona felt very vulnerable ducking up the rickety stairs— the wind suddenly blew upward so hard as she mounted the second staircase that she thought she would fall backward and off—but she pulled herself along doggedly. It seemed to her that her entire brain now lived somewhere in her forehead. Her body knew it was tired, but it was as though someone else were feeling it; or maybe that she weren't feeling it at all.

Honesty lived in what had used to be a utility room, so it didn't have any numbers on the door. Honesty always said he found that comforting, staying in an unlisted apartment. She hammered on the door, and when nobody answered, she despaired. She hammered again and hissed, desperately— "Honesty, it's me! Let me in!"

There was still no sound from within. What if Honesty had gone out? But then the door cracked on a rusted chain, and a watery blue eye was visible in that seam between door and frame, and she heard his familiar hoarse voice—

"Nona?"

"Honesty, *please* let me in," she said.

"I can't."

"Will you talk to me, then? Just here at the door?"

His eye flashed one way, then another. He said, more conversationally: "I mean, it's not—it's not like I don't *want* to, Nona, but . . . you gotta understand, it's that . . . well, you see . . ."

Nona knew immediately, and was miserable. "You've talked to Hot Sauce."

"Is it true?" said Honesty. "*Are* you a zombie?"

"Even if I said I wasn't, would you go against Hot Sauce?"

"Hell no," said Honesty.

"Good," said Nona, "I would think less of you if you did, you know, Honesty, because—because even if I'm not in the gang anymore, I want you to know, I think it's important to believe Hot Sauce first."

Honesty looked backward and forward again, his pale eye roving restlessly over her and her surrounds.

"You've cut your hair," he said.

"Camilla did it."

"It makes you look mean as."

"I know," Nona sorrowed.

"It'll grow back—maybe," said Honesty cautiously. "If you can push a bullet out your head your hair's probably okay. What do you want, anyway?"

"It's—it's the Convoy," she said, wringing her hands. "I need to know where you saw them. What street you went down, when you went on that job with the Convoy. Honesty"—for he had tried to shut the door on her—"Honesty, this is a matter of *life*."

The chain rattled and the door hesitated.

"You're s'posed to say 'and *death*,'" he supplied.

"I have started to not believe in the other one," said Nona. "It's stupid saying 'and death' when most of the people who die get up and walk around again. Maybe if I said 'a matter of *life* and *double death*.'"

Honesty said, "How about, 'Life and death where you don't come back'?"

"That's so long," said Nona. "Honesty—*please* tell me the name of the street and I'll go away—I'll go away forever, I think. And I want you to know that if I go away forever, and you go into the Building and someone lets you into my room, I want you to have all the coins in my ceramic fish, and if you check at school they keep my old wiping rag in the desk."

Honesty said, "What the hell would I want with your ole wiping rag?"

"Sometimes they put drops of turpentine on it, and you might be able to sell it to get someone high," said Nona pitifully.

The door closed in her face. Nona felt like a failure. But before she could try again—stave the door in with a good solid shove, hoping that she wouldn't wimp out at the last moment—it opened again.

It wasn't Honesty. It was Hot Sauce.

Honesty was right there behind her shoulder, saying mulishly, "I don't care—I don't *care.* She's always gonna be my friend, boss. I won't ditch a girl like that, a girl who thinks of my business like that. I'd go into business with a girl like that, boss, okay?" but Nona had no eyes for him.

Nona stood on the threadbare, filthy carpet and looked at Hot Sauce, and Hot Sauce looked at her; her heart trembled in her throat.

"Come in. Sit down," said Hot Sauce.

Nona sat down on one of Honesty's chairs, which consisted of a big square of cardboard on the floor. Hot Sauce sat on another. Nona drew her knees up to her chest and said, "I can't stay, so please don't shoot me, because it'll take up time."

"Don't shoot her anyway," said Honesty, "bullets is expensive."

Hot Sauce ignored him, and said—

"Are you going away?"

"Yes," said Nona. "So are the other necromancers—zombies. I guess there won't be any more here for a while."

"There'll always be more necromancers."

"I suppose, eventually," said Nona, feeling wet and depressed.

Honesty had spread the map that had hung in the classroom out on his sleeping bag. "Nicked it," he said, to Nona's quizzical glance. He was following something with his finger. He said, "Gimme a moment." Then he said, "There, 'cause that's the alley where the winos were, it's the only one that ends in the triangle."

Hot Sauce said, without looking—

"Write it down, idiot."

"You know Nona can't do written stuff, boss."

"It's not for her."

"Fine. I'll print," he added generously. "My joined-up writing's too sophisticated to read."

Hot Sauce and Nona were left together. Nona kept stealing glances at Hot Sauce—at her closed-off, silent face, with its ridges like

strange waves on the sea. Hot Sauce met her gaze levelly, and Nona
said—

"Will you tell Born in the Morning and Beautiful Ruby and Kevin
I love them? You don't have to say 'Yes' or 'No,' but think about it,
please. And will you tell the nice lady teacher I'm sorry that I had to
leave work, but at least I didn't die at the water treatment plant, and
if they get a new Teacher's Aide they have to be specially nice to the
tinies? It's not their fault they're small."

Hot Sauce said, "The Angel?"

Nona swallowed. "The Angel's important, Hot Sauce."

"Well," said Hot Sauce, "we knew *that.*"

Honesty said, "Finished," and he folded up the bit of paper, and
he deposited it in Nona's waiting hands. Nona immediately shoved
it into her pocket, in case the wind wanted to blow it away. Honesty
said, "Don't get involved in the Convoy, you know what, Nona. That
shit's creepy."

Nona decided not to tell Honesty that the Convoy was probably
full of zombies.

"Don't *you* take jobs like that again," she said. "There's lots in my
ceramic fish, okay?"

She scrambled to her feet and brushed some of the wetter cardboard off her black trousers. Hot Sauce also rose to stand—Hot
Sauce always stood so beautifully—and she walked Nona to the door,
which took two and a half steps.

Nona looked at Hot Sauce. She was terribly afraid she was about
to cry, but then she burst out—

"Hot Sauce, *why* are you called Hot Sauce?"

Hot Sauce blinked at her. "You really want to know?" she said.

"Yes," said Nona. "Yes, yes. Terribly, yes."

Hot Sauce looked up at the chipped ceiling of Honesty's apartment, then down at the carpet, and then at Nona.

"Because I really like it," she admitted.

"What?"

"You can put it on anything," said Hot Sauce. "Spicy food's always
better. You can put it on rice but you can also put it on bread."

Nona reached out. She wrapped her arms around Hot Sauce. She whispered, "Hot Sauce, forgive me—forgive me so I can know what it feels like."

Hot Sauce was as still as a statue in Nona's arms. Then she gently perambulated Nona toward the door—bumped her gently over the threshold—looked her dead in the face.

"We're cool," she said, and, awkwardly: "I'll always love you, Nona."

Nona found that huge tears were dripping out of her eyes, making it hard to see Hot Sauce.

"Can I be in the gang again?" she whispered.

Hot Sauce wavered.

"Yes," she said, "but you're on Kevin bathroom duty forever for being a zombie. That's fair." And she shut the door.

27

THE THUNDERCRACKS HAD INCREASED tenfold, with no rain to be seen—the night had grown so hot that everyone in the big truck had started to sweat. The moment Nona had moistly thrust the note into We Suffer's hand, the commander had barked into her headpiece: "Go. All units not on barracks duty are now deployed. Inter-wing rules no longer apply. Ctesiphon Wing cells, repeat, this is Cell Commander We Suffer and We Suffer. We have recommenced Operation Lock and Key—repeat, we have recommenced Operation Lock and Key." There was a ragged cheer from the drivers and a powerful *oo-RAH* from deep in Pash's chest, one hand steadying herself against the rattling car seats as she pulled a pair of tough rustling overalls up over her day clothes. We Suffer continued, "No speeches. All I shall say is, revenge is a dish best served ice, *ice* cold. Cells Saaftinge, Zoar, Birmingham, Troia, Maputo, Taree, proceed. Memphis, Takṣa, Calakmul, Valencia, Opava, Dundee, proceed."

There was an aerial screech far overhead, another long, whistling crack of something atmospheric. The commander levered her headset away from her face, sighed nigh-hysterically, and said: "I never thought her operation would begin afresh by extracting *Housers* from another Blood of Eden wing . . . and yet, it is unmistakably the first step."

Pyrrha said, "It's not one she would have taken."

We Suffer looked at Pyrrha inquiringly, tapping her fingers on one knee. "I have noticed you love to make these statements," she said. "'Commander Wake might have said this. Commander Wake would have thought that.' I have come to the conclusion that you are not simply trying to annoy me and others like me, but I have no idea what you are doing otherwise."

Next to Nona, Pyrrha gave an ineloquent shrug. "Maybe I just like talking to other people who knew her."

"And should they wax so nostalgic with you—her murderer?"

Pyrrha was unmoved. "I like to think I knew her as well as anyone else, Commander . . . as well as anyone *could* know her."

Pash viciously snapped shut the clasps on her trousers and pulled a vest over her head, putting her brightly dyed hair into complete disarray. "Say one more word on this fucking subject and I swear to all fuck, I'll do for you."

Pyrrha said, "Wake had your photo, you know. She kept it on her."

When Pash's head whipped around, Nona could see that this had shaken her badly. Her bird's-beak features had all scrunched together toward the front, as though clustering for safety, and this made her scars zigzag up her forehead and her nose. She said, "Oh, *shut* your *mouth*," but there was a desperate note to it.

"Knew it the moment I saw you. What were you, nine? Ten?"

We Suffer said, "Lyctor . . . Dve . . . I ask you to stop, from one alive human to another more or less so," but Pash was saying quickly— "Let her. She's bullshitting. Con artist stuff."

"This might be my only chance to say this," said Pyrrha comfortably, "and I'm seriously nicotine-deprived, which makes me sentimental. You're the kid in that photo . . . She kept it folded up in her pliers case. You're holding an automatic three sizes too big for you, right? One of your front teeth is gone. She holds up that photo to me and she goes, *If it wasn't for filth like you, nice kids like this wouldn't have to hold these.*"

Pash's throat was working. Pyrrha continued, "I mean, I was all, *I'd buy this a lot more if you weren't so obviously proud as hell,* and she only laughed in that mean-ass way she always laughed and said, *That's my submachine gun she's holding.*"

Pash closed her eyes. Nona held her breath, but Pash wasn't mad or upset. She looked as though she were having a religious experience.

"I remember asking if you really were a nice kid," Pyrrha said. "She said, *No. She's my flesh and blood. She takes after me.* After that . . . I kept thinking about you for a long time. Sister?"

Pash swallowed once. Twice. Three times.

"No. My mother was her sister," she said gruffly. And, "Not that it means shit to you, wizard. If you're lying to me, I swear—"

Palamedes said mildly, "You know we're conversant with the concept of *family* in the Nine Houses, right?"

Pash seemed genuinely surprised. "Why the hell would it matter to you?" Then she checked herself and said, "Scratch that. Why the hell would that matter to *me*? You don't give a fuck about families when you're carving them up—"

At a warning glance from We Suffer, Pash scowled expressively. She said, "Well, I'll leave you with this: fuck you," and then her vivid blue head disappeared under a helmet, her bright eyes beneath a visor.

Nona found a sigh escaping her chest. All her noises seemed to surprise her now; it was as though her body were capable of shocking her by doing things that did not seem connected to Nona. Pyrrha reached over and touched her hand gently, and said, "How're you holding up?"

Before Nona could answer, there was another high-pitched whistle— far closer to them now, outside their truck, shockingly close—and a dull *thud,* and a huge pattering of stone. The truck screeched to a halt, then lurched forward again, and everyone inside held on to their seats as the truck juked left. It said quite a lot about life in the city that no-body really freaked out about this the first time, nor the second time, nor even the third time when they heard yelling coming from the front of the truck.

We Suffer's headset crackled to life, and she brought it back down to her mouth. "Report," she said, then: "*Pardon?*"

Pyrrha stood, swaying with the swerving movements of the truck, and picked her way along the handholds to the back where the cover had been lashed down tight. There was a clear window of soft plastic you could look through, so long as you didn't want to see much or clearly. It would have been bad looking out of it during the day; at night, with a lot of the streetlights gone, it was basically impossible. Over the headset, We Suffer said, short and clipped, "Keep us together. Do not reroute either package. Do not engage. Take the first off-ramp you can find and get us underground."

Pyrrha had gotten a long look out the window. She suddenly squatted down, working at the pegs that kept the cover tight at the back. A corner flapped free and slapped violently at itself, letting in gusts of hot, muggy night air, which in that space felt like a breeze. Strong, yellow lights from the headlights of the truck behind strobed over them all. Palamedes moved to clamp his arm around Nona's and Nona held on to her seat and the armrests tightly as Pyrrha leant out—the truck behind them honked in alarm—and stared out at the street.

When she leant back in, Nona was profoundly upset by her body. Pyrrha was so sinewy and tough, and she was so calm—unbunched, unhurried, unaffected by most things, sweet and slouchy and always the least afraid person in the room, even if that room had Cam in it— but now she looked at Palamedes and Nona with her deep dark eyes, and she had an expression Nona hadn't seen there before.

"Sextus," she said, "game over, I'm afraid."

An air siren was wailing—the one they only used in the rainy season to announce a problematic amount of waves or water. Palamedes looked at Pyrrha and said crisply— "It's not . . . ?"

"It must have retracted a while ago," said Pyrrha. "We never could've got out of here in the shuttle, no way, no how. The first wave is here."

We Suffer said—

"No planet-killer has attacked a planet like this in my lifetime, or in the lifetimes of any of my superiors."

"Number Seven—Varun the Eater—always was lively," said Pyrrha. "But after killing my necromancer, I'd assumed the damn thing would go dormant for a good century. That's how it was after it ripped apart Cassiopeia."

"Is it after the Lyctor?" We Suffer said urgently. "If we neutralised *that* body, then . . . ?"

Palamedes held out his hands helplessly. "If it were responding to the soul of Ianthe Naberius, wouldn't it have responded days ago? From what I gather, it doesn't take a Resurrection Beast that long to spin up—the slow part is getting in position, and it's been in position for months."

"It doesn't matter why. There's Heralds out there," said Pyrrha impatiently. "If Number Seven's blown, it's blown. We'd need a Lyctor to lead it away—a fully instantiated, experienced, *serious* Lyctor, who'd need a start point halfway across the galaxy, preferably with two other Lyctors to engage it in the River . . . and if we had all that, we'd hope to God it rerouted the Heralds the moment it found better prey. You want Cyrus, Augustine, Cassiopeia . . . You want Gideon the First, and Gideon the First is dead. He's not coming back. Oh, God, Gideon," said Pyrrha, suddenly. "Gideon . . . G——, you died for *nothing.*"

Suddenly the Captain started violently trembling. Crown immediately moved to hold the Captain's hands away from her face—said, in low tones, "Come on. Come on, Deuteros. I'm here. Fight this, goddamn you. Stay awake and fight," and the Captain made a noise like *ah, ah, ah.*

Nona made her body stand on its two feet. Two feet—the worst number for feet; not so many that they were ever useful, not so few that you didn't have to think about them. She walked to the end of the truck and stood where the wheels burred beneath her, and she pushed Pyrrha aside—Pyrrha fell back flat on her back on the bottom of the truck, and she was sorry immediately, but she didn't have time—and she stood in front of Crown, and she held out her hand.

"Sword," she said.

Crown said, falteringly, "Nona . . . ?"

She took too long. Nona took her sword. She had to use her hands to bend Crown back, enough to get at the scabbard. It wouldn't pull free—it was at the wrong angle—so she cut it out of its scabbard. The blade parted the scabbard and came out. It was very heavy on her wrist, and dragged a little on the truck floor with a bright, awful screeching.

There was a gun trained on her. Pash had jumped to her feet. We

Suffer was saying, "Passion, do *not* shoot—" and Palamedes was saying, in the other body, "Nona, stop. Nona, talk to me," and it was too
much. Nona had to get out.

She pushed the flap aside—the truck behind them honked again—
and she found the side of the truck with her hand. It was too hard
to climb with the sword in her other hand—she needed two—so she
sheathed it in her hip, making sure it wedged in firmly. Some of the
shirt went with it, but it came out the other side. Nona was glad it
was someone else's shirt instead of her Salt Chip Fish Shop shirt. She
wasn't able to think on her love for her Salt Chip Fish Shop shirt—she
had clambered up to the top of the truck and was standing there, in
the hot wet blast of the wind in the night, with the truck roaring down
the street, fishtailing occasionally, and she could see everything.

There was a rain of blobs falling out of the sky. They were shaped
like teardrops, twirling crazily as they drove through the atmosphere,
lodging themselves in buildings and in the road and in the tops of
cars, coming down with an almighty splatter of thick grey mucus.
Within these blobs, trembling—the truck was going too fast—Nona
saw a thick pod thing like the miniature sleeping bags worms made
for themselves before they bust out as moths. The pods and the mucus were transparent, wreathed in smoke, and there were irregular
shapes inside—irregular and shivering shapes—and some of the
pods had wings poking through, flexing, pushing.

Nona looked at the truck ahead, which was about one truck
length away, and the truck behind, which was about one truck length
behind. She walked forward to stand on the hard shell driver's cabin,
and with a little run-up she jumped forward and sailed through the
distance to land on the truck in front. This hurt her feet briefly—it
also hurt the thin metal shell on top of the truck, which dented. She
looked up at the sky, and she bellowed: "You *said* you wouldn't do
anything *weird!*"

Nona unsheathed her sword from herself, and nearly wept from
fury. She put both her hands on the hilt. She did not know how to
hold a sword, and she didn't care.

She could see the broad main drag, with the fisheries off to one side and the harbour far beyond. Her eye, desiring the familiar, looked to where the Building probably was, her home a little grey block among the other grey blocks. The truck made a sudden left turn, veering. The trucks were the only vehicles on the road, but big seething pods had splattered onto the asphalt, and the trucks were having to drive around them. Nona stared around herself as the things kept twirling out of the sky like huge and terrible drops of rain—made hard landings on the buildings, or on the road, or soft landings thudding into the far-off ocean. She could hear yelling—glass breaking—screaming—and the air siren, all at once.

Nona turned around. On the truck she had emerged from, someone was now standing where she had stood, on top of the driver's cab. It wore tattered old trousers and a thin old shirt, and it was the Captain.

The Captain opened her mouth and said, "Get him. Get him. Get him. He flees."

"I can't," said Nona. "I can't do anything. I don't want to do anything."

The Captain moaned, sharply. "All for nothing—you asked for help—you asked . . . and all for nothing, only pain. You asked . . . I gave you blood for blood."

Nona, grief-stricken, hollered—

"Not like this. I love this place."

"Do you love?" said the Captain's mouth.

Nona struggled. "Yes—no—yes," she said, then: "I don't know what it means. I say it, and I don't know what it means . . . Did I ever know what it meant?"

"Green thing," said the Captain. "Green-and-breathing thing, big ghost, the drinker, transformed, what will you eat now? Where will your body go? What did he do to you, to make you this way? You eat yourself. I gorge on unliving marrow."

It was true; the Captain looked as though she were withering before Nona's eyes. She cried out in haste: "Don't . . . *stop* that! I can't stop it, but you can stop it. Stop hurting her . . . She doesn't know what you're doing."

"You cry mercy?" said the Captain.

"Yes—mercy—yes," said Nona.

"I have crossed the face of the universe," said the Captain. "I poison it to match my grief."

"Yes," said Nona, "but—but stop *this*, stop hurting the Captain . . ."

She rooted around wildly to find a phrase, and fell back on Cam— "You're acting out. Maybe you should take five."

"For eight thousand unjust bodies I will stop," said the Captain.

Nona said, "*No.* I want you to stop *now.*"

"They concoct their own vengeance," said the Captain. "Their justice is not my justice. Their water is not my water. I came to help. I am made a mockery. The danger is upon you, and you do not even know . . . they are coming out of their tower, salt thing. There is a hole at the bottom of their tower. I will pull their teeth. I will make it blank for you."

Nona said—

"Hot Sauce never did anything wrong, or Beautiful Ruby or Born in the Morning or Kevin, and Honesty"—here she was compelled by the truth—"Honesty doesn't know any better. Camilla and Palamedes never did anything wrong . . . Pyrrha says she did a lot wrong, but at least she knows it . . . and we don't like the Captain, but we pity her. Stop hurting the Captain . . . don't do this." And Nona found herself saying— "I'm ready to die . . . really ready."

"Nothing is really ready to die," said the Captain.

Nona took a running leap as the truck rounded another corner; she misjudged—she bounced off the side of a building like a ball— she came to a rolling stop in front of the Captain, and knocked her down, and they both fell together. Nona looked at the Captain's face with its closed eyes—still wasted, but not dead, and looking a little less like a piece of fruit someone had sucked all the juice out of.

Nona lay on her back atop the stretched canvas, and Nona's mouth said— "Just wait. Just help me . . . help me do this. I might be different . . . soon."

The big dark shapes were still twirling out of the sky, silently it seemed, although there were mismatched *boom—CRACK*s distantly resounding at the very tops of the tall buildings. Nona watched them anxiously—the sky was so thick with them—but were they thinning? Were fewer falling?

Nona stared up at the sky. She felt movement next to her. The Captain was looking at her, eyes open: normal eyes—the whites covered in little red spindles from where the veins had burst, the ring around the iris deeply black, the iris deeply brown. One of her hands was clasped to the back of her neck, as though it hurt her.

"Harrowhark?" said the Captain doubtfully.

Nona looked up at the sky. She was very tired—or at least, there was a tiredness happening to her: a huge, neighbouring exhaustion that lived, when she sought it, beneath her neck. It was hard understanding how her body fit together. She had to deliberately think about its different parts, when she wanted to feel a sensation.

She closed her eyes. "No," she finally admitted. "And I never was."

JOHN 1:20

IN THE DREAM they breached what he called the reception area and were confronted with a series of long corridors. At intervals down the hallway were more tidal heaps of furniture and stone—and bones, but the bones had been moved by the water and settled far away from where they had originally fallen. Bones and bodies and parts of bodies. He lingered by them and he said, "Those shitty fucking barricades," and caressed the edges of desks and broken chairs. There were huge black scorch marks on everything, fragments of metal and bone embedded in the walls. Pockmarks everywhere. Little round holes. It was barely traversable.

After a while he hesitated and some of the bones got up. They assembled themselves into wet, splinterous heaps. Chips flew out of the walls and out of the water and they were perfect again, softly white and glowing in the darkness. They scrambled past him and her and started clearing a path. A slow way to do it, but he didn't seem to mind.

He said, We couldn't get anywhere near political conferences anymore, physical or online. But the guy I was walking around was still invited, so I got in for free. He was my eyes and ears. Nobody was arguing about the FTL plan at that point, Wave One was in place and getting ready for final international inspections. They were all arguing about us. How to deal with us. Who should deal with us. Always thought it was funny when I had to puppet my guy into doing speeches about how his government thought I should be brought to justice. I didn't mind.

He said, What I *did* mind was the fucking state of the first wave of evacuee ships. I saw the inspection reports, I saw the questions about second-wave logistics, about exactly who was getting to ride those ships out of here. None of them could pass any kind of muster. See, back in our headquarters we thought the worst they would do was set up some kind of fucking pay-for-preference system to get the richest bastards out first and save everyone else for second wave, maybe third. I can't believe how naive I was. It was M— who came to me one night looking like she'd seen a fucking ghost. Apparently A—'s little brother and her nun had been obsessing over bank movements and assets. Going crazy checking manifests. M— said, *I've worked out what they're doing. I've worked out the plan. I thought they'd merely make people pay to see who got to jump the queue, but there is no queue.*

She said to me, *John, there is no second wave. There is no third. They're escaping. The trillionaires have converted everything to material resources. Half these passenger manifests are made up, these aren't real people. They've fucked everyone, even the governments. There'll be one single ship of internationals who think they're on Wave One to Tau Ceti, and everyone else will be corporate, or have bought a ticket, or be* useful. *They're leaving us to die.*

I had to have her breathe into a bag for a while, because she hated it when I tried to fix her anxiety attacks with necromancy. When she could talk I was just all, *Are you sure.*

She said, *John,* there they go!!

And I said, *Not as long as I have breath in my body.*

At this point the skeletons had freed some debris from an entryway and they could both get through. It led to an equally tumbledown, fire-smoked wreck that had not been improved by spending a few weeks underwater. More bodies everywhere—lots of them still with meat on their bones—another assemblage of furniture and a big cracked table with more holes in it. He said, "God, this kitchen's fucked." He stepped over bodies as his skeletons fought him a path toward a set of cupboards, and he squatted in front of them and opened a cupboard, and more foetid water came out. She was feeling light-headed by then. Eventually he returned with his arms full of cans, saying, "Hey—peaches in syrup." He did not seem to know how to open the can. One of his skeletons came over and he fused their fingerbones into a kind of saw, and he sawed through the top of the can. In that dank and awful room they ate peach halves together, slippery and yellow and squashy, with their fingers. They were so sweet she stopped tasting them after the first bite, but they made her feel better.

After half a can of peaches he stopped and said— Our last chance was to talk to our government, tell them everything we knew. It wasn't like they'd stopped listening, but we got the impression that they couldn't listen to us unless we all came in with our hands up.

He said, We never should have talked to them at all. What we said spooked someone, who told someone else, and word got through to the fucking FTL project, who started moving like their asses were on fire. The timeline changed. We were down to days, not months. Our intel said they were getting their people on board, setting up the elevators to get to the orbital launcher, which we were told was fully operational. I was going to have to physically stop those ships from launching. Problem was, they were launching from multiple platforms, and I didn't know if I could stop every single one.

C— had been saying, *Can't we gin up some kind of miracle? John, can't you do an act of* good *wizardry? Any way to stabilise the North America glacier? Any way to trap atmosphere over the Northern Territory, show them we can fix things here?* But A— said, *That's for later, first things first, bum-rush the ships, pull the bastards out, make them do the cryo plan instead. Get the population safely out, and we can stay behind and clear the planet. If John's up for it.*

He said, I was *trying.* I was so close to cracking this third thing, the soul. I'd realised there was the energy you produced from being alive and the energy you produced when you died, but the fact that energy was produced *when you died* meant there was another phase. I could get a corpse's heart beating and get all the neurons firing in the brain, but it wasn't producing the alive stuff anymore. It wasn't an on-off switch. I'd stopped sleeping and I wasn't eating much, I was keeping my body going just by fiddling with the processes.

He said, It made sense that every human had a well of this energy, this soul energy, but I couldn't distinguish it from anything else. Even on the day I'd killed all those cops there was too much noise and I couldn't work out what the noise was. I could tell it was the thing I was looking for, but I didn't understand why it seemed so *big*. And I didn't know what to do with it, or how to use it.

So I said to everyone, *I can't stop them myself, not yet. We have to stall them. We know they need Pan-Euro's orbital gate access, so let's make sure they can't get it. Let's make sure nobody wants to give them orbital gate access.*

He said, And all of us looked at the floorboards.

He said, None of us wanted to actually nuke anything. But a nuke's good blackmail, right? A nuke adds a lot of pressure, right? The people who knew it was there, they knew that if we talked about having a nuke everyone would find out *who gave us a fucking nuke*. So we said to our client, Pan-Euro cannot be allowed to let these people through. They're cutting and running. They're leaving ten billion people behind to die, having stolen financing and support and materials. They're leaving us to drown. And we said, We don't want to make a scene, but . . .

They said, *Okay, okay, but hand the fucking nuke back, we've changed our minds. We'll stop Pan-Euro, we'll put our whole weight into making sure they don't get out of orbit. But we want the bomb back before you do something crazy.*

He said, They took so long that the ships were counting down to launch. We were about forty-eight hours away from Wave One at that point. A couple of nations were all, *Hang on, this is early, this isn't to schedule,* but the FTL project said they were doing a mock run because preparation was going so well. How the hell did anyone buy that? How much money was changing hands? Didn't they realise that if these bastards were giving away insane amounts of cash it was because they didn't think cash was worth anything anymore?

He said, So here's us, planning to meet these agents in neutral territory, across the ditch, over in the huddle where the Territory refugees were. They wanted us to pass the nuke back. We all voted to trust them, but A— and G— and M— and I came up with a just-in-case plan. Forty-eight hours became twenty-four so quickly. G— fixed up the case and carried it over alone, with caveats. Nobody liked that. They were all, *Shit, John, send someone dead, send a puppet.* But I wanted G—. P— volunteered to go with him, but G— said he wouldn't arm it if P— was in range. P— went off at him, but it was one of those times where he held his ground against her. I remember. She called him a stupid kid.

He said, I had—I had this weird gut feeling before we sent him off, on that private plane. And I was getting pretty good at that time, even if I wasn't good enough. I took G— downstairs and I got him to face the wall, and I took his arm off.

He said, He didn't feel any pain, and I grew him a new one then and there. Bit of a gamble, but I was sure I could do that by then. I wanted his arm . . . his material. He didn't even ask me to explain. That was the kind of guy he was. He and I had grown up on the same street. I'd spotted him for mince pies all the time as kids, so stands to reason he let me cut off his arm and carried a nuke for me.

He added contemplatively, Should still be around here. The arm, I mean. I stuffed it in the morgue so nobody would find it. I've got plans for that arm.

Then he took a moment to eat another bright yellow wedge of peach.

After the peach wedge he said, Where was I? G— on his way with the nuke. The ships on the launchpad, twenty hours to go now, less. So much waiting around. Me in my bedroom with a nun and a migraine, her thinking that if she pushed me enough we'd instantiate the Trinity and we'd all be saved. Everyone else drinking. The clock ticking louder than ever before. C— admitting out of nowhere she's dating N—. All of us like, *What? We've known for a year? Go ahead and get married already, we've got a nun.* N— was all, *That's not legal.* C— of all people said, *Who cares.* That's how bad it was.

He said, C— and N— got married right over there, you can't see it now 'cause of the rubbish. I made flowers grow for them out of the garden, but they came out . . . weird. Some of the roses had teeth. C— and N— thought that was hilarious.

He said, The dome meant we hadn't had full sunlight in a while. It was beautiful anyway, I cried the whole service. I couldn't remember the last time I'd eaten food.

He said, An hour and forty-two minutes later, G— landed and made his way to the meetup, and that's when I had to tell everyone that the nuke was armed and G— was a dead-man's switch. First I told our contacts, then I had to tell C— and N— and P— and everyone.

He said, They went apeshit. Which I don't think was entirely fair.

I said to them, *You think they weren't just going to shoot him first thing? You think there aren't six snipers with beads on G*—right now? But they weren't only aggro about G—, they were aggro that a nuke might go off and kill a couple million people. I was like, *Guys, it's fine, they're Australian.*

He said, Wow. Talk about jokes with no hope of landing.

He said, The contacts stayed pretty calm though. They said, *John, we're not doing anything until you dismantle the switch and disarm the bomb. It's not a fair conversation if you have this nuke on the table. Also, you will not be hurting any of us with this suitcase nuke. We are not even sitting in that country, so where would that get you? Who would you be hurting, John?*

And I said, *Yeah, I thought about that.*

They said, *Did you?*

I said, *Yes. On that note, do you remember the dead guy you've mocked up to look alive, the one who still has executive power over your own nuclear codes, who you gave me* total access to?

He said, By that time I had him in position. It was pretty easy. I just made sure that everyone around him wasn't part of the conspiracy, that nobody around could stop me, and I locked the doors. They gave him—me—the codes. I had his finger on the button. I told them: *You have thirty minutes to tell Pan-Euro that there is no way those gates are opening for those ships.*

They said, *You wouldn't. It would be nuclear war.*

I said, *I'd do anything. You know I would. Cows exhibit mourning behaviour for other cows.*

He said, At this point my people were like, *John, what the fuck? What the fuck is happening?* We were all yelling at each other. First time I'd ever seen C— angry. N— and P— were having a go at me too, and the nun and A—'s hedge-fund-manager brother had teamed up to try to mediate, which as per usual made everyone pissed off at them instead. A— and M— were on my side, kind of, or at least the side of *this will be fine, we can walk this back, nothing's going to happen, right, John.* I was pissed. I told them it would work. N— was all, *It's not going to work. This is going to end with the ships launching and G— getting shot, and you're going to kill millions of people for nothing. We followed you to save the world.*

I said, *We're doing that. This is how we save the world. Believe me.*

C— said, *John, your problem is that you care less about being a saviour than you do about meting out punishment.*

I said, *C—, I was just your best man!*

C— said, *You still are. That doesn't change the fact that you can be quite the most appallingly vindictive person I have ever met.*

He said, Things went from bad to worse. The other side scrambled pretty quickly. Like, what you've got to keep in mind is that we've got hundreds of cultists on both sides of the cow wall, and quite a lot of these guys are One Nation nutbars who think they're going to see out the end of the world in a bunker and live to build a beautiful paradise that looks a hell of a lot like *The Moon Is a Harsh Mistress.* And those guys have illegal semiautomatics. We've still got Wi-Fi, more's the fucking pity, and those guys are talking to their people on the outside, and they flip. So while me and the others are having this massive fight, we get the message that a hundred of these guys have changed their minds about us, and they've surrounded the inner building with guns and we're going down. They've taken a hell of a lot of the other cultists hostage, so if I start killing anyone the hostages are dead meat.

He said, We kept on yelling at one another, but we mobilised while we yelled, making barricades. I *didn't* just kill them all. It would have looked completely fucking shitty, and I was trying to win an argument that I didn't solve all my problems with murder. Everything always happens at the worst time. We got everyone in the building on lockdown, using a bunch of procedures we developed in case some of the cryo stuff leaked. Shutters down, fire doors locked remotely, that kind of thing. And we built the barricades. You saw those.

He said, We tried talking to them, saying, *Wow, this is not the time. Be chill.* They didn't listen.

A— said they'd sold out. I didn't think so. They'd seen me fuck up once, killing the cops, and once people see you do something and come to an opinion about it, there's nothing you can do. People don't forgive, not really. Once they doubt, you've already lost them. That's what was scaring me about the others. Had I already lost my best friends? The only people I needed? I'd just caught the fucking tooth bouquet at C— and N—'s wedding. What if that didn't *matter*?

After a moment he said, Anyway.

The outside force of ex-cultists with guns were trying to force their way in, said they'd open fire if I didn't walk out, and I said, *Okay, do you want me to walk out, should I go,* and A— and M— and the others said, *Don't you dare, John.* Instead I sent out a couple skeletons to try to save the hostages. Lot of fighting, lot of confusion. We got some of the hostages inside the building, but then they charged us. We sealed up the hall when they busted through reception. You saw the front doors, right? They had Molotov cocktails. I was all, *Next cult, let's go for teenage girls instead, write that down somewhere.* M— was all, *Are you kidding, at least with these guys we have a chance of getting out alive.*

I was still on call with G— the whole time. He was holding up well, dealing with a lot of negotiators telling him pretty awful shit. He was immovable. That was why I wanted him in: G— only listened to two people in his fucking life. He wasn't going to listen to some white-collar asshole in a Kevlar jacket preaching about cost analysis. I was pretty sure he was safe: they were too scared to do anything to him. I was more freaked out about the guys hammering on the barricades. I couldn't even take them down, because I was trying to do sixty fucking things at once. I was walking around a dead politician, I was having six conversations with people I was trying to negotiate with while making a barricade out of lawn chairs, and the hour was ticking down and I didn't—I didn't know what to do anymore. I'd lost my nerve. I didn't know what I was going to do when the hour ran out. I had to admit that to myself. It was taking a lot of effort not to ice everyone within a kilometre, if only to get some fucking peace and quiet. But I figured that'd lose me the moral high ground.

He said, They were skirmishing down the hall when I *did* freak out and lock myself in the bedroom. I didn't let anyone in except Ulysses and Titania, because they wouldn't fight with me. Here. Let me take you.

He took her from the kitchen, the can of peaches forgotten. The skeletons moved to clear all the rubble from their path. At one point they reached a solid mass of bone, and as he approached it collapsed into dust so that he was walking through a bad-smelling mist. She followed him. The hallway behind it was clear, no piles of broken furniture or broken walls, but everything was filthy with water. The walls bowed. The lights had been ripped out of their housings, and parts of the ceiling had torn open and revealed big black gaps above the roofing panels. At last one of the skeletons opened a door so that they could stand on the threshold of a room, just a few steps away from what on first blush looked like a pile of wet brown clothes. So much of what was left looked like wet brown clothes. But there was a body inside those clothes that had not come through the water well. She looked at it, but he didn't; he looked anywhere but at it. He covered his face, he uncovered his face. He looked away. It took him a long time to talk.

When he could, he said, M— and her nun spent a while yelling through the door at me. Well, M— was yelling. M— kept saying this was too far, she knew I didn't want to do this, I could walk this back. She told me everything could be okay so long as none of those buttons got pushed. She said the ex-cultists had made it as far as the

labs, so what were we going to do? I didn't respond. Eventually M—
gave up and went away.

He said, more dreamily, Not much left of the hour. Everyone would
have been inside the ships, everyone would have been in place, they
would have been doing last-minute checks. There was G— waiting
in the middle of a city centre across the ocean, definitely half a dozen
sniper beads on him, a nuke in his hand. I could feel it. I was there
with him. I was with a dead body in a command room, security detail
none the wiser, with three guys with codes and their fingers on the
buttons, everyone who knows this guy's a walking stiff locked out of
the room. A nun praying for my clarity outside my bedroom door.
A bunch of scared ex-cultists exchanging fire with the faithful down
the hall. It was only a matter of time before someone I loved caught
a bullet that I couldn't bring them back from. I needed to do something. I couldn't do anything.

He said, Eventually it was the nun who changed things. She knocked
on my door and said very nicely, *John, how are you doing?* And I said,
Not great, honestly. She said, *John, how close are you to finding the soul?*

And I said, *I can't, Sister. It's too big. I don't understand why it's so
huge. I can't find the soul inside the body, I don't know where to look.
I don't know what I'm doing.*

She prayed over me, and then she went away for the longest five
minutes of my life. Call came down the line that they were trying to
evacuate the city around G— but I was all, *You took too long, you
know that won't work.* And they didn't talk to me again.

Then the nun came back and knocked on my door and said, *John,
I think I have it. I know you're very scared right now, but I'm going to
help you. Please let me in.*

He said: I let her in. She'd brought P—'s gun.

As they stood in that filthy hallway, he looked down at the brown
collection of clothes and body. She did too, recognising, dimly, what
she was looking at. He said, "Don't. This isn't what she looks like."

And he said, as though he were underwater with the rest of everything: I guess in all the confusion P— didn't notice it was missing. I
thought she was there to kill me. Titania and Ulysses were there, but

I didn't have them jump in front of me, I didn't have them stop her. I guess I almost—I was feeling pretty bad, you know? I was feeling pretty shaken.

He said, She just smiled at me. She said, *John, don't misunderstand. I want to help you. I truly believe that in our most terrible hours we don't instinctively reach out to God; we push ourselves away from Him. Don't feel bad for not rising heroically to the occasion right now. Fear doesn't help us achieve a state of grace; it deafens the heart. John, I truly believe you can save everyone. So concentrate, please.*

She said, *Holy Mary, Mother of God, pray for us sinners, now and at the hour of our death.* And she shot herself.

He said, Her soul hung there, for a second, nothing more. And I tried to keep her—all I was thinking was that I had to save *her*, had to stop this fuckup if I couldn't stop any of the others. I'd got a huge injection of the death energy close up, and it was like getting meth injected into my eyeballs. For the first time I could hold a soul and see its edges, pin it down. It was like a tiny atom bomb. I could tell immediately that this was the missing link. If I could only control it. I should have been able to take that bullet out of her brain and undo the damage. Fix the soul back in. Bring her back to life.

He said, But I held her soul in my hands and I knew why it had been so hard, because I was tuned in. I was looking at the code. I knew why I hadn't been able to see anything.

He said, When I touched her soul, I touched *you*.

He said, You were the noise that was everywhere. It was like trying to talk to someone down a phone line with someone screaming through a megaphone in the same room. You drowned everything out. You were so huge and so complicated, and you were screaming. You wouldn't stop screaming. You were so scared. You were so goddamn mad.

She said, "I was?"

He said, "It wasn't your fault."

He said, But that's when I realised you were there. And I realised the soul of a single human being was incredible, but at the same time—incredible *small potatoes*. I wasn't holding two nukes on the line. I was holding three. And compared to you, the other two were birthday candles.

He said, I left her dead in the bedroom. Did I take something? I don't think I took anything, not even Ulysses and Titania. I didn't have much blood on me. I wiped it off on a jumper and left the jumper in the bedroom too. Nobody noticed. We had the next problem to hand. While the crazies made us wait, they'd flipped some of the faithful *inside* the dome. Told them I was busy plotting nuclear war or something else wildly unfair. When I walked back into the kitchen they were all shooting each other.

He said, I just kind of stood there and watched it happen, I think. It wasn't like people shooting each other in a movie. You'd have someone shoot someone. Everyone would yell about it. Then someone else would shoot *that* person. It was all awkward, like they were angry but taking turns. A—'s little brother was there . . . dead in the middle . . . shot from both sides. Nobody likes a peacemaker. The more they shot each other, the angrier they got. I don't think they even noticed me watching them. It was like I was invisible. They made each other dead in front of me, and I felt each one . . . like popping bubble wrap . . . only I held on to them, I collected them up. In the next room I found C— and N—. They'd shot C— first . . . and right in front of my eyes they shot N—. Pop. Bubble wrap. I don't know what happened to them. This part gets a little weird, you know? Like I dreamed it. I remember P— behind a barricade . . . not dead yet . . . telling me, *John, run.* I remember A— and M— . . . they were alive . . . we all hid behind a kitchen table. I remember their hands in my hands . . . I remember A— telling me something, and M— saying, *We're together. We'll go together.*

But they found us, they were already there. They shot A— right in front of us . . . hauled me out . . . M— said, *Take John alive. He's worth more to you alive.* And they shot her.

He stood there and he said: "Do you remember what I said was coming?"

She said, "Yes."

He said, "This is the part where I hurt you. Are you ready?"

She said, "Yes."

He said, You were screaming. I wanted you to stop, I wanted . . . I wanted you. I wanted you like a caveman wants a wildfire . . . or the sun. I thought you were going to take me, somehow. Purge me. Use me as an instrument. But you didn't say anything . . . I was babbling, Show me. Come on. I'm ready. You kept screaming and screaming . . . like a baby in pain. So I tried to hurt you—I *did* hurt you. I reached out for you, and it hurt you . . . but I wasn't strong enough. The caveman. The wildfire. The Neolithic priest staggering in front of the falling star.

He said, I felt P— go. G— was the last one alive. I reached out and stopped G—'s heart.

He paused and said, I'm still sorry it was Melbourne, honestly. Love a working tram service.

Abruptly, he turned around and walked out of the room, passed back into the kitchen. The skeletons knocked holes in the crusted-up glass so that air came rushing through to them, and he rattled the handle of the glass doors until they opened up and he could stand outside on the tiles. He stood there, his eyes glowing like lamps in the shadowed air, and he looked out at the sky.

He said, God, that hurt you. That stung. I ate every single death.

He said, I let go. In the body they'd paid me to puppet, I gave the command. That command was heard round the world . . . so many men with so many fingers on so many buttons. The world went down in dominoes. Launch one nuke, you'll get twenty thousand anti-air missiles in response. SAM sites open up all over the earth, like wildflowers. One little nuke . . . then a lot of bigger nukes . . . Christ, why'd we have 'em? Nukes into nukes into nukes. They came out of subs and bunkers and scrambled jets. The funny thing is, it was all to try to make the other ones stop firing . . . like an old comedy sketch.

He said, First, I became a demigod. I nearly fell out of my body. I put my hand around half the world's throats. Some of them I managed to snap before they were melted away by nuclear fire. I did them clean. Everyone died, but I helped a hell of a lot of them go before they knew anything had happened. I drank them in, and it wasn't enough. I needed those ships. I needed to extend my hand. I got it around the throat of the other half. I made them go away too. Then I had control of everything on the surface, but not the ships . . . birds flying above the fire . . . kids playing keep-away.

He said, I put my hands around your neck.

He said, I cupped your soul in my hands.

He said, I took you into myself and we became one.

He said, meditatively, I mean, I *tried*. There was so much of you— you weren't the small, stained soul of a normal human being. You were so much bigger than that. I opened my mouth and tried to cram you inside . . . you didn't fit. I dropped to my knees—here, I believe.

He strode forward. She saw what he was pointing at: a pile of grassless dirt.

He said, So I dropped to my knees here, right . . . I scooped dirt into my mouth . . . ate until I vomited. I gathered up the bloody earth . . . I realised you were too much for me. This is the problem, the incorporation, this is the hardest part . . . It's the human instinct, to take. When you burn your thumb, you stick it in your mouth, right? And there was still too much of me that was just a human being . . .

He said, I didn't stick my thumb in my mouth. Had more sense than that. Fuck knows what would've happened if I tried to absorb you all the way; I probably would've burnt to death. But I needed a house to put you in, if I wasn't going to put all of you in *me*. I made you one on the fly . . . I wasn't even thinking . . . I ripped half my ribs from my body and made you from the dirt, my blood, my vomit, my bone.

He said, I wanted to make you the most beautiful body I could think of.

He paused and said: "But I was stressed, okay? I was insane. Most of what had made me John had gone somewhere else. There were a few little thoughts left . . . a handful of things that made me *me* . . . a couple scraps of id. It's not fair to judge me, right? I didn't do this *thinking* . . . I didn't do it like *art*. When I was seven, you know, all Nana had to play with in her house was some of Mum's old toys. And my favourite out of all of them . . ."

He gave a long, shuddering sigh.

"My favourite was her old Hollywood Hair Barbie," he murmured. "I loved her little gold outfit and her long yellow hair. She was the best. She got to have all the adventures. There was also a Bride's Dream Midge, but Mum had cut Midge's hair into this weird mullet. It was Barbie for me."

She looked at him. He looked at her.

He added, "*Not* Hollywood Hair Ken. Mum had him too, but he was a creep. I gave him to Nana's dog to eat."

He said, From my blood and bone and vomit I conjured up a beautiful labyrinth to house you in. I was terrified you'd find some way to escape before I was done. I made you look like a Christmas-tree fairy . . . I made you look like a Renaissance angel . . . I made you Adam and Eve . . . Galatea. Barbie. Frankenstein's monster with long yellow hair.

He said, As the world went up I remade us both. I hid me in you . . . I hid you in me. And when we were together . . . once the shaman had claimed the sun . . . I became God.

He said, It wasn't enough.

He said, The ships . . . the ships were still full of people. I reached our hand out into space. I extended. I struggled.

He said, I bit through the sun first. It's human nature. *That* started things going. Once you take down the sun, you're cooking with gas, pardon the pun. I sliced through Venus, Mercury, Mars . . . by that point a couple of the tugs had already launched through the Kuiper. I had to kill Jupiter and Saturn in a fucking hurry. I reached . . . they blinked away from me . . . all I could do was hope that they'd watched what I was doing and all died from fucking terror.

You and I went full fucking Hungry Caterpillar. We took Uranus . . . Neptune . . . crunched down Pluto . . . found every satellite and craft, reached in, crunched up all the humans, moved on. I didn't know how to look, you see, only how to touch. The moment I found the fleet spinning up to enter FTL, it was too late . . . I could only grab one of them . . . and you and I held it in the palm of our hand. I was in there with them. All those frightened people. All those runaway rats.

He stopped.

She said, "Then?"

He said, Then they were gone . . . lost to me in time, forever. That'll teach me not to hesitate.

She folded her arms across her chest. She wasn't cold, but she felt as though she ought to be. Standing out in the shadows, in the dust and the dirt, with the reeking concrete shell behind them, she wanted to be cold.

He said, lightly— "That's it. That's the story. That's what I did."

"Oh," she said.

Then he said— "Do you remember what you said to me once I had done it? When we stood here together?"

She looked at him and she said, "Yes."

He said— "You said, 'I picked you to change, and this is how you repay me.'"

She said— "What else did I say?"

He said: "You said, 'What have you done to me? I am a hideousness.'"

She said— "What else did I say?"

He said, "Where did you put the people? Where did they go?"

She said, "I still love you."

He said, "You said that too."

28

NONA WOKE ON THE COLD, shoe-smelling surface of the back of a truck, in the dark mostly. The seats seemed to close in on her arms and legs, and she panicked briefly, thrashing her head this way and that, until somebody said, quite gently—

"Chill."

The back doors of the truck were wide open—the air was cool and damp and reeked of oil and cold road. From far off there were the familiar peppery sounds of gunfire—a yell, occasionally—metal creaks and moans that echoed sharply all over the place, as though she were stationed in a deep tunnel. This was because she *was* stationed in a deep tunnel, she realised. She sat up and looked out the back of the truck and saw blackness stretch before her—blackness occasionally relieved by pockets of pale pink light, the spluttery try-hard light you got from solar power, offering little relief to the eye. Much bigger spotlights had been placed at points on the road, like windows to some other world—big luminous rectangles, suckling on cables that were lying in thick coils over the painted concrete, in heaps and snarls. Some of them led back into the truck; and there was Prince Kiriona Gaia, stretched out on the seats, lying flat, looking at her from the shadows with those golden eyes like a dead animal's.

Nona looked at her; she looked at Nona. They looked at each other for a very long time. The scarf at Kiriona's neck had been tied back up, and her jacket had been buttoned up, so that you couldn't see her wounds. The corpse prince looked at her, and her expression was flat, and cool, and metallic.

Kiriona said, "Where is she?"

Nona didn't know what to say. The corpse prince urged—

"Come on. Where'd she go? Where is she?"

"I don't know who you're talking about," said Nona miserably.

"Listen, she can be in hell for all I care, I won't get mad," said Kiriona. "She can be at the bottom of the sea or at the bottom of space. I just need to know—*where*."

When Nona didn't answer, the corpse prince said—

"Okay. Different question. Do you love her?"

"Take a walk, Nav," said a new voice.

It was Pyrrha, at the back of the truck, looking stretched thin and worn out. There were long, healing grazes going up both of her arms, like she'd taken a tumble since Nona last saw her, extending up to underneath her neck. Her stubble was a glittery scrape of red across her cheeks and on the underside of her chin and upper lip. Her hard, familiar face looked impossibly tired.

Kiriona said, "Kind of pretending to be dead here."

"All right. *We'll* take a walk. Don't go anywhere, and stop being a little shit," said Pyrrha.

"It's genetic," said the corpse prince.

Pyrrha got up into the back of the truck, making it jolt and jostle, and shifted cables away from Nona.

Nona said, trying to find the words: "The fingers—the things . . . ?"

"The Heralds have us pinned down in here," said Pyrrha. "Not that many of 'em, but even a handful is more than enough."

"Oh, yeah, those things are bastards," said Kiriona. "I fought a handful up close, back on the Mithraeum."

"Yeah, well. We fight those things up close, the fight's over. You have to take them out long range. Couple of BoE cars are taking potshots at them from the on-ramp, about two kilometres down. No— don't move, kiddie . . ."

Nona had tried to slither her way up into the halo of Pyrrha's arms, and found her legs felt like blocks of marble. They had never felt that way before: sort of fizzy and numb. Sometimes her gang had given each other dead legs and arms, and she had offered herself up for this treatment, but to her disappointment it had never worked on her. Pyrrha cradled her in her arms and worked her way, very carefully, out the back of the truck. It was dark and echoey outside, with small sanctuaries of light here and there on the oil-smelling road.

There was a barrier a little way from the truck, a waist-high slab of concrete. Pyrrha put her down with her back propped against it, then crouched next to her.

Nona said, surprised: "I can't walk."

"Do you remember what happened after you blacked out on top of the car?" asked Pyrrha.

"No," said Nona.

"Maybe that's for the best," said Pyrrha. Then she opened her mouth and said quietly—

"A . . ."

"Don't," Nona found herself saying. "Don't. Don't call me that or anything like that . . . don't make me remember. I don't want to . . . You won't like it. Don't. Don't make me do it."

Pyrrha said, "Don't freak out, junior. Cool it," but she didn't feel cool at all, she felt horribly hot. Something itched wetly and warmly on the back of her neck, and she raised a trembling hand to touch the spot, but Pyrrha took her wrist and said, "Don't smear it. It's meant to keep . . . to keep you in the body as long as possible."

The grip on Nona's wrist was firm and gentle and totally normal— how many times had Pyrrha grasped her wrist, before crossing a road, or helping her stand, or twirling her around to songs on the radio? But from some hole in the back of Nona's cupboard behind a fake plank of wood in Nona's brain, her voice said roughly: "Don't touch me."

Pyrrha dropped her wrist, and Nona's voice went on and on:

"Did you think this was *fun*, Pyrrha Dve? Did you think this was lovely? Family. Blood. Together. Kiss, kiss. A child's game. You say nice words and everyone pretends they are the words you say. Here is a house. We live in it. Worms slithering over each other . . . Did you *like* playing pretend? Did you like being mother and father? You should have given into your desires and eaten us. Chew and swallow. More natural. Would have respected you for it . . ."

The voice died away and Nona, in agonies of hatred and repulsion and embarrassment, tried to curl up in on herself, only it didn't work. She felt as though she had been interrupted in the bathroom. White-hot, fatal shame seemed to start in her middle and travel outward, and she got her own voice and she said—

"Don't, don't, *don't.* Don't do this to me, Pyrrha . . . Pyrrha, just let me die. It's nicer. I can't bear it."

Nona cried for a little while. The tears oozed out of her eyes and landed in her lap. Her face felt hot, and the back of her neck was sore and itchy. After a while the tears subsided, and Pyrrha said— "Better?"

"Yeah," said Nona, and felt her voice tremble, but said more steadily: "Yes. Can I have a tissue?"

"Wait till Cam and Sextus get here. You don't want any tissue that's been in my pockets."

"Did they find the Sixth House?"

"Yes—thanks to you. And the megatrucks weren't hard to stop either. The moment Ctesiphon grounded the first one, the others pretty well gave up. It's . . . extenuating circumstances."

This cheered Nona up a little. "That's good, isn't it?"

Pyrrha's face did not look as though she thought it was altogether good.

"Nona," she said carefully, "what if I told you I thought this was the end of the line, honey? I'm not sure any of us are getting out of this one."

This cheered Nona up a lot, but she hesitated before saying so. It was an awful relief . . . that she and Pyrrha and Cam and Palamedes were all together, and nobody had to worry about the next day, or the day after that; that she could put everything else out of her mind— violently put everything else out of her mind—and she did not have to try anymore. But her relief was hard to articulate in a way that did not make her sound awful. So she simply said, "I'll behave."

"Let's go see the others," said Pyrrha. "You okay to be picked up again?"

Pyrrha's boots crunched on the shiny black surface as she carried Nona. A megatruck loomed out of the darkness, blizzarded over with luminous strips, bigger than any truck Nona had ever seen. It was as tall as a house. If it had been driven up somehow next to the classroom building you could have stepped out of the window and stood on the top. It rose up out of sight, its top lost to the blackness, and was so wide that it took Pyrrha something like twenty seconds to walk around its bumper. A huge shutter had opened, and a ramp had been laid down, and there were people milling around next to a much smaller Blood of Eden truck with the soldiers laying people down on rollaway beds: checking them over, doing something medical, fluttering in the darkness like moths. Nona noticed many of the people being helped had wide, watery white eyes just like the makeup that Nona had gotten earlier: the sticky, filmy gazes that had so terrified Honesty's crew.

Camilla was sitting in a chair. The chair had wheels. She had a clipboard in her hands, and the body of Ianthe Naberius was there behind the chair, as Palamedes in his shoulders and the line of his head as ever. Various people tottered down the ramps, assisted by Blood of Eden soldiers—Crown and, astonishingly, Pash, helping an extremely feeble and aged person, about Nona's size. Palamedes looked very distracted as they approached. He was saying— "Cam, can we get any update on the tunnels?—For fuck's sake, can someone please stop my mother from walking around talking to Blood of Eden? Someone's going to put a bullet in her head. Go ask Kester Cinque to do it; he can actually talk to people, though I think right now he's wishing he never left Koniortos. *Where* are your fathers? Why is this like herding chickens? Nona, how are you?"

Nona felt very lost and astonished and weary. "Are *all these* your family?" she asked.

"Metaphorically yes, literally it's complicated," he said. There was a great calm relief in his body, which Nona did not expect. Cam was slumped in her chair and she was about six degrees paler than she had ever been. "My mother wanted to meet you—too bad for her, I assume she's off asking one of the junior officers about the philosophy of violence and how these trucks work and what everyone does for a living."

Most of the people being helped could not stand, and they all looked thin and crumpled and haggard, though quite cheerful in many cases, Nona thought. Pyrrha looked around and said, "Sextus, any Heralds get down here, I'm not sure these people will survive."

Camilla said, "They wouldn't."

Her voice was thin, barely a whisper. Palamedes supplied, "They're in pretty poor shape, yes . . . but there's also everyone in the city to think about. I've tried to explain to them what's happening, and they've got the gist, but before you ask about necromancy, that's right out. The Master Archivist says any display of aptitude on their part crocks them for days—blinding themselves nearly killed them, and that was when they were much stronger. There's no hope of us taking anyone back to the barracks to work on something as fine-grained as those wards Ianthe left."

Nona felt herself being shunted around in Pyrrha's arms, her weight shifted from side to side. Pyrrha said, "And Ianthe . . ."

"Kicking," said Palamedes. He smiled again. "She's getting lively now. And quite shockingly angry."

"Sextus," said Pyrrha, "I'm not used to saying this, but I'm fresh out of plans, and either you're so completely high on lovey-dovey cavalier shit that you've taken leave of your senses—and, you know, fair do's, I've been there—or you know something I don't."

"It's not that I *know* anything, Pyrrha," said Palamedes. "It's that I'm feeling ready to gamble. In a couple of minutes—once the commander gets back to me with the manual—I'm loading everyone here back into the truck. They're going over it now, in case Merv Wing left anything untoward inside."

Nona peered around into the truck, into the big well of dim light, and tried to be positive but cautious.

"Palamedes, you know I get motion sick."

"I know. I'm sorry. You'll only have to put up with it for a bit, Nona, I promise."

Pyrrha said, "Look, I know this thing has the tonnage you usually find in spacecraft, but if your plan is to hoon around the city squashing Heralds as you go I have to tell you: that's *not* going to work."

"Didn't think of that," said Camilla.

Palamedes said, "No. Don't worry, Dve, my ambitions don't extend to the city surface. Hang on—here comes the committee."

The commander and someone that Nona had never met walked into the big yellow square of light in front of the ramp. The commander looked normal, except Nona was struck afresh by the enormous contrast between her and Palamedes: We Suffer looked a *lot* more like Pyrrha, in that she was stressed and wild-eyed and had a fatal, brisk focus that was completely at odds with Palamedes's cheerful anticipation. Palamedes was acting as though he were a tiny at show-and-tell who had brought in his favourite toy with the expectation that he was about to get two minutes all to himself to tell the whole room about it, even the big kids. The crumpled, blind-eyed woman next to We Suffer, who walked with one hand on her gracefully extended arm, stopped in the light. She had quick features and a very long braid of dark, silvering hair, so long that it made Nona wish to have her own braids back. She looked quite old—maybe older even than We Suffer, marks of deep care delineated on her face—and wasn't glamorous, and wouldn't have been even had she been in fresh clothes.

"Here's the numbers, Master Warden," she said, and leant out with a sheaf of paper. "I haven't been able to double-check them—I did an initial calculation, but of course, the basic mathematics *can't* be relied upon. I will say that my computation has come along wonderfully in the past couple of months. We were having quite a fun time in my corner doing quadratics out loud until the Chair threatened to toss us out of the truck. How are they?"

Palamedes squatted down to check the papers with Camilla. Cam said, "If we could get inside the dome, this wouldn't matter."

"I can't navigate like that, Cam. I'm not sure anyone can. I never knew where I was, spatially, and exiting and entering must be hell—we're going to have to do this on the fly. Gideon's ponied up some of the inside layout. Our best bet sounds like their landing platform—if we get anywhere even slightly near it . . ."

Pyrrha cleared her throat. "Commander, casualties?"

We Suffer sighed. "Out of the frying pan," she said, "into another frying pan—falling out of that frying pan—into the underworld, where there is a huge frying pan where the devils dance, and say, 'Fuck to you.'"

"You always had a way with words," said Pyrrha. "Are they everywhere, or localised?"

"Ctesiphon is at the mouth of the tunnel and further inside. I cannot get good reports. We are doing fine—but we will run out of bullets in a few hours. They are having a veritable orgy out there, and we cannot use explosives unless we want to collapse the tunnel. And I do not want to collapse the tunnel, because there is no getting out."

"Roger that," said Pyrrha.

The archivist said, "That's a new voice," and Palamedes said cheerfully, "Archivist, this is Pyrrha Dve, whom Cam and I credit with keeping us alive . . . please be very nice to her. The Sixth House owes Pyrrha Dve everything barring tenure. All right," he said, and tapped a knuckle on the sheaf of papers. "That's all we're going to get. Commander, I'm about to ask that we put the Sixth House back on this truck—we don't need to be too worried about living space, this is temporary. If you want to pack anything on here yourself, tell me now."

The commander stepped forward into the light. The archivist, plait twitching, stepped with her.

"Palamedes Sextus," she said, "how do you hope to get out of here?"

"We're heading through the River," said Palamedes. "I plan on getting everyone to the Nine Houses, and—once we complete the mission—heading back to the Sixth House. Which, so you know, is parked on an exoplanet just outside the star system."

Pyrrha demanded—

"Are you a fantasist, boy, or only out of your mind? Your cav's the one with no blood left, so there's no excuse for *you*."

"I believe it will work," said Palamedes.

"I know it won't. You can't travel the River. You've never been trained, for one thing."

"That *is* the tricky part," admitted Palamedes. "But Pyrrha, I've spent time in the River . . . I've studied it, albeit in a strange and partial way. I think I can accurately navigate."

"I don't care how much you learnt in that bubble. You're not a

Lyctor," said Pyrrha. "You can't keep the ghosts off. They'll strip you to the bone."

"Not this time," said Palamedes—very lightly.

Nona felt Pyrrha's arms suddenly lose their normal untrembling strength and let her slip down a couple of centimetres until she said urgently, "Pyrrha, you're dropping me," and Pyrrha gathered her back up.

We Suffer said, "I need you to tell me you can do this with a certainty."

"I can give you ninety percent," said Palamedes.

"Prove it."

Palamedes passed the sheaf of papers back to We Suffer. He said, "Mum, can you get Kiana? She should be here . . . and Cam's dads—"

"No. Just Kiki," said Camilla. "Just my sister. They won't . . . They might not understand, Warden."

The archivist was saying, in quite a jaunty and familiar way, "Ah, family matters—would you give me your arm, Commander?—Are you a family woman yourself?—Oh, and when was the divorce . . ."

Palamedes wheeled Camilla into the dark, back toward the truck that Nona had woken up inside. Pyrrha looked after them, her face and eyes wild; she followed without being asked to, and Nona clasped her arms around Pyrrha's shoulders. She did not understand.

The corpse prince was sitting on the back step of the truck when they got there. Palamedes had hit the brakes on the wheeled chair and Camilla was slumped back in it. Even in the darkness of the tunnel Nona could tell that she was in a terrible way. She was very calm but very feeble; her mouth had gone dark.

"No. No more medication," Nona heard her say clearly. "Need my head . . . want it clear."

Pyrrha sat Nona on the truck step, blindly, despite Nona's warning squawk; Nona very much did not want to be sat next to the shimmering white figure of the dead Kiriona Gaia, who was watching the proceedings with the lively interest of a spectator at a ballgame. Pyrrha practically stumbled away—she dropped to her knees before the chair and Palamedes—she reached out and took

Palamedes's hand, and then Camilla's. Her face and hands showed only dumb despair.

"I've loved you two," she said. "Not well. Not even wholesomely. I don't have it in me. But I've loved you—in a better world I'd be able to say, 'Like you were my own,' but I don't know what that would even mean anymore. You've been my agents . . . you've been stand-ins for something I haven't had for longer than either of you can understand. Which is why I'm saying—don't do this. Please, don't do this."

Neither of them answered.

Pyrrha continued urgently: "Understand that once you do this, you can't take it back. It's better to die. There's a power to dying clean . . . dying free. It's not love, what you're about to do. It's not beautiful and it's not powerful. It's a mistake. We didn't even do it right . . . we were children—playing with the reflections of stars in a pool of water . . . thinking it was space."

Palamedes stood, and Pyrrha stood with him. He reached out and grasped her wrist strongly. "Whatever you think we're doing, we're not," he said.

"Whatever you think you're doing," said Pyrrha, "you shouldn't."

Camilla said, "Just watch us."

Pyrrha tugged her wrist free of Palamedes's hand. She reached down, and tilted Camilla's chin up, and looked at her for the longest time. Then she leant down—she kissed her brusquely and briefly on the forehead—and, startlingly and even more briefly, on the mouth. Nona, who even then could never ditch the lessons of the hand and the mouth, watched that kiss and felt very sad. It was like watching Pyrrha stealing something she didn't want to take—reaching out for the juicy, cherry-red part of the oven, even when she knew that all it could give her was a burn. And Nona saw Camilla, with her cold, navy blue mouth, and could tell that Camilla understood.

Camilla said, "Could you try not to be such a chicken hawk, Pyrrha?"

Pyrrha reached out, ruffled the perfect hair of the body of Ianthe Naberius, and leant in to briefly kiss Palamedes too—Palamedes said, tolerant and amused, "You are an appalling old roué, Dve,"—and Pyrrha said, "Call me if you need me. Otherwise, see you around."

Pyrrha crossed over to the truck, to Nona, and leant heavily into the interior; Nona could see that she was sweating, in exactly the same way she had sweated after the bottle of bleach. She mumbled, "You knew this was happening. You knew this was happening *months* ago," and when Nona put her hand on Pyrrha's, it was like Pyrrha hadn't even noticed her.

By now, other people had filtered through to stand in a ragged semicircle around the wheelchair. There was the birdlike lady with the braid, We Suffer, a tall, lanky, creased young woman in grey whose face looked so startlingly like Cam's that Nona wondered at it; her hair was nearly all shaved off on both sides, and unlike the others her eyes weren't milky-white at all, they were set deep and dark in a face like a hawk's. Crown joined them too, golden, shining Crown, another ragged lamp in the darkness. She was tying her fingers in knots, then untying them, over and over.

Nobody said a thing. Camilla's head was lolled back against the chair, but she abruptly stood—stood on her own power, rolling her shoulders, cracking her neck. Palamedes drew her to sit down on the cold road, and they sat facing each other, cross-legged. It took Camilla a long time to fold her legs, and when she did, she made a kind of deep *oof* noise that told Nona it had cost her. She drew one of her knives from its holder, and laid it down between them on the concrete.

All at once, the ragged watchers closed in—just a few steps—so that they formed a ring: not tight enough to smother, but like they were trying to shut out the rest of that vast, empty tunnel, the far-off echoes of bullets. Nona instinctively moved forward, and nearly fell out of the truck; Pyrrha caught her up and they sank to the ground together. Kiriona Gaia was staring politely at the side of the truck, as though there were something really interesting on the paintwork.

"Camilla, we did it right, didn't we?" Palamedes said, and now Nona knew he wasn't speaking to anyone else in the universe. "We had something very nearly perfect . . . the perfect friendship, the perfect love. I cannot imagine reaching the end of this life and having any regrets, so long as I had been allowed to experience being your adept."

Camilla Hect stared at him stolidly, and then burst into tears. She made very little noise, but the tears were violent anyway; Palamedes took her hands and said in distress, "Cam—dear one—don't."

"No," said Camilla, after an obvious struggle to master herself. "No. I'm crying because . . . I'm crying because I'm relieved," she said, frankly mulishly. "I'm *relieved* . . . Warden, I'm so relieved."

"Not long now," he promised.

Camilla took a couple of gasping breaths—it was obvious how much they hurt her—and then she said: "Warden—will she know who we are, in the River?"

"Oh, she's not stupid," said Palamedes lightly. "In the River— beyond the River—I truly believe we will see ourselves and each other as we really are. And I want them to see *us*. I am not saying *this was our inevitable end* . . . I am saying we have found the best and truest and kindest thing we can do in this moment. Tell me no, and we'll go on as we have been . . . and we'll go on unafraid . . . but say yes, and we will make this end, and this beginning, together."

Camilla shivered all over. Then she was at rest; she relaxed her head—the lines of her neck drooped like a flower—she raised it again.

"Palamedes, yes," she said. "My whole life, yes. Yes, forever, yes. Life is too short and love is too long."

He demanded: "Tell me how to do it, and I'll do it."

Camilla said, "Go loud."

Palamedes took her knife, and he cracked open an invisible seam on the end of the handle. A thin trickle of something white and grey and powdery dribbled into his palm. He held it out to her, and Camilla opened her mouth and—to Nona's horror—ate it, whatever it was. He took the knife and he scored her finger, saying, "Not much longer," and he pressed her own bloody finger to her cool and bloody mouth, and he said, "Don't look back. Whatever you do, don't look back," and they huddled their heads together, they rested their heads on each other's shoulders.

Nothing particularly interesting happened, until Camilla burst into flames. She blazed like a white candle—she rolled away from the body of Ianthe Naberius, booted the inert figure away to roll over and over across the road—and stood, stumbling, completely ablaze, a hot white pillar of fire. Nona watched her open her mouth as though she were calling out, but no sound came. She sizzled: her bandages and clothes and injuries all sizzled, her hair sizzled, she blackened and wasted right in front of them. Wherever she staggered, she left bloody black footprints, and those footprints curled up in flowerlike wreaths of smoke and flame before dribbling to nothing on the road. She dropped to the road as though dying, rolled around in the agonies of the dying, until Nona thought she too would die of watching: that she had finally found something so horrible she could die just from seeing it, the worst thing you could ever see in your life.

The whole tunnel was filled with sparking, sparkling flame, and the crackle of roasting human flesh, Camilla's body dancing gruesomely trying to put it out—a black thing within the fire—then something red within the fire—and then she tried to stand; she arched, trembling, featureless; the flames died.

In the darkness, the figure was naked and whole and unhurt. It crouched in on itself—elbows to knees, clasping itself, curled up in a kind of C—and then it said: "Clothes, please?"

Nona watched as Kiriona started to unbutton her jacket, then thought better of it. The hawk-faced stranger shimmied, completely unembarrassed, out of her trousers, leaving herself in shorts; We Suffer was taking off her heavy coat. As both of them approached, Nona could see that the stranger's hawk face was stony and emotionless but that there were wet tracks down her cheeks. The naked figure shrugged on the coat—hastily pulled up the trousers—said, "Thanks," and buttoned itself in.

And it was just Camilla, after all—Camilla having lost all that fringe and most of her hair except for a charred inch or so—Cam with new eyes, and a new face, for all that they were the same-shaped eyes and the old familiar features. But the eyes were a different colour, though Nona could not see *what* colour from where she sat. All she could see was that they were different. And the features, though

in the same order, were making such a different set of expressions—
not Camilla's, not Palamedes's—that it struck Nona all at once: they
were gone—they had left her—they were no longer there.

Nona lifted her voice, and wailed aloud.

The new figure broke past We Suffer and the hawk-faced woman,
and rustled through the pockets of the inert dead body of Ianthe Naberius, alone and still on the road—loped over to Nona in a way that
neither Camilla nor Palamedes had ever moved but was filled with
both of them, long in the leg, easy in the stride, spare and efficient.
They held out a lavender silk handkerchief.

Nona sniffled thickly, and recoiled. "I want a tissue—that's too
fancy," she mumbled.

"That's the point," the figure said, and looked at her with a grave
smile. "We know there's not going to be a big birthday party anymore, but: happy birthday, Nona."

Nona mopped her eyes dolefully with the handkerchief. "Thank
you," she said. "It's a relief you didn't get hair ties."

The new person suddenly whirled around in one movement. They
dashed toward the abandoned body of Ianthe Naberius—an abandoned body that was now propped up on its elbows, staring out with
pale, distrustful eyes, an expression on its face of commingled hate
and despair.

"So there was another way, Sextus, after all," the body murmured.

The figure crouched down and extended their arm.

"I know how hard it is for you to kick against the goad," said the
new person. "But there are more worlds than this. Come with us. We
are the love that is perfected by death—but even death will be no
more; death can also die. There's still time, Ianthe. Time for you, and
for Naberius Tern."

The abandoned body stared at what had once been Camilla's hand,
at what once had been Camilla's face, then at the hand again. After
which it said brightly—

"I bet you say that to all the boys."

The body collapsed and was empty; staring up at the top of the
tunnel, its eyes strangely white and silent.

29

THEY LOADED EVERYONE BACK into a single truck. Nobody seemed annoyed about this, even though Nona knew they had been on the trucks for months. Maybe once you were on a truck long enough, you forgot that there was anything but the truck. To Nona, it did not seem like a nice kind of home. She kept thinking in a welter of heartbreak about *her* bedroom, *her* mattress, *her* blankets. She had started thinking of bed in a kind of longing, desperate, hungry way.

Pyrrha had taken the wheeled chair that Camilla had used and sat Nona inside it. Camilla—Palamedes—the new person—did not need any kind of wheeled chair anymore, or pain medication, despite having been nearly dead. With enormous energy, few words, and a clipboard clutched in their hands, Palamedes-and-Camilla herded all those bent-down, exhausted people. They stopped every single one briefly, and patted them over, and said things like, "Rehydrated," or, "Try walking on that," or, "Fixed the kidneys. Take better care of them." Somehow simultaneously they took measurements, all while moving like someone Nona had never met. She fell back entirely on Pyrrha, who seemed as absolutely out of her element as Nona was.

"How much to ride the merry-go-round?" said someone familiar.

It was the Angel. The Angel and Pash appeared in front of Nona's chair, before the truck, and with them—most wonderfully—Noodle; Noodle, sitting on the ground, opening his mouth and panting, closing his mouth and rolling his eyes with displeasure, obviously as past the events of the day as Nona herself. Pyrrha said with a flicker of old humour—"How much to get *off*?"

"More than we can afford, I guess," said the Angel. She was looking composed in a long canvas coat like the one We Suffer had given up, with a long bag slung over her shoulder. Pash wore two of the same, one over each shoulder, with a third in her hand. "Sometimes I feel as though I were born on the merry-go-round—I worry I won't know what to do with myself when it stops. *If* it ever stops."

Nona, having seen the bags, and Noodle, and the leashes, found eagerness enough within her to say— "Are you coming with us?"

"Probably not, kiddie," said Pyrrha, but Pash said unexpectedly: "This is the fucking stupidest idea in the world, but yeah, we are. I go where *this* goes"—a violent jerk of the head in the Angel's direction—"and I guess *this* one is getting on the bus."

"To the Nine Houses," said Pyrrha slowly.

"Yes," said the Angel.

"The very centre of the Emperor Divine's power," said Pyrrha.

Pash said, "Don't even start. You'll set me off again. We go where we're sent . . . and this city's a death trap. I don't know, I would have moved out into the tunnels and tried to get clear of the city that way, but . . ."

"But I exist," said the Angel. "Pardon—*we* exist. And as long as we exist, we are a terrible liability. The commander will get some breathing room if she doesn't have to take us into account with every movement."

Pash said roughly: "The commander's probably dead the moment we walk out of here."

"We have left many wing commanders behind to die," said the Angel calmly. "This wing commander is particularly cunning and particularly brave and particularly determined—but get used to it, Passion . . . We've been weighed," she shouted out, and waved her hand at the figures of Palamedes-and-Camilla and We Suffer in the distance, and they waved back.

Nona said: "Who *are* you?" Then she explained, "Everyone asks me the same question, so—I feel like it's my turn."

"You don't get to ask," said Pash roughly; which Nona thought was a wonderful and very cool answer she wished she had come up with herself.

But the Angel leant down and looked at Nona. There was something settled in her face: a calmness that had not existed there before—a kind of immovable, fixed-concrete resolve. She had never seen the Angel look like that. Every furtive, fleeting, mercurial spark had gone, leaving something hard and old, something that touched light to some paper deep within Nona. She suddenly reached up and grasped the Angel's hand, and the Angel grasped hers, and the Angel looked at her.

"I'm the Messenger," said the Angel simply. "We are the Message . . . the message has two parts left, and you are looking at one of those parts. The name for this part of the message was 'Aim' when the message was passed to us through my forebear Emma Sen. The message is too simple for human beings like us to understand. What do you think the message is?"

Nona couldn't guess.

"I hope you hear it one day," said Aim.

She reached out—she ruffled Nona's hair—she smiled. Then she said, "Noodle, let's go," and she stepped resolutely up the ramp and into the truck.

Pash dithered behind a little—a more subdued and unsure Our Lady of the Passion. She said, "I have to shoot you now," and then she burst out, quickly, "Joke—that was an actual fucking joke, you don't even need to pay for it," and she followed the Angel up the ramp.

Pyrrha leant down and plucked Nona out of the chair. Nona was bewildered to find that her arms were now betraying her too. When she tried to place them around Pyrrha's neck again, they too had become something more like rocks and ice. Pyrrha put them around her shoulders and said— "You've been very calm."

Nona found herself saying: "It's not long now, is it? Are we going to find me?"

"Yeah," said Pyrrha. "I think it's time to wake you up."

The megatruck, on the inside, was a long corridor of little cubicles.

Pyrrha avoided these cubicles and instead travelled up a short flight of metal stairs to another compartment. She opened a door and she brought Nona into an enormous cockpit with wraparound windows, the most complicated car insides that she had ever seen. Pyrrha sat down on a chair made of shiny, soft, cracked stuff, worn at the seat from too much sitting down. The windshield was a huge black expanse, strung with the few lights lit in the tunnel and otherwise looking like the blackness at the bottom of the world.

The corpse prince was already in the cockpit. She had apparently walked there under her own steam—if anyone from Blood of Eden had noticed, they had kept it to themselves—and now she was strapped into one of the sideways seats, her sword beneath her feet, legs splayed carelessly wide at the knees, arms folded over her chest. She did not speak to them, even when Pyrrha said, "Hey, kid." She had not said much of anything since Camilla and Palamedes had become Camilla-and-Palamedes—seemed withdrawn and lost in thought, unwilling to look at anyone or anything.

Camilla's body appeared at the doorway. The commander was there with it, and Crown was close behind, with the Captain's arm around her shoulder. The Captain seemed to be able to stand up now, but was staring, dumb and dull, as though she didn't understand her surroundings. Supporting her must have been awkward, but Crown didn't seem to notice. Crown flashed a smile at Nona—she even smiled at Kiriona—before sitting down in one of the front-row chairs. Camilla-and-Palamedes selected the biggest chair of all, right at the front, before the enormous wheel.

"Mind showing me how this thing starts?" they said to the commander.

"Oh, dear God," said the commander. "For what I am about to do, I will go down as history's greatest monster." But she leant over, and she said: "Ignition is there—those are the three brake lines. The lights will need to be green before you hit the ignition. This will start the automatic checks. Press this button to indicate you have read them. If you flip that switch—and *do not* flip it before everything else has gone green—it will free this lever, which can be manipulated forward . . .

and the wheel turns, although it will also turn automatically with the wall detection . . . Do you have that?"

Pyrrha said, "Please let me drive."

"No chance," said Palamedes-and-Camilla comfortably. And: "Commander . . . thank you. Leave everything to me."

"I do—I have," said We Suffer. And— "Every single hope of Eden now rests within this clapped-out vehicle."

"Same for the Nine Houses," said Palamedes-and-Camilla.

"You know what I want," said We Suffer. She turned to address the rest of the driver's cockpit. "To complete what she started. Troia, listen to me. Every so often there is invoked a Blood of Eden mission protocol—we call it Protocol One. It is used in times of either terrible joy or the worst possible outcomes. Protocol One means there are no more formal orders—if given in the field of battle, often it is understood as 'Scatter. Retreat. Disunite,' but it is not quite that. There is a different protocol that is simply used for retreat, protocol that means 'Save yourselves.' I received the order to save myself when I was young . . . and I saved myself, which is why you hear me now, starting this terrible truck, putting my life's work in the hands of my enemies and of strangers I do not understand. But now I give you Protocol One . . . and Protocol One is 'Live.'"

Crown saluted. Pyrrha looked at the commander, and she saluted too, a slightly different salute with her hand over her heart. Palamedes-and-Camilla turned around in the seat, and they said— "What mission protocol are you about to give Blood of Eden?"

We Suffer flapped her hand dismissively. "Oh, a very common one. It is basically 'Fight like hell and do not shoot any civilians.' We can do that one any day of any week. I only wish civilians were not so dumb, like rocks are . . . Lieutenant Crown Him with Many Crowns, good luck. Pyrrha Dve . . . I am amazed to say this, but I wish you luck. Nona . . . I wish you luck. You . . ."

We Suffer paused. Camilla-and-Palamedes cocked their burnt head to one side.

"Paul," they suggested.

"Paul. Good luck, Paul," said We Suffer. "Now . . . you have my coat, which you can keep, but my wallet is in the breast pocket, so hand it over."

Palamedes-and-Camilla—Paul—obediently dislodged the wallet and handed it over. We Suffer said, "Now I will give final orders to Aim and Lieutenant Our Lady of the Passion. I will also say goodbye to Juno Zeta, who I understand is your mother, and who is an extraordinary lady who has already memorised the names of various people in my family."

We Suffer turned around and walked out without ceremony; she paused only for one long, last look at the corpse prince. Nona noticed that Crown held her salute for a long time after the door shut behind We Suffer, and only reluctantly let her hand drop.

"Buckle in," said Paul.

Pyrrha tested and tightened the seatbelt over Nona's arms, and asked, "How long were you planning this one?"

"They had a lot of rainy-day backup plans."

"Yeah, but—*Paul*?"

"Just Paul," said Paul.

Crown suggested, "Paul . . . Hect?"

"Just Paul," said Paul.

"U Lap," said the corpse prince, from the back of the cabin.

"Thanks for your contribution," said Paul.

"Aulp," said the corpse prince.

"No," said Paul.

A light started flashing on the megatruck control board. Paul leant over and touched the button, and We Suffer's voice crackled through.

"Troia cell, do you read? You're clear. Goodbye, and good hunting."

"Troia cell copy. Good luck," said Paul, and, a little laconically— "See you soon."

"You have a big ego," she said. "I enjoy that. It is a good and terrible sign. Ctesiphon-1, out."

Paul settled back in the chair and buckled in. Nona watched as Paul depressed a button until the lights flickered green; a pleasant *ding* sounded as a screen rolled across the front of the big blackness—as the lights in their little cabin dimmed into nothing, and as a long squiggly readout filled up fully a third of the glass. Paul tapped a button—the readout shifted smoothly over to one side—and flipped a switch, then freed a lever.

There was a deep, smooth *clunk* all around Nona, insulated by dint of being in Pyrrha's lap and also by her body feeling so strange and numb. A huge light swept out in front of them—the headlights from the megatruck had come on automatically—so that there was the darkness, and the road, and the beams of light.

The truck began to roll forward. Pyrrha leant back in the chair and said, "Okay. What now?"

"This," said Paul.

Paul released a lever, and the truck lurched forward into the darkness. They settled their hands on the wheel. There was nothing in their face but easy surety, not one trace of pain or fear or worry. *Everyone* had at least a slight trace of anticipation or pain or fear or worry, but not this new person called Paul. Nona felt the truck accelerate—the light ate away the darkness—and a huge, heavy chill settled into the cabin.

Nona's breath started coming in frosted pants that hung before her face. An urgent whirring started at the front of the cabin—a white, thick fog of condensation had started to build at the bottom of the glass, and then the heater kicked in and it melted into rivulets of water that pooled down, then abruptly started to run *upward*, up the windshield glass.

Paul leant forward on the accelerator, and then—

JOHN 5:4

I N THE DREAM they were back on the beach with
their backs to the sea. The sand was soft and wet
and grey—so fine that it dried as they plucked
at it, then crumbled through their fingers like ash. The beach was a
long, smooth stretch relieved only by hummocks, here and there, of
thin grass and silvery driftwood sticking out of the dunes like exposed
bone. He was scooping indentations in the sand, making big, print-
block child's letters with the tip of his forefinger. As she watched,
he made a pothook—*J*—then the finned spine of *E*. He wiped that *E*
clean, and replaced it with *A*. He wiped that clean, and he drew the
prison bars of *H*. This *J* and *H* he barred around with an uneven heart.

She watched, and she said—

"Teacher, may I ask a question?"

"Sure," he said, surprised, and he shook his fingers free of clinging
sand. "Shoot."

"What does it mean to love God?"

"Decent dinner and a bottle of average rosé. Maybe a movie. I'm
not picky," he said.

She said, less patiently: "Teacher, what does it mean for a child of
the Ninth to love God?"

The razor-sharp grasses lay in a shivering mat, cuddled like fearful
animals, as the wind swept over them. Fine salty fragments got inside
the corners of her mouth. He said, finally—

"You live in a darkened house, and in your darkened house are
infinite rooms. By the light of a dying candle you cross the room—
knowing that when you reach the threshold of the next room you'll be
gone—the candle passed to someone whose face you can't see clearly."

She urged, "Is God the flame? The light? The candle?"

"The love of God is the trust that you won't have to illumine that darkness alone," he said.

She said—

"After this, you'll resurrect them."

"Yes," he said, as though halfway dreaming. He stuck his finger in the sand and made a hole so deep that water glimmered at the bottom. Hypnotized, he did it again. "Yes. Once we've rested. No, we'll do it before you've rested. You can rest afterward . . . *resurrection* is different from *waking up*. We'll get them all back . . . some of them, anyway . . . or at least, the ones I want to bring back. Anyone I feel didn't do it. Anyone I feel had no part in it. Anyone I can look at the face of and forgive. And my loved ones . . . The ones I left, I'll bring back. I know I can. Even G——. In fact, G——'ll be easiest—he won't remember the compound—none of them will have to remember anything. I know where remembrance lives in the brain, and he won't have any of it. You know that too, don't you? It's the easiest thing in the world . . . to forget."

She said, "To forget . . . everything?"

"Yes," he said, and more sharply— "Yes. It's the only way."

"Teacher, why?"

"They won't forgive themselves," he said. "They'll spend the rest of their lives asking what-ifs. 'What should we have done? How could we have done it differently? Did you *need* to do it?' And—I did need to do it, Harrow. There was no other way. Once those bombs were going off, there was no hope for Melbourne anyway—G—— was dead meat."

She said—

"You said that G——'s bomb went off first."

"Yeah, it did," he said impatiently. "Of course it did . . . Look—what does it matter? In the end, why the *hell* does it matter? Only one thing matters now."

He smoothed over the holes—covered them up in a slight, leaden depression, a wave of his hand across the surface. Wet sand banked up on either side.

"I still have breath in my body," he said. "They are still out there. There can be no forgiveness."

"For whom?" she asked.

For a long time he did not answer.

Then he said, "Do you remember what happens now?"

Harrowhark Nonagesimus stood up. She brushed a few traces of sand off her trousers. She wiped tiny motes of rock from her eyes, and she heard the sea behind her, moaning soundlessly as it ate into the beach. She looked up to try to find the poisonous yellow fog; the degraded land; the torn-up buildings and flooded skeletons of towns; but there was nothing—just the beach, and some foothills below the beach.

"Yes," she said. "Through her, I've seen it. You resurrect some of them. You wake up fewer still. You start out with a few thousand, then, later, some hundred thousand, then millions, but never more than millions. You teach them how to live all over again. You teach yourself. You work out how to repopulate the installations on each planet—or to finish the work begun before the bombs, or to improve on it. It's easy. You're God. Your energy is limitless and you can sustain your theorems without a thought—forget about them—because she is so enormous, and you and she are one. She understands at this point that she does not have to die—that she can never die, if you're alive. And she's scared to die. You're afraid of so many things, but she's only afraid to die. Then, when the disciples come to you and say the word *Lyctor,* she does not understand that they want the thing you did to her—she watches as you watch . . . watch them misunderstand the process."

He looked up at her, squinting his eyes against the white and merciless sun. "God must be able to touch all of creation," he said.

"I don't—"

"You said it yourself. I can't die if she's alive; she can't die if I'm alive. Why would you let something like that run around, Harrow? Why would you let someone go—away from you—untouchable—*two* people? I couldn't—I loved them too much—I saw the face of Earth and choked the life out of it and ate it whole. Oh, I knew I was on the clock for the Resurrection Beasts. I pretended she was the

only one, but I knew the others were coming. I needed my loved ones
to be something I could touch . . . needed them to be my hands . . .
my fingers."

"But—"

"There can be no forgiveness for those who walked away," he said.
"Just as there can be no forgiveness for me—even though I rip the
very fingers from my hands . . . throw them into the jaws of the monsters who hunt me . . . as I run from them across the universe, end
to end. Something will satisfy them eventually, but nothing satisfies
me. Nothing."

He drew his gaze away from her—his black-and-white, chthonic
stare—and looked out over the dunes. He said, "But that's the grace
of it, Harrow. If I'm God, I can start over. The flood, you know?
You can wash things clean. That's all the end of Earth was . . . making things clean. It gets dirty again, you clean it again. Like those
old power-washing ads. *Spray and walk away,* right? Sometimes I
think the only reason I haven't done it already is that I can't bear the
idea that I wouldn't be able to touch them—that they'd still be out
there . . . maybe that's why I made the Tomb, Harrow. It *is* the death
of God . . . it is the apocalypse . . . because it's my self-preservation
in a box."

She said, "Teacher, there's one thing I don't understand."

"There're multiple things I don't," he said.

She said— "I want to understand why she was angry—I want to
understand the mathematics, now that I have seen them for myself. I
want to know how many of the Resurrection are left, and how many
you began with, and what the discrepancies are. I want to know where
you put them. They didn't go into the River. I want to know why she
was angry . . . and why you were terrified."

She looked away from him, and she said: "I want to journey to
find God. Maybe, at the end of that road, I will find God in you,
Teacher . . . the God who became man and the man who became
God. Or, perhaps, the child of the Nine Houses will recognise a dif-
ferent divine. But I am the Reverend Daughter—I am the Reverend
Mother, the Reverend Father—I must find God, or some aspect of

God, and understand it for myself . . . even if she lies, right now, within the Tomb."

He stood. He was taller than she was. She was not afraid. He reached out a hand to her, and placed it upon her shoulder, and looked at her, wondering, with his ordinary face; if she had suspected his fear might manifest itself, yet again, as an act of murder, she could not see that in him now.

"God is a dream, Harrow," he said very gently. "You all dream me together—and she's dreaming me too. In a way, her dead dreams of God mean more than all your dreams put together. In this dream of yours, where will you seek out God? Where will you go?"

Harrow turned away from the hand, and crunched out, barefoot, over the wet sand—her feet slapped with each step—and she stood ankle-deep in the River, disbelieving.

Before her, the waters parted, speared-through and mute, for the enormous lance of a tower—a tower that had never been there before; a tower that soared, impossible and deadly grey, out of the waters—a tower of grey bricks, lurching out of the River as though gasping for air. An impossible, cone-capped tower—a belled tower; she could see the steeple, but the bell cot was too far from shore to see the bell.

"I'll start there," she said.

And she stepped into the River. She took another step, and she walked, and she walked.

WHEN NONA'S EYES OPENED, it was still dark—but then the darkness changed. It thickened, then resolved, then turned grey, then turned transparent. There was a huge roaring *pop!* within her body's ears, and then they weren't in the tunnel at all. They weren't in anything. The space between the windshield and whatever was out there wasn't space at all: it was as though someone had thrown a bucket of grey paint over the windshield. She couldn't see out.

Nona stood up—or at least, her body stood up: she was nauseous, and thought that if she stood something would be left on the chair or stuck within Pyrrha's arms. The belt of the chair broke as she stood. Pyrrha reached out for her. She brushed Pyrrha's arm away. Her legs still felt like distant nothing, as did her arms, and her trunk, and her neck, but her eyes could still see and her ears could still hear and her tongue could still taste. When she opened her mouth so that her tongue could taste, it helped her to see a little better. Everyone was talking, talking, talking. Pyrrha was saying something—Paul was saying, in calm repose, "No. I've bubbled us," and all Nona caught of Pyrrha's response was:

"—not *enough*, I'm not saying velocity exists here but—"

"—untethered, but—"

"—if you want to get into the current you'll—"

Crown was whispering in her softest and most coaxingest voice, "Judith? Won't you come back to me—Judith—Jody?" and of course the Captain wasn't saying anything back. Pyrrha swung around to the corpse prince and said, "Kid, you still in there?" and Kiriona said scornfully, "It takes more than *this*." Nobody was speaking to, or noticing, Nona.

Until Nona's hand tapped Paul on the shoulder. Paul looked up into her face with a grave play of understanding flashing across Camilla's once-familiar features, the unfamiliar eyes with their deep slate dot in the centre.

Nona took a long time to examine those new eyes and decide what she thought of them: whether she liked the pupil that was that cool grey-brown, the iris of clear and limitless grey. Her mouth said— "I'll take it from here."

Paul looked at her one final time, then unbuckled—moved aside—steadied themselves as Nona sat in the chair. It was made for someone longer and her leg did not reach the accelerator, so Paul extended one leg and pressed down with a foot, and braced against the chair and the side of the console.

Nona said, "Your thing. The outline. Won't work. Don't ask me questions."

Paul said, "That skin's all that's lying between us and certain death."

Nona's eyes dazzled. Her body shuddered beneath her. For one of the first times she acknowledged it, she felt the body as something *with* her, on top of her, but not *her*; her sense of living outside it. There was a fragile, pulpable ecstasy in that body. It was like one of the soft blue jellyfish in the harbour, with all its stings and promises, and now Nona's self, Nona's thoughts, were a hand closing around the jellyfish, unbidden, feeling it undulate blindly between the fingers. And the more she felt like fingers, the more she closed down.

Somewhere, in that shimmering space between fingers and palm, she heard a voice: Pyrrha saying, "Kiddie—stay with us."

So Nona stayed.

"Don't say things that are questions but aren't said like a question," she said eventually, letting her voice rush out without thinking about it. "Take it away. Take it. We don't need it. If you ask more questions— I'll want to answer them— Take it away, I said."

Paul considered this. "Okay."

Pyrrha said, "Wait. Hang on—" but Paul had already obeyed. Nona felt it, the *pop*. The grey flapped and peeled away from the windscreen—pale light poppled in, and the whole windshield exploded into vision.

Before them was water, and the megatruck drove along its surface. There was limitless nothing above its surface—something that wanted to look like a night sky, maybe, or a purpling storm with winking lights like stars or lightning—and it stretched without relief over and above that water. Dirty gouts of foam were being spun up by the megatruck's tires and undercarriage as it sped along, on top of the water, and that obscured the space and the water and everything, until Nona heaved herself forward on the wheel and spun it hand over hand. It was good to let her hands do things: they knew how to do things she did not know how to do. That raised a huge cloud of foam; the megatruck lurched to one side, and everyone was holding on to things, and everything that hadn't been secured tumbled to the other side of the cabin. Yells echoed softly through the door behind them. Paul, light on Cam's feet, reached forward over Nona's shoulder and the windscreen wipers started a huge *SCREE... SCREE... SCREE* across the windshield.

Pyrrha said, "This is impossible. We should be flayed alive," and Paul said, "Yeah."

Nona tried to explain.

"The water doesn't want to touch us, that's all."

Crown was saying urgently, "Judith—stop, come back," and Nona vaguely heard unbuckling; and then shadows fell over her, people standing behind her seat. Lots of people had crowded around behind her now; Nona wasn't sure she liked it.

Pyrrha sucked in her breath, and she said: "What the fuck is *that*?"

"Told you so," said Kiriona Gaia.

As the megatruck spun around, the wide rippling grey waters resolved into something totally different. There was a big structure standing up out of the River—that water was the River, after all—a tall, cold cylinder of what was unmistakably stone. The waters parted around it, and each bulgy wave slammed into it as though trying to bring it down, but it was as hard and inexorable and real as the water and the skies seemed faint and fantastic. Nona thought it looked like something out of a picture book, and held on to that thought, that *middle-of-the-brain* thought. There was a thought above and below that knew what it was, but the moment she looked at either thought she'd lose the game.

The Captain's voice was like old teeth. "He left them too long— you left them too long, my salt thing."

"You *are* here," said Nona, finding talking was hard, that her voice sounded drowsy in her own ears. "Okay, good—the water really won't touch us. I was worried about our back end."

Paul and Pyrrha flinched hard away from that voice—dived to the other side of the cabin, wheeling away as though struck. This meant that there wasn't a foot on the accelerator, and Nona had to slither down in her chair until she was pretty well staring at the top of the windshield just to keep the megatruck going. A recorded voice said, "Auto-acceleration enabled," and a little bell made a nice little tinkle, so she slithered back up and left it.

The tower was so big—as the megatruck approached she began to realise *how* big, as big and as broad and as tall as any crane or building in the city—stretching higher than their Building at home, even. There was a clear mark where the water reached up it, where the stone was wet black rather than the dry-stone grey above. From inside the megatruck, she could not see how high up it went.

For some reason this tower scared Nona's top and bottom thoughts so terribly that her heart went *ker-CHUNK* in her chest—there was a terrible pain in her side and all the way down her arm. The pain was good, because she couldn't think about anything but the pain. The more she thought, the more problems she had.

"The hole," said the Captain, "the hole in the road, the hole, the hole, the hole."

Crown was saying something, scrabbling against the back of Nona's chair, scrabbling. Pyrrha and Paul were collapsed on the floor. Nona knew that skidding across the surface of the water was no good, so she looked for one of the big, cresting waves, and with the auto-accelerator dinging in her ears, she ploughed the megatruck directly into the water.

The River swallowed them up. It felt very heavy. The truck's wheels spun against nothing—the truck groaned horribly from the pressure, creaking like Nona's hurting heart—and they sank like a stone. The cabin darkened as they sank—the windshield wipers bowed and sagged away from the windshield, and then were suddenly ripped off, sucked into the current—and a soft white starry crack appeared at the edge of the glass.

Nona slithered again, fumbling for the accelerator with her foot, but she couldn't take her hands off the wheel. She was exhausted. She did not want to drive anymore. Seeing the tower had taken the fight out of her top and her bottom, and now out of her middle too. She looked down the side of the chair, and there was Paul, struggling across the floor and shaking blood out of Camilla's right ear—Paul, face calm and even and only a little cross-eyed. Paul reached out to put one hand on the dirty accelerator and looked up at her, not beseeching, only waiting.

"Can you get us to the Ninth House?" they said.

There was another awful shriek of metal somewhere in the back of the megatruck. The windscreen darkened all the time—the water was turbid and filthy and the air in the cabin was getting weirdly chill—lots of people were yelling. She could hear Pyrrha in the background, Crown struggling with the Captain.

"Yes," said Nona, "but—"

"But?"

How could she say that she was so tired—that whatever was going on in her chest was so incredibly urgent that if she closed her eyes and let it happen, she could probably die right there, right then? How to say that she wanted to go as *Nona*—with all her thoughts and feelings being Nona feelings, which might only be about six months old and therefore not very good, but were still her own? What could she do with the little selfish thought that now Camilla and Palamedes were gone—even if they had left behind Paul, which was probably quite nice of them—and Pyrrha was broken somehow, it was hard to want to live, hard to want everyone else to live, even lovely Crown? The Captain was gone, forever probably, and it didn't matter about the corpse prince, who was dead already and therefore used to it.

Nona swallowed. She let her eyelids nearly touch, which would have been the end.

"But maybe we shouldn't," she said, holding the eyelids to that little slit—watching the onscreen scribbles flash urgently on the truck glass, watching the widening white crack, watching the river water pound itself into the place where it wanted to be even if the River itself didn't. "If we end here, it'll be just like . . . a bad dream, won't it? And maybe we'll wake up somewhere else. I know we won't," she explained, "but we don't have to *know* that . . . maybe if we all go, it'll be quick."

Paul looked at her, with those dark grey-brown pupils widening, slightly.

"Nona," they said, "Noodle's in the back."

The middle thoughts surged. The slit widened all the way.

"Oh my God," she said, in a panic. "I forgot about Noodle."

The windshield cracked all the way across the middle. Paul leant their full weight on the accelerator. Nona drove the truck home.

IX

$\mathfrak{Z}$1

THE WATER DISAPPEARED. There was a huge squealing of tires—Paul eased off the accelerator just in time—and a big gravelly noise as the tires, going from water to pressure to nothing to a big field of gritty stone, spun the stone in all directions. The windshield cracked all the way through, and the truck bounced—once—and a whole stream of red text blinked up on the screen overlay. But the light that came through the windshield wasn't grey light, and in fact wasn't very bright at all. It was a thin electric yellow light that did very little to pierce the darkness. The megatruck horn honked itself, and Nona was only aware of the sound, its echo, the blaring wail.

Then she became aware of something else; an insistent tugging at top thought, bottom thought, and middle thought. She wanted something. She didn't know quite what it was, only she wanted it—quite like a bathroom thought in its insistency.

"Headlights," someone was saying. "Get the headlights."

Paul had staggered up from behind her and was moving to the back cabin, unlocking the door. Pyrrha said, "We've equalised. We're on level ground," and then, in the corner of Nona's vision, the corpse prince rose.

She leant over the driver's seat, through the electric light, peering out at whatever was there. Then she suddenly cut off a word in her mouth—she followed after Paul—Pyrrha was saying, "Where are we? Back in the tunnel?" and Nona felt Pyrrha's strong, ropy arms circle around—felt herself lifted up and out of the driver's seat—found she was mucky with sweat, which embarrassed her, and that the warmth of Pyrrha's arms was distant and faraway. She could barely remember walking, moving her body in the chair, doing all that driving. She was grateful now for being carried. She felt lifted through the cabin, floating above a high chatter of voices in the megatruck behind:

"—forget to check on the engine, a big hit like that and the fuel cells—"

"—all right? Sprained, not broken, surely . . ."

"Thanergenic," someone else was saying. "I felt it immediately. Like a warm shower."

"Since when have *you* had warm . . . ?"

There was a shrill volley of barks. Noodle; Nona was weak and grateful to hear Noodle. There was a big release sound—a metal sliding door—and, "One, two—heave," followed by a great metal clashing. Nona struggled to sit up in Pyrrha's arms and open her eyes, and she saw the blackness out the other side of the door, and heard the sizzling, steaming sound as water boiled off the sides of the megatruck, and felt a blast of arctic air—black, cold, dust-smelling air, the blackest and coldest she had ever felt in her life.

The Prince strode down the platform. She stood on the gravel, haloed in the underlights from the wheezing megatruck, and she said—"Home, sweet home."

Pyrrha clattered her way down the platform. Nona looked up: they were standing at the bottom of some enormous rocky shaft—there was a tiny square of light way up top, as though they were standing at the bottom of a hole. All the steam was boiling off the truck upward. There was a soup of white cloudy stuff, and then a navy expanse of night—of space. She knew she should feel cold, as her body was feeling cold, but it was more the memory of a sensation than sensation itself.

Paul trotted up alongside Pyrrha, and stared at the filigreed back of the standing, gazing Prince, and said, "Gideon, where are we?"

"Top tier—shuttle field," said the corpse prince. "Smack bang in the middle."

"Nona," said Paul, "well done."

Nona did not feel as though she had done anything warranting a *well done.* She had just driven the truck, and she nearly gave up on that. She said drearily: "I didn't do it on purpose."

Pyrrha said, "No Lyctor could have taken us here that precisely. I'm not sure *John* could manage it . . . then again, I'm not sure of John, period. Gideon and I couldn't have—though for one thing, this field wasn't around in my day, you used to land at the installation they made the prison out of and go down from there in the elevator . . . What the *hell* was that, in the River? That wasn't Number Seven."

Prince Kiriona Gaia had walked several steps away from them into the darkness, and now seemed to float in the gloom, ghostlike in her pure white clothes. She had drawn her sword, and she didn't turn around.

"Quiet," she said.

Noodle ignored her totally: inside the truck he was doing the regular *bark—bark—bark* of a dog alerted to a nearby threat. Everyone else obediently stayed silent for a few seconds.

"I don't hear anything," said Pyrrha neutrally.

"Nor I," said Paul.

Kiriona made a noise that sounded almost amused, and said, "Fine. I'm going. Keep up or you're probably dead." Then she crunched away over the gravel and dwindled out of sight.

Pyrrha and Paul exchanged glances. Paul scrambled back up the ramp of the truck and said something to the people inside. There was a short discussion—Nona's hearing had gone very fuzzy and she couldn't make out any words, but no one was shouting—and then Paul dropped back down and the ramp began to scrape upward into its housing. Pyrrha adjusted her grip on Nona's body, shifting her weight, and then set off with Paul in the direction the corpse prince had gone.

"No Pash?" asked Pyrrha.

"She has to stay with Aim," said Paul, "and Aim got knocked around in the crash. They'll be fine."

"Honestly, I was hoping for another gun," said Pyrrha. "How are the Sixth doing? Is your—is Juno—"

"We're out of the Beast's radius. There's enough thanergy to go around. That truck has multiple highly capable necromancers and a dog. Worry about us instead."

"I do," said Pyrrha.

They walked for a long time. Nona felt like she wanted to sleep, but she was very frightened of sleeping. Somewhere in her spine was that same weird insistent urge or twinge. She noticed, vaguely, that Paul and Pyrrha weren't talking to her anymore. They weren't talking to each other either, just trudging steadily on through the darkness. Once upon a time Pyrrha would have jollied her along—made bad jokes or said things like "Right, kiddie, another minute and then you're carrying me." Now it was almost like they didn't think Nona was awake, even though her eyes were open.

The only time anyone spoke during the journey was when Pyrrha suddenly said—

"Fucking dark in here."

"Yes," said Paul, as if this was something intriguing that Pyrrha had been clever to notice.

"Ninth House ambiance, you reckon?"

"No."

"Someone should've told Anastasia that a string of fairy lights wouldn't have gone amiss. They could shape 'em like little skulls, stay on-brand. Then again, she always said the skull was the least interesting bone . . ."

As they walked farther, Nona felt the twinge getting stronger, and she felt something else: something at once familiar and unpleasant, squirming far off in the darkness. She strained her thoughts toward it. Many things—small things—things she'd seen before, once, but didn't feel up to seeing again. Grey shapes swam in front of her eyes in the darkness—she thought she saw the side of Pyrrha's face—she *did* see the side of Pyrrha's face, because it was getting lighter. They were walking toward a light: a cold white glow somewhere ahead of them, down a tunnel, getting closer and closer.

They arrived in a room. It was a big circular room with dark stone walls: there were arched niches in the walls, and each one held a seated skeleton in a dark shapeless robe. Nona could see all of this because there was a powerful electric lantern, rather like one of the truck's headlights, placed on the floor throwing long spiked shadows out in all directions. The corpse prince, Kiriona Gaia, was standing in the middle of the room with her drawn sword turned wet and red partway up the blade. There were crumpled dead bodies discarded around her—six or seven that Nona could see, all bundled up in black fabric like the skeletons were wearing. At the back of the room was a rectangular cage, taller than a man and made of wrought iron like the park fences. Slumped against the outside of this cage was a large person in strange, battered metal armour, tangled in his own black robes. He was quite simply the *oldest* person Nona had ever seen, and Nona had always collected old people in much the same way as she collected dogs: the old people at the dairy and the old men at the fishmonger's and the old women who worked at the car repair place. He was older than any of them. His whole face looked like it was trying to escape its skeleton. Dark red blood had spread out around him in a pool.

His antique head rolled sideways to look past Kiriona at Pyrrha—at *Nona*—and he said, in a voice that creaked with agonised, reverential awe—

"My lady . . . my lady, you have come home to us . . . at last."

Paul dropped to the ancient man's side and started looking him over—pulling away the tangled black cloth from the body, revealing a series of livid gashes down the neck, a puncture mark through the chest. The old man raised a hoary-looking fist and, without saying a word, boxed Paul soundly around the ears.

"Leave me," he wheezed sharply. "Interloper. Stranger. Fool . . . Do nothing for me. Touch me not."

"Leave him," said the corpse prince.

Paul said, "No. I can save him easily. It's only shock and blood loss."

Kiriona wiped her sword clean on one of the black-shrouded bodies. Then she kicked it over with her beautiful polished boot. "Look at that," she said, "and trust me on this one."

Beneath the light of the powerful lamp, the dead person's face was startling. The eyelids hung slack, and there were rows of dark purple pinpricks above and below them—like something fine and sharp had come through. Hanging out of the eyelids—Nona at first did not know what she was looking at—was a shrivelled object, wet and red, like a slug. Like a muscle. The tongue hanging out of the mouth was a lot longer than a normal tongue—and pointed, triangular, deep blue in death. For some reason, the sight started a shudder at Nona's feet that carried on all the way up to the top of her head. The awful pain tightened in her chest, and nearly shuddered her out of her body. The back of her neck itched so badly it felt as though it were bleeding.

Pyrrha said a word so terrible under her breath that it startled Nona back into the middle ground of her thoughts. She rebuked, "Pyrrha," and then— "No, I'm sorry, you're allowed to say whatever you like at this point."

Paul was crouched, staring thoughtfully at the dead, empty-eyed face in a way that would have been strange for either Palamedes or Camilla. Nona thought Camilla would have looked with eyes like stone and given away nothing, and that Palamedes would have reached out to touch. Paul did not reach out to touch, and Paul looked as though it were interesting.

The corpse prince said tightly, "They shouldn't be here. We would have gotten word if they were back in the home system. They're confined to Antioch—he said they'd only be on Antioch. God damn it, he *said*!"

Paul said, "Gideon, I've seen this before. My memory's split. Where?"

"Silas Octakiseron's poor bastard cavalier," said Kiriona. "Colum Asht. I didn't understand then . . . we call them devils. I mean, Dad calls them devils—this is what we're facing on Antioch. Fuck me, I didn't think . . . this is mental. They can't be here. He said they couldn't travel—he said . . ."

Paul said, "Gideon, cool it. Why can't I heal this man?"

"Like this I am undesirable to them," croaked the figure.

"They bit him," said the corpse prince, as though nobody had spoken. "I mean, they hit him—they don't have to bite. It's revenant magic. They're waiting for him to die so they don't have to work so hard. Heal him up now, and they'll still ride that wound all the way into his hideous old body and I'll get to kill him myself."

The ancient old man turned his single rheumy, hateful eye to the corpse prince.

"I would that you had been carried back here on a stretcher," he said. "I would that you were stretched out before me, dead in the rudeness of you . . . your niche is ready, Gideon Nav, and now I cannot clasp the joy of laying you within it." He coughed fretfully—batted another metal-fisted hand at Paul, who had instinctively surged forward—and he said, "Look at you, you cock-o'-the-walk, you filigree piglet, you scum. A whited sepulchre . . . Ninth blood on your foreign sword . . ."

Nona was distracted from her lazy enjoyment of the word *piglet* by a flicker in the dark archway, the one from which they'd just emerged. She felt again that strange sense of the familiar made awful—like coming back to your own bed and finding it covered in stains and slimes that hadn't been there when you left it. She clutched feebly at Pyrrha's forearm. "There's more," she said. "More outside."

Pyrrha's muscles tensed. Paul and Kiriona both looked back at the archway. Something moved, deep in the shadows.

"Thanks, kiddie," said Pyrrha. "Nav—let's get that cage open and head down. Sorry, Gramps, we're on a clock."

Paul crossed to the metal cage and started fiddling with a sort of heavy latch mechanism on the front. Kiriona hovered, sword still in her hand, staring at the archway.

"Nav, come *on*," said Pyrrha sharply. "Any kid in the Cohort knows the mission comes first. Or did you get that uniform out of the dress-up box?"

Kiriona rounded on Pyrrha, her gold eyes cold and haughty, but instead of saying anything she shoved her sword back into its scabbard and moved to the cage as well. Paul had freed the latch and was hauling back the barred gate with an echoing clatter. Inside was a bare and empty metal box, a bit smaller than their old bathroom back in the apartment.

Once the gate was partly open, Paul and Kiriona set about dragging the dying old man into the box. This was a messy and difficult process: not only did he leave a great smeared slick of blood behind him, but he kept coughing, flailing his arms, and calling them both *dunghill pups in need of a sound whipping* and other things that were clearly not meant to be kind. Nona felt bad: not only could she not help, but she was keeping Pyrrha from helping. She risked a glance back at the archway. There was a figure there—dark robes topped by a pale face, not moving forward, but swaying slightly on the spot. It looked as if it were watching them. Its eyes writhed.

Paul positioned the old man against the back wall of the metal box, then snatched the lamp. Kiriona retrieved a sword that had been left lying in the blood nearby, brought it in, and dropped it unceremoniously in the man's lap. Then Pyrrha carried Nona into the box, and Kiriona heaved the gate shut with a clash. Two more figures had appeared in the archway, flanking the first.

"Hope we've still got power," Paul said.

"The breaker," said Kiriona. "Big switch there on the wall. Ought to work, unless they've killed it from below."

Paul yanked the handle she had pointed at. A small glass bump above the handle lit up with a sickly red glow. There was a heavy mechanical *clonk,* the floor jolted, and the stone floor started to rise up the side of the bars; blood trickled over its edge and dripped down, a few drops spattering on the metal tiles. The floor went higher and higher until it closed off the window of bright light from above, and they were all in darkness except for the faint redness from the indicator bulb. The old man's breathing rasped and laboured, and machinery rumbled somewhere over their heads. There was a low, whirring moan, and a rush of freezing cold air. At first Nona thought she would never see again; then she found her eyes adjusting after all.

"Please, sir," Paul was saying patiently. He had crouched back down next to the old man, in the blood. "If you stop trying to hit me, I can at least do something for the pain."

"The marshal loves pain," said Kiriona. She was staring fixedly at the red bulb.

The old man gurgled, *"Seneschal, you fool."*

"Oh, congrats, I forgot Nonagesimus left you in charge," said Kiriona. "Where's Aiglamene?"

"Dead," the seneschal said.

Kiriona became very still. The seneschal wheezed with relish at her expression. Even in the darkness Nona could still tell, and surprised herself by saying to Kiriona, "He's lying."

"Dead—as far as I care," he amended. "She went on ahead. To the monument."

"Nav, talk to me," said Pyrrha. "Antioch. You've been fighting these—things? How long?"

"Fuck knows," said Kiriona, highly distracted. "Three, four months? Took us a while to work out what they even were. Thought they only had a weird disease."

"And how long have they been on the Ninth?" This was addressed to the seneschal.

"A night. A day," said the rasping old man. "You hold the Reverend Daughter, so I must answer. We shut them away . . . locked some of them inside their cells. They riot. Their touch consumes . . . they hunger for the youngest of us."

"Boy, are they out of luck," said the corpse prince, sotto voce.

"Their bodies twist—they do not know how to use their bodies," Crux rasped, as though Kiriona had not spoken. "Some of them are dead walking. Those are the weaker kind . . . Sisters Lachrimorta and Aisamorta plied the art, to some effect. The constructs . . . the constructs were safe . . . fleshed corpses they took, but the bones they wanted none of . . ."

Paul said, "How many are like this?"

"Too many."

"Can I get 'too many' in numbers?"

"Over two hundred. Full forty lie dead at the bottom of the tiers where they were pushed, in the first hour . . . it was all we could do to secure the tier. More have died . . . the marshal reckoned we lost a full hundred already. And," added the old man sourly, "now those seven above are added to the bier, by my own blade and the stripling's . . ."

"Those were dead already," Kiriona interrupted. "The dead ones move differently. You realise the ones you shoved off the tier probably just got back up again?"

"Can the living ones be cured?" asked Paul.

"You can't *cure* this," said the Prince. "It's spirit shit . . . possession. You can ward people so they don't get grabbed—if you're really good—but otherwise, chop them up and burn the bits. That's the cure. Civilian or Edenite or House, it makes no difference."

There was another great jolt that shook the metal box. The seneschal grunted. Nona realised they were no longer moving downward.

The cage doors opened to a floor of more cages, like the world's strangest zoo: machines of a kind Nona had never seen—nothing like the nice normal machines back home—enormous edifices gated behind iron bars, as though someone were afraid they would get out. They all droned away. Their bars had been strung with long streamers of black cloth that seemed so old and tattered and frail that they might dissolve if you breathed on them. Pyrrha murmured, "God, this place has gone downhill," but thankfully only Nona heard it.

The dying old man rasped: "We barricaded behind the Anastasian. Sister Canace and Deacon Davith were left here. Why have they abrogated their duty?"

"Holy shit, Sister Canace is still alive?" said Kiriona, startled. "She used to oversee me on oss duty. If you're using Sister Canace as a last line of defence, how bad off *are* w—you?"

"Sister Canace, you cancerous gosling—you bloodied slime—has what you have always lacked," burbled Crux wetly. "Faith, and loyalty."

"Probably, but I have what Sister Canace always lacked, which is knees that work," said Kiriona.

The old man ignored this. "Nobody down here was touched. Nobody down here was taken. Canace and Davith should remain. This is our place of safety—it has never been breached," he added, with a look that said he thought the assembled and unlovely throng in front of him were in danger of counting as a *breach.*

Pyrrha said, "Well, the chambers down through the main artery ought to hold up—there's that long tunnel with the blast doors on either side."

This seemed to fox Crux.

"Who are you, foreigner, that you know the mysteries of the Anastasian?"

"I was here before it was the Anastasian," said Pyrrha absently. "Painted a nursery. Mint green. Look, if your watchers aren't here they've pulled back behind whatever bailey you've set up. Let's keep moving. How are we going to move . . . ?"

But Paul had already gone to the old man, lying bloodied on the bottom of the platform. The huge, horrible ancient dwarfed Camilla Hect's lithe, solid form easily, but—much to Nona's surprise—Paul heaved him up to standing as though he were Nona, or even smaller, like he was Kevin.

Crux howled out, "This shames the Ninth."

"Not possible," said the corpse prince.

But Paul said—

"We can move this way, but I can't fight at the same time."

"Nav, take point. I'll take the rear," said Pyrrha, to which the corpse prince said, "Nice," and Nona laughed out loud. She felt a little drunk and strange.

At that laugh, the old man stared at her in frank dismay and reproof—then his face closed up somehow, left off its look of horror and awe, and he looked at her with a totally different expression. He really did look like a skeleton mask, with his age-spotted pate and his deeply shadowed, bitter eye. Nona looked away, and found that the corpse prince had looked at her briefly too, again with an expression even Nona couldn't translate. Pyrrha held her close and said: "Can't be doing that badly, if you're going to laugh at an ass joke."

Nona did not want to tell her that something terrible was going on in her body and had been ever since the period where her heart and her arm had hurt. She snuggled down into the halo of Pyrrha's arms for warmth—she was starting to feel blue all over—and the zip fastener of Pyrrha's jacket caught her arm and scratched her. She stared mildly at the rough red graze and the little square flaps of skin that had risen off her arm. The corpse prince held the lantern before her as they moved down that long, toe-curlingly cold tunnel—the strong white light glimmered off rough unfinished stone and the softer gleam of very old metal and paint—and Nona got the fright of her life, seeing shapes on the walls, until she realised that it was more bones that had been glued into the rock face. It was awful.

A yell echoed down the tunnel, and they all startled—but they reached the end of the tunnel, where what seemed to be huge white bars had been pressed into service over the doorway. As the light from the end of the tunnel and their light dazzled each other, Nona realised that what she had taken for painted white metal was fresh, slightly pink bone, redder at either end where it had planted itself into the doorframe. There were more huddled, black-wrapped old people peering between the bones, their anxious faces blurred with painted masks: white bone, black background.

"Halt," quavered someone, but the corpse prince said, "It's me. Where's Aiglamene?"

The most asymmetrical person that Nona had ever seen in her short life stumped to life behind the bars. At her barked command, the bars parted—sort of twanged away and opened up in the exact way that bars shouldn't, exposing the cortex of the bone. Now Nona could see her clearly. Most of her face had rippled in the way that Hot Sauce's would someday ripple when she was eighty to two hundred years older, like a candle that had burned for hours before someone blew it out. A proud, keen-eyed face peered out behind that melt. One of her legs wasn't her own (it went on funny at the hip, Nona noticed), but she held herself as tall and as proud as Crown. In her hands was a huge black-metal pike about the same height as her, with an edge that gleamed in the light. Nona couldn't stop herself looking at that edge: for some reason it made her palms sweat, and the back of her neck itch again.

The woman barked, "The seneschal needs help. Get Asya and Brother Clement, now . . . !"

"You're a fool and a twit and your brains have turned, Aiglamene," rasped the old man. "*I* would have kept the doors barred against me, in case I had been compromised."

"Good point. Get someone with a spear—treat him at arm's

length. Spear him through if anything happens. Spear him through if anything doesn't," the woman added, beneath her breath.

"Yes, Marshal," said one of the robed onlookers— "Yes, Captain Aiglamene," said another, robed over rusting armour. Crux lashed out at them as he had lashed out at Paul, though at least he had left off lashing out at Paul.

He snarled, "Canace—Davith—they have abandoned their post . . . they have been taken, or fled . . . they have gone back up another route, perhaps the blocked-up ways, or the peep, or . . ."

"Cease worrying. Sister Canace and Deacon Davith are not the types to abandon their post," said the old soldier. "I'll send people to check. We're safe down here—so leave your maunderings, or the youth will start to think your dotage is on you already. You see secrets and conspiracies in every corner now."

"Brat—toy soldier—harridan," ground out Crux; and then he was hustled through the arch, with Paul supporting. The old soldier they called Aiglamene watched him go, with her face caught up in some worry.

"He's too old to walk that one off," she muttered to herself. But then she shook herself back to the situation at hand, and looked critically at Pyrrha—her gaze swept over Nona—her gaze fixed briefly on the corpse prince; then back to Nona.

"I've never seen this many nuns before," said the corpse prince, who didn't sound excited about it.

Aiglamene said, "Sister Berta—hold," and passed the pike on to a rather gloomy-looking girl who looked not much older than Honesty. Berta could barely hold the thing, and someone else came up to help her struggle with it. Then the old woman said, "The Ninth House welcomes back its Sainted Reverend Daughter."

To Nona's horror whole and entire, Aiglamene dropped to her one native knee. Behind her, in ones, then twos, then threes—every robed old person, or medium person, or even quite young person glancing sidelong at their fellows, dropped to the floor. Only hapless Sister Berta remained upright, and her fellow helping her with the pike. The call moved back through the broad, dark room behind them—"Reverend Daughter," "the Reverend Daughter," "the Sainted Daughter." Nona's horror only grew when she realised that it was not Kiriona Gaia they were referring to, but *her*.

Aiglamene rose from one knee—it took a long time, but she quelled with a look anyone who offered to help—and then stumped forward into the ring of light flung by the corpse prince's lantern. She reached out—she touched the side of the Prince's face—they both recoiled.

Kiriona Gaia recovered first.

"You always said I'd come back in a box, Aiglamene," she said lightly.

"They killed you," said Aiglamene.

"Crime of opportunity," said the corpse prince. And: "Don't tell Crux—I absolutely, positively cannot give him the fucking satisfaction."

Aiglamene shoved her square in the chest, with the palm of one gloved hand; Kiriona tottered a little and wheezed, "Don't—that's where my heart used to be," but the old soldier's gaze had already fallen upon Nona.

Nona cringed back in Pyrrha's arms, because the expression was as bad as every single time Camilla had caught her putting a mouthful of chewed-up food in the potted plant or elsewhere. She could read this very old, very furious soldier like a book: the woman was angry, and blamed her. Kiriona Gaia could read her too, because she insinuated herself between them, and said coolly—

"It's not her, Captain—it's only her body."

Over the Prince's shoulder, Aiglamene looked at Nona, long and suspiciously; then she sighed, and wheeled around, and said: "Get inside. Now. Complete the gate," she told a few of the other robed people.

With her back still to the group, she said— "Nav, rest assured I would give you the beating of your life *and* death if we were not under terrible siege. I don't know why you're here—I don't know why you came back—but if we have the time later, and the Ninth House survives, I will ask pertinent questions. For now, only give me information if I need it."

"We need to get through to the rock," said Pyrrha.

Aiglamene turned to look at Pyrrha, but Pyrrha—as per usual—was completely unmoved by any hostile, gimlet-eyed expression. Aiglamene said slowly: "You ask me, in the middle of the worst emergency my House has ever faced, to let strangers through to our holiest of holies?"

"Yes. We have a Lyctor's rights," said Pyrrha.

The old soldier sharpened, face alight with something that Nona could tell wasn't hope, but was in the same room—at least the same building. She looked over Pyrrha again, Pyrrha in her ordinary jacket and her ordinary clothes with her very ordinary guns and her extraordinary scruff on her jaw, and she said dubiously, "Your Grace . . ."

"I said a Lyctor's *rights*. Not a Lyctor's prowess, sir—Captain?"

"Marshal," Aiglamene corrected, but— "I ranked Captain, before discharge."

"Territorials?"

"Strike force, for my sins."

"You look too sensible for a Brandishment Baby," said Pyrrha, her most winning smile in her voice, and the old soldier made a noise that was second cousin to a laugh.

"An' there's a term I haven't heard since I was a child." Then Aiglamene bristled, as though she had dropped her guard too far, and said: "Can you save us, or not?"

"If you let us through to the rock, maybe."

"But where's the Reverend Daughter, who we have taken as Saint and Lyctor? Why the *Tomb*?"

There was no smile in Pyrrha's voice now; in fact, she sounded a lot like We Suffer, with her best radio voice on. "Captain, perhaps you'll understand me if I tell you this is a matter of the Emperor's Intelligence."

But this just made Aiglamene laugh again, and not with a bit of humour in it.

"Hah! Don't come over all intelligence agent with *me*, you young fool. The Bureau's not welcome in the House of the Ninth. Last one we had—thirty years back—we dropped off eleven hours from the prison with ten hours' worth of air and told 'em to hurry up."

Aiglamene looked at Nona. Nona felt unhappy again, hot in her cheeks and under her shirt. The old soldier looked at her critically, like a stranger, and added: "Take her in. Get her to a heater—slowly—and warm her through. She's taking a chill."

"Nona doesn't chill," said Pyrrha. But she shifted Nona around in her arms, and in a slightly different voice said, "Fuck me. Nona, you *are* cold."

Before Nona could protest that in fact she felt quite warm now—too warm for her jacket—Pyrrha moved into the depths of the room. It was a long oblong, and resembled nothing so much as a graveyard for rusting swords and things; rocky niches carved into the walls were filled with old, tarnished rubbish, and long fearsome slabs of rock, only there were robed people of all kinds perching on top of them, which gave them a kind of picnic aspect. Dim overhead lights hung in cages just like the machines of before, and bright lamps—no candlelight, though Nona could see branches of old, dribbly candles with black tapers and horrible brownish tallow—made weird shadows of everyone. Pyrrha shouldered her through surprised skeleton faces and surprised skeleton people. Nona was deeply horrified to see *actual walk-around skeletons* mixed in with the crowd, when she had mistaken them in the dark for people who were very thin. When they turned around they were skulls with pinprick red lights dancing in the hollows of their eye sockets—she was fascinated, horribly so, but had no time to be. Pyrrha broke the soft, worried hush by saying: "Palamedes—Paul," and then Nona was laid down next to a glowing red bar heater that smelled like oil and burning hair, displacing a couple of creaking old people who couldn't get out of the way fast enough because they kept bowing to her. One kissed her shoe. Even Kevin knew better than that. She said reproachfully, "That's unhygienic—there's germs," but they were gone already.

The terrible old man was there too; he was being tended to by Paul and continuing to heap great curses upon their head, which

Paul was taking with calm imperturbability. Another, shorter person stood alongside, holding a knife as though they wished very much that they weren't.

Nona was laid down on the hard, cold rock—Pyrrha had taken her hands and was warming them between her own. Nona's were a strange, livid colour. Nona could see confusion in the shape of Pyrrha's eyebrows and mouth, and when she ran her hands up Nona's forearms, the confusion changed.

"When did you get this?" she demanded.

She was pointing at the very slight mark on Nona's forearm, still a little pink from where the skin had lifted. "I got it off your zip," she said, and then she realised—

"My first wound."

"Paul," said Pyrrha, desperately, but Paul had already transferred his attentions from the old man to Nona. Paul was touching the back of her neck—checking her eyes, behind her ears, sticking a finger briefly in her mouth—moving down to slide a hand underneath her armpits. Nona looked away, and found the hideous old man looking directly at her, with that same expression in his bleary, pain-trammelled eyes of—recognition. He wanted something, from her specifically.

"Lady," he said, in a much softer creak, "you've gone away again, my lady; where have you run? Remember your catechism and your lesson, and remember them well now: this is where you come back to—you have your little escape. You'll feel better for coming back . . . you remember that, Harrowhark."

Nona whispered, "I'm sorry—I'm not Harrowhark."

"Ay, and you've said that before," said the old man. "Who are you this time, if not my Lady Harrowhark?"

Nona shut her eyes. The darkness closed in around her, unrelieved by the bar heater, and the lamps set all around, and the caged lights swinging overhead, and the press of people crammed into that long, dusty, abandoned room. She was outside the room—she was outside the great tunnel—she was looking down at the terrible dead grey-and-white surface, the great hollow pores set into rock. Then she went back down, pulled down into each cavern—the long central shaft—deeper and deeper.

Her middle thoughts crawled into her top and bottom thoughts. For a moment she thought she'd die of it.

"There's a box," she said, "and . . . there's someone in the box who isn't me. *I'm* me. I don't know who's in that box, not really, only— when you open it—I'll be gone, because I can't survive . . . knowing. And I think—inside that box—there's something that looks like a girl . . ."

The face of the old man blurred. Paul was saying—

"Her healing mechanism's stopped. The body doesn't have enough of anything to keep going. Her brain's seizing. A couple of organs have collapsed. Massive trauma. Interesting."

"Paul," said Pyrrha, "your bedside manner is bullshit."

"It's interesting. It's not *great*. Nona, how do you feel?"

"Good," said Nona. "Fine." Honesty compelled her to say, "Worried and a little sad, but—good. *I'm* fine. The body's . . . not."

"Okay. Ecstatic seizure. Anyway—she's static, not regressing. She's not healing, but she's not going downhill. We have to get her soul back in . . ."

"Now," finished Pyrrha.

"Five minutes ago, for preference," said Paul.

Nona reached out. She found Camilla's wrist—a wrist she had loved so keenly, attached to hands that had bathed her and flipped the pages of magazines to read to her and spooned out food she didn't want to eat. She looked up into the face of the woman who was gone, which had been shared by a man who was also gone, a face taken by someone new. She said—

"The more I go back—the more I'm made to go back . . . it'll hurt her. She wasn't made for it, she's not . . . not the right shape."

"Don't talk. Don't stress yourself," said Paul, but Nona didn't want to be interrupted.

"I might not help you when . . . I'm back," she said, not quite un-derstanding *I*. "I'll be different. I'll remember everything . . . I'll re-member the thing I'm trying to forget. And Palamedes—I won't *love* him. I won't love Camilla, or Pyrrha, or Hot Sauce, or even Noodle. I won't love anything . . . I won't know how. I won't be *me* at all, or . . . I'll be the me who knows the thing, and *knowing* the thing means I'm not Nona—I'm someone else."

Paul, practical, clasped one of her hands between them, and used the other to rub a rough section of black frieze over her sides to try to warm her up.

"Okay. Don't worry," they said.

Nona felt hot and cross.

"I've just told you why I'm worried, in detail, and I think that matters quite a lot."

"Camilla and Palamedes were loved by Nona," said Paul. "Pyrrha was loved by Nona. It's finished, it's done. You can't take *loved* away. We loved you too. Palamedes and Camilla loved you."

Pyrrha was there too, floating into view above Nona's head, in the darkness. Her mouth was set in that unmistakable *need-a-cigarette* shape.

"Don't worry, kiddie," she said tiredly. "I'll keep loving you—my problem is I don't know how to stop. And, you know . . . who you are . . . were . . . you're capable of more than you think, right now. I liked you. He liked you—Gideon liked you. My necromancer and I always liked you . . . and hey, what's *like* except a love that hasn't been invited indoors?"

She reached down and ruffled Nona's short hair. Nona felt her borrowed heart go *thump-pa-thump-pa-thump.*

"But you didn't get me a six-month birthday present," she whispered pathetically. "I didn't get the beach party, or a cake, or any dogs."

"Honey, of course I got you a birthday present," said Pyrrha instantly. "I bought one the morning of the broadcast. I went and got you a new T-shirt—the expensive kind, not the ones that dissolve when you wash them. I hid it in the sink cabinet."

Nona sucked in a breath. "Tell me about it," she whispered. "Describe it exactly."

"Uh," said Pyrrha, and flicked her eyes up at Paul. "Okay, so, I hadn't cleared this with the powers that be, but it was a picture of a moustache—like the facial hair, but a cartoon?—and then there were words below. Look, you had to see it, I'm not sure I can describe it in a way that . . ."

"Pyrrha, I want to know what it said."

Now Pyrrha avoided Paul's gaze.

"It advertised cheap moustache rides," said Pyrrha. "We're talking low prices."

Nona started to cry softly, overwhelmed.

Paul said, "Palamedes wouldn't have let her wear that outside the house." Then: "Camilla wouldn't have let her wear it inside, either."

"Yeah, but what about *you*?" said Pyrrha.

"Her choice," said Paul. "I think moustache rides should be free."

"It would have been my favourite present except for the handkerchief," said Nona breathlessly. "I'm going to go back and fetch it. I'll remember. I'll make myself remember. And I'll wear it all the time, inside the house and outside the house, and then you'll know it's really me. I'm not going to be gone forever . . . I'm ready. I'm ready. Let's go."

32

AIGLAMENE MET THEM at a little nondescript door out of the oblong. Paul had supported the awful old man—he had demanded his rights as seneschal—and they had met the corpse prince, who was pacing at the doorway. Pyrrha had wrapped Nona in one of the big black cloaks, which were much warmer than they looked but smelled as old as the room—sort of dusty and fusty and mildewy—but she was finding she had to smell quite consciously now, to make her brain understand what she was trying to do. It was like having your feet slip off the pedals of a bicycle. Aiglamene, lantern held high, led them down a long, winding passage. She took endless back-and-forth turns, until, at one last door, she stopped. She turned off the lantern and plunged them into a big black icy darkness.

Pyrrha said, "We going in blind?"

"There is no light of electric or fat in this place," croaked out the old man. "There is no light but that which was given to us. Not before the rock and the Tomb. This is the place you should not be travelling . . . none of us but the Daughter, and her cavalier."

Nona could make out nothing in the darkness, but the corpse prince's voice was unmistakable.

"The Reverend Daughter has no cavalier living."

There was a metal sound. The door opened, and Nona was carried over the threshold into a big empty void. The air changed, cold as ice, black and blue as paint. Everyone's feet suddenly made a big *squelch*.

A light flicked on—a tall bright lantern with a huge glowing bulb within. They were standing in a huge room, a cathedral cave, with

463

a great roundish cold stone rock placed at what was obviously the mouth of a tunnel leading away—a rock the size and height of a big car and probably the weight of multiple cars. And standing before the rock—a lantern by one booted foot—was Crown.

Nona's eyes had been tricked by the light. It wasn't Crown. It was someone exactly Crown's height, someone with Crown's face, but like someone had washed her in hot water and soaked the colour out—a Crown who gangled, without any of Crown's lovely curvy softnesses or bignesses, a wretched white Crown. A Crown with an arm that was all bones—metal-shod bones, real moving bones, with bony gold fingers holding a tiny pinpoint of orange light. Nona realised that it really was her arm; that it really was a cigarette. Pyrrha startled forward—but there was another *squelch;* they had all stepped into a soft, jammy yellow field of what looked like canolene but more transparent. And Pyrrha was stuck fast. Paul stuck fast, and Crux with them, and Aiglamene stuck fast, and the corpse prince—

"How'd you get here before me?" she demanded.

"Didn't—got here after," said the thing, and it had Crown's voice too: the same silvery, musical sweetness of Crown's, but not nice at all. "*I* simply looked for any signs of God and slithered downward—easy pappy. This place is like a neon sign saying *John Gaius Was Here.* And now, I am afraid . . . I am here to scotch all your plans. Don't move, please—Sextus—Hect—Hectus," they suggested silkily. Paul had moved to support the horrifying old man; the yellow stuff was creeping up above both of their ankles, holding them fast. "I don't know what you are yet, but you know what *I* am, so . . . stay put, Sext."

"It's Paul," said Paul.

"I respect that, but can't admire it," said the new person, taking a long drag.

Paul said, "This is interesting stuff underfoot, Tridentarius. What is it?"

"Adipose fat and mucous membrane," said the not-Crown modestly. "It's my own recipe."

"Oh my God, Ianthe, barf," said the corpse prince.

The only person not stuck in this mix was Nona, who was being carried; but the field spread out far enough in front of them that Nona, who did not think she could walk anyway, would probably get one step before sticking and falling over. Pyrrha shifted Nona to her other hip—the eyes of that pale mirror face fell on them—and Pyrrha said, "So, what, John sent you?"

The person—Ianthe—the real Ianthe Naberius, after all, not the lovely-chinned corpse with the perfect hair—crossed over to them, lit from behind by the electric light. Up close she had skin like Honesty's, if Honesty had been put in a cave for maybe a million years, or perhaps like Noodle's skin when you parted the crimpled, curdly fur at the back of his neck.

"Who are you, really?" she asked, sounding genuinely curious. "You had me fooled that you were the Saint of Duty with bits missing—I wasn't paying attention."

"Number Seven got him. I'm his leftover cavalier parts. Pyrrha Dve."

"Does that happen—normally?"

"No."

"Phew," said Ianthe, and then, finally, "No. No, John Gaius didn't send me."

She came to stand in front of Kiriona Gaia, and they stared at each other, evenly and coldly, one hand on the handles of the rapiers each carried on their hip: for Ianthe Naberius carried a rapier too, worn on a jewelled belt atop her beautiful leather breeches, with a parchment-coloured shirt all swirled over by the softest-looking white material Nona had ever seen. It was like a rainbow had been put in the fridge, then woven into fabric. It settled over Ianthe Naberius's shoulders like a mist. It was so beautiful. She stood there, before the corpse prince, looking barely more alive than Kiriona was.

Pyrrha said lowly, "Don't do anything stupid, kid."

"Are *you* ever too late to come into my life and say that," said Kiriona.

Ianthe, ignoring this interchange, said merely—

"Prince Kiriona Gaia."

"Prince Ianthe Naberius," said her opposite. And: "Can you not fucking smoke in here?"

"It's a filthy habit," admitted the other prince. "I didn't think you cared though."

"I don't, but there's like a million fire detectors."

In a show of obsequious obedience, rolling her eyes, Ianthe took her gold fingerbones and stubbed out the cigarette on her real, thin flesh hand, then tossed the discarded butt over her shoulder, where it smouldered on the stones. Crux started to make a noise like a teakettle filled with soup. Ianthe ignored him; a terrible hunger had sharpened her like a knife.

"Did you bring my sister?"

"Upstairs," said the corpse prince, and thumbed vaguely somewhere over her shoulder. "You can pick her up whenever. She came on her own—I didn't have to use my attraction or my charm."

"You don't have either. God, it's like she *wants* me to catch her," marvelled Ianthe. "That ill-shampooed slut."

"Sixth House bigwigs are up there too, don't know if we want 'em," said the corpse prince laconically. "The rest of the House is parked outside the Ur system, should be easy enough to sweep them up. Not that we've got the people . . . Anyway, I don't think Dad even wants them, they'd only depress him."

It had slowly dawned on Nona—by the look of everyone else caught in the yellow muck, it was dawning on them too—that this conversation was not being carried out in a way anyone had expected. Ianthe reached out—her sleeve fell away from her wrist—and Nona saw a strange fat bracelet ringing her bony wrist: a braided, hyper-coloured cord in shades that were somehow even uglier than the cords she had seen before—in her class—and on the wrist of—

"Friendship bracelets," she fairly shouted. "They're wearing *friendship bracelets.*"

Ianthe grasped Kiriona's wrist, and Kiriona pulled free of the sticky yellow muck as easily and as neatly as if it were dust. They stood there, hands clasping each other's wrists, in their beautiful polished boots and their jewelled white swords—a matched pair of princes, one dead and one barely looking better. They tapped each other on the knuckles, did something complicated with their thumbs, and stood angled toward each other, easy and familiar, as though they had stood beside each other a million times.

Paul said quietly—

"Harrowhark's body is nearly dead. Are you going to get us inside the Tomb, or not?"

Long straps of that sticky, taffy-textured fat snapped out and wrapped around Nona's ankles. She was jerked out of Pyrrha's arms, rolled up in a thick wad of it, and rolled over and over, nauseated and panicked, until she came to a stop right beside that polished boot. It shone so highly that Nona could see her face in it, and the distorted reflection looked terrible: a blue-lipped, haggard version of herself she had never known—the face of the other girl, maybe, not hers: a face distorted with fear. The fat dissolved, leaving nothing but a weird moist feeling on the insides of her wrists. Ianthe was saying— "I'm simply doing exactly what I think Harry would want me to do . . . Harry *adores* this ghastly old rock and its ghastly old inhabitant. Harry would be the first to say, 'No. I'm not worth it. Leave it shut.' Don't you think, Ninth?"

"I try not to," said Kiriona modestly.

Both Ianthe and Kiriona briefly fell about laughing. They slapped each other's shoulders in what seemed to be genuine mirth. Nona rolled an eye desperately toward Pyrrha, and Paul, and the two ancients: Pyrrha and Paul were still as statues.

"Good to see you," said Ianthe, quite kindly, to Kiriona.

"Yeah—same," said Kiriona, with infectious good cheer. "Anyway—let's open the Tomb and get out of here."

For a moment Ianthe kept laughing, and then she said— "Wait. What?"

"That Tomb's opening, now," said Kiriona.

"You can't possibly be— Ninth!"

For Kiriona had taken a few steps backward, away from Nona, in no danger of tripping over her, bathed in the yellow glow of the electric light reflecting off the fat. She drew her sword with an oily rattle, and Ianthe drew hers. Nona stared, transfixed, at the edges of their swords.

Ianthe said, "You little three-way double-crosser."

"Haven't double-crossed anybody, let alone three times," said Kiriona.

"You've double-crossed God, for one—"

Kiriona said, "What? John *sent* me, you overgilded doorknob."

Pyrrha said, "Like hell he did."

"My sentiments exactly expressed," said Ianthe.

"No. He did," said the corpse prince. "I didn't sneak onto that ship for my health. Don't you see? This is my chance. We go in there, we open up the Tomb, I take down whatever's inside—Alecto, Annabel, I don't care, whatever her name is—*boom*, we're done. Dad won't be immortal anymore, but he says he doesn't care about that, and I believe him, Tridentarius . . . I'll be his cavalier. I'm the First. Hell, I'm his child and heir. Isn't this the neatest way? Are you going to help me, or not?"

Ianthe had withdrawn. Even from below, Nona could see the horror and disgust writ large on her face: it had a lot to do with the chin.

"Oh my God," she said softly. "You can't believe that. You're very stupid when you want to be, Gonad . . . but you can't believe that."

"*You* know he's never recovered."

"Yes," said Ianthe. "Oh, I know."

"If we weren't around, I don't know what he'd do."

"I do," said Ianthe. "Exactly the same thing he's doing right now, without trying to hide it. Drowning his sorrows in whatever or whoever comes to hand . . . Do you know who I saw creeping out of his bedroom the other day? Grand Admiral Sarpedon, I shit you not."

"Oh, God, *yuck*," said Kiriona, looking highly diverted. "That's sick—"

"—following a grand cavalcade of Cohort officials, ensigns, et cetera—"

"Yeah, but Sarpedon is old!"

NONA <del>THE NINTH</del> / 469

"*That's* your problem? Kiriona, you fat-headed wreck, John's older than our recorded time," said Ianthe.

"Yeah, but he doesn't look it, does he," retorted Kiriona. "Sarpedon's, like, in his fifties? Sixties? It's nasty! They should know how it looks! It looks suss! Anyway, that's my *dad*!"

"You haven't had to live through an atom of the worst of it," said Ianthe. "You are an exasperating child and a moron—stop making me argue with you! The *important* part of this, you gibbering bozo, is that the moment that door opens, you're not killing the monster inside—"

"Give me five minutes—"

"—you're not becoming his *cavalier*—you're not fixing anything! You're signing our doom," snapped Ianthe. "He gets her back, you don't know what he'll become! You have no idea, and you've deluded yourself into believing him, and he's just tricking you! You know that, don't you? Are you trying to kid yourself? Is this about Harry, after all?"

There was a deep indrawn breath; Ianthe laughed and said—

"You don't have to breathe, you know."

"You're so goddamned boring when you talk about Harrowhark, so don't," said Kiriona. "Listen to *you,* big lady of the First. 'Leave Harrow to die, don't open the Tomb, mneh mneh mneh.' What'd you come here for? Stop playing the good son. You don't give a shit about anything except your own plans, you know. Your sister's upstairs. Take her and go—let me fight this thing and win, or die trying, who cares?"

"You let that monster out of its box," said Ianthe, "and you start us down a path nobody can save us from. If God truly wants her out . . . if Teacher set this all up . . . if he wants her . . ."

"Wants her? He told me to kill her. He said, *Make it quick, but kill her,* said me with my blood could do it—said me with my blood, I was the only one . . ."

Ianthe rounded on the corpse prince, and she gave her a ringing slap straight through the face. Kiriona did not stagger.

"He *loves* her!" Ianthe howled. "John *loves* Alecto—John *needs* Alecto! Without that piece of goddamned fridge meat, he's *nothing*— and we need to *keep him that way!*"

The secret was told: the secret was out—the middle brain disappeared. Nona unravelled.

The first thing that happened was that a big slit opened up above her baby heart—she gushed up blood against the front of her black shirt; then more slits through her middle—then in and out of her mortal insides, her unshapely organs. All the stuff inside her guts was hammered through. She was slit a thousand times—a million. Her skin erupted in blood through all the pores of her face. It poured out behind the backs of her knees, her ears, her armpits. Anything glandular. She choked up blood; both Tower Princes had whirled around—dropped down to their knees beside her—one said, "Her neck—get her neck," but as fast as she could be stitched together, she came apart. The baby body was coming apart. A slim brown hand was at her cheek: "Keep it together. Wherever you are, idiot, I know you can hear me. Keep it together . . ."

Above their voices, and the blood, and the dim sweetness of the pain, she heard Paul say—

"Pyrrha, go."

A gunshot. The pale yellow figure crumpled over next to Nona's bust-up body, covered in Nona's fluids—she jerked and went into a spasmodic fit, shuddering and juddering, as though she could somehow vibrate out of her skin. Paul dropped to Nona's side with a clinical glance at Crown's frothing, screaming sister, and said nothing more than, "Effective."

"I was saving that bullet for John," said Pyrrha. "Herald bullets don't grow on trees. Wake made that for me . . . Or I stole it from her . . . same difference. Paul— Can we— Is there still . . ."

Paul sounded detached, strange above her. It was as though she were underwater. She yearned to be underwater. "Open the door," they said. "Now."

Nona felt herself lifted—Kiriona's arms beneath her shoulders, Pyrrha's beneath her hips. Why were they carrying her that way?

Why was Pyrrha saying, "Keep her arm—Paul, her arm's coming off." The rock loomed so big above, so awful in the electric light. There were so many people standing above her, her body, the baby's body. The baby with the big black eyes. The scrap of meat with the purple mouth.

Pyrrha was saying, "This isn't the real entrance, right? It can't be," and someone—the old soldier—was saying, "No. The true rock, so it is said, is down a corridor. But I can't lift this—I'm no adept . . ."

An enormous sound. The rock, rolling away. A great, grinding noise. Paul saying, "Not a problem," but the old man, hoarsely— "The traps . . . the thieves' traps, the snares . . ."

Again, Paul: "Let me."

She had been down this corridor: she had squeezed through this crack in the rock—not a passageway, not at that point. John had told her he had something to show her. He had said, It's very pretty. You'll like it.

Paul's voice again—Camilla's voice, Palamedes's voice— "Most of them are disabled. Neat work, whoever did it."

Maybe the body blacked out. The next thing she heard was Kiriona, urgently saying, "Take it. Take it from anywhere. Take all of it."

"My lady," the old man was saying feebly. "My lady . . . my girl-child . . ."

"I don't need all of it—but I need to keep it wet . . ."

Pyrrha was saying, "You can't spoof this. Cass and Mercy and I worked on cell thanergy—we need thanergy, *fresh* thanergy, to activate . . ."

John loved her. She was John's cavalier. She loved John. For she so loved the world that she had given them John. For the world so loved John that she had been given. For John had so loved her that he had made her she. For John had loved the world.

"Kill me," said Kiriona.

"No. You're dead," said Paul. "You won't produce a reaction."

"Me," said Pyrrha. "Take me and Gideon. If Wake had just asked me, I might've done it in the first place—died here, with her, for this . . ."

"Take *me*, you fools," said Crux.

She hadn't come on purpose; the scrap of black-eyed meat had asked for it—the chain of a kiss: the ice that burnt the flesh of the mouth that had stuck to the mouth that was frozen. The teardrop on the hand. The hand that John had fashioned.

Someone said something. The old man, Crux—the child Crux, barely one hundred years old—was saying hoarsely: "Fix me, and I am taken by the unknown. Kill me, for the love of the Reverend Daughter. Oh, do you think you are the only one who knows how to die, Nav? I knew you were dead to see you . . . I will commit this apocalyptic sin. I will die for her. She is my nurseling. I am the only one who knows how to die for the Reverend Daughter Harrowhark Nonagesimus."

"Good," said someone, so savagely that it sounded like a new voice altogether. "Good. Die. Die for her . . . it's the only goddamn good you'll ever do her. It's all any of you ever knew how to give her. You could have *lived* for her . . . but you didn't know how."

"You never knew wot of what you talked of, but ran your tongue anyway," said Crux. "All our sacrifices . . . our scrimping . . . the blood of the tomb-keeper . . ."

Paul was saying, "Are you certain?"

Aiglamene said, "Marshal, you have a duty to Drearburh and to the oss. This is my duty as your—" and Kiriona, "No. No. I won't let you," and Crux, "My *rights* . . . my *rights* . . . I am dying anyway."

"Oh, just let him go!" snarled Kiriona. "He wants to die—I'll do it. I've wanted to do this for years."

John had said, It's so beautiful. Come and look.

She had said, There are almost no beautiful things left. Where is Anastasia? Let me talk to Anastasia.

"Then do it, coward," Crux said. "Do it—the knife is before you; the work has been done."

"Did you know I'm God's child?" Kiriona demanded. "Did you know all the things you did—all the shit you pulled—every single thing you did, every lock you snapped on me, every cuff you put on me, every—every crappy plate of food you put in front of me, every word—every look—did you know I was the real, true-blue daughter of the *Emperor*? I want you to know that—I want you to know what I *am*!"

"You remain—what you are," said Crux. "A worthless millstone hung about my darling's neck. You were born to make her suffer. You died as you lived, Gideon Nav—a disappointment to me—*and* to God."

There was a wet, meaty sound. The old man exhaled. It was dark. Then there was light, bright, cold, electrifying, like death; and the noise of another rock—slowly—agonisingly—grinding away.

And Kiriona kept saying— "It didn't feel good . . . Fuck . . . It didn't feel good. Why didn't it feel good?"

A rising, hysterical note. "Why didn't it feel good? You fucking old . . . You hideous, cruel . . . you *bastard* . . . Why didn't . . . Why can't I . . ."

Glowworms, she had told John.

Technically beetles, said John, but I always loved them.

Narrow beetles with long strands hanging off them—a carpet of shifting, dead, winking lights at the top of the grave. Greenish, orangeish, yellowish, moving over one another silently with those long filaments hanging down. (Something came off the baby's body; a foot, maybe. Paul jammed it back on.) And the water—the huge pool of real salt water, where she had knelt and drank—

She moved the baby's body apart from the others. They could not stop her. She stepped into the water: A-a-a-ah! That was good. The water was ice-cold—it froze the baby's heart in its tracks—but she was moving her now and did not need her heart. Someone said, "Let her go. It's gravity. Let her go," and those voices were dim now—she could no longer distinguish them. Most human voices sounded alike, after all. They were not beautiful. The waters parted for her and it became possible to walk, crunching through the bones at the bottom. The bones at the bottom; what did they make her think of?

John and she had swum to the centre hummock rising out of the pool. Not an island, not really. An outcropping. With the marble pillars, and the marble top, and the long low marble table. He said he thought it was a nice place to be. To lie down. She had liked hard things to lie down on. It was hard to endure having a spine. And there she was—

A long echo down the tunnel. The Lyctor with the broken body, screaming still in crazed agony, but getting closer.

There she was; John had made her so ugly, so unbearably ugly. The terrible face, with the terrible arms and legs and the terrible middle part, and the terrible hair, and the terrible ears: the nose too short, the ears too brief. But there she was—and within her the child, asleep, with the strange sword. The sword—her sword—her own edge had been pushed out, her swinging edge, her toy. Her plain bladed sword. And her body was chained up . . .

"No!" someone howled, from the shore. "No—no!"

She looked back beyond, and she saw Anastasia, tucked where nobody would find her: Anastasia, all bones. Not really Anastasia. But Anastasia's body without the meat on it, snuggled right into the curve of the rock, ready to close the door whenever it was opened. She remembered Anastasia.

Her vision swam: her heart was in her throat.

"Well, happy birthday to me, I guess," sighed Nona.

And Nona tumbled forward onto the icy dead breast of the Body.

EPILOGUE

WHEN THE ROCK THAT had been made meat awoke in a body, it cried out aloud, saying—You.

Then it broke the chains that were upon its right wrist, and the right wrist broke with them. It broke the chains that were upon its left wrist, and the left wrist also; so followed the chains upon the right ankle and upon the left, until its arms and its legs and the chains were broken all as one. When it raised its terrible head the chains around the neck collapsed into dust, and it cried, Ah, ah, ah.

At the breaking of the chains and of the bones, one of the children there offered violence to her, appearing on the altar and raising her weapon high. But the black-eyed infant collapsed on the altar chid her sharply in a clear voice, saying, What is this that thou wouldst do, Tridentarius? Touch her and our vow will come to nothing, and I will slay you where you stand.

To which the first child said, Thou knowest not what thou dost.

And the second child answered, Not lately, but now.

And the first child asked: Dost thou oppose me, and thou half-dead?

And the second child said, I am as one half-dead, but you would be two-halves dead, bitch.

To which the first child said, My sweet, I only die of longing for thee.

And the other child said, Then perish.

Upon which the body that had been rock rose from the altar and struck the child who had offered violence to her with one broken

475

hand, forgetting the sword in the other, so that the child who offered violence was not slain, but was cast into the water like a detestable thing. And many skeletons emerged from the bones of the bier, and from the walls of the tomb, but when the sword was raised, they fled. When the broken feet touched the stone around the tomb, they were mended, and when the broken hands raised the sword they were mended also, but the body itself was not fully awake, and stumbled on the steps at the bier, crying, John, John; but did not fall.

And there was a crowd of dead children there. They were striving loudly against living children on the far-off shore of the tomb. The body did not understand how this had come to pass, yet when one on the shore called, Alecto, Alecto, then the body remembered, and was mightily dashed in the memory of Alecto, so that all their sleep was perished with a noise.

And Alecto said, Pyrrha, he laid me down as an appeasement to them; he fed you to them as an appeasement to them; but he has never appeased me, and now all he has done was teach me how to die.

But Pyrrha did not hear above the noise.

Then Alecto remembered the vow, and turned back upon the altar to face the second child and raised the sword with wrath in her heart, for they meant to bring destruction upon her. But when the black-eyed infant showed her countenance to Alecto, Alecto recalled her, for it was a face once dreamed in Alecto's dream. And Alecto stayed the sword.

The child rose and said, O corse of the Locked Tomb, I have loved thee all my life, with mine whole soul, and with mine whole strength. I would to God that I find grace in thy eyes. Destroy me according to thy word, for I love thee.

Alecto was angry, and raised her up, and kissed her. The child did not cry out, though blood fell from her lips and tongue, and she was wounded sore. For Alecto knew not how to kiss, except such as it involved the mouth and teeth.

And Alecto said to her, Why are you not appeased? That is how meat loves meat.

The child was silent; but her blood was on Alecto's lips, and through that blood Alecto was made to understand what it was, and was astonished exceedingly. Alecto put away wrath and said: Thou art the blood of the tomb-keeper.

The child answered, Yes.

Alecto said, The line of Anastasia is unbroken yet.

The child answered, Through sin and iniquity, yes.

Alecto said, I am very sorry about Samael.

The child made no answer. Alecto said, I remember my vows. As I swore to Anastasia I swear to you. I am in your service until you bid me the favour, and whatsoever you appoint I shall perform, and consider the vow rendered. This is what I promised, until such a time as you deal with me as you see fit.

The child was afraid and said, My hands are too stained, and I am too lowly.

So Alecto, wearied of talking, kneeled upon the rock and offered up the sword to her, and placed the child's hand upon the blade, so that it received also the red blood of the child. This made the child exceeding faint, but it did not swoon of weariness.

Which strength pleased Alecto, who said: Notwithstanding, I offer you my service.

To which a voice on the opposite side of the shore was raised, exceeding wroth, and Alecto heard it shout in a very great shout: Get in line, thou big slut.

* * *

Afterward Alecto went down to the ship and stood before John, purposing to travel through the River, and was grieved to find it yet dead. John was asleep, and not in his garments, unshaved and still drunken. The child who accepted the blade and thereupon fainted with hunger and thirst was thrown over one of Alecto's arms, a deep sleep like death upon her, and in Alecto's other hand was the iron sword. And so Alecto took that iron sword, and with one hand pierced John's chest with it, even to the heart.

At which John awakened and said, Annabel, good morning.

Hell Will Break Loose In

ALECTO THE NINTH

ACKNOWLEDGMENTS

Many people were bewildered when *Nona* sucker punched her way into the world, throwing *Alecto* into total disarray. Nobody was more bewildered than my agent and my editor, two people whom I imagine will have ascended to a state of higher consciousness by the time this is all over. I'd like to thank my agent, Jennifer Jackson, the unstoppable and the ever-gracious; I'd also like to thank Carl Engle-Laird, my editor. Carl, I finally found a way to thank you properly. In this book, there are almost no memes.

Thanks must go to the whole of Tordotcom, but to these in particular: Irene Gallo, Caro Perny, and Matthew Rusin; the indefatigable marketing team of Michael Dudding, Renata Sweeney, and Samantha Friedlander; and the wonderful Christine Foltzer and Jamie Stafford-Hill, without whom my books would not look remotely as good. On that note, I got impossibly lucky when Tommy Arnold got designated for cover work, although after all those bones I'm not sure Tommy's wrists will thank me back. Thanks to Lauren Hougen for catching all the fiddly errors. And thanks to my copyeditor, Melanie Sanders, who catches all the massive ones.

I would also like to thank the patient Michael Curry from DMLA, and all the wonderful knowledge we have gained about double taxation treaties.

I rely upon the kindness of my first readers and friends Clemency Pleming and Megan Smith, who also constantly feed me. On that note, this book was brought to you by Clemency's ice-cream machine.

To all the other people who have listened to me complain while *Nona* was being worked on—grateful thanks to the West family, the Helens, Beau and Charlotte Diffey, Lissa Harris, Bo and Ben, Ben Raynor and Monty, Chris Douglas, Malloreigh, Ray, Tim and Joe, Lottie and Alexis. Thank you to Avery and Martha, and thank you to Waverly

March (in other words, the whole Rat Compartment). Thanks always to Isabel Yap, the series's fairy godmother. As per usual I'd like to thank my family, but I haven't seen them since the pandemic started so I've only been able to interact with my brother in *Animal Crossing*. Thanks, dude, and please send me some pears because my island doesn't have those.

My final thanks to Matt Hosty: I lied! There was another book!! Sorry!!! You were Nona's cheerleader even when I was ready to punt the whole book into the ocean. You've dragged me over the finish line for three books and you'll drag me to a fourth. I know exactly what I would do without you: die of loneliness and also starvation.